CRITICS FIND THE LIFE OF THE PARTY LIVELY READING!

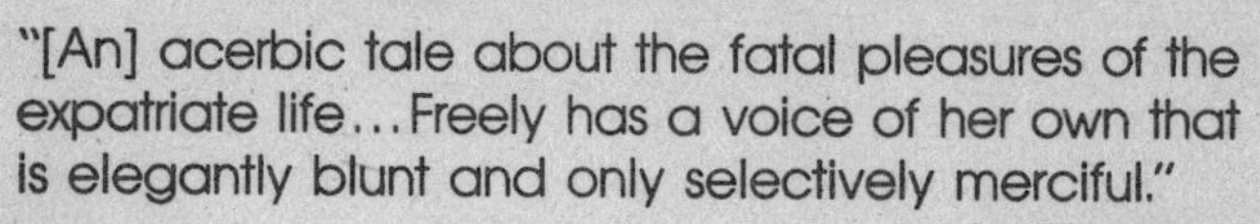

"[An] acerbic tale about the fatal pleasures of the expatriate life... Freely has a voice of her own that is elegantly blunt and only selectively merciful."

—Newsday

"Wickedly satiric."

—ALA Booklist

"Stimulating reading.... The collision of incompatible social standards that Ms. Freely ironically describes is both grim and comic."

—Atlantic Monthly

"A complex, funny, and shrewd satirical novel."

—Kirkus Reviews

"Hector Cabot may be one of the great rogues of contemporary literature.... The whole story is cloaked in deadpan humor filled with funny observations and a rich sense of place."

—Richmond Times-Dispatch

MAUREEN FREELY grew up in Turkey and graduated from Radcliffe College in 1974. She currently lives in Oxford, England, with her husband, novelist Paul Spike, and their two children, Matthew and Emma. Her first novel, Mother's Helper, was published in 1979.

THE LIFE OF THE PARTY

MAUREEN FREELY

A Warner Communications Company

All the characters and situations in this novel are inventions of the author's imagination, and there is no reference intended to any living person

WARNER BOOKS EDITION

This Warner Books Edition is published by arrangement with Simon and Schuster, A Division of Simon & Schuster, Inc., Simon & Schuster Building, Rockefeller Center, 1230 Avenue of the Americas, New York, NY 10020

Cover art by Fred Marcellino

Warner Books, Inc.
666 Fifth Avenue
New York, N.Y. 10103

Printed in the United States of America

First Warner Books Printing: May, 1986

10 9 8 7 6 5 4 3 2 1

To John, Dolores, Eileen and Brendan

Acknowledgment

The author would like to thank the National Endowment for the Arts, whose support made the completion of this novel possible.

I

The Ghost

THERE once was a man who tried to find out the truth about Hector Cabot. His name was Peter Brooks, and he came to Istanbul in 1979, during the worst of the troubles.

He came to teach at Woodrow College, where Hector himself had taught, on a rustic hilltop campus reminiscent of dozens of New England prep schools and colleges, except that this one was perched above the Bosphorus, looking across the straits at the ancient hills of Asia. Like most of its New England counterparts, Woodrow College had been founded by Protestant clergymen—missionaries, in this case—in the latter half of the nineteenth century. Over the decades, it had acquired a well-deserved reputation as one of the two finest institutions of higher learning in Turkey, with a mixed faculty of Americans and Turks, who conducted their classes in English. However, much had changed in the years that separated Hector's departure and Peter's arrival.

In 1971, the university had been nationalized, with the Turkish government taking over from the Protestant missionary board back in New York. The American faculty had been gradually replaced almost entirely by Turks. Classes were no longer conducted exclusively in English. In fact,

Woodrow College no longer existed. It was now officially Boğaziçi Üniversitesi, or the University of the Bosphorus. Whereas Hector had been a tenured professor in the mathematics department, Peter had been hired out of Berkeley on a one-year contract, renewable on a year-to-year basis, at a salary so low few Americans would have been interested, unless they, like Peter, had at least a small income of their own. In Peter's case, this amounted to less than ten thousand dollars a year.

Peter first heard about Hector from Margaret, who was later to become his wife. While paying her a visit one afternoon, he came across a framed photograph that interested him. It was hanging over the sofa in the library, dwarfed by a Bengali dagger and a Konyali *kilim*. It was a picture of a group of people sitting at the bow of a caique. From the hills and the castle in the background, you could tell they were sailing on the Bosphorus, between Rumeli Hisar and Bebek. Peter could pick out a number of his new neighbors in the group: Amy, Meredith, Ralph—and Stella, who was Margaret's mother. Thomas (Margaret's father) was sitting at the front of the group, holding Margaret, aged nine, by the shoulders.

Standing behind the group was a man Peter didn't recognize. He was about to fall into the sea and none of the people sitting in front of him seemed to realize. He was drinking out of a flask, with his head thrown back and his back arched, waving his free arm in a vain effort to regain his balance. He was laughing, but he had an air of doom about him.

"Who's that?" Peter asked.

"That's Hector Cabot," she replied.

"Does he still teach here?"

"Oh, no, he's long gone."

"That's too bad. He looks interesting."

"You would have liked him," Margaret said. "In fact, you remind me of him." She smiled in such a way that it was not clear whether she intended this as a compliment or an insult. "He was a mathematician, you know, just like you. He taught here back when it was still Woodrow College."

"Where did he end up? Do you know?" Peter asked.

"It was very sad," Margaret said. "He drowned."

"Not right after that picture was taken!" Peter cried.

"Oh, no, it was years later. Right at the foot of that tower." She pointed out the window at Rumeli Hisar, the majestic castle built by Mehmet the Conqueror in 1452, prior to his siege of the city. "It was a great loss for all of us," she said. "Especially me."

"Why?"

"Because I was the one who pushed him over the edge."

"You're not trying to tell me you threw him in?"

"Of course not," she said. "I was speaking in moral terms. Morally, it was my fault. I'm trying to say I was too moral with him. You know what I mean."

"I'm afraid I don't."

"Then let me try to explain," she said, and she launched into her confession.

Hector Cabot, she began, had been her father's best friend. He had, in fact, been everyone's best friend. Although he had been, for years, the most popular professor on the Woodrow College campus, he was best known and best loved for being the life of every party he ever attended.

When he was sober, he was a good husband, a kind father, an inspired teacher, a generous friend. But when he was drunk, he was a horror. Some of the things he had done while under the influence were simply beyond belief. He was the world's worst driver, for one thing. And he would go off on binges for days at a time. It would have been enough if all he had done was destroy himself, Margaret said, but he insisted on dragging his friends down with him, too. Margaret's father was a case in point. Before coming to live on the Hill, Thomas Ashe had been a God-fearing, hardworking man. But then he met Hector, and Hector had completely changed his character, eventually turning him into a hopeless alcoholic. If Thomas Ashe ever died of cirrhosis, Margaret said, it would be Hector's fault.

Hector had much the same effect on all his other friends, she claimed. But because he was so much fun to be with, everyone forgave him. Everyone except, perhaps, his wife and children, who had too much to remember, and Margaret, who was best friends with his daughter and had therefore witnessed many atrocities.

One night, when Margaret was sixteen, Hector had turned up at her house when her parents were out. He had announced that he loved her, and suggested that they run away together, to Greece. Outraged, she had repulsed his advances in the most cruel way possible. Heartbroken (and very drunk), he had driven down the hill and plunged his car into the Bosphorus, where he drowned.

Hundreds of people had attended his funeral, which was arranged by the missionaries. The chaplain of the Dutch Chapel, who was a newcomer, officiated. When he got Hector's name wrong, there was almost a riot. The Turks in the congregation, many of whom were Hector's former students, were particularly appalled. There were many reasons for the decline of the good life on the Hill, she said—years of double-digit inflation, the nationalization of the university (and with it the end of dollar salaries), the growing anti-American feeling in the country as a whole, the shortages, the political turmoil. But nothing had ever had as devastating an effect on the community as the sight of the two swarthy gravediggers dragging Hector's coffin down the aisle of the chapel as they conversed in guttural Arabic, or the hollow thud the coffin made when they dropped it down the hole.

It broke people's spirits. Before a year was out, five of Hector's closest friends had died. Many others left Turkey never to return. And all because Margaret had judged a man too harshly.

Peter could not help himself when she said this. Without thinking, he reached across the table and took her hand. "I think it's yourself you're judging too harshly," he said.

She did not withdraw her hand immediately.

At this point, Margaret's mother burst into the room, and Margaret went back into her shell. But this brief glimpse into what he took to be her soul had the desired effect upon Peter. Over the next few days, his curiosity and vague interest in Margaret changed into an aching—a yearning—he could only describe as love.

This would probably have happened anyway. Margaret had a mysterious air about her and he had always been attracted to mysterious airs. She was also beautiful, beautiful without knowing it, or perhaps she was so accustomed to being admired that she just didn't care. She had long, dark brown hair, delicate features, translucent skin, a sudden smile, and large, asymmetrical eyes that seemed to look through him. She had the added advantage of being the only woman Peter had met so far who wasn't middle-aged.

It took ages for him to seduce her. It wasn't until the end of October, when her parents went to Greece for a long weekend, leaving them alone in the house, that she finally warmed to him.

Too giddy to sleep that night—and perhaps too drunk—he went upstairs for a beer toward dawn and found himself standing once again in front of Hector's photograph. The more he stared at him, and the more he tried to see through the shadows that obscured his face, the more he felt he understood him. Here was a man who, like himself, refused to do things halfway. A man who had decided to die rather than face life without Margaret. Peter regretted the man's death, and marveled at his own good fortune. How was it that he had succeeded where a greater man had failed? He longed to ask Margaret more about him. Where in Greece had he wanted to take her? Did he smoke? What kind of laugh did he have? In what ways did she find Peter like him? But he didn't ask, out of respect for her feelings. He assumed that the reason she never mentioned Hector again was that the memories were too painful. He was badly shaken, therefore, when he found out she had been lying.

He made this discovery in the most embarrassing way possible.

It was late in January, not long after Peter and Margaret had announced their engagement. Amy Cabot (Hector's ex-wife) was throwing a dinner party in their honor. Everyone was feeling gloomy because of the weather and the mud, and the pipes that had burst during the recent cold snap. But Amy had tried to compensate by serving hot toddies made with the whiskey she had bought at Heathrow Duty Free over Christmas, and hors d'oeuvres she had brought back from Fortnum & Mason.

This was not enough to cheer up Ralph, whose nose was out of joint because of the engagement announcement. Ralph was in his late sixties, a man of great dignity who made much of not having lived up to his early promise. He had once taught music at Woodrow College, but he had moved to the Community School a few years after the AID money ran out. The Community School was a primary school that had been founded for the children of Woodrow College faculty, and that now served the foreign community as a whole. Amy, Meredith, and Margaret also taught there. Ralph was the only male teacher at the school. A homosexual, he had become Peter's friend and confidant, more or less by default. Although their friendship had always been platonic, it clearly injured Ralph's *amour propre* to think that Peter could allow his head to be turned by a woman. All week he had been calling Margaret "the other woman."

"And how is the other woman on this fine morning?" he would say. "Did she have her beauty sleep or did you keep her up all night with your disgusting groping?" He made a point of saying these things in front of Margaret's mother.

Tonight he was determined to make trouble again, but he had changed his tack. He was going to infuriate the women by bringing up politics, a subject he knew they regarded as unsuitable for dinner parties, especially dinner parties intended as celebrations. He did not have to look far for material.

That day there had been yet another riot downtown—Saturday being the favored day for riots. Fifteen or twenty Leftists had been killed. That meant funerals in a few days, new solidarity marches in honor of the dead, and new reprisals on the part of the Left; hence new casualties for the Rightists, then Rightist funerals, solidarity marches, and reprisals.

"Where will it all end?" Ralph wanted to know. "And do we want to be here when it does?"

As usual, Meredith rose to the bait. She had intellectual pretensions that had never been quite satisfied in this small community. A tall, handsome woman who wore her blonde hair in a bun at the nape of her neck, she had aged considerably since her husband's death of lung cancer that autumn. She still smoked herself, quite heavily, in fact. Now, as she prepared to answer Ralph, she put out one cigarette and promptly lit another.

"Of course it would be preferable to miss the debacle,"

Meredith said, pronouncing debacle the French way. "But we have no choice. Our work is here, and here we must remain."

"I knew you would say that," Ralph snarled. He glowered at her. "You have no political sense whatsoever."

"Come now," said Meredith. "I read the same newspapers you do. I know what's going on in the world. It's simply that I don't sensationalize."

"Sensationalize? Is that what you call it? Bullets flying everywhere, not a week without a bloodbath, and *you* think that if you just keep your mind on your little job it's going to all go away? We're sitting ducks here. Damn it! We're cultural imperialists! It's a colossal joke! The question is, what are we doing here if they don't want us? Why am I risking my life? So that those spoiled consulate brats at that school of ours can have a well-rounded Yankee education?"

"I'm afraid that's a question you'll have to answer for yourself," Meredith said. "My own answer is simple. This is my home. Here I stay."

"This is *not* our home. This is *their* home, and *they* don't want us anymore."

"To each his own point of view, Ralph, dear."

"You goddamn Candide," he snarled. "We'll see how long they let you tend your own garden!"

"We *shall* see, shan't we? In the meantime, we shall be interested to learn from your example."

"What do you mean?"

"Well! I don't see *you* rushing for the first plane out, do I?"

"Bitch!"

That was when the power failed. The argument was interrupted as they all scurried about lighting candles. When they returned to the table, there was an uncomfortable silence as they watched the candlelight flicker in each others' eyes. It reminded Peter, just a little, of the way his mother's dining room table looked during a seance. His mother was a spiritualist. One of the reasons he was in Istanbul was to get away from his mother and her News of the Otherworldly.

It chilled his spine, her preoccupation with the dead. That was why he nearly jumped out of his chair when Amy, who was usually so unassuming, so eager to please, made the party seem even more like a seance by rapping sharply on the table.

Her soft blue eyes grew hard suddenly, and her nostrils flared. Her lips clamped shut in a way that reminded Peter of a clam. In an unnaturally shrill whisper, she said, "I am going to tolerate no more politics at my table. We have come together for a pleasant evening, not a forum or a junior college debate!"

She went into the kitchen and came back with a bottle of champagne—not Turkish but French. She refused to say where it had come from. "I procured this bottle," she announced, smiling, using her normal voice now, "in order that we might make a toast. Here's to Peter and Margaret. May they live happily ever after.

Have you decided," she asked, after they had clinked glasses, "on a suitable date?"

"We were thinking of June," Peter said. "My mother wants to come, and she can't take the cold."

"Well! That's one thing we have in common! I look forward to meeting her."

"I wouldn't, if I were you. She's really pretty awful."

"Oh?" Amy said, as if it were inconceivable that a mother could be less than perfect.

"She may not come anyway," Peter blundered on. "She'll have to consult her spirits. She's a spiritualist, you see. She became one after my dad died. She and her friends have seances every Friday night. It used to drive me crazy. Why is it," he said, getting carried away, "that widows feel compelled to communicate with their husbands' ghosts?"

There was an uncomfortable silence in the room, broken only by Meredith and Amy lighting cigarettes. Oh, God, Peter thought, I forgot how many widows were in the room.

"Well, for one thing," Meredith said, in an injured voice, "they might take some comfort in it."

"I can't buy that," said Peter. "There are plenty of other ways to find comfort. She could do volunteer work in a hospital, for example. Make herself useful, instead of sitting at home rapping on tables. It's obscene!"

"My dear boy," said Meredith, "it is clear that you have never been bereaved."

"I think that once you've been married to someone for that many years, he stays with you forever in one form or another," said Amy. "He's part of your personality, for better or for worse. That's a good thing, don't you agree, Meredith?" Meredith nodded. Amy knocked back the rest of her champagne, then smiled nervously at Peter. "For example, I still speak to Hector now and then. I find it's a comfort. In fact," she said, "I spoke to him only last night!" She smiled her craziest smile. "I told him about the upcoming wedding, and he sends his very best wishes, Margaret. Did I tell you I spoke to him? No? I suppose I forgot. He's in excellent form, anyway. He says he's in seventh heaven."

Peter's heart sank when he heard this. He thought he had gotten away from all that nonsense. Now here he was, seven thousand miles away from home, sitting with yet another middle-aged woman who talked to her dead husband.

Later, when he was sitting in the Ashes' living room having a nightcap, Peter asked Stella when it was that Amy had become a spiritualist. She looked at him, startled.

"Why do you think she's a spiritualist?" Stella asked.

"Because she said she had spoken to Hector," Peter said.

"How does that make her a spiritualist?"

"Well, I thought . . . I was under the impression that Hector was dead."

"Who told you that?" asked Stella.

"Margaret did."

Thomas and Stella looked at their daughter.

"Margaret!" Stella said.

"This is preposterous," Thomas said. "What exactly did she tell you?"

"She told me he drove his car into the Bosphorus and drowned."

"Margaret!" Stella said again. "Aren't you a little old now for making up stories?"

Margaret flashed her mother a brilliant, guilty smile.

Picking up a strand of her hair, which she wound around her finger, she said, "I suppose I am." Then she cleared her throat and regained her composure. "I'm sure that's not exactly what I said to him, anyway." When Peter spoke, she startled, as if she had forgotten he was in the room.

"That *was* what you said, though. You told me he had drowned."

"Are you sure I didn't say he *almost* drowned?"

Peter shook his head. "No, you told me he drowned. There's no doubt about it, because you also told me about the funeral."

"I did?" Margaret said, still twisting the strand of hair around her finger. "Well," she said, smiling to herself, "I suppose I mixed things up. There were a lot of funerals in those days."

"She's always made up stories," Stella explained to Peter. "You could say it was her tragic flaw. If you're going to marry her, you'll have to get used to it." She opened her mouth as if to say something else, but then she shut it again.

"What *did* happen to Hector?" Peter asked, when it became clear that no one was going to volunteer the information.

"The night Hector went into the water?" Thomas asked. "Oh, you'll have to ask Stella. She was there."

"Oh, God, I couldn't tell you either," Stella said. She laughed. With her eyes shining and her cheeks flushed, you could tell for a moment how beautiful she had been when she was younger. You could also tell how miserable she had once made life for Thomas. He was clearly remembering her transgressions now, as he sat in his easy chair, his bad leg propped on a gout stool, his deep-set brown eyes fixed gloomily on his drink.

Thomas cleared his throat. "Apparently he's made quite a life for himself in Connecticut."

"Who has?" Peter asked.

"Hector." Thomas turned to his wife. "Did you hear Amy say he was in seventh heaven?"

"Self-righteous bastard," Stella said.

Later that night, Peter tried to force the truth out of Margaret. "We're supposed to be getting married in a few months," he said. "We have to be honest with one another. How do you expect me to trust you otherwise?"

But she wouldn't tell him much, beyond the fact that Hector had indeed driven his car into the Bosphorus one night, that he *had* almost drowned. In fact, she said, there were people who said that he had deserved to drown.

When had he left Istanbul? Peter asked. A year or so later, Margaret said. And his reason? There had been no reason, Margaret claimed. He had just left. Couldn't they talk about something else? she asked. She was tired of talking about Hector. She was sorry she had made up that silly story about him. She would try not to make up stories for the fun of it in the future. It was childish. "And now," she said, wrapping her arms around him, "it's time to go to sleep."

She was lying naked on his quilt, and so he forgave her, temporarily. But as he covered her with kisses, he noticed she was smiling at him, as if to say he would never possess her. Her mind was her own: he would only know what she wanted him to know. She did not want him to know about Hector. She was not alone.

"You ask such broad questions," Ralph said the following afternoon, when Peter went to pay him a visit. He waved his arm with theatrical exasperation. The gesture was from another era and dated him. "How could I possibly tell you all the sordid little reasons why people hated Hector Cabot?"

He paused to take a sip of his tea. Earl Grey—his very last teabag, he had said. He was savoring it as much as he savored the conversation. He picked up the silver tray of bacon cheese on toast and offered it to Peter. It was his very last bacon cheese until his next trip over the border to Alexandropolis.

"The fact is," he continued, pausing to take a bite out of his own piece of toast, "the sad truth is, we were all glad to see Hector go."

"But why?" Peter asked. "I thought he was so popular."

"Oh, he was, he was. But then he made a fatal mistake."

"What was that?"

"He lost his nerve. He saw the error of his ways and tried to make amends. Imagine trying to make amends in this den of iniquity, just imagine. What nerve! We are none of us terribly good people. It's impossible to be a good expatriate, you know. It's a contradiction in terms. I suppose that's why he went back. He must have realized."

"What's he doing now? Do you know?"

"Well, he came into all that money, you know," Ralph said, peering over his glasses. "So he doesn't have to worry about making a living. Which is awfully convenient if you want to live a virtuous existence. Oh, he works from time to time for some snot-nosed charity. Something International. International something. You know what I mean—those people who are against the death penalty. Imagine being against the death penalty!" Ralph snorted. "The thing is, he became impossibly moralistic at the end. None of us could stand him. Not even Stella. They were lovers, you know. That was why Hector's car ran off the road into the Bosphorus. It was a terrible scandal. So you see, your wife-to-be was not, after all, telling a complete lie. She was merely twisting the facts. As we all do. And why shouldn't we? What do we stand to gain by admitting to ourselves that the good old days when Hector was in his prime were not so very good? God knows the man was no saint. And when you think what he did!" Ralph put his hand over his mouth.

"What *did* he do?"

"How darling you look today," Ralph said, evading the question. "It is eerie, sometimes, how much you remind me of Hector. It's not the physiognomy so much as your expressions. The way you move your eyes. Your smile. That disarming grimace. Why must you waste yourself on a woman? But if that's what you want, how can I stand in your way? Just promise me one thing."

"What's that?" Peter asked.

"Don't do what Hector did."

"What exactly did Hector do? It would help if you told me."

For a moment it looked as if Ralph were going to tell him. But then he sat back with his Cheshire-cat smile.

"Don't let the bitch talk you into growing a beard."

What Hector did. Over the course of that spring, Peter was able to compile a vast list of the man's misdeeds. There was scarcely a woman about whom someone did not eventually say, "She and Hector Cabot were lovers, you know." There was scarcely a restaurant, a hotel, a bar, a house, where Hector had not disgraced himself. Landmarks were pointed out to him: the exact spot from which Hector had hurled a bottle of Johnny Walker Black, the police station from which Hector had once stolen a flag, the classroom where the Woodrow College trustees had discovered him teaching his students how to dance on the desks. Then there were the more serious allegations, usually on the part of Turks who claimed to have known him well but seemed to bear a grudge against him. "He was, of course, an agent for the CIA," they would say. Or "I have been led to understand he was in the pay of the KGB."

There was no end to the rumors, but the rumors did not add up. Some said he was a good man who had gone bad. Others said he was a bad man who had turned good. Some people called him two-faced, others called him transparent. But no one would tell him why Hector had left Istanbul, why he had gone from being the most popular man on the Hill to the most disliked. There was something they weren't telling him. Was it, perhaps, something that did not show them in the best of lights?

Or did they withhold this missing information because he was a newcomer? Friendly as they were, as desperate as they were for new blood on the Hill, they found plenty of ways to let him know he would never really belong. He had arrived too late. He had not been there during the golden days, when their lives had really been Something. They worshipped the golden days. He could never belong to those, nor share fully in the secrets of that era.

Instead, they teased him. Oh, the things they had done that he would never do, the things they had seen that he would never see, the places they had gone at prices never to be duplicated. Scarcely a week passed without someone saying, "What a pity it is that you never met Hector in his prime. Did I ever tell you about the time when . . ." They would go on to tell him some anecdote that said nothing about the man. "Yes," they would say, "he was quite a character before he went sour." That was as far as they would go.

And then the comparisons. People were always saying, "How like Hector you are!" He was like Hector because of the way he moved his eyes, because of the way he sometimes lost his temper in public places, because he often drank too much, because he loved animals. Sometimes—particularly on mornings after he had misbehaved at dinner parties—they didn't tell him how it was that he had reminded them of Hector. They would just give each other looks, like worried parents. It was as if they were afraid he might become even more like Hector than he already was, that he might commit the same unmentionable sin. It was as if they withheld the key to the story of Hector Cabot so as not to alarm him.

And so the silence continued, until Meredith's son, Eric, blurted out the truth, on the day after Peter and Margaret's wedding.

Amy's son, Neil, who had gone AWOL from the army to attend the wedding, was an amateur photographer, and so they had many photographs of the occasion. The best ones now adorned the walls of Peter and Margaret's small apartment.

There was one of the actual ceremony, which had taken place on the Ashes' wisteria-covered terrace. (It had been a perfect June day: sunny, with warm breezes carrying the scent of wildflowers. Downtown there had been a bombing, but they did not hear about it until the following day.) The other photographs were of the bride and groom embracing each other (a beautiful bride, a handsome groom, an ideal couple); the bride with her eyes closed; the bride cutting the cake; the bride with her parents; the bride with her old schoolfriends, the Cabot and Lacey children, who had come so far to join the festivities.

There was a beautiful picture of Peter with his mother, who had also traveled thousands of miles to be there. She looked radiant in this picture, as well she might, because everyone had been extremely kind to her. Everyone except Peter, that is. She had arrived at the beginning of the month and had been driving him crazy: gasping and hanging on to telephone poles if he made her walk farther than half a block, going through his chest of drawers when he was not at home, telling people embarrassing stories about his childhood, and quoting dead people until he wanted to wring her neck.

In the beginning, he had complained about her to the

others, only to discover that these hard-hearted expatriate sophisticates took his mother's side. Why they liked her he could not say. She was not a very interesting person. But like her they did. "You should really try and be nicer to Greta," they would say to him. "She loves you so much. With your father gone, you're all she has. And she's not as dull as you make her out to be. If you'd only stop and listen to her. You should really try and make an effort, you know. Think of all the thousands of miles she traveled."

And so he had tried. The picture was a testament of how successful he had been—at the beginning of the reception, at least—at keeping up appearances. In the picture, his tie was askew but otherwise he was the devoted son, with his arm around her shoulder, and his head leaning to one side, brushing affectionately against her large, floppy, purple hat.

There were several other pictures of Peter alone in which Margaret claimed to see hints of what was to come, but that was only because she knew him so well. These pictures were of Peter holding a bottle of champagne (Turkish, not French), Peter toasting the photographer with a glass of champagne, Peter holding his champagne glass close to his chest as he stood at the edge of the wisteria-covered terrace, apparently admiring the beauties of the Bosphorus. This was a particularly good photograph: it had been taken late in the afternoon. It was of Peter's profile. He looked tanned and deep in thought. In the background was the garden, and beyond it the castle and the Bosphorus. Although the images were blurred, the colors were perfect. The water was a deep, deep blue, the crenelated castle walls a luminous yellow, and the hills leading down to the castle a misty blue-green.

There was only one photograph in which Peter was actually misbehaving, and that was a photograph of the entire wedding party. They were huddled together at the corner of the terrace, laughing, with their arms around each other. Peter was standing behind the group, on the terrace wall. In his hand was a glass of champagne, which he was pouring on his mother's head.

His back was arched. He was waving his free arm as if to keep from falling—although no one could remember whether or not he had fallen at that point. He had definitely fallen later, but he had not hurt himself. It was not much of a drop.

Neil, the photographer, had used a fast shutter speed because no one would stay still. Thus, it was a dark, sharp picture of captured motion. The champagne hadn't landed on Peter's mother's head yet, and so she was smiling sweetly, completely unsuspecting. Peter's face was in shadow, but if you looked closely you could detect a crazed glint in his eyes. He had that lopsided smile that Margaret said was a sure sign that he had been drinking too much. And his tie was loose and flapping over his right shoulder. He looked like the ghost at the feast, chuckling as he set out to dampen the high spirits. He had, Peter thought (whenever he found the courage to be honest with himself about the picture), an air of doom about him.

He did not remember pouring the champagne on his mother's head. In fact, all but the first two hours of the reception were lost to him. He woke up in his apartment the following afternoon with a splitting headache, with no idea how he had gotten home. He had no idea, either, why neither his mother nor his wife were at home with him. He was all alone.

He found them later, at the Ashes'. Or rather, he found Margaret, who was sitting in the living room, looking drawn and bleary-eyed, as if she had spent the whole night crying. Her parents were hovering in the doorway. They looked uncharacteristically grim.

Oh, my God! he thought. What did I do last night? he knew how hard it was to shock Stella and Thomas. These were people who had seen everything—drunken brawls and men on destructive binges, infidelities of every variety, homosexual strip poker parties, the defiling of flags and others acts of sacrilege. . . . They had seen their friends involved in countless perversions, and had forgiven them, but last night, it seemed, they had witnessed something so terrible that they had drawn the line. They could hardly look at him.

They offered him a beer, but only out of politeness. Then they left Peter and Margaret alone. "Well," said Peter in a small voice when the silence became unbearable, "how are you feeling today?"

"All right, considering," Margaret answered.

"Would you like to come home with me? Or are you going to stay here?" Peter asked.

"Oh, I suppose I'll come down to the apartment sooner or later. But I think your mother wants to stay here."

"Where *is* my mother? By the way," he added hastily.

"She's napping in the guest room," Margaret said. "She's exhausted after what you put her through last night."

"What did I put her through last night?" Peter asked. He tried not to show his panic.

Margaret gave him a long, weary look, as if she knew more about him than she would have liked to know. "Oh, threats, mostly. You're very big on threats."

"I didn't hurt her, did I?"

"No, there were too many people protecting her."

"Too many people protecting her!" Peter cried. "Protecting her from what? You make it sound as if I went stark raving mad!"

She gave him another of her weary looks, as if to say he had. "Why don't you go home now? I think it would be better if you weren't here when she wakes up. I'll be down later. In any event, I'll give you a call." Peter slunk off down the hill, mystified, horrified by all the unanswered questions, feeling like a dog with its tail between its legs.

At the bottom of the hill, he paused outside Osman's. Osman's was a restaurant across from the Rumeli Hisar ferry station. It had once been a gathering place for fishermen. Now, with inflation, it had become too expensive even for teachers with dollar incomes. But he paused today, because he was in desperate need of another therapeutic beer. His head was killing him. God only knew how many bottles of champagne he had gone through at the reception. He was happy to see Eric Lacey waving at him from one of the outside tables.

Eric Lacey was a big, tough Viking type who had, to his mother's distress, never gone to college. He worked, from time to time, in the merchant marine. He was going for his captain's license. Between jobs, he drank rather heavily, but he was better than Peter at holding his liquor. Peter had not liked him when he'd first met him. He had been too gruff. But today he looked as if he might be an ally.

"Well," Eric said, when Peter finally got his hands on a beer. "I bet Margaret is putting you through some changes today."

"She sure is," Peter answered.

"It doesn't surprise me. She was always a martinet."

"It's not only her. It's everyone. They're all treating me as if I were some sort of criminal."

"That's typical," Eric sympathized. "They used to treat me like a criminal, too."

"It's a strange place, this Hill," Peter said.

"You're telling me. I grew up here."

"This obsession with Hector Cabot, for example."

"Well," Eric said, "I'm sure you could have understood that better if you'd met him. He was quite something."

"Do you think we're alike?" Peter asked.

"Do I think you're like Hector, you mean?" Eric asked, lighting a cigarette. For a moment, he looked exactly like his mother. Then he resumed his Viking persona. 'No," he said, exhaling through his nose. "No, not particularly."

"They're always telling me I'm like Hector. And sometimes they don't mean it as a compliment. Sometimes it seems as if they're afraid for me. As if I'm almost too much like him. As if . . . as if . . . I were going to make the same mistake that Hector did. Sometimes I feel like they're almost daring me. It's unnerving."

"It *must* be unnerving," Eric agreed. "You should tell them to lay off. They're playing games with you, you know. Because you're not really all that much like Hector. They don't have anything better to do, stranded up on that Hill of theirs, and so they make up games to chase away the boredom. But it's not fair. I mean, you were pretty goddamn foul to your mother last night, but you're not planning to kill her, are you? Because that's what Hector did, you know. He killed his mother."

Peter gagged on his beer.

"Of course," Eric continued, lighting up another cigarette, seemingly oblivious to Peter's coughing fit, "it was—technically speaking—an accident. But still, the whole thing hit him very hard. He was never the same after that. He was a changed man."

"How did the accident happen?" Peter asked, when he

had managed to stop coughing. His voice was hoarse and his hands were shaking.

"Oh, God, it was so long ago. I can't remember the details. If I remember correctly, he had been drinking that night, and things got out of hand. You know how it goes," Eric said. "You start out thinking you'll just have a beer or two, and then, before you know it. . . ." He paused and lifted his arm to attract the waiter's attention. They were in need of another round of beers. But Peter jumped to his feet before the waiter reached the table, and said in the loudest whisper he could manage that he had to be going. He did not want another beer. He did not want to hear the end of Eric's sentence.

Peter's mother stayed in Istanbul until the end of June. After a few days of recriminations, she forgave her son. The rest of her visit went smoothly, despite the hijackings and the shootouts and the bombings that they read about in the paper but happily did not witness. Peter gave up drinking after his conversation with Eric and so was able to control his temper better whenever she did any of the little things that annoyed him. They had no arguments. After their initial discussions, she never again referred to the wedding night catastrophe, until it almost seemed as if it hadn't happened. When the visit was over, they parted on the best of terms.

Peter stayed on the wagon for a time after his mother's departure, but slowly he started drinking again. Social life on the Hill being what it was, it was impossible not to. What happened was that he became a more careful drinker. Oh, yes, there were nights when he overdid it. Occasionally, there were nights when he had blackouts. But never did he disgrace himself as completely as he had on his wedding night.

Life improved as time passed. That October, the military took over, making it safe to walk the streets again. For a while, it even seemed as if they would mete out justice equitably. And even when the news of torture chambers and political prisons reached the Hill, there were those, like Meredith, who felt compelled to add that, even though such rumors were dreadfully shocking, one had to admit that the common man was happier now than he had been during the

Anarchy. In '78 and '79, she said, they had all lived under a gigantic shadow. The shadow of fear, she said, choosing to overlook what they all knew: that for any Turk involved in politics, that shadow still existed, greater and more ominous than ever.

But for Peter, it had receded.

He had come into his own, he thought, with the embarrassed regret of a man whose personal destiny has proved much happier than the destiny of the country he is living in. Yes, things had worked out well for him. He enjoyed teaching, now that he had more experience. And now that they had resolved their minor differences, he and Margaret had a happy life together. They were beginning to think of having children. He knew that, with the way things were going, they would not be able to live in Turkey forever, but for the time being, he loved it, and thought of it as his home.

Although he saw plenty of the Ashes and Amy and Meredith and Ralph, he was not completely dependent on them. He had friends of his own now, people closer to his own age. But the best thing of all was that, as time passed, he could go for weeks without once thinking of Hector Cabot.

Hector! That heartless cad, he would say to himself. Well, he had finally shown himself in his true colors. No wonder his friends hated him. No wonder they were glad he was gone. Imagine killing your mother—just imagine! So what if it had been an accident? That was no excuse, no excuse at all.

Sometimes Peter had dreams about having a fistfight with Hector and knocking him out cold. Sometimes Hector appeared to him as a specter, mocking him with a hollow laugh, daring him over the precipice. He would wake up from these nightmares crying, "No! Keep away from me! You're mistaken! I'm not like you at all!"

Even during Peter's waking hours, Hector took on the attributes of a monster in his mind. And so it was a shock when Peter finally came face to face with the real Hector. He startled, as if he had seen a ghost.

It was a surprise visit, though not a spur-of-the-moment one. No one on the Hill was expecting him. Hector had been gone for thirteen years.

As luck would have it, Peter was the first to come across him. It was a summer afternoon, in the garden outside the building that housed the lower grades of the Community School—a green-shuttered, red-roofed, white clapboard house that looked as if it belonged in New England. It had been built by the missionaries who had founded Woodrow College. Before becoming a school, it had been a private home. It was now badly in need of a coat of paint.

It had a beautiful walled garden on four or five levels. It had a pine forest, two ponds, a grape arbor, a manicured lawn overshadowed by an ancient yew tree. It was under this yew tree that Hector was standing when Peter came in through the gate. (Peter was coming from the Upper School, where Margaret was helping out in the office. He was on his way to the Ashes' with his copy of the *International Herald Tribune*.)

He recognized Hector immediately. Why, he did not know, because Hector looked different in real life than he did in Peter's imagination. He was tall and thin, and deeply tanned, still youthful-looking despite the gray in his hair. He had bright blue eyes. He was looking at the Lower School and squinting. In his expression was pain, even regret, and resignation—none of the qualities his former friends remembered him for. Either they had never understood him or they had misrepresented him.

Why? Peter asked himself. Was it that hard to know the truth, to tell the truth, about a friend? He lingered at the gate, temporarily unable to find the courage to walk across the lawn and introduce himself.

It was July 6, 1982.

II

Hector's Odyssey: The Beginning

Saturday, June 14, 1969
Morning and Early Afternoon

HECTOR did not notice Peter right away because his mind was in the past. His mind was on an earlier summer day, the day his troubles had begun.

What year was it? 1968? 1970? No, of course not. It was 1969. June 1969. What day in June? He could not remember the date, only that it was a Saturday.

It was a Saturday in June, and school was over for the year. At least classes were over. Perhaps they were still giving exams. They had not had graduation yet, at least Hector thought not.

It was a beautiful summer day: sunny, with warm breezes carrying the scent of wildflowers. The first thing Hector had seen when he woke up that Saturday was the yew tree swaying in the breeze. Because in those days the house he was standing under had not been the Lower School. It had been his home.

His bedroom had been upstairs, next to the balcony. He could remember it perfectly: the bed with its worn green corduroy bedspread, the scuffed-up chest of drawers, the chintz curtains, the goat-hair rugs on the floor. The Penguin mystery story on the bedside table, and next to it an ashtray, a half-empty pack of black-market Marlboros, and one of Amy's tea cups or coffee cups from the night before. And next to the windows, the blue chaise longue where Hector would end up spending most of that summer.

He could not remember what he had done that morning in June 1969, and so he imagined doing all the normal things: waking up to the aroma of bacon and eggs, getting out of bed, stretching, standing at the window for a moment to admire the fine day before going into the bathroom to shave. Waiting until the last moment to go downstairs—"Hector? Are you coming?" He could hear the annoyance in Amy's voice even now. Dashing down the stairs two at a time, whistling as he burst into the dining room, where the rest of the family was already assembled.

At the end of the table was Amy, still annoyed but happy to see him. She was dressed in a bright summer shift, and her face was flushed from standing over a hot stove on a warm day. Or had the maid been there to help her? He could not remember if Kleoniki had come on Saturdays. Nor could he remember if they had liked the way Kleoniki made eggs. What he could remember was Amy with the stack of warmed plates in front of her as she dished out the eggs and apportioned the bacon.

Their son, Neil, was sitting to her left, busily buttering his toast. Chloe, their daughter, sat on Amy's right. She was reading a book which Amy now wanted her to close, but Chloe was paying no attention to her. How old would Chloe have been in 1969? Sixteen, at the very most seventeen. An awkward age, at least for Chloe. She had seemed buried in her black hair.

Sitting next to Chloe was Hector's mother, Aspasia. When Hector took his place at the head of the table, she jumped to her feet and came around behind him with the coffee pot. As she poured him a cup of coffee, she asked him how he was feeling. She asked the question in Greek; although she had lived in America for forty years, she still felt more at home speaking Greek.

What had they talked about at that breakfast? Probably their plans for the day. Amy had told him she was going to spend the morning at the Community School filling out report cards. And then, in the afternoon, she would go to the hairdresser's. What was the name of the man she had gone to? Kerim. That was his name. "I want to be at Kerim's by two at the latest," Hector heard her say, as she (or the maid?) gathered the dishes. "Do you need the car, or can I take it?"

"I was planning to go downtown, actually," Hector answered.

"Oh, really?" Amy said. "What for?"

For obvious reasons, Hector told some lie or other. He could not remember which. "I'll be back by seven at the latest," he assured her. "Unless I get held up in traffic."

"Well, eight at the latest," Amy said. The Ashes were having a big party that night and they were due at eight.

How had he passed the rest of the morning? Reading in the garden, perhaps, or grading papers in his study? Lunch had been outside, that much he remembered. Tuna fish sandwiches and lemonade which was weaker than usual because Amy had made it in a hurry. Report cards always took her longer than she thought they would. He remembered how she kept looking at her watch as she ate her sandwich.

Aspasia had gone to the hairdresser with her. Had they all gone down to Bebek together? No, he thought not. He remembered leaving the house alone. Most probably, they had called a taxi and he had taken the car. He remembered, very clearly now, driving along the shore road that Saturday in his new Citroen and shuddering when he passed the spot where he had driven the Peugeot into the Bosphorus.

He had left the house in midafternoon. His appointment had been for three? Half past three? He pictured himself taking a last look behind him before closing the door—at the library, with its leatherbound classics on the high shelves and the Penguin paperbacks on the lower ones; at the living room, with its shabby college furniture, its Oriental carpets (some worn, some brilliantly colored, some common, some priceless), its copper trays and tea services. That Aliye Berger print of the fisherman was on the far wall, and on the wall behind the blue easy chair was his rifle collection, which hung there idly except for the occasional boar hunt, and which had led many people (Meredith's old schoolfriend,

Ginger, for example) to the conclusion that he lived his life in Hemingway's shadow.

He remembered taking in every detail of the entryway. He remembered looking up the stairs toward the door of his study. He remembered looking into the music room and seeing that someone had left a half-eaten apple on the red piano. He remembered taking one last, searching look at himself in the large mirror that hung between the living room and the dining room doors, but in fact he had done none of these things. He had rushed out the door without even bothering to make sure it was locked, because Meredith and her old schoolfriend, Ginger, were waiting for him, and because he did not realize yet that his days in that house were numbered.

He had gone downtown not in his car but in Hamdi *efendi's* taxi, which he shared with Meredith and Ginger. The women were going downtown to buy sandals. There was also some talk about a new passport for Meredith, because Ginger had noticed that her old one had expired. But Meredith was sure that the consulate was closed on Saturdays.

Hamdi *efendi* had taken the shore road into the city. In the small coastal town of Bebek, they ran into their first traffic jam. As they inched past Kerim's Beauty Parlor, Hector's mother, Aspasia, who was sitting next to the window, waved at them, but they did not see her, because the Venetian blinds were only halfway open.

Aspasia was having her hair frosted, on a hunch. Kerim Bey was standing over her, applying the complicated treatment, looking up only when he needed one of the boys to fetch him a pin or a comb. He was pleased that Aspasia had agreed to have her hair frosted. He had been after her to have it done for weeks.

From time to time he would ask her a question. "Aspasia Hanim," he would say. (He always addressed her the Turkish way. He refused to lump her with his foreign customers by calling her "Madame.") "You are finished with your magazine, Aspasia Hanim. Shall I have the boy bring you another?" Or, "Another tea, Aspasia Hanim? Or perhaps you would prefer a coffee. Let me send out the boy.

No, I insist, it is no problem. It is a pleasure. Coffee, did you say? Medium sweet? No? Extra sweet. Ah! I take coffee extra sweet myself. Most foreigners don't like it that way. But you are not a foreigner, are you, Aspasia Hanim? You are one of us."

Next to Aspasia sat Amy, her shampooed hair quickly drying. She was rereading her magazine for the third or fourth time. She seemed annoyed that Kerim Bey was taking such a long time frosting Aspasia's hair. Beyond her was a row of wealthy Turkish women, most of them also awaiting Kerim Bey's attentions. But instead of reading magazines, they had their faces close to the mirror. As they scrutinized their reflections, their fingers traveled over their faces, pressing, tugging, stretching, in an unabashed search for signs of middle age.

The one who had just had her hair bleached looked particularly worried. Kerim Bey's top assistant was taking out her curlers. "He went to Europe again," she said to the assistant. It was clear that she was talking about her husband.

"He was only going to Munich, he said, but now he's called me to say that he will have to go to Paris. He says it's for business, but Rozet Hanim told me that Ajda is also finding herself in that city at this moment. Ajda is the one I was telling you about. She was in *Ses* last week, do you remember? There was a picture of her dancing with Ferda Hanim's nephew at that wedding. She was wearing a red décolleté dress made of crepe de chine."

"It had sequins on the sleeves, didn't it?" the assistant said. "And her hair was in the Twiggy style."

"Yes," said the woman. "That's Ajda."

She leaned forward to examine her eyes. "They've been using an apartment in Maçka," she continued. "A friend of Rozet Hanim's lives across the street and has seen them come and go."

"Shame on them," said the assistant. "Isn't she married, this woman?"

"Married for less than two years, and already she's putting the horns on him. He's a surgeon, poor follow."

"She should be ashamed, this Ajda."

"What can I say to you? Morals are changing."

"And she's not even beautiful," the assistant continued. "She has a nose like an Arab."

"There's no accounting for taste," said the woman. "And furthermore, she has certain advantages. She's very young. She's a Dame de Sion graduate. Class of sixty-seven."

"Allah, allah, Nüket Hanim!" the assistant protested. "As if you yourself were old!"

"I'm getting wrinkles around my eyes," said the woman.

"Nonsense," said the assistant. "Those are simply from squinting in the sun. If you wear sunglasses, no one will notice them. And furthermore," he said as he began to tease her hair, "this new shade of blonde makes you look like a newlywed."

Aspasia had only been back in Istanbul for two years, but her Turkish was already good enough to allow her to follow conversations. At first her memory of the language had resisted her, but then the defenses had crumbled, and the words had come tumbling back into her consciousness, bringing with them a host of sun-filled memories. How sad it is, Aspasia thought, as she looked around the beauty parlor, at these people she had once considered murderers, and whom she now considered to be her friends. How sad it is that I didn't come home sooner.

Aspasia Palaeologos Best Cabot was a native of Istanbul—or Constantinople, as the Greeks called it. Her family had lived in the City since the days of the Byzantine emperors. They had two restaurants: a winter place in Galata and a summer place on the island of Büyükada, then better known by its Greek name, Prinkipo. Both the summer and the winter restaurants were famous for their music. All the best singers sang there. But when the singers had departed, the customers would stay, because if her father was in the right mood—if he had *keyif,* as the expression went, he would take out his guitar and sing *kantades* until the early hours.

All sorts of people came to the restaurants—large Greek families and groups of single men, elegant foreigners, fair-skinned Turkish officers who knew all the dances and all the songs but who did not like to admit in public that their mothers were Greek, or Bulgarian, or Albanian, or Russian, or whatever their uniform said they weren't. The restaurants were part of Aspasia's mother's dowry. If things had gone smoothly, they would have been part of Aspasia's dowry, too.

Aspasia had fond memories of Galata, especially of Galata in the early evening, when the light was golden and the streets were teeming with people in their finest clothes. But her favorite place on earth was Prinkipo. From the sea, Prinkipo looked like a green crown rising out of the water, a green crown studded with beautiful Ottoman summer villas. Prinkipo was an hour's ferry ride outside Istanbul, in the Sea of Marmara. There were no automobiles allowed on the island, only horses and carriages.

When Aspasia's family arrived at the end of May the restaurant would smell of dust. The furniture in their house would be draped in white sheets. The fine villas along the shore would have their shutters closed, the sea would be a desolately empty blue, and the wind would be far too chilly for evening promenades. Then, in the course of one weekend, the island would come alive. The wind would turn warm, the sunlight golden. The families and their servants would pour off the ferries. The shutters of their fine villas would fly open. The windows would fill with servants shaking dusters, servants beating rugs, servants shaking out the white sheets that had covered the furniture during the winter. The little shops near the ferry station would reopen. The streets would fill with horses and carriages, and elegant strollers wearing the finest fashions from Paris, Geneva, and London. The sea would fill with rowboats and the air would fill with music. Music from the *laterna,* music from the blind accordionist, and singing from the rowboats. There were few moments without sound. Years later, when the silence of the New England countryside threatened to chill her to the bone, she would close her eyes and pretend that she was back in Prinkipo on a summer night, basking in warm breezes, floating on the never-ending waves of music and footsteps and horses' hooves and people's voices.

It was a paradise for a young child, a paradise that came to an abrupt end in 1923, when Aspasia was thirteen. It was a bad year for Greeks in Istanbul: the first year of the Turkish Republic.

It was the year after the sacking and burning of Smyrna

and the catastrophic defeat of the Greek army in Anatolia. It was the year Aspasia's mother's restaurant in Galata was broken into by a group of men and Aspasia's mother was raped. Aspasia's aunts later said it was her father's fault.

The previous evening, he had tried to cheat a group of municipal officials. It was the old trick: adding the date to the bill. In the ensuing fight, Aspasia's father had called the youngest member of the party—a recently arrived Anatolian—a barbarian. Not only had he called him a barbarian, he had spat in his face. You did not do that sort of thing to a proud Anatolian on his first visit to a Greek taverna and go unpunished.

There was a difference of opinion as to whether it was the Anatolian municipal official who had sent the thugs to rape Aspasia's mother or whether it had been a spontaneous act. It was possible that the thugs had been walking past the restaurant the next day and been angered by the sight of the Greek flag Aspasia's father had hoisted over the door in an act of defiance. At any rate, Aspasia's family fled the country that same day, because they feared more reprisals.

They went to Athens, where Aspasia's father's brother had already established himself in the pastry business. Aspasia's father pleaded poverty and was taken in as an employee.

Eight months to the day after their arrival in Athens, Aspasia's mother gave birth to a baby boy. Because it was eight months and not nine months, there were hopes that he was not the rapist's son. But with every day, he looked more Turkish. He had large Eastern eyes and a darker complexion than the rest of the family. One day, when Aspasia came home from school, she found her mother trying to suffocate the infant. She rescued him just in time. Her mother then locked herself up in the outhouse with a kitchen knife.

Aspasia had shown great promise in school, but after her mother's death, she stayed at home to care for her father, her older brother, and the little boy. She hated the Turks more than ever, blaming them not only for the loss of her city, her happiness, and her dowry, but also for the loss of her dear mother, and the loss of the opportunity to better herself through education.

Although seething as she was with hatred for the Turks,

she could not bring herself to make the little boy suffer for the transgressions of his barbarian ancestors. He was a beautiful child and became Aspasia's first love. She baptized him Ektor, after her maternal grandfather.

After working in his brother's pastry shop for eighteen months, Aspasia's father took the money he had secretly smuggled out of Istanbul and opened up a pastry shop right across the street from his brother's. His brother was outraged. A terrible feud ensued. Asapsia's uncle went so far as to poison the milk Aspasia's father used in his rice pudding. One of the people made ill by this rice pudding happened to be a deputy in Parliament, and he almost had Aspasia's father's permit taken away. At the very last moment, Aspasia's father was able to dissuade him with a bribe.

As usual, Aspasia's father made too much of his victory. he had a big celebration and offered free ouzo to all his friends. He sang *kantades* until the early hours of the morning and shouted insults at the windows above his brother's pastry shop, which was where his brother lived. A few nights, later, Aspasia's father's pastry shop burned to the ground.

So, in 1925, her father, her brother Andreas, and little Ektor moved on to Alexandria.

This time they had no resources. The only relation they had in Alexandria was Aspasia's mother's half-sister. She could not forgive Aspasia's father for his part in the tragic events that had led to Aspasia's mother's death, and so she put him in the position of having to beg for assistance. Once she had humiliated him thoroughly, she agreed to put him to work in her grocery store. She treated him like an Arab lackey. Aspasia's brother, Andreas, looked around and quickly saw there was no future for him in this grocery store. He quickly found and courted the twenty-five-year-old daughter of a nightclub owner, whose dowry was a large villa overlooking the sea.

Until now, Andreas had been a dutiful brother. If things had gone smoothly, she was sure he would have continued to look after her, and refrained from marrying until she was herself married to a suitable man. But she could not blame him for breaking with tradition. Her chances of ever finding a husband were slim now that she had no dowry. She didn't care: she had Ektor. She gave Andreas her blessing, not realizing how his marriage would change him.

No sooner had his wife stepped out of her expensive wedding gown than she took control, not only of Andreas but of the entire family. Dimitra was as ugly as a witch, and jealous of Aspasia's fierce beauty. Under the guise of generosity, she put both Aspasia and her father to work in the nightclub. She arranged for Aspasia's father to take care of the billing (but not the actual money) and for Aspasia to sell cigarettes to the clientele.

Aspasia went out into the nightclub on the first night completely innocent of what people thought she was. Without her brother's protection, she found out in a matter of hours. It pleased Dimitra to watch what happened.

But then her plans to humiliate Aspasia backfired. Dimitra's father, the nightclub owner himself, began to take an interest in Aspasia, too. Not only in Aspasia, but in the little boy, Ektor. Dimitra began to make life even more difficult for her. She accused her of being a prostitute. Aspasia countered by saying that if she was a prostitute, it was Dimitra's family that had made her one. Aspasia then accused Dimitra of being barren. That sent Dimitra into such a rage that she devised a way to hurt Aspasia more than any other woman has ever hurt another woman.

One day, when Aspasia came back from an assignation, little Ektor was gone. Dimitra had disposed of him. Aspasia never found out what happened to him. She didn't know if Dimitra had had him killed, or given him away, or sold him. Aspasia combed the orphanages for him. She even went to the police, but they wouldn't help her. She was so beside herself when she returned from the police station that she took Dimitra by the throat and threatened to strangle her if she didn't tell her where Ektor was. "What do you care about that half-Turkish bastard?" Dimitra said. "I'm not having any half-Turkish bastard in my house."

When she saw the meek way her brother and father took this treatment, her opinion of men as good-for-nothings became unshakable. It was then that she left home, if you could call a house with that Medusa living in it a home.

She was forced to go to the siren's father, the nightclub owner himself, for help. He set her up in a flat, making it clear, of course, that he expected daily favors in return. She obliged him but made plans to escape. During this period, she had the misfortune of becoming pregnant, but the other women who lived in her building, who were accustomed to such things, helped her to abort.

She kept her eyes peeled for someone who could take her away from Alexandria. Eventually, she found him—a young, painfully innocent businessman who had no business wandering around the red-light district. He was British, but was also from Istanbul, as it turned out.

The City was the subject of their first conversations. He had grown up on the Asian side of the City, in Moda. His family had once owned an import-export firm there. He was in Alexandria working for a distant relation. He acted as if he were not worth much money, but Aspasia assumed the opposite because of the gold fillings in his teeth.

And so she set to work on him. While she was forced to sing for her supper every afternoon with the nightclub owner, in the evenings she played the virgin. Slowly she gave in, and methodically set about the task of making him happier than he had ever been in his life, with all the expertise she had gained during her few months of prostitution. When she became pregnant, she had no trouble convincing him to marry her.

The firm for which Phillip Best worked was not pleased with the match. They asked him to reconsider, and when he refused, they asked him to leave. Aspasia didn't mind, because that had been her plan all along—to leave Alexandria.

And so, in the spring of 1929, they set sail for New York, where an old schoolfriend of Phillip's had offered him a job in an investment firm. Their son was born a few weeks after their arrival. Aspasia baptized him Hector, after both her grandfather and her lost half-brother.

To tell the truth, the child was baptized twice, first in a Greek Orthodox church made warm by the anger of his absent father, and then in an Anglican church made cold by the scorn of his absent mother. Sad to call the birth of a son the beginning of the end, but it was true for Aspasia and Phillip, because when they looked at the little baby in his bassinet, one saw a Greek and the other an Englishman. The tug-of-war began before he even learned to walk.

If things had gone smoothly—if the stock market hadn't crashed, if Phillip hadn't lost his job, if Aspasia hadn't been forced to support the family by working first as an assistant to an abortionist and then as a housekeeper, if Phillip hadn't drowned his shame in drink—Aspasia was sure she could have turned the marriage into a harmonious one. She would not have minded the boisterous friends, the all-night card games, the overflowing ashtrays and broken glasses if he had been bringing home good money. And if he had been bringing home good money he would have been too busy to worry about the details of his son's future. But, as it was, their small apartment became a battlefield, with Hector the prize. When he was five years old, they were divorced. Although Aspasia was granted custody of the child, Phillip was granted the right to supervise his education. And since Aspasia knew what that meant—it meant boarding school in England, it meant they would take him away from her then and there and never give him back to her—she decided to take Hector outside New York, to a place where his father would never find him.

Through friends of friends of her employers, she found a job with a retired diplomat and his invalid wife in Woodstock, Connecticut. On the train from New York, she told her son that his father had been run over by a trolley.

Mr. Cabot was a kindly and deeply religious gentleman in his mid-fifties. He had retired early on account of his wife, who had been bedridden since the age of thirty-seven. The first time Aspasia laid eyes on this frail, watery-eyed woman, who reminded her of an old, cracked bar of soap, she said to herself, Aspasia, prepare yourself. This woman is going to die. Do not let this opportunity slip through your fingers.

And so she was careful. In laying out the groundwork for her illustrious future, she drew upon the wisdom she had gained at the expense of her first marriage. She knew now that it did not pay to speak your mind. Honest, brave, passionate women were thrown out of their homes. They lost their sons to English boarding schools. They became the laughingstock of drunken friends. Whereas no one was better loved than an obsequious servant, a groveling friend, a willing convert. Once Aspasia had proved herself to be an invaluable housekeeper, cook, nurse, valet, and lady's companion, once she had earned the trust of her ailing mistress and the admiration of her kindly master, she began to play her cards.

She loved her new country so much, she told them. She wanted to become an American citizen. Could they help her realize this dearest wish? They did. Mr. Cabot was present at the naturalization ceremony. He had tears in his eyes. When they returned home, he read her a Walt Whitman poem. For a few years he had been reading fine works to her. He had been touched that a woman of her background would have a taste for literature. "How extraordinary you are," he would say to her, as he caressed her forehead during their late-night trysts. His happiest moment—and Mrs. Cabot's happiest moment—was at breakfast one morning, not long after Aspasia had become an American citizen, when she expressed a shy admiration, a humble curiosity for their beautiful Episcopalian church. Could she, perhaps, if it was not too much of an imposition, accompany them one Sunday? And Hector—could he, perhaps, receive religious instruction? She was received into the church in 1937, the same year Hector became an acolyte. In 1938, when Mrs. Cabot died, her last wish was that her husband take "dear, dear Aspasia" as his wedded wife. "I can go in peace if you promise me that," she said. "I know she'll look after you." And Mrs. Cabot was right. Aspasia was the perfect wife, the darling of all Woodstock, until Mr. Cabot himself passed away in 1950.

How shocked her neighbors were when she stopped attending church after the funeral. How outraged when she had a Greek Orthodox chapel built on the property before her husband's body was even cold. Rumors circulated about the goat she had slaughtered for the laying of the cornerstone. Even the shopkeepers would not talk to her. But Aspasia laughed at them.

On the day she brought the priest down from Boston, she stood on the flagstone terrace and stared at the gently rolling hills of the estate—her estate—and imagined it as it would be one day, with Hector and his lovely young wife sitting arm in arm on the lawn, surrounded by a flock of little children who filled the air with the melodic chimes of Greek. "Grandmother, Grandmother, tell us a story," they would say. And she would tell them about their ancestors, the Byzantine emperors. They would listen with bated breath, their eyes shining at her tales of glory and magnificence, and then clouding over at the mention of that infamous Tuesday when Mehmet the Conqueror brought the empire to its knees. "But who knows, my children, what the future has in store for us? Perhaps, one day, Istanbul will be ours again, and we shall all return."

Standing on the flagstone terrace that day with the priest from Boston, she imagined sailing into her beloved city on a glistening ocean liner, watching throngs of jubilant Greeks toppling minarets while Aghia Sophia emerged from the shadows like a golden orb. What would she have thought that day had she been able to see into the future? February 18, 1967: a woman defeated by ten years of loneliness stepping off a Pan Am jet at dusty, grimy Yeşilköy airport, fighting her way through a throng of flat-headed Anatolian porters and customs officials, and seeing at the other end of the ill-lit room a large, red-faced, hawk-nosed American waving a beer bottle at her, and wondering who it could be. That had been her worst humiliation, not to recognize her own son.

The city she saw through the car windows on their way home looked just as foreign to her. So many Turkish signs, so many Turkish faces, so many dilapidated cars, so many old buildings about to crumble, so much dust—it was a hopeless cause, she decided, but she did not give up her fight.

One of the first things she did after unpacking her bags was to make arrangements to be buried in the Greek Orthodox cemetery in Balikli. Oh, the hours she had spent haggling with the priests at the Patriarchate, bargaining with the undertaker, choosing the tombstone, and the choir, and the clothes, and insuring that her grave would be properly tended and her bones exhumed at the proper time. Oh, the joy she had enjoyed. Even if the city itself would never again be Greek, she told herself, she was staking her claim.

The project had kept her busy for weeks. Finally, there was only one thing left to do, and that was to find someone trustworthy to leave the instructions with. But who? Her son, the American? Her wretched daughter-in-law? Her grandchildren, who never talked to her? The neighbors, who looked right through her, as if she were a window? No, she couldn't trust any of these people to carry out her wishes. Of all the people she had met on the Hill, there was only one person she could call her friend.

And who was this person who listened solemnly as Aspasia explained the funeral arrangements in all their grisly detail, who put the instructions into a manila envelope and filed them away in a safe place, who insisted that Aspasia stay for coffee, who asked, with genuine concern, after Aspasia's health? This person was her son's secretary. Her name was Feza Hanim, and she was—it went without saying—a Turk.

A Turk, and therefore an enemy. But an enemy who cared for her and wished to help her. Oh, Aspasia! she said to herself that night. What kind of world is it you live in, when your enemies are kinder to you than your own people? Oh, Aspasia! You are planning your own funeral. Your soul is dead.

No, not dead, but dying. Perhaps there is a chance for you, now that you know that your real friends are the ones you always thought were your enemies. Look how much you trust them now! Look into the mirror and watch Kerim Bey come up behind you, smiling, flashing a pair of scissors. Do you shudder at the sight of him? Do you think, for a moment, that he is about to slit your throat? No, of course not. No, not for long. You shudder, but only for half a second. And then you smile, and let your hand drop from your neck, and remind yourself that he is your friend, that he understands you better than your own people do, because he, too, is a child of the City.

Look at yourself in the mirror and say, There is hope for you. You have lifted the curses on your enemies, and perhaps one day your enemies will lift their curses on you.

Perhaps, one day, you will feel a hand on your shoulder and hear that voice from the past. You will turn your head and he will be there, reformed and repentant. You will look young and beautiful, with your frosted hair. He will whisk you away. When the angel comes to take you to the other world, and asks you what you have achieved in your lifetime, you will be able to say, "In the autumn of my life,

I knew love. My life—my senseless odyssey—fell together like pieces in a puzzle."

And who knew what other glories awaited her? Perhaps, one day, her son would come and ask her, "Mother, why have you never taken me to see the house where you were born? And what about the church you were baptized in? And the restaurants?" There was no knowing what miracles awaited her. Who could tell? Perhaps, one day in the distant future, her daughter-in-law would show her some respect.

Looking at Amy now (her hair was dry: Kerim Bey, having offered his apologies, had moved on to rescue a flushed Stella Ashe from the hairdryer), Aspasia thought, how weak this woman is. She's not happy with her life, and yet she endures it. She never fights back, except in small ways, like a petulant child. Look at where she threw her magazine. She threw it on the floor because she was tired of looking at hairdos, tired of waiting and being passed over. But her impatience had gone unnoticed, except by Aspasia. Aspasia had never been fooled by Amy. From the very beginning, she had known that the girl was not strong enough to be her son's wife.

A woman's face told no lies when her hair was up in curlers. Her smiles lost their charm, her eyes their power to captivate. Watching her mother-in-law's reflection in the beauty parlor mirror, Amy could read her naked thoughts. A frown: she was recalling an injustice, one of tens of thousands. A fleeting smile: she was planning her revenge. And now, doubt. She was turning her head from side to side, looking for that double chin that Amy could see so clearly. She was looking into her eyes. Recognition: she sighed. She turned to Amy's reflection, scanning it for flaws. Her lips curled. She sat back.

One of these days Amy was going to learn to trust first impressions. With Aspasia in particular, she could have saved herself so much trouble. Because there was another time when a woman's face told no lies, and that was when she did not know she was being observed.

All the signs had been there eighteen years ago in New London, on that cold Sunday afternoon in March. Remembering her first encounter with Aspasia, Amy felt like a fortune-teller gazing into a crystal ball. There it was, spread out before her: her future.

The train was pulling into the station. Her face pressed against the window, Amy was scanning the crowd on the platform, while Hector, who was sitting across from her, hid his face behind a newspaper. "Do you see her?" he asked. "She has black hair and she's probably wearing a fox coat."

"Yes, I see her," Amy said, "In fact, she's standing under our window staring up at me."

"Oh, God. Well, just stare back at her as if you're insulted."

"Lower the paper a little. You look too obvious. You know, I think she's caught on already. She's staring at your hands. Don't you think she recognizes that?" She pointed at his class ring.

"Oh, God, you're right. Why didn't I think of it?" Holding the paper with one hand, Hector removed the ring from his other hand with his teeth. Amy suppressed a giggle. En route between her humdrum New Jersey home and her humdrum college, she was delighted to find herself in the midst of an intrigue.

She had struck up a conversation with Hector between Penn Station and New Haven. She was not in the habit of talking to men on trains: she had been something of a snob even then. But he had looked right, with his Brooks Brothers clothes and his leather briefcase full of serious-looking mathematics textbooks. After Bridgeport, they had retired to the club car for a few martinis.

Outside New London, which was his destination as well as hers, he had suggested that they continue on the train to Boston, for dinner. The idea had appealed to her. She had been looking for a reason not to go back to college anyway. Her closest friends had all dropped out to get married. The only reason she was still there was to please her parents—dull, earnest, hardworking people who believed in education the way other people believed in the Second Coming, while she herself had always suspected that there was more to life than final exams. What if she had said no to Hector's invitation? Where would she be now? She had said yes, she would be happy to join him for dinner, so long as they had lobster. He had liked that.

It did occur to her, as she locked eyes with the distraught black-haired, fur-coated woman who was so clearly Hector's mother (that same hawklike face, that same disaster-seeking glint in her eyes), it did cross her mind that Hector's motives in asking her to dinner were not as romantic as she would have liked them to be. But that was part of the romance—to be the other woman.

"Is she alone?" he asked.

"No, she's not," Amy said. "She's with a younger woman. Dark, heavyset. Long, curly hair. She looks sweet. Her legs are like tree trunks, though."

Behind the newspaper, Hector sighed. "Yes," he said. "That will be Eleni."

"That will be Eleni." That was all he had said. She had guessed the truth: the poor girl was his fiancée, of course. But Amy had not discovered the whole truth for a long time, and when she did she felt truly ashamed. Aspasia had had Eleni brought over from Greece, just for Hector. They were to have been married that June, after Hector finished his exams. When the engagement fell through, Eleni had to go to work in an uncle's pizzeria. It was typical of Hector that he had let his mother bully him into the engagement, only to slip through her fingers at the last moment. This was Hector to a T: pliable and good-natured on the surface, a rebellious adolescent underneath. No one was going to tell him what to do. Rules were for other people. He was the exception. Amy supposed she had known that about him from the start, but she hadn't minded in those days because they had been breaking them together. Now, eighteen years later, Amy was the rule Hector took exception to.

The conductor rang the bell and the train began to move. "Is the coast clear now?" Hector asked. He put down his newspaper just a moment too soon. "Phew," he said. "That was the longest three minutes of my life." He glanced out the window. He let out a horrible moan, as if he had seen a ghost. His mother was walking alongside the train.

She was looking at him and yet she was not looking at him. She was looking at him as if he were an ocean she was scanning for signs of life. She was looking at him as if he were lying dead in a coffin. Her eyes were filling with tears. As the train picked up speed, she put her hands over her mouth to stifle a scream. At the end of the platform, she stopped, put her hands on her head, and looked up at the heavens as if to exhort the gods. This was the true Aspasia, Aspasia the tragedienne, whose existence was a mere shadow of itself unless she was being cheated, abandoned, or betrayed. Only then was life big enough for her. Only then could she feel the full brunt of not only her own misfortunes but the misfortunes of all her forbears, all Byzantium, Greece, and Christendom. She was happy to suffer for them all.

This was the true Aspasia, and not the woman who turned up at Amy's door eighteen months later: contrite, tentative, soft-spoken, and loaded down with presents. The joke had gone out of Amy and Hector's life by then. No more club cars, no more bars, no more restaurants they couldn't afford, no more last-minute parties. They were married and living in Morningside Heights, in an apartment the size of a closet. Actually, it was only Amy who lived in the apartment, because Hector was working on his thesis and therefore lived in the library. That was like him, too. It was all or nothing with Hector. He was either working himself to death or not working at all. Friendless, pregnant, suffering from morning, noon, evening, and night sickness, Amy had considered packing her bags and going home more than once. It was only the prospect of her parents' smug faces (the I-told-you-so's, the lectures on the virtues of Planning Ahead) that stopped her. Amy had been glad to find Aspasia standing at the door on that dismal September morning, almost eighteen months to the day after their first encounter.

At lunch (the Plaza), Aspasia had sat across from her with a tired, wise, and understanding smile (how hard it must have been for her to keep quiet) while Amy confessed to confusion and remorse. "My child, you must allow me to help you," Aspasia had said. "I have money. I can make life comfortable for you. Let Hector finish his thesis in New York, and come back with me to Connecticut. I can look after you." And Amy (never one to think things through—she and Hector were a perfect match in that respect) had consented on the spot.

Hector, to his credit, had tried to talk her out of it. But she had not listened. She had enjoyed those first months in Woodstock. She had to admit it. The food, the clothes, the servants—it had been just like a fairy tale, with Aspasia playing the fairy godmother. How innocent Amy had been. And Aspasia—how wise, how serene, how giving. At times Amy would remember her own mother and think how selfish and small-minded she was in comparison to this marvel of motherhood and femininity. She wondered now if Aspasia had deliberately set out to fool her, or if, in her search for an idol, she had fooled herself.

It was when Amy went into labor that the trouble began.

Amy had been seeing a doctor in the nearby town of Putnam. She had assumed that when the time came Aspasia would either call him or drive her to the hospital. Such a sophisticated woman, who quoted the poetry of Walt Whitman and spoke in reverential tones of her son, the mathematician, would certainly have a respect for the innovations of science. But no. Amy had misjudged her. Too late—twelve hours into a thirty-hour labor—she realized that Aspasia planned to deliver the baby herself.

Amy tried to get to the phone to call the doctor herself, but she was too weak to walk. As Monday turned into Tuesday, she had to fight sleep as well as pain. Every time she drifted off, Aspasia slapped her. Amy would open her eyes and think she was in hell: a thin line of daylight shimmering like a flame in the gap between the curtains, the table piled high with sheets and scissors, a gray and moldy rectangle where the mirror had been, tubs of water on the floor, and standing over her, her features thrown into relief by the lamp, the true Aspasia, grim, muscular, and glowing with purpose, rolling up her sleeves with relish as she prepared to plunge her arm into Amy once again to stretch the cervix around the baby's head.

When the time came to push, Amy was too angry and exhausted to cooperate. Aspasia swore at her in Greek and told her in English that she was not a real woman. She got up on the bed and sat down on Amy's stomach. Amy thought she was going to burst.

And that was how she had given birth to Chloe, with Aspasia sitting on her stomach. Another glimpse into the crystal ball: her next two years in a nutshell. It was Aspasia who became Chloe's mother, not the sick, weak, shell-shocked woman whom Aspasia did not let out of bed for forty days. It was Aspasia who decided Amy's milk was not rich enough for Chloe, Aspasia who filled the house with incense and placed a broom against the front door at night to keep out the devil, and Aspasia who decided that even though Chloe's legal name was Chloe she should be baptized Aspasia. It was Aspasia who announced to Hector that mother and child wanted to spend the summer in the country, and Aspasia who decided in the fall that she could not allow mother and child to return to the city without her. She rented a grand apartment on Riverside Drive and moved them into it one afternoon while Hector was at the library. Hector's protests were met with contempt. What kind of father was he, Aspasia had said, to expect his own family to live in a shoebox? Hector had shrugged his shoulders and walked out. Amy had followed him to the elevator.

She had put her hand on his shoulder. "Hector," she had said. "Please." She had wanted to say more but was unable to find the words. They had stared at each other. Two strangers. "Well, this is what you wanted, isn't it?" he had said. It was indicative of her confused state of mind that she had nodded.

It was as if Aspasia were still sitting on her, telling her what to do and think. If ever a small voice inside her tried to disagree with what Aspasia thought was right and good, she would feel shame and suppress it. Amy wondered how long it would have taken her to fight back if it hadn't been for Meredith Lacey.

August 1955: Hector had received his doctorate that June, and Aspasia had brought the family to Greece as a graduation present. They were staying in her brother's summer villa outside the village of Tigani, on the island of Samos. Every morning after breakfast, Hector would disappear with his sketch pad. Art was his new hobby, his new excuse. He would promise to come back in time for their morning swim, but he never did.

They would wait for him until eleven, and then they would set out for the beach with their tubes and beach blankets, hats, pails and shovels, watermelons and cold meatballs. All of them: Aspasia, Aspasia's brother, his wife and son, Amy, Chloe. Birds would rise up in panic-stricken flight as they walked down the path. They made more noise than an army. There was a taverna at the far end of the beach and this was where Amy would sit while the others swam, because she was two months pregnant that August, and pregnant women were not allowed to go swimming.

It was at this taverna that Amy met Leslie and Meredith Lacey. They had already been living in Istanbul for six years by then—they were in Samos for a late summer vacation. Their children were not with them. They had left them at home with the maid. They were not the sort of people Amy would normally have befriended. Cold and angular, with pretensions of intellectual superiority, they were the sort of people who had made her life miserable in prep school and college. But in contrast to her Greek relations, they were as refreshing as a glass of ice water after a trek in the jungle.

She had been playing her favorite game that morning, watching her family on the beach and pretending she had never met them before. That short, compact woman in the black bathing suit was not her mother-in-law. That spoiled, fat little monster who talked baby-talk and crossed her eyes to attract attention was not her daughter. That fat, balding man, that fat, ugly woman with all the moles on her face, that conceited playboy of a son—how dreadful they looked, how glad she was she didn't know them.

When Leslie and Meredith, who were sitting at the next table, started talking to her, she continued the pretense. And that was why Meredith had made that tactless remark.

During a lull in the conversation, they had all three of them gazed out to the beach, to see Aspasia reduce little Chloe to terrified screams by dunking her repeatedly in the water.

"What a dreadful woman," Meredith had said.

The pretense had not lasted long. The family had descended upon them, shaking the taverna walls with their loud requests for fish, cold drinks, and service. Aspasia and the Laceys had had a tense little conversation, which came to an abrupt end when Aspasia found out where they lived. Later in the meal, she had corrected them when they ordered Turkish coffee. "No," she said. "Not Turkish coffee. Greek coffee.'' Amy had been mortified. The Laceys soon stopped speaking altogether. Having finished their lunch, they excused themselves. ''Do look us up if you ever are in Istanbul,'' they said to Amy. ''Hah! We'll never go to that stinking place, not while there's even one Turk left in it,'' Aspasia told them. It was their look of distaste that lingered in Amy's mind, paving the way for the first doubt.

Could it be that Aspasia was not always right? She played with the idea the way a child without appetite plays with a fork.

It was not long afterward that Aspasia's nephew, the conceited, philandering, brainless Manolis, was arrested as a member of the Communist Party and taken off the island to prison.

If there was one thing Manolis did not care about, it was politics. It was laughable to suspect him of being a Communist. Even Aspasia, who was, she bragged to Amy, responsible for spreading the rumors that had led to his arrest, thought it was stupid of the police to have believed her. But that was all for the good, she said. She had had her revenge. Long ago, she said, her sister-in-law had sold her half-brother to the white-slave trade. Now she was going to suffer for her sins. Her son Manolis was on his way to a prison island where they would knock some sense into him. If he didn't act right, there would be ''accidents,'' and he would die.

Manolis' mother, Dimitra, was insane with grief. Although she had no proof, she knew it was Aspasia who had turned him in. She had also decided that it was Aspasia who had put a curse on her, and caused her to suffer the many still births and miscarriages that had left her with a single living child. She threw Aspasia and the rest of them out of her house. The next day she came to their rented rooms and told Aspasia that she had better keep a close eye on Amy's baby when it was born, because if it turned out to be a boy, she had plans.

This sent Aspasia into a panic. She decided they should leave the island at once. It was almost August 15, the date of the festival of the Assumption of the Virgin Mary. The boats were full of pilgrims traveling to sacred shrines, so there were no tickets available. Aspasia went into the main port to see if she could twist any arms.

After Hector had woken up and wandered off, oblivious as always to the household confusion, Amy took Chloe to the sweetshop on the waterfront. Neither she nor Chloe had been out that day and the child was getting cranky. They sat outside at a table overlooking the harbor. Amy ordered two lemon sodas and two ice creams and then she combined them to make ice cream sodas.

As they sat there, they looked across the channel at the distant mountains of the Turkish coast.

How quiet it was without Aspasia. She could not remember how long it had been since she had been out alone—alone with her child, and without her mother-in-law. Chloe was not acting hateful for a change. She even exchanged some words with Amy in English. After she had finished her ice cream soda, she put her chubby little hand on Amy's arm and said "thank you" in a thick Greek accent. It broke Amy's heart. She wondered if they might have been friends if Aspasia hadn't invaded their lives. She thought about the life that awaited her in America—in Washington, where Hector was due to start work, at the National Bureau of Standards. She thought of the upcoming birth: Aspasia standing over her, Aspasia removing the baby from her body, the forty days in bed. And Hector, out of the house or asleep, letting his mother do whatever she wished.

Then she looked across at the wild, dark, inviting mountains on the Turkish coast. She looked at Chloe, who seemed at a loss. "Where's Mama?" she asked Amy in Greek.

Amy paid up and took Chloe by the hand over to the fishing port. She found the man who had taken the Laceys across the channel to the Turkish town of Kuşadasi, and arranged for him to take her there immediately.

She had money and documents in her purse. She didn't go back to the hotel for her clothes, because she didn't know how long she was going to stay in Turkey. If she knew deep down that she was going to remain a lifetime, she didn't want to admit it to herself. August was a windy month, but fortunately they were between storms, and so Amy and Chloe had a smooth passage.

Amy never forgot what Turkey looked like when she stepped off the boat. After Greece, it was quiet and relaxed.

The people on the streets moved about in blissful slow motion—such a treat to the eyes after the frenetic activity on the other side of the channel. The sun was not as bright. The cobblestones in the streets of Kuşadasi lacked the hard shine that comes from constant scrubbing. After they had checked into a hotel, Amy took Chloe out to a little restaurant, where they had the same meal they had been having all summer on Samos: grilled fish, potatoes, and salad, except that the potatoes, peppers, and onions were finely diced—a welcome change from the large, careless chunks they had been getting on Samos. Lazy Oriental music poured into the street through shop doors and car windows—a perfect antidote to the lively, almost hysterical music that Amy had once loved and lately come to hate. All summer on Samos they had been playing the same five songs over and over (two by a man who sang through his nose and three by a woman and her shrieking chorus) until Amy had thought she was in purgatory.

Aspasia had told her that Turks were rapists and murderers who would rob her blind the moment she set foot in the country. It pleased Amy no end to discover that Aspasia was wrong. The Turks she met on her way up the coast could not have been more considerate.

The manager of the hotel in Kuşadasi insisted on arranging her travel to Izmir. He found her a taxi driver who was married to his cousin and was therefore trustworthy. On the way to Izmir, they stopped for lunch at a friend's restaurant. The friend refused to accept payment. The taxi driver had a friend who worked in the ticket office of the Turkish Maritime Lines, and he was able to find her a first-class cabin on the ship leaving for Istanbul the following day, even though the ship was supposed to be fully booked. The taxi driver didn't leave her until she was settled into a hotel that was known to be respectable.

On the ship to Istanbul, she was able to rest, because the staff on the *Marmara* could not have enough of Chloe. At supper, the captains insisted that she sit at their table. They taught her how to say "Allah allah allah." Every time she said it, they burst out laughing and pinched her cheeks. The bartenders in the first-class lounge never tired of giving her soft drinks and twirling her around the barstools and teaching her Turkish words. When they sailed into Istanbul, while the bartenders looked after Chloe, Amy was able to stand on deck and watch the city sweep before her eyes.

She saw only the best things from the ship—the city walls, the palaces, the minarets and Byzantine churches, the European city on one side, the Asian city on the other, the Golden Horn, and the blue mouth of the Bosphorus. Nothing she saw later—not even the things she saw later that day—could sway her from her first impression of Istanbul. It was the most beautiful city in the world. It was her city. Even if the Laceys had not taken her in, Amy was sure she would have managed to stay.

It was a lot to ask of strangers: to take in a pregnant woman with a spoiled two-year-old daughter who had only one dress and a scuffed-up pair of shoes to her name. But the Laceys did so with good grace, even pretending it was a pleasure.

To tell the truth, pretense had become the operative word by the time March rolled by and Amy checked into the hospital to have the baby. Was this woman never going to leave? they asked each other. True, they had said she could stay as long as she wanted. True, they had pooh-poohed the idea of her working as a governess to their children to pay off the medical bills. True, also, they were terribly fond of the poor thing. Such an exquisite sense of humor, and she had been through so much that one could not *not* sympathize with her. And yet she had no plans, no hopes, no dreams. (They did not realize she had fallen in love with her obstetrician: a hopeless infatuation from the beginning—he was engaged to one of the richest women in Istanbul.) It was to force the issue that Meredith did what was, after all, the decent thing.

> Congratulations stop you are the father of a healthy boy stop Neil Bartholomew Cabot was born at the American Hospital on the eleventh of March weighing in at two and three quarters kilos stop mother and child both doing well although Amy is still recuperating from hopefully minor exclamation point complications of

caesarean delivery stop what do you want me to do with them question mark please advise post haste stop write care of Woodrow College yours very sincerely Meredith Lacey.

Thanks kind telegram stop my mother requests custody both children stop how soon baby fit for travel yours Hector.

Sorry no dice dear comma Mom says absolutely not although she could use some assistance with bills exclamation point yours Meredith.

Thanks prompt reply my mother adamant on custody issue ready to wage legal battle stop means it stop ask Amy what advise yours Hector.

Sorry answer still unchanged stop but what about bills question mark Meredith.

Sorry must resolve custody issue prior funds forthcoming Hector.

Your wife almost dead of hemorrhaging comma your son jaundiced and your daughter houseguest at home of perfect strangers and here you are squabbling about bills exclamation point what kind of father are you underlined question mark Meredith.

Arriving first week April settle all disputes sincerely Hector.

"Did you ever hear the story of how Hector came to Istanbul?" Meredith said to Ginger as Hamdi Bey's taxi crawled through the coastal town of Arnavutköy. The traffic was terrible. Hector glanced at the clock on the back wall of the Yapi ve Kredi bank. He was already late for his appointment.

"No, I don't think I *did* ever hear that story," Ginger said.

"I'm sure I put it into one of my letters. You did know that Amy came first, didn't you?"

"Vaguely, yes. Didn't you meet her on some island?"

"Yes, that's right. We never expected to see her again, of course. And then lo and behold—"

"I remember that story. She stayed for about a year, right?"

"Well, almost. When is Neil's birthday, Hector? April? May?"

"March eleventh," said Hector.

"And you arrived . . . ?"

"Early April."

"Yes, that's right," said Meredith, turning back to Ginger. "And now here's the good part. His mother—you know, Aspasia—sent him here to kidnap the children."

"Goodness," said Ginger. "How extreme."

"She is, rather. Even now. Don't you agree?"

"Hmmm. Yes. I know what you mean. Quite a temper for a woman her age."

"She's Greek, of course."

"Yes, I know. Greeks are awfully temperamental, aren't they?"

"Oh, indeed they are." Meredith pursed her lips. "I don't think I could ever live there. Greece, I mean. I'd be a nervous wreck in six months. No, I prefer the Turks. They're so much calmer."

"Hmmm. Yes," said Ginger.

"You never really *intended* to kidnap Chloe and Neil, did you, Hector?" Meredith asked, turning to him abruptly, as if she had just remembered he was in the car.

Hector shook his head.

It was true: his mother was a difficult woman. But he did not like the breezy way Meredith and Ginger dismissed her as a crank. If you had only seen the death in her face the day Amy and Chloe went missing, he wanted to say to them. If you had only heard the sighs and broken sobs floating down the corridor night after night after night after night. How were we to know that they were safe and sound? For all we knew, they might have drowned or been kidnapped. And how do you think I felt, he wanted to ask them, when I showed her that first telegram announcing Neil's birth, and she bowed her head and went into the room where she kept her icon, and fell to her knees, and took off the diamond ring she had promised to give the Virgin Mary if she answered her prayers?

And then to watch her make plans—yes, they were totally

unrealistic, but they had brought her back to life. As she bustled about the Riverside Drive apartment, making lists and conspiratorial phone calls, humming songs, cleaning up the nursery, advising Hector on how to mix formula, change a diaper, and bribe officials, she had the inner glow of a bride on the eve of her wedding. There is nothing, Hector thought, worse than false hope.

He had never intended to kidnap the children for her. He had been hoping, instead, to make some sort of compromise with Amy—shared custody, perhaps, in exchange for financial support. He would never have gone along with his mother's plans if he had not had another reason for wanting to visit Istanbul. Yes, he wanted to see Chloe and the new baby. But what was foremost in his mind at that time was his father.

He had known his father was alive since his freshman year in college. It was a secret he had shared with no one. He had found out from a man he had met in a bar in Greenwich Village. This man claimed to be a friend of Phillip Best's, and he also said he had known Aspasia during the thirties. "Around the same time she was doing abortions," he recalled. He even said he remembered meeting Hector as a toddler. The man did not have kind things to say about Aspasia, or, for that matter, about his friend, Phillip Best, whom he had last seen in 1944, when he was "up to no good, as usual." But he was kind enough to take Hector back to his pigsty of an apartment and rummage through his things until he came up with a postcard from him. It was from Bombay, and it contained the address of a paper company for which he claimed to be working. Hector had written to that address, and after a year he had received a response.

This letter was from Kenya, where Hector's father claimed to be working as a farm machinery distributor. It was the beginning of a polite, strained correspondence in which much attention was given to the choice of words. "You must come and visit me here," Phillip Best would write in his postscripts, which were carefully placed to look casual. He would sometimes preface the invitation with "By the way!" or "Come to think of it!" The "here" where Hector was to visit him changed with regularity. Phillip Best went from Kenya back to London, and then to Beirut, Athens, Nicosia. The last letter had been from Istanbul, where he said he was working for a pharmaceutical company. He had written:

> It is so nice to be home again. Did your mother ever tell you that both of your parents hark from this enchanted city? It is still as lovely as ever, with its sparkling waterways and splendid pleasure palaces. I do so hope you'll find time to visit me here. I am living on the Asian side, in Moda, which is where I grew up. I still have family here, though I must admit that the only ones who remember me are a handful of aunts and uncles who are not much longer for this world. Still, it is fun for a rolling stone like myself to gather moss. . . .

Hector often wondered what course his life might have taken if he had arrived in Istanbul by air—if his first sight of Turkey had been that expanse of barren hills. If his first Turks had been a pair of sleepy, round-shouldered customs officials marking his bags with chalk. If his first view of the Galata Bridge had been the dusty red and white Yapi ve Kredi signs, seen through the grimy windows of a slow-moving bus. If he had arrived the sensible way, if his first impressions had been of the slowness and the dirt, he might have remained the detached, cool-headed mathematician. If he had been sober and jet-lagged when he arrived at the Laceys', instead of wild-eyed, euphoric, and drunk, they might not have befriended him, or forced him to make up with Amy. She might have agreed to a divorce, perhaps even joint custody of the children. And he might have found his father.

But Hector did not arrive in Istanbul the sensible way. He arrived in a Belgian-registered Peugeot whose trunk his mother had thought would be big enough to hide the children in. From the moment he passed under the stares of the two ferocious soldiers who guarded the Edirne border station with rusty submachine guns, a nightmarish logic took over his life, forcing Dr. Jekyll into retirement and replacing him with Mr. Hyde.

The customs people kept him for four hours, during which time they searched every inch of the Peugeot for contraband. They filled up his passport with huge stamps and clumsily written riders. They asked him questions in Turkish, and when he did not answer they slammed their fists on their desks and shouted at him. Then their superior arrived, his hands clasped behind his back. He took Hector's passport, examined it the way a housewife would a dubious-looking piece of fruit, put it down on his desk, and then redirected his attention to another pile of official documents. After an hour had passed, he looked up and said to Hector, "You may go."

As he drove off down the road, watching the watchful border guards in the rearview mirror, it occurred to him that he had fallen off the edge of the earth.

The road was lined on both sides with wrecked cars, smashed wagons, burnt-out gasoline trucks, overturned buses with people climbing out of them. Halfway to Tekirdağ, a bus began to race with him. There were only two men on the bus—the driver and a fierce-looking man with a huge mustache and flashing white teeth. He looked like the Terrible Turk his mother had threatened him with as a child, the kind who walked through the night with a knife between his teeth and chopped Christians into forty-two pieces. Every time the bus passed him, the Terrible Turk would do a triumphant belly dance. Wild music was playing on the radio.

First Hector tried to lose the bus by slowing down, but it would just stop at the side of the road and wait for him to go by, and then pass him again. So Hector tried speeding up. The faster he drove, the faster they drove. Cars coming from the opposite direction had to run off the road to avoid them. The faster Hector went, the better he felt. He got into the swing of it. When he passed them, he began to belly dance, too.

First he did it with one hand on the wheel. Then he let go of the wheel altogether. The bus driver followed suit.

On the outskirts of Tekirdağ, there was almost an accident. Hector swung around a corner to find the bus blocking the road. He screeched to a stop. His Peugeot spun around three hundred and sixty degrees. The bus driver and his

Terrible Turk companion thought this was very funny. They got out of the bus, walked over to the car, reached in and patted him on the back, and, using sign language, invited him to join them for lunch at a nearby gas station restaurant. It was at this lunch that Hector had his introduction to *raki*. When he got up from the table, he could hardly walk.

How he had managed to get to Istanbul that afternoon without killing himself or someone else, Hector didn't know. He must have gone ninety miles an hour the whole way. He remembered flying past the crumbling walls of the old city, the Gypsy encampments, abandoned horse carts and idle fishing boats, tanneries, crowds of veiled women, clouds of dust, mosques. He remembered hearing the muezzins calling the faithful to prayer from their minarets and shouting back at them, the way a cavalry officer shouts before charging. He had actually believed he was conquering the city.

He drove around in circles, across bridges, up and down cobblestone streets, along the Golden Horn, the Bosphorus, and the Marmara. God only knew for how long. He had no idea where he was going and he didn't care. He arrived at the Laceys' in the same way he had arrived at so many other turning points in his life—by accident.

They were cold to him at the outset ("Oh," they said. "Yes. You. Well, I suppose you'll have to come in."), but before long he had conquered them, too. "And to think," they told him at breakfast the next morning, "that we expected you to be dull."

There was a disappointment awaiting him that morning when, before going to visit Amy in the hospital, he tried to reach his father by telephone. A surly secretary at the pharmaceutical company informed him that Phillip Best had been "let go." She gave him an address in Damascus.

Damascus. Another thousand miles. he wouldn't have time to go—not if Amy was in as bad shape as the Laceys said she was. He went to the hospital that afternoon with a heavy heart. It was with great relief that he saw Amy was infatuated with her obstetrician.

His name was Fehmi Bey. He was a handsome man despite his receding hairline. He had liquid black eyes and the demeanor of a Roman senator. Amy blushed when he entered the room.

When the obstetrician saw Hector, his face darkened. He shook Hector's hand, congratulated him on the birth of a fine son, and made it clear that the infatuation was mutual.

Hector felt almost proud of Amy. He hadn't thought she had it in her to be so naughty. Now, this was the Amy he had married. Although he could not bring himself to feel any affection for her—not after what she had done to him and his mother—he wished her well.

"Tell me the truth, Amy. Do you need me here or would you prefer me to go?"

"I'd prefer you to go," she said. He went back to the Laceys to pack his bags, so that he could leave for Damascus first thing in the morning.

But the Laceys had other plans. They were not about to let their new friend slip away.

They wanted Hector to apply for a job at Woodrow College. There was an opening in the math department and they had already been on the phone to the dean and the vice-president arranging interviews. They were sure he would get the job. They even had a house lined up for him and Amy. (They assumed he and Amy were getting back together: they did not know about the obstetrician.) The house was a beauty: it was right across the street from the Laceys'. There was another couple after it, but Meredith wanted to beat them to it, because they were teetotalers and very dull.

"I've invited the chairman of the math department to dinner," Meredith announced. "I'm sure you'll have no trouble charming him. He's Turkish."

Hector remembered sitting back at one point during dinner that night, looking around the table and shaking his head in disbelief. Why was he allowing these people to boss him around? They were just the sort of people he had hated most in prep school and college. He could read them like a book. Leslie was the sort of man he could imagine telling his son to go make a killing on the stock market. Meredith was the sort of woman who ran charities and Girl Scout meetings. They were fish out of water. Hector couldn't imagine what they were doing in Istanbul.

Until Hector got drunk, it was a very boring dinner party. Emin Bey, the chairman of the math department, and his wife, Roksan, did their best to keep the conversation going, but their eyes were heavy with sleep. When Hector blacked out, they were discussing the Marshall Plan.

Sometimes entire evenings were lost to Hector, but on this occasion there were a few highlights that had stayed with him, that made him cringe and hide his head under the pillow the next morning. First there was his memory of lambasting his fellow dinner guests with his unorthodox views on the Marshall Plan. He could see the four faces looking at him across the dinner table—intent, sober, concerned. He also remembered going after Leslie Lacey, holding him personally responsible for the sins of the social class he represented.

Then, somehow, they had gotten him upstairs to the living room, where he danced the *hasapiko* (without music). He remembered the four puzzled faces watching him as he circled around and around the living room floor, to his own beat.

Later, he was kneeling beneath the window, clapping his hands to his own beat, while a miraculously animated Emin Bey did *his* own dance to *his* own music, his suit jacket nowhere to be seen and his shirt half unbuttoned. He had a *raki* bottle inserted in his belt and he was doing the *çiftetelli*. From time to time, he would remove the bottle, and he and Hector would take a swig or two. Emin Bey's wife was trying to convince him that they should go home. Hector remembered pushing her away.

He had even vaguer memories of waking up Chloe and bringing her downstairs to show her off to the company. She was screaming with terror. There was another isolated image of him telling Leslie to go to make a killing on the stock market and Meredith to go make some Girl Scout cookies, and yet another memory, which made him shudder the next morning, of throwing his arms around Meredith and trying to push her into the bedroom.

He didn't remember a thing after that, but he feared the worst. He decided to leave for Damascus immediately.

He waited until both the Laceys had left the house, and then tiptoed downstairs with his luggage.

He wrote out a large check to the Laceys and an even larger one to Amy. He put them in an envelope with a note of apology and left the envelope on the kitchen counter.

Then he steered his Peugeot down the cobblestone streets of Rumeli Hisar, turning right on the shore road, in the direction of Bebek.

He had a dreadful hangover. It was because of the hangover that he decided to stop for a beer in the attractive open-air café that he passed on his way into Bebek. He took a table under a plane tree, next to a ruddy-complexioned man in a fisherman's sweater who was eating a fish.

This man was Emin Bey. When he looked up from his fish and saw Hector, he let out a loud, joyful cry. "My friend. How are you? Come and join me for a plate of fish." Emin Bey had a hangover, too, but this did not lessen his memories of the enjoyable evening they had just passed together.

Emin Bey had never met an American as open and genuine as Hector. Most Americans were like unripened fruit, but this man had a great soul. Not only did he know how to enjoy himself, but he was a farsighted thinker. Emin Bey had never before met an American who shared his unorthodox views about the Marshall Plan. For despite the fact that Emin Bey was pro-American, he could foresee, as Hector did, the negative effects that this massive injection of American aid would have in the long run, if it continued to be administered by arrogant men who knew nothing and cared nothing for the local culture.

It took courage for an American to be openly critical of his country, and Emin Bey admired this quality in his new friend. It did not matter that Emin Bey's wife, Roksan, who claimed Hector had pushed her rudely the night before, thought the man was crazy. That was a womanly view of things.

To think that this man would be joining the mathematics department! He was a gift from heaven. Because of certain recent events in his own life, in which his wife was not entirely uninvolved, Emin Bey had grown tired of the smiles which concealed insincerity, the empty gestures of friendship, preserved only for the purpose of self-advancement, the hypocrisy in every facet of university life. There was nothing Hector did that was insincere, calculated, or hypocritical.

He was upset, almost up in arms, when Hector told him that he was not, after all, going to be staying in Istanbul. When he found out why, he was mortified.

Hector told him that he had decided to leave because his wife had fallen in love with her obstetrician, and he did not want to stand in the way of her happiness. "If there were any way to talk her out of it," Hector told him, "I would do it, but I'm afraid there's no hope."

Hector kicked himself later for saying this, because when Emin Bey insisted on coming to his rescue, there was no way of getting him to stop without admitting he had told a lie.

The obstetrician, it turned out, was a friend of Emin Bey's family, and the woman he was engaged to marry was Roksan's cousin. Emin Bey was appalled to discover that this man had been making promises to a married woman, with a newborn child he himself had delivered, at the same time that his fiancée's family was sending out invitations to his wedding. Emin Bey insisted that he and Hector go down to the hospital at once.

Emin Bey and Hector made two stops on their way to the hospital. The first was at Emin Bey's house, where Emin Bey changed into his city clothes. The second stop was at a florist, where Emin Bey purchased a fabulous bouquet of roses. When they arrived at the hospital, Emin Bey had the flowers taken to Amy's room. Then they went to pay a social call on the obstetrician. When Emin Bey introduced Hector as "my dear friend and future colleague," the obstetrician's eyebrows shot up in surprise. He begged them to sit down and ordered coffee.

While they were waiting for the coffee, they discussed the weather, the hospital, the rising birth rate, with Emin Bey dwelling on a storm that was bothering him, that was probably going to interfere with his weekend plans. Apparently, clouds were gathering to the north of the city, and by tomorrow they would reach Istanbul, bringing to an end the unseasonably warm weather they had been enjoying. The obstetrician was surprised to hear this, but then he added, as an afterthought, that he had neglected to listen to the weather report on the radio that morning.

It was only after the coffee had been served that Emin Bey asked the obstetrician about his fiancée. The obstetrician, his eyes hooding over, said that she was fine. He then asked after Emin Bey's wife, Roksan.

"She is in excellent health," Emin Bey said. "When she heard I was coming to see you, she asked me to thank you for the invitation to your wedding, which we received in the mail yesterday. She will be accepting through the normal channels, of course. But she wanted me to pass on her warm congratulations and wish you many years of happiness."

The obstetrician smiled, but his eyes remained impassive. "You are most kind," he said. "Please thank your wife on my behalf and tell her that Gülbanu and I will be honored by your presence."

There was a pause.

"And your presence also," the obstetrician said, turning to Hector. "I shall see to it that you and your wife receive a formal invitation."

Hector thanked him. There followed an even longer silence, during which they all smiled politely at one another. Finally, Emin Bey sighed and clasped his hands regretfully.

"There is, however, a small problem remaining, and I must confess that it is this small problem that is the reason for my visit this afternoon."

The obstetrician stiffened. Emin Bey smiled at him and took a last sip from his coffee. He placed his coffee cup on the tray and then, smiling again, he folded his hands.

"The problem is this. We now have living with us my wife's maiden aunt. She is an elderly woman, and we do not like to leave her alone."

"My dear fellow," said the obstetrician. "This is not a problem at all. It goes without saying that she will be most welcome at our wedding. Was she insulted that the invitation did not include her name? Please forgive us. I shall make sure Gülbanu telephones her tomorrow and apologizes personally."

"That is very kind," said Emin Bey. "But there is another related problem we have yet to resolve. I would like to know your candid opinion."

"Of course," said the obstetrician.

"My wife's aunt is an old-fashioned woman. I'm afraid she has not been able to keep pace with the new ideas. Unfortunately, this poor woman, who has never been married herself, is upset when traditions are ignored. She had decided—for some unknown reason—that this wedding will be highly unconventional, like another wedding she attended recently, and that the boys and girls will not show respect for one another when they are dancing, and that the vows exchanged between bride and groom will not be taken with due seriousness. I told her she had nothing to worry about, and reminded her that both parties came from good families who would not permit such transgressions. However, I thought it would be wise if I spoke about this matter with you first. Her age is advanced, and I would not like to upset her unnecessarily."

The obstetrician stood up, breathed deeply, and straightened his shoulders. "Please tell your aunt," he said, with a tragic finality, "that there will be nothing at the wedding to upset her."

On their way down the hallway to Amy's room, Emin Bey asked when Amy would be ready to leave the hospital. The obstetrician said that she could leave at once if they wished. Financial and bureaucratic matters could be left for another day, he assured them. They were all friends.

Just before they reached Amy's room, the obstetrician took Hector aside and said, "You must understand. I had no idea. No idea at all."

When the obstetrician told Amy she was going home, she looked first at Hector with horror, and then at the obstetrician as if he had condemned her to the guillotine.

Hector carried his crying son to the car, and tried to remember how long it had been before Chloe slept through the night. Emin Bey carried Amy's suitcase. Amy lagged behind like a sullen schoolgirl. "How can I thank you?" Hector asked weakly.

Emin Bey looked hurt. "There is no need to thank me. We are friends. It was the least I could do."

There was one last hope, and that was that the Laceys would be so furious at him that they would never want to see him again, let alone help him get a job and have him move next door. But they, too looked back on the previous evening as a success. They hadn't had so much fun in years. "And to think we felt sorry for Amy on account of her dull husband," Meredith said. Over the course of that evening she gave him so many special looks that he was not left in any doubt as to what had gone on in that bedroom he had pushed her into.

That evening, he discovered he had been wrong about the Laceys. Leslie Lacey, far from being an advocate of the stock market, spent cocktail hour defending Trotsky, and Meredith, it turned out, was the daughter of an anarchist. Although it was true she had had a rich girl's childhood, having been brought up and sent through school by her grandparents, she said she didn't even know what a Girl Scout cookie looked like. She had studied with what's-her-name, the famous modern dancer, at Bennington, and had once danced almost naked on whatever that street was in Paris.

They invited all their friends over to meet the new life of the party. That night was nothing more than a blur of bright-eyed drunken faces, but over the ensuing weeks, these people regained their individuality as Hector entangled himself in the bonds of friendship, reckless promises, and atonement for offenses committed while intoxicated. He made a fool of himself that night, which everyone, even Amy, seemed to welcome.

Not long afterward—it could not have been more than a few weeks—he wrote to both his mother and his father. His mother wrote back a letter full of curses. She said she never wanted to see him again, but time would prove her wrong. His letter to his father was returned. Phillip Best had moved on, leaving no forwarding address.

And so Hector and Amy were given the second chance neither of them had asked for. They moved into the beautiful white house next door to the Laceys and tried to learn to love each other, Amy because she felt she owed it to the Laceys, and Hector because he knew he owed it to Emin Bey.

Thirteen years had passed since then, and they were still together.

But had they learned to love each other? Hector didn't

even want to think about it. He shifted his weight, sorry that he had not sat in the front seat of the taxi with Hamdi Bey. He looked idly out the window, at a banner hanging from the window of an apartment building. It said, "American murderer go home." He stifled a yawn, refusing, as always, to believe that the message was for him.

Meredith was showing off her Turkish.

"You see that one on the wall over there?" she said, nudging Ginger in the ribs. "That says, 'No to the bridge,' and it's everywhere these days. They're referring, of course, to the bridge they want to build over the Bosphorus. I can't quite understand *why,* but there are those who believe the money should have been spent on the poor, when it's perfectly obvious, isn't it, that the bridge will help the economy. And over there, you can see 'Imperialist Americans go to hell,' and right underneath it—in white paint, not red—one of my favorites: 'Down with cultural imperialism.' Did you know we were cultural imperialists? *I* never knew I was a cultural imperialist. Did you, Hector?"

"No," Hector said.

"What *I* always wonder is what the hell they think we hope to achieve. They probably think we take our orders from the CIA. 'The Department of Cultural Imperialism, Langley, Virginia. Directive 984A. Subject: Brainwashing of Turkish Youth. Method: Exhaustive Textual Analysis of *House of the Seven Gables*.' I mean, I ask you!"

She laughed, but no one joined her. Ginger looked alarmed. Having arrived only recently, she had not yet recovered from the shock of discovering that the entire world was anti-American.

"There's another good one over there," Meredith said. "An old standby. 'Death to the Sixth Fleet'—not that our dear old Sixth Fleet would *dare* come within a hundred miles of us these days. And that banner over there, hanging from the window. I think that's a school, but I'm not sure. 'Long live the People's Army,' the banner says. Now, what did they tell me the People's Army was? It's not really an army, is it?"

"I don't think so," Hector said.

"Well, at any rate," Meredith said. Hamdi *efendi* turned

at the stadium and headed up the hill toward Taksim. As they approached the first curve, Meredith craned her neck to look into the stadium. "Oh, dear, a game," she said. "We'll have to go back another way. Perhaps through Nişantaş. *If* we can find transportation. They weren't planning a rally today, were they, Hector?"

"I don't think so," said Hector. "If there were a rally today, the traffic would be much worse."

"Right you are, right you are," Meredith said. "Well, that's one thing to thank our lucky stars about. I don't think I can stand another rally. All those angry faces. I know it's a terrible thing to say, but they remind me of restive cattle. And they're so goddamn rude. One of them pinched me last time. Can you imagine? Oh, look," Meredith said, pointing at a modern building farther up the hill. "More banners. What does that one say? Something about Nixon. I can't make out the other word. Oh, yes, now I can. 'Nixon is a son of a donkey.' That's a good one. Did you know that whenever they mention Nixon on Radio Tirana, they say 'capitalist pig Nixon'?"

"What's Radio Tirana?" Ginger asked.

"The Albanian station. They broadcast the news in English. It's the strangest English you're ever heard. It's a riot."

Across the street from the Park Hotel, Hamdi *efendi* pulled to the curb to let Hector out. Hector paid the fare, despite Meredith's protests.

"So!" Meredith said, beaming at him through the open window. "I take it we'll see you at the party tonight?" Hector nodded and turned away.

The Park Hotel was a drab stucco building set back from the road that led to Taksim. It had a circular driveway bordered by forlorn flowerbeds, and a brown-suited doorman. The lobby was dark and shabby, but the dining room was one of the grandest in the city. Almost Art Deco, Ralph had once called it, "with hints here and there of a Bulgarian train station." The food was continental—wiener schnitzel, beef stroganoff, filet mignon, that sort of thing.

The most famous part of the Park Hotel was the bar. Dark and wood-paneled inside, in the summer it opened out onto the long, narrow terrace that overlooked the winding streets of Cihangir and, beyond them, the Bosphorus. The bar had been a favorite haunt for spies during the Second World War.

The terrace was full when Hector reached it—not entirely with spies, although he spotted one or two, but with newspapermen, consular officials, foreign businessmen, and a few tourists. There was a gypsy with a dancing bear directly below the terrace, and you could tell who the tourists were because they were the only ones upset about the painful bit the bear was wearing. The others gazed blankly at the view beyond.

There was a haze over the Bosphorus, which was wider here. The haze made the opposite shore look gray. To the right, the sun sparkled lazily on the Marmara Sea. Shading his eyes, Hector scanned the row of tables for a clerical collar. As he did so, he wondered if there was still time to get out of this meeting.

It had begun in March, with a letter—a letter he had hidden well but which he was not sure he had kept from the all-seeing eyes of his mother. "Dear Hector," the letter had begun:

> I'm sure you never thought you'd hear from me again. Well, then, surprise, surprise. To tell you the truth, I had given up hope of ever finding you!
>
> Perhaps it will surprise you to hear that I am no longer that shady character who scraped by writing copy for disreputable British firms who were busily exploiting the destitute peoples of those unfortunate lands that were once part of our much overrated Empire. No, dear boy, all this has changed, and miraculously so. After a longish stretch in hospital some seven years ago (a kidney ailment), I saw the light, as they say, and life, I must say, is all the better for it! It is useful to have sinned oneself before taking on the task of advising sinners, although that, perhaps, is taking too dim a view of my vocation.
>
> I have spent the past four years in an excruciatingly virtuous corner of Devon, but enough of that. My long-standing ambition to return to my former haunts is finally to be realized. Through assiduous cultivation of

certain influential members of the clerical hierarchy, I have been able to secure what is not generally considered a desirable appointment. I was overjoyed when informed of the Istanbul posting. You may remember that my family has a long-standing connection with the city.

Not long after this welcome news, I was fortunate enough to welcome a dear old friend to my dull little Devon parish. His name—and I think it may be familiar to you—is Nikolai Kadinsky. As you may already be aware, he is a longtime resident of your lovely city. In the course of a discussion about the foreign community of which I am soon to become a member, your name came up. Naturally, I kept my surprise—and my joy—to myself, preferring to advise you of this unexpected development personally rather than to allow the news to pass inevitably from gossip to gossip.

I hear you have a family now. I look forward to meeting you all. Never fear—it need not be a rushed reunion. You may depend on my eternal discretion—not a bad quality, don't you think, for a priest. I hope this letter finds you in the best of health.

Your devoted father,
Phillip Best

At first, Hector had thought the letter was a practical joke. He could not remember his father's handwriting well enough to verify it. Neither could he remember meeting any longtime Istanbul resident named Nikolai Kadinsky. But then one day Thomas Ashe had mentioned Nikolai in passing. "Don't you remember him?" Thomas said. "We went to a wild party he gave about seven years ago. He lives in that strange neighborhood below the Russian Consulate." But Hector did not remember. He supposed, ruefully, that on the evening in question, he had been one over the eight.

Then, in late May, Phillip Best arrived, and the telephone calls had begun.

He was anxious to meet his son, he said. Would Friday do, or Monday, or Tuesday? At first, Hector begged off with imaginary illnesses. Then he claimed to be busy with exams. This week he had finally run out of excuses.

When Hector finally spotted his father—a frail, white-haired man wearing an Anglican collar, sitting at the far end of the Park Hotel terrace—his first reaction was one of relief. The man looked familiar to him. It said something for blood ties, Hector thought, that a father could still look familiar after thirty-five years. Or had he seen him more recently?

He was saying his farewells to another man whom Hector half recognized—a tall, elegant, boyish man with short blonde hair, arms that seemed too muscular for his build, and a loud Oxbridge drawl. "*Do* help yourself to a Sobranie," he was saying. "It was positively wicked of you to bring them. I shall have to give them all away before I get hooked."

"I'm sure that bulldog fellow wouldn't mind replenishing your stock," Phillip said. Hector recognized his voice.

"Don't even remind me of that dreadful man. You shall ruin my afternoon. But what have we here? My goodness, if it isn't Hector Cabot. Where have you been hiding, you disgraceful thing? What in God's name are you bothering with Hector for, Phillip? He hasn't converted to the C of E, has he? Goodness, I hope not. Bulldog and company would never recover. They would have to found a rival place of worship. Well, my dear fellow, it has been some time since you last darkened my door with your shadow. In fact, weren't you involved in the fracas, Phillip? I think you may have been visiting at the time. Of course you were. Seven, eight years ago, it was. Or was it nine or ten? It was before your reform. I think you were pretending to be a journalist at the time. And *you*, my dear boy," said the Oxbridge man, turning to Hector, "you broke all my lovely china. *Not* to mention a circa-five-ninety terra cotta figurine. B.C., mind you, B.C. I shall never forgive you your monstrous behavior, never. I hope you have learned to moderate your drinking. What *would* you want with this incorrigible brute, Phillip?"

"Oh, do shut up, Nicky," said Hector's father. He gestured for Hector to take the seat opposite him. "Nikolai was just leaving. I take it you know one another? Well, then, no need for introductions. Bugger off now, won't you, Nicky? Hector, what will you have to drink?" He crossed his legs, lit a cigarette, and smiled. It was a kindly smile, and suddenly Hector remembered where he had seen it before.

He remembered everything: the apartment in that strange neighborhood below the Russian Consulate; Nikolai, the nonplussed host; his disapproving guests, most of them British. The broken china, and Amy and Thomas apologizing for him. And the bedroom where they had gone to fetch their coats, where they had discovered Phillip Best *in flagrante* with the houseboy.

Phillip had not been at all rattled. He had aided them most courteously in their embarrassed search for the coats. It went without saying that they had not exchanged names.

As Hector sat across from his father now, he even remembered what Thomas had said to Amy as they were helping him down the stairs: "I guess that's what people call having a stiff upper lip."

And now he was a minister. God help us, Hector thought.

"Have you decided what you'll have?" his father asked, as courteous as ever. "Do feel free to order anything. I'm in pocket, for a change. It's all on me."

Hector cleared his throat and tried to find his voice, while the waiter hovered above him with an inquiring smile.

"They make rather nice screwdrivers here, you know," his father said. "You would do well to consider a screwdriver."

"That's what I'll have, a screwdriver," Hector said. Turning to the waiter, he said, "I would like a *vodka portakal.*"

"One *vodka portakal,*" said the waiter, smiling. He turned to leave, but Hector stopped him.

"No. Bring me two."

III

The Party

Saturday, June 14, 1969
Late Afternoon and Evening

WHILE Hector sat with his father on the terrace of the Park Hotel, Stella Ashe made her way down the main street of Bebek, making the final purchases for that evening's party.

The little coastal town of Bebek had its moments. There were the restaurants whose terraces hung out over the Bosphorus, and the narrow stucco houses between them, with their private landing stages. There was the old Egyptian Consulate—a graying nineteenth-century palace—and the little wooden ferry station, which was painted light green, and next to it the mosque, which had only one minaret and which everyone said was architecturally uninteresting, but which Stella liked, as things of architectural interest were lost on her. And in the back streets, tucked away among the treeless neighborhoods of new apartment buildings, you could still find a few of the beautiful old wooden houses.

But the main road was—Stella had to admit it—seedy. There were potholes in the road and gaps in the dusty, uneven pavement. There was a traffic problem, and the clouds of black exhaust that came with a traffic problem. The storefronts, with their Venetian blinds and lopsided signs, lacked that glossy European sophistication. But Stella loved them.

She followed her usual itinerary, starting at the kiosk in Little Bebek, where she picked up the blackmarket Winstons the man had saved for her, and crossing the street to look at the publicity photos outside the Gaskonyali Nightclub. From there she went to the butcher. The butcher was a soft-faced, patient man whose understanding of her halting Turkish and vague illustrative gestures was unmatched in the city. He had saved some lungs for her (for the cat). But he didn't like the look of his beef filet, so he sent her across the street to the other butcher, his dearest friend.

Her next stop was the haberdasher's. The man there had saved her favorite shade of stockings. At the pharmacy she picked up some aspirins, knowing she would need them in the morning, and from there she went to Nick's for sausages and black-market cheese. Nick's was run by a family of Albanian Greeks who allowed Stella to run up her account for as long as a year, so long as she deposited an American check into their Athens bank account every August.

Most of the time she bought her fruit and vegetables at Nick's, too, but today she had some money for a change, so she went to the vegetable stand across the street. He had the best produce in Bebek—the largest oranges, the least-bruised peaches, the juciest cherries, the crispest lettuce, the thinnest, shiniest eggplants, the cleanest potatoes—and even if you turned your back he wouldn't tip the scale or sneak a rotten vegetable into the bottom of the bag. He was an Arab. He wrapped his produce in old college business correspondence, which an enterprising college employee sold him in bulk. Often these letters were confidential and therefore good for a laugh.

Her string bag loaded down with peaches and cherries, she crossed the street again, stopping first at Yalter's for the paper and then at the old bakery for a loaf of warm bread. Her last stop was Tandir's Pastry Shop. Stella always stopped here for croissants and European coffee before taking a taxi home. The owners were her friends. All she had to do was walk through the door three times a week and they liked her. She felt more at home at Tandir's than she did at any house on the Hill, where she never measured up when the talk turned clever.

Hamdi *efendi*, her favorite taxi driver, was not at the taxi stand when she came outside. She decided to wait for him. To kill time, she walked slowly back up the side street and paid a visit to the church.

It was a small French Catholic church with an adjoining orphanage. It was in no way as grand as the church she had attended as a child in New York, but it still brought back memories. There was the smell of old incense. There was the basin of holy water at the back. There were the polished pews, and the dark flimsy confessional, with the old priest clearing his throat behind the screen. There was the likeness of Jesus hanging in the narrow arch behind the altar, desperately trying to soar above it, and the altar itself, which, to Stella, was facing in the wrong direction.

She had come here once on a Sunday morning. The congregation consisted of three old ladies with black veils, one well-dressed couple who looked Italian, a handful of American consular types with rigid crewcuts, and the orphans, who looked wan and sad in their gray coats and kerchiefs. They all turned around because she came in so late—after the Agnus Dei, which was a sin, Stella recalled.

She had pretended to be abject with guilt. She had knelt down in a back pew, covered her face, and muttered a few Hail Marys.

Today the church was empty, so she took a seat near the altar. She made a point of not crossing herself before she sat down. Glancing at the empty confessional, she was tempted to go tell that doddering fool behind the screen that she was an atheist. But of course it was impossible. She didn't speak French and the doddering fool spoke no English. And hadn't they changed what you had to say before you made confession? It would be embarrassing to get it wrong.

On one of their first times together, Hector had told Stella that her husband's nickname in certain uncharitable circles was "the Priest." It was assumed that, coming as he did from an Irish working-class neighborhood, Thomas was a devout Irish Catholic. This was not true. Thomas was not even Irish. Although it was true that he had been brought up

Catholic, he was now an atheist, and so was Stella. In fact, it had been their common lack of faith that had brought them together.

Thomas became an atheist after what he saw in Germany after the war. The army should never have sent him there, because his family was of German extraction. He was born Thomas Aschenbach, but his parents, who ran a grocery store in Stella's neighborhood, and who both played the organ in the parish church, had changed their name to Ashe during the war in order to prove their patriotism.

Until he was drafted, it had seemed to Thomas and his mentor, the parish priest, that Thomas might have a vocation. Peer pressure had made him join the army instead, and to tell the truth, the decision had taken a great weight off Thomas' shoulders—until he got to Germany, where what he saw threw not only his vocation into question, but his faith in God as well.

When he returned home, he tried to discuss Germany with Father Johns, and Father Johns' intransigence in the matter only served to deepen his doubts. But it took four years in college, scores of books, and countless conversations with strangers in bars before he admitted to himself that he was an atheist, and it wasn't until he met Stella that he stopped going to church.

Stella became an atheist because she was perverse; even she knew that. She was perverse because she was desperate, and she was desperate because she was a romantic who dreamed of opera and world travel, in a family where the only music considered worthy of the name was played on the bagpipe, and the only dream for the future worthy of consideration was one that included a steady Catholic husband and a nice house, which, by the time Stella was of age, was supposed to be in the suburbs.

Stella's father was a policeman, a pleasant enough fellow despite his habit of falling asleep halfway through dinner and his fondness for firing holes in the kitchen wall when he got drunk. Her mother was a pleasant enough woman—a recent immigrant from County Tipperary—a beautiful woman, in fact, despite her permanently pursed lips. She kept control of the household by never doing anything to cover up the bullet holes in the kitchen wall, and by letting her husband snore peacefully every evening with his head on his dinner plate while she cheerfully cleaned up the rest of the kitchen, until finally the mashed potatoes he was resting in made his cheeks so cold and clammy that he woke up.

There were five children in the family, of whom Stella was the youngest. Like Stella, the older children had entertained lofty ambitions, but the parents had held them back. One or two rungs up the social ladder—that was fine, but anything more smacked of false pride. Stella's mother in particular had brought with her from the Old World a deep suspicion of excessive achievement.

And so, the brother who had wanted to be a lawyer had followed his father into the police force, and the brother who had wanted to be a physicist became an electrician. The two sisters who had dreamed of college became secretaries and married early. By the time Stella herself became engaged, her older sister was a war widow with four children to support, and her other sister, whose husband had survived the war, was unable to have children and therefore considered herself a failure. Stella vowed not to follow in their footsteps.

But what choice did she have? No child of her parents was going to be a la-di-da opera singer, or deplete their savings by insisting on a la-di-da college education. They sent her off to work for the same firm where her sisters had worked. The only way she had of fighting back was by doing her job poorly. Thus, she was never promoted from the position of file clerk.

When she was nineteen, she became engaged to James, the biggest troublemaker in the neighborhood, who had spent his school years wearing the dunce cap in the corner and had almost been excommunicated for playing practical jokes while serving as an altar boy. With the exception of the army, the longest time he had ever held down a job was two months. Never had there been a man less likely to be given a mortgage in Yonkers.

Two days before the wedding, James came rushing into her parents' kitchen, his cheeks flushed. "Our problems are over," he said to Stella. "They'll have me after all. I'm joining the force."

Stella nearly had a heart attack. It was what her parents

had always dreamed of for her—a husband on the force. She spent that night in a panic, trying to think of a way out.

At breakfast the following morning, she told her parents that she could not go through with the church wedding because she had suffered a crisis of faith during the night and no longer believed in God.

This caused an uproar the likes of which Stella, a connoisseur of uproars, had never seen. Her mother became hysterical. Her father shot a few more holes in the kitchen wall. James himself made a sullen appearance later that day in the company of Father Johns. When all else failed, Father Johns sent James' oldest childhood friend, Thomas Ashe, to reason with her.

Thomas was himself an atheist by then, although he had not yet broken the news to Father Johns. He was determined to get out of Stella's house with the fewest possible lies. So he sat at one end of the living room, cold and silent, while Stella stood at the other end and raged at him.

She acted as if Thomas were the parish personified. She accused him of jamming religion down her throat, of trying to murder her soul, of being a hypocrite. The more she spoke, the more beautiful she looked to Thomas, until she seemed to be twice her size and Amazonian in her courage and defiance. Finally, he broke down and told her he agreed with everything she said.

During those early years of their disgrace (which was aggravated by a civil wedding attended only by Thomas' brothers) they had often stayed up until the early hours of the morning discussing what they did not believe in, and what new humanistic ideals they thought should replace the old religion. Now—now that they were living in a community where everyone agreed with them—they didn't talk about such things. It seemed to Stella that they had gone on automatic pilot.

She wished now that she had listened more carefully to Thomas' brilliant arguments in defense of the new way and in repudiation of the old. Perhaps his thoughts might have cast some light on the mystery as to why, when Stella most emphatically did not believe in heaven, she was certain that her affair with Hector was going to land her in hell.

You goddamn hypocrite, she thought, glaring at the cramped

likeness of Jesus in the narrow arch behind the altar. Trying to scare me with fire and brimstone. When she left the church, she deliberately neglected to cross herself with holy water. She marched down the side street, the handles of her string bag of groceries cutting into her hand.

And there was Hamdi *efendi,* waiting for her. He smiled as he opened the door for her. He drove her up the Aşiyan Road, and then all the way up the little alley to their front gate, which was something most taxi drivers refused to do. Stella cheered up when she saw the house, and her thoughts returned to the party.

The Ashes' house was perfect for parties. It was situated on the empty side of the Hill and had few neighbors to speak of. Its walled gardens were bordered on one side by a Moslem cemetery, on another by a whorehouse and a tea-garden that turned into a nightclub after dark, and on a third side by a museum—the former summer home of a famous Turkish poet—where, in 1964, a watchman had chopped another watchman's head off with a hatchet in a fight over a stolen suitcase.

The house had begun its life at the turn of the century as the summer villa of a poetess. Her son had abandoned it during the twenties after an angel came to him in a dream and told him that the house was under a curse. When the Ashes moved in, it had been empty for almost forty years. The roof leaked, the pipes had burst, the central heating system was broken. There were rats living between the walls and in the attic. Every morning at dawn, they had a soccer match. A bloodthirsty cat kept them from venturing into the main rooms, but very little was done to correct the other problems, and for years, it had rained in Margaret's closet.

The house had once been painted white, though by 1969 its color was closer to mustard. It had a widow's walk, and two sagging balconies, one on top of the other, each with a magnificent view of the Bosphorus. Directly below the balconies was an oval pond stocked with goldfish the size of carp. At either end of the pond was an islet out of which grew a palm tree. Below the house were the tangled terraced gardens, spilling down the hill to the cemetery. There was a greenhouse with only half a roof, a circular terrace shaded by an ancient plane tree that stood at its center, a field of unpruned grapevines, an abundance of pomegranate trees. Only a few of the old footpaths remained passable.

The house had three stories. At the top were the bedrooms and Thomas' study. On the middle level were the living room, the dining room, and the library, all furnished with the usual Woodrow College combination of antique and Turkish modern, with Oriental rugs and wall hangings and copper trays providing the warmth the rooms would have otherwise lacked.

On the ground level was the small bedroom where the maid and her family slept, and two kitchens. One was large and airy, with a black and white tiled floor and a five-windowed alcove into which the Ashes' round table fit perfectly. The other was cramped and cluttered. This was the maid's kitchen, and it was where Seranouche now sat with little Beatrice Ashe on her knee.

Usually Seranouche fed Beatrice in Madame and Monsieur's kitchen, but today she had been asked not to. Madame had already put out the punchbowl, and what would she think if her little daughter, her sweet little daughter who was said to be the bastard child of Mr. Cabot, happened to break the precious crystal punchbowl by accident? Would Madame blame it on the child or on Seranouche? Of course she would blame it on Seranouche, who would have owned God knows how many Cadillacs by now if the bloodthirsty Turks had not burned her grandfather's store during the Armenian massacres; who would have traveled all over the world on an ocean liner by now, like Madame and Monsieur; who would have had her own servants instead of washing other people's clothes. *Vah, vah, vah,* she said to herself as she watched Madame descend from the taxi, how they cut us, how they cut us. How they cut our throats, our hands, our hearts. May the devil take them.

Seranouche was in her thirties, but she could have passed for fifty. She had curly red hair, a rubbery complexion, and buck teeth—she was no beauty, even she knew that. But she was fixing herself up, little by little. Her cousin washed hair in a chic beauty salon, and one day she was going to have the *patron* fix up Seranouche's hair for free. "Oh, how nice," said Seranouche, with spiteful thoughts for the fools who had to pay for such pleasures. If you had brains, like Seranouche, you could get things done for free.

As soon as she could wheedle a raise out of Madame and Monsieur, Seranouche was going to get some false teeth, straight ones. There was a dentist in Bebek who pulled out teeth on the installment plan. Every two weeks, one tooth. He kept them in a box, and then, when they were all out, he sent them to a tooth factory where a proven expert made false ones with a perfect fit, except that they were straight. That was what Seranouche called genius, and you could have it on the installment plan. In a year or less, she would have a mouthful of perfectly straight teeth and be the envy of all her relations. Then she would finally be ready for America.

Sooner or later, Madame and Monsieur were going to return to America, to their houses and their Cadillacs and their fancy yachts, and when they left, Seranouche was planning to go with them. Not only Seranouche, but her son Avram, the most handsome man in the world. And perhaps her good-for-nothing drunkard of a husband. She was sure she would be able to convince Madame and Monsieur. Because how could they ever get along without her? Madame didn't even know how to wash a plate. She didn't even know how to feed cereal to her own child.

For all their laziness, they were not born to their money, and if it were not for America where gold grew on trees, they would be nothing, absolutely nothing. They didn't even scrub each other's backs when they took their baths. If there was one thing Seranouche had learned in her years with Madame and Monsieur, it was that they were no better than she was. And yet here she was working for them.

Seranouche was a hard worker. There was not a living soul in Rumeli Hisar who did not know what a hard worker she was. It wasn't for nothing that her family had once been the envy of all Kumkapi. Her grandfather had owned six carriage horses, and her grandmother had owned five hundred silk gowns. They had all burned, burned, burned, and now their granddaughter was taking care of someone else's house. But she did a fine job of it, even if Madame was too busy smiling at other women's husbands to notice.

She dared any of Madame and Monsieur's friends to come to this party tonight and find one speck of dust on the furniture. She dared them to tell her one place in the city where they would taste a better *börek*. But what was the use of it? Her work would vanish under the trampling feet of Madame and Monsieur's careless friends. By the morning it would look like an abandoned *meyhane*. *Vah, vah, vah,* what a waste. All that money for champagne, for shameless men and women to say, "Ha, ha, ha, I feel so dizzy," and "Ha, ha, ha, come dance with me, I am so beautiful." Wives embracing other women's husbands, may the devil take them. What a waste of money. If Seranouche had that money, she could get her false teeth in one month; she could buy her son, Avram, the most handsome man in the world, a new jacket, and herself a stylish pair of shoes that would make her the envy of all her relations. She could . . . she could . . . but she couldn't and for all the old reasons.

"Oh, my little Beatrice," she said, prying her mouth open affectionately as she forced down a spoonful more of *makarna*. "Oh, you will never know the troubles we've suffered. Oh, how they cut us, how they cut our throats, our hands, our maidenheads. May the devil take them."

Her thoughts turned to all the things she had yet to do for the party. There were the *böreks* to make, and the *sosi kokteyl,* and the cheese and the olives to set out, and the punch and the napkins and the glasses and the toothpicks and the devil only knew what else, and there was Madame getting out of the taxi, smiling as if she had not a care in the world. *Ptuh!* said Seranouche to herself. She was probably overpaying the taxi driver.

But when Madame came inside, she swallowed her anger, greeting her with false warmth. "Oh, Madame, your hair looks wonderful," she said, because Madame had been to the hairdresser. It was only the thought of the Cadillacs she would own one day in America (where her son, Avram, would have no trouble finding a millionairess), only the thought of the grand houses she would live in and the multitude of servants she would have under her thumb, that kept Seranouche from spilling out her true thoughts with all their venom.

* * *

Upstairs in the study, Thomas Ashe could hear the two women discussing the last arrangements for the party. He tried to block it out, but Seranouche's voice took on a strident note when she switched to pidgin English. Finally he put his hands over his eyes and surrendered to it.

"No worry, no worry," she was saying. "I put the baby sleep sleep now, then making *börek* plenty time."

"I realize I'm late, and I'm sorry," Stella said, her own voice veering dangerously close to the cadences of pidgin English.

"No worry, Madame, I'm saying you truth. Maybe *sois kokteyl* little not so much cooked. . . ."

"That's fine, Seranouche. You just do what you can."

"First thing put baby sleep sleep," Seranouche said again. Really, Thomas thought, it was a shame about her English because it made her sound like a moron, when really she was so very bright.

"I'll put baby sleep sleep if you like," Stella said.

"You put baby sleep sleep? Ah, how nice. Beatrice, you go to Mama now; she put you sleep sleep. I going downstairs making *böreks*. Ah, Madame is very generous. I'm tanking you *viel dank*."

"Oh, it's nothing," Stella said. Thomas thought, Did she have to be so obsequious?

They were up at the top of the stairs now. Thomas listened to his wife trying to take his daughter out of Seranouche's arms. Beatrice screamed. Stella laughed nervously.

"No worry, Madame, is little not so feeling good today. I put her sleep sleep right now, then going downstairs finishing work, no problem. You take rest. Big night tonight, you need beauty sleep."

Sometimes Thomas was amazed by the hatred in Seranouche's voice. He couldn't quite understand it. Certainly they had gone out of their way to do well by Seranouche. Certainly they had overlooked many little transgressions, and some big ones. For example, the time they had come home from a spring vacation early, to find Seranouche and her husband hosting an Armenian Easter party. There had been about fifty relatives in the house. Their shoes were under all the beds. Anyone else would have fired Seranouche then and there, but Thomas had not. He knew that they would never have thrown that party (and charged all the food to their account at Nick's) if Thomas and Stella hadn't always been so liberal. It was their lenience that had created the problem.

If only he liked the woman.

It wasn't fair to dislike her, Thomas realized. Seranouche was a good woman, and a hardworking one, and she had had a rough life, so no wonder she hated them. When you really thought about it, there was no good reason why the Ashes should have so much while Seranouche had so little. It was just a difference of opportunity. She was just as intelligent as they were. What a pity Margaret had not been able to teach her how to read.

And she did a marvelous job with Beatrice. Beatrice loved her. If only Seranouche had a softer voice. If only, if only, she did not insist on wearing Margaret's old party dresses.

Thomas was grading exam papers. That was why he was in such a bad mood. He loved his students, but their English was often infuriating. This, too, was unfair. After all, how well would he do if he attempted an essay in Turkish? But if he had to read one more sentence about something hitting the nail on the head, he was going to scream. He knew how good the English prep department was—it had to be, to bring students up to college-level English in one year—but sometimes they were old-fashioned about idioms. Thomas did not think people hit nails on the head anymore even in America.

He sighed and looked at the pile of exams that he had yet to grade. "Hell!" he said. He looked out the window at the hundreds of golden windowpanes on the Asian shore, and wondered if it would be foolhardy to start drinking before sunset.

When the setting sun is reflected on windowpanes, the Turks call it *yangin*, which means fire. If you lived on the European shore of the Bosphorus, the sun set behind you, so that was all you saw of the sunset from Woodrow College—the hundreds of little fires in the windows across the water in Asia.

It was Chloe Cabot's favorite time of day, although she

had never found the words to describe the love that welled up inside her as she watched the flickering windows cast a lemon light on the hills and the water, the castles and the ferry boats. Once, long ago, her father had dismissed her rapture as pantheism. She had looked the word up in the dictionary and found it to be inadequate.

This evening she and Margaret were watching the sunset from a bench on the college terrace. They were already dressed for the Ashes' party, their hair carefully arranged, their highheeled shoes well polished, their stockings fresh from the haberdasher's, their clothes a poor but respectable imitation of thc French fashions sported by the wealthy Turkish girls they went to school with at the American College for Girls. They had taken the precaution of dressing early so that Chloe's mother would not have the chance to tell Chloe that she really would prefer it if Chloe did not attend adult parties.

Chloe thought her mother unfair. For God's sake, she was going on seventeen. Margaret had been attending her parents' parties all her life, and she was still in one piece, wasn't she? Year after year she had been reporting the scandals she had witnessed in minute detail. There was no immoral act that Chloe was not prepared to witness.

They had to do something with their Saturday night. They were both in disgrace because they had no dates. Chloe was between boyfriends, because none of the Turkish playboys she went out with could stand the way she talked back, and also because they had heard so many locker room stories about her sexual prowess that they never failed to take the news that she was a virgin as a personal affront. Her reputation had matured without her, she was fond of saying.

Margaret did have a boyfriend, an attentive yet often unfaithful boyfriend to whom she was unfailingly loyal. He was rich and snooty, and Chloe hated him. His name was Can, which was pronounced "John." Can often called up at the last moment to say that he had to go to a business dinner with his father, that he really had to study that night, that a maiden aunt was coming to dinner and would be offended if he was not there. On Monday morning, however, Margaret would discover from the socialites in her class that Can had been seen at the Club 33 with a Swedish model, or on the

Hilton Roof with a French stewardess, or at the Hidromel with an older woman known for her loose morals.

Chloe would have wrung his neck if she were in Margaret's place, but Margaret believed in enduring bad news of this sort with martyrlike smiles. It was as if she thought Can's infidelities were intended to test her character. They saddened her, she told Chloe, but it was important to be patient. It was important to understand. Everything she said was a complete lie. Ever since Margaret had met Can, she had been playing a part.

Once Chloe and Margaret had been such close friends that they had shared their every waking thought. Now Margaret told her nothing. She just posed, and smiled, and looked mysterious. Chloe was damned if she could tell what was going on in Margaret's head at this moment, as she smiled her infuriatingly mysterious smile at the young man who was sitting on the wall opposite them. Blake was attracted to Margaret—Chloe could tell. And *she* was encouraging him, even though Can would triumph in the end. Why did she bother? Just to make things harder for Chloe? Chloe was interested in Blake. She had told Margaret so earlier that afternoon. And now Margaret was trying to make things harder for her. You would have thought they were enemies instead of best friends.

Blake Moffet was a Peace Corps worker. Before being posted to a little village west of Bursa the previous autumn, he had attended a summer training program at Woodrow College, and that was how they knew him. He was tall, broad-shouldered, somewhat clumsy but affable, attractive in spite of his unruly hair and his broken nose, or perhaps because of them. He was from Kansas City and was painfully sincere about wanting to help mankind. He was a romantic. That April he had done something reckless: he had become engaged to the *muhtar's* daughter in his little village. He had only seen the girl twice: once when he caught a glimpse of her at a window, which was when he had fallen in love with her, and once at the engagement ceremony, a magnificent feast which many people from Woodrow College had attended. The marriage was to take place the following year, just before the end of Blake's tour of duty. The girl was illiterate, but Blake planned to educate her in America.

Margaret's Can had no patience for Blake. "What is this?" he would say. "Building schools for villagers he has never met in his life? Who asked him to do this?" The engagement itself made him almost speechless with disgust. "This is a typically American blunder," he had told Margaret and Chloe. "In fact, it is a travesty."

Chloe remembered the time and place of this conversation very clearly. Can had picked Margaret up after school and had offered Chloe a lift home out of politeness. When the subject of Blake came up, Margaret's mysterious smile changed into a vaguely contemptuous one. But she had said nothing, as usual. It had been Chloe, as usual, who had spoken up.

"But he loves her," she had protested.

Can had waved his arm impatiently. "Such love is for children. It completely denies the realities of the situation."

Margaret had smiled and nodded, as if in agreement with her officious boyfriend. Now she was smiling and nodding in agreement with Blake. Whom did she really believe? Or was making the right impression all she cared about? Chloe felt like shaking her, to see if the old Margaret she had once been friends with was still inside.

They were discussing Blake's upcoming wedding. In reaction to Margaret's bland, encouraging smiles, Chloe found herself becoming more and more outspoken. "You're just like your father," she could hear her mother saying. "You never know where to draw the line."

"What are you going to do on your wedding night," Chloe asked, "if your beloved takes off her clothes and is grossly overweight?"

"I hadn't given much thought to it," he replied.

"Are you going to go through with that disgusting ritual of displaying the bloodstained sheet out the window?" she then asked.

"I suppose so," Blake said. "If they really want me to. It's their village. I don't want to offend them."

"But what if she doesn't bleed?' Chloe persisted.

"Oh, for Christ's sake, Chloe. What a question."

"I'm serious. What will you do?"

"Show them a sheet without a bloodstain, I suppose.

"You can't do that. They'll think you're not a man."

"You know," Blake said, showing some annoyance now, "as long as *I* know I'm a man, I don't give a damn what anyone else thinks."

"That's just the kind of attitude that's going to land you in trouble."

"What kind of trouble?"

"The kind of trouble you don't need," said Chloe. "You see, you're going to have to make up your mind. Either you do as the Romans or you don't do as the Romans. Either you don't show them the sheet at all or you let her prick her finger on something if there isn't any blood forthcoming."

"You make it sound like a cattle show," Blake said.

"It is."

"Oh, for crying out loud!"

"You still have time to get out of it," Chloe said.

"No, I don't," Blake said sharply. "You know what would happen to that girl if I walked out on her now. Her life would be over. She'd be in disgrace. Even if I decided today that I didn't love her, I'd have to go through with it. But I do love her, as it happens."

"You haven't even talked to her," said Chloe. "You're not in love with her. You're in love with an ideal."

"So what?" he said. "Whatever way you look at it, I'm committed."

As if to emphasize his point, he took out a handkerchief and blew his nose. The handkerchief had a cartoon figure printed on it, and beneath it was written, "Blow me." The handkerchief was so inappropriate that Chloe began to giggle. At first it seemed as if Margaret was going to side with Blake again. But then, miraculously, her aloof smile faded away. She exploded into giggles so loud they sounded like hiccups. So she was right, Chloe said to herself. Her old friend Margaret was still there, hiding behind that infuriating front.

"You two aren't very nice sometimes," Blake said, putting his handkerchief away. Chloe wondered if he had forgotten what was written on it. "I mean, what do you care about, besides yourselves?"

...re too sophisticated to care about anyone,'' Chloe

...at's perverse.''

''Of course it's perverse. We're perverted. We were born and bred in perversion. We have no morals. We live in abandonment.'' Chloe spread her arms. ''We lurch from hedonistic pleasure to hedonistic pleasure. We wallow in pantheism. We answer to no god.'' She looked at Margaret and they both giggled again. Blake looked disgusted. ''For two people who are supposed to be sophisticated, sometimes you act awfully immature.''

''I'm sorry,'' said Chloe in a fake high voice.

''Sure you are,'' he said, standing up. 'I've had enough of this ridiculous conversation. I'm going back to the house for a shower.'' And off he went. He was staying with the Ashes. Chloe and Margaret followed him at a distance.

On their way down the hill, they passed many landmarks. The spot on the road where Chloe, who could not see without her hated glasses, had accidentally snubbed her first love by walking right past him, thus bringing the flirtation to an abrupt end. The tennis courts where Margaret had broken off with a former boyfriend so ugly that she winced now at the mention of his name. The bench where, aged eight or nine, Chloe had first told Margaret about the horrors of rape. She had read an article entitled ''Rape and the Single Woman'' in *Readers' Digest,* and it was such a frightening article that they had vowed to each other that they would never be single. They had made many vows to one another, and broken almost every single one.

They walked through the Hisar Gate and headed toward the Aşiyan Road, losing Blake and then finding him again as they walked past Rapist Hill.

Rapist Hill was a shrub-covered mound at the foot of the tower. At the top of the mound was a rock shaped like a chair, which Margaret and Chloe called ''the Wishing Rock.'' From the Wishing Rock, you could look down the Bosphorus almost as far as the Old City in one direction, and almost as far as the Black Sea in the other. If you did so three times, they had once believed, you could make a wish.

Margaret and Chloe had made many wishes here that were no longer important to them. Wishes about bra sizes and leg shapes, wishes about the kind of men they wanted to marry, the kind of engagement ring they wanted these men to give them.

The Wishing Rock was also popular with courting couples, and that was why Margaret and Chloe had given up on it at twelve or thirteen, not so much because of the couples themselves but because of the grimy vagabonds who would hide in the bushes in order to watch them. There was a band of them. They even came out of hiding from time to time for cigarette breaks. They occasionally exposed themselves to Margaret and Chloe, or tried to attack them, or chased them down the hill, but the girls had long ago learned to kick, or to scream, or to scare them off by pretending to be spastics. They had treated the whole thing as a joke until one day Meredith Lacey had explained to them that these men were not funny at all, but victims of an unjust economic order, as well as being homeless, unloved, and confused by Western dress and morals. "Most of them are upright citizens in their own villages. It's just the conditions of city life that have changed them." This revelation had confused them. It was easy to kick a rapist in the groin, hard to kick a lonely and culturally bewildered man.

The sun had set by the time they reached the little alley that led up to the Ashes' house. The streetlamps were on and the air was tinged with blue. Blake was sitting on the cemetery wall, swinging his long legs back and forth as he gazed at the tombstones. He turned and smiled at Margaret as they walked past, and Margaret smiled back at him. The mysterious smile again. Chloe sighed, feeling very lonely.

Looking over her shoulder at Blake, she was forced to admit to herself that, arguments about bloodstained sheets notwithstanding, she was still interested in him. She pictured herself in his arms, kissing him. She pictured herself passionately dizzy, and going almost all the way. She would stop at the last moment, and confess to having no birth control. Had Margaret ever gone all the way? She had no idea. She wondered what it felt like to go all the way. She wondered what conversational contortions she would have to put herself through tonight to end up in Blake's arms.

Margaret had once told Chloe that she degraded herself

when she flirted with people. But what else could she do? How else could she hope to win in a world full of women with mysterious smiles? So what if she degraded herself, if by midnight she ended up in Blake's arms?

She admired him. She admired his moral tenacity. Imagine sacrificing your happiness for an ideal. Imagine having the strength, the amazing blindness, to refuse to admit you'd made a bad promise. Imagine believing in exactly the same thing for two days in a row. "I wonder," Chloe said to Margaret after they were out of earshot. She hoped to draw her out again, if only for a moment. "I wonder if he knows he's a tragic figure."

"Drinks? Drinks, anyone? Would anyone like a drink?" Meredith's high-pitched voice rang through the house as she went from room to room, flicking on lights. Her children, who were upstairs in Eric's bedroom, smoking hashish, knew that it was sunset without even looking out the window.

"Leslie?" Meredith said, as she walked into the study. Leslie was sitting at the desk, grading papers. He looked up. "Yes?" he said. He was a thin, frail man with thinning gray hair and sunken cheeks. His face spoke of the tragedy of wasted intelligence.

"Are you ready for a drink, darling?" Meredith said.

"No, I am not," said Leslie. "I want to finish these papers first, if you don't mind."

"Of course I don't mind. So long as you don't mind if I have one."

"Of course I don't mind," Leslie said.

"Do we have any of Ginger's gin left?" Meredith asked. "I'm in the mood for a martini."

"Then go ahead and make yourself one. You can do anything you please, just as long as I can have some peace and quiet."

"Fair enough!" said Meredith. She went over to the window that looked out over the balcony and opened it, with some effort. Ginger, who was sitting in a lounge chair reading the *New Yorker,* jumped at the noise. "I just wanted to know if you'd like a martini."

"I don't drink martinis anymore. They're *démodé.*"

"Your obsession with fashion overwhelms me, my dear. What makes a martini unfashionable?"

"It smacks of Madison Avenue," said Ginger.

"Oh, goodness gracious, we can't have that, can we? Well, I'm having one anyway. What can I get *you?*"

"Nothing, thanks. I'll save myself for that party."

"Fair enough!" said Meredith. She slammed the window shut. She went downstairs and made herself a double martini. She drank half of it in the kitchen, then went back upstairs and established herself in the other lounge chair on the balcony.

She longed to turn off the light so that she could see the view better, but of course she couldn't, because Ginger was reading.

"What are you reading about, pet?" Meredith asked.

"China," Ginger said.

"Oh. How interesting."

"Yes, it is," Ginger agreed. "And if you wouldn't mind, I'd like to finish it before we start talking."

"Forge ahead, my dear. I didn't mean to be a nuisance." Meredith retreated to her drink. Why was everyone so sour this evening? She was the only one looking forward to the party.

It wasn't Ginger's abruptness that bothered her. Ginger had always been abrupt. Ginger was Meredith's oldest, dearest friend. They had gone to Northhampton together, they had gone to Bennington together. Together they had tried to break into the dance world, and together they had failed. Together they had come out to Istanbul to teach at the Girls' College. But then their paths had diverged. Ginger had lost her head over the male lead in a campus play and followed him back to America. Meredith had married Leslie—on the rebound, really—and stayed in Istanbul. They had not seen each other for nineteen years.

Now, suddenly, Ginger was back—tanned and divorced, with a doctorate in Art History—to work on the excavation of a Byzantine church. She was staying with the Laceys until her foundation money arrived—unless Leslie kicked her out first. Leslie and Ginger had not been getting along.

When had it started? The day Ginger suggested Leslie wash out the gray in his hair with henna, or the day she told him he ate too many eggs? Or was it the night she had tried to drag him off to the bushes? (He had demurred.) She had taken to calling Leslie names. Closet queen, wimpy dick, eunuch, misogynist . . . usually out of earshot, but sometimes loud enough for Leslie to hear.

It was so unkind. It was true, to a degree, what she said about him, but did that excuse her? Meredith did not like to see her husband hurt. So what if he was bad in bed? She had married him for his exquisitely cynical mind.

She had married him because she needed a companion and wanted a family. His reasons had been much the same. Their sex life had been purely procreational. Bang, bang, bang, and before she knew it, she was the mother of two. Satisfied, she and Leslie had returned to their respective beds.

For a while, she did not know there was something missing in her life, until one night at a cast party (*A Streetcar Named Desire?)*, when drink had eroded her moral fiber to the extent that she allowed a man she did not know very well to escort her up to a vacant bedroom, where she had her first orgasm.

Now, in the midst of the progressive era, it shocked her to remember how little she had known about sex. It was shocking, really shocking, to think that no one had bothered to tell her, in all those years of top-notch schooling, that humans were capable of orgasm.

It was criminal to keep people in the dark. And what happened when you wrenched a poor, unsuspecting creature out of the middle ages only years before she herself reached middle age? You created an insatiable beast whose only thought was orgasm.

Now her primal urges had diminished somewhat. It was age, Meredith thought, and there was something to be said for it. Her only regret was having confided too much to Ginger. Because it turn out Ginger was indiscreet. Only the other night, she had blurted out—at the dinner table, in front of everyone—"Well, you two haven't fucked in years, so how do you know?"

So long as Ginger didn't tell any of her tales tomorrow.

This evening, for the first time in months, Meredith was in one of her wild-animal moods. What a bore to be sitting with a group of spoilsports when she herself could hardly sit still. She stood up, took a deep swig of her drink, and then moved her chair closer to the railing. She swung her right leg impatiently, then locked it under her left leg. She tapped her fingers on the armrests. Humming a half-forgotten tune, she lit a cigarette.

Down below, just outside the living room window of their garden apartment, Ralph and Theo were enjoying their first drinks of the evening. Theo was having a Hill cocktail, which he made with his lethal homemade lemon vodka, while Ralph nursed a simple lemonade. Ralph was under doctor's orders not to drink, having recovered recently from hepatitis. He blamed his hepatitis on Amy, who had (he said) forgotten to wash the lettuce twice for a salad she had made at a dinner party that winter. Ralph had done an informal survey of the dinner guests, and as far as he could determine, everyone who had eaten the salad had come down with hepatitis.

Theo was not one of those people. He had had a difficult spring looking after the invalid Ralph, and his patience was almost gone. He had been looking forward to some free time tonight, but now it seemed as if Ralph was going to accompany him to the Ashes'.

Theo owed Ralph everything, so he was not about to protest. A large, bearlike man—more bearlike than ever now that he was approaching forty—Theo had once been a lifeguard, a football player, a small-town hero, a Rhodes scholar with political ambitions. He had suffered a nervous breakdown halfway through his first year of law school. His family had hushed it up. The next year he had arrived in Istanbul to teach French at the Academy, but he had been fired in 1964 for indiscretions. He now taught English at a little language school downtown. It had been Ralph who had found him the job, and Ralph who had taken him in as a companion. It was assumed they were lovers, and Theo did love Ralph dearly, difficult though he was. What no one would have believed was that they had never (apart from the odd orgy) made love.

Ralph was a good twenty years older than Theo. He had been teaching music at Woodrow College for thirty years and was soon to retire. Although he had not lived up to his early promise, he had the bearing of the distinguished pianist he ought to have become. He had a high, bulging forehead, gray hair swept back majestically, oversize glasses, a firm yet overwide jaw, a pouting lower lip, a large repertoire of dramatic gestures, and a voice that was deep and authoritative even when he was only being catty.

Noise filtered down from the Laceys' balcony, where Meredith was shuffling her chair. As it scraped against the painted wood, it sounded like fingernails on a blackboard. Looking up at Meredith, Ralph grimaced. Then, crossing his legs with disdain, taking a drag from his black-market cigarette, he said, "The Horse is in heat."

"Not again," said Theo.

"Oh, yes," said Ralph. "Just look at her. Can't sit still."

"Poor Thomas," said Theo.

"Do you think we should call ahead and warn him?" Ralph said.

Theo didn't answer.

Ralph took a sip of his lemonade. "Did you put *any* sugar in this lemonade, Theo, or did it slip your mind?"

"I put in plenty," said Theo.

"Not plenty enough," said Ralph.

"I'm sorry. I'll try and remember to put in more next time."

"You do that," said Ralph. He sighed. "God, I'm dreading this party. Do we have to go? I'm not in the mood for watching the Horse pursue Thomas. I've seen it all before."

"Why don't you stay home, then?" Theo asked.

"You know I don't like to be alone," Ralph snapped.

"Come, then. No one's stopping you."

"Whom are you meeting there?" Ralph asked.

"No one," Theo said.

"I don't believe you."

"Don't, then. I didn't expect you to. You never believe me anymore. You're a jealous old fart, you really are."

"Don't you dare call me a fart."

"Then don't act like one," Theo said.

"You're being disrespectful," Ralph said. "You never used to be disrespectful. You used to respect me. What have I done to deserve this?"

"I'm sorry," said Theo. "It's been a long day."

"It's not over yet."

"Perhaps you would like some more lemonade," said Theo.

"That would be lovely," said Ralph.

"I'll make it sweet," said Theo as he stood up.

"Would you?" said Ralph. His voice seemed to echo in the failing light.

Ralph was upset today, but not because of the doctor's ban on alcohol. Whatever his friends might think, alcohol was not an obsession with him. He could take it or leave it. In fact, he was enjoying the lack of hangovers. Nor was it jealousy that had ruffled his feathers, as even Theo seemed to think. What Ralph was upset about was the boys.

Neil Cabot had not turned up for his piano lesson again. He had been turning up less and less. When he did turn up, he cringed whenever Ralph sat down next to him on the piano bench. He seemed to expect Ralph to make a pass at him, to abandon the strict professional standards Ralph had upheld for over thirty years. Neil overrated his charms. If Ralph felt strongly about anything, it was Neil's promise. If Ralph loved anything about Neil, it was his beautiful hands. He was Julliard material, or would be if he worked. Now he had stopped working, and all because his wretched mother suspected Ralph of ulterior motives.

How dare these harridans seek to isolate him from the children! They were just as much his as they were their parents'. In fact, they were more his than theirs, because he did not take them for granted as their parents did. He agonized over them. He worried constantly about the effect their parents' indiscretions were having on them. He thought they were extraordinary. He dreamed of escape for them. He saw them leaving their nests for great accomplishments. And so it hurt him when they turned out not to have the stamina to do as they ought. When Neil allowed his mother's suspicions to keep him away from Ralph's piano. When Eric Lacey limped home a high school dropout and retired to his room to smoke hashish. When those girls swallowed their pride to please their moronic boyfriends.

If Ralph had had authority, he would have packed up and taken them all back to New York or London—someplace where people aspired to more than cirrhosis of the liver. The Hill was not good for adolescents. It taught them false values. But Ralph had no authority, and so he had to sit silently and watch these extraordinary children turn into prematurely middle-aged pseuds.

Eric wouldn't even say hello to him these days. He looked a wreck, when only two years earlier he had been an angel. Now he never washed his hair or his clothes, and his face was covered with a fuzz that made him look like an apricot. Beards! Ralph thought they should be outlawed.

By the time Theo returned with the tray of drinks it was pitch dark. The trees of the garden had receded into the black shadows, and when Ralph looked at the Cabot house without his glasses it looked as if the windows were suspended in midair and not connected to a house at all.

One by one they disappeared as the bitch Amy went from room to room flicking off lights. She paused at her daughter's window to smoke a cigarette. She was dressed in a low-cut blue cocktail dress Ralph remembered Hector buying for her in Beirut a few years back, but she had left off the gauze cape that had given the dress distinction. Her hair was a shade or two blonder than Friday. Putting on his glasses, Ralph saw that her face was caked with makeup.

"Dressed to kill," Ralph said to Theo. "Dressed to kill and going nowhere."

"I suppose you could say that about all of us."

"Couldn't you, now," said Ralph. He took out a cigarette for himself, and then offered one to Theo. He lit them both with his gold lighter. "Well, thank God I'm getting out for the summer."

He closed his eyes and thought about the delights awaiting him. St. Paul de Vence. London. New York. Tanglewood. Perhaps even Santa Fe. Oh, how delicious it was going to be, to spend time with people who read *The Times,* who cared about music and drama and art. Oh, what a letdown it would be to return to the Hill. Damn the Bosphorus, he thought. It was the Bosphorus that had lulled him into thinking that a life in beautiful surroundings was better than a life of concert triumphs. The Bosphorus and the confounded charm of his first Turkish friend, whose untimely death he lamented as much as the most impressionable, patriotic schoolchild—though for different reasons. Mustafa Kemal Atatürk. Now, that had been a man with an intellect. Now, that had been a man with musical taste. Why Ralph had lingered on in Istanbul after his death was beyond him. Why he still remained was even more of a mystery. Taking a sip of his lemonade, which was sweeter than the first but still not sweet enough, he looked at the oppressive black shadows of his beloved garden. "What in God's name," he said, gesturing with his cigarette arm at the night, "what in *God's* name are we doing here?"

Standing at her daughter's window, Amy gazed across the street, where Meredith and that awful friend of hers were immersed in a passionate conversation on the balcony. Amy half expected them to embrace each other, or to raise their voices without realizing, as lovers will often do when they have a quarrel.

It was clear to everyone on the Hill that Meredith and Ginger were lovers.

In the garden below them, Amy could see two burning cigarettes moving shakily in the darkness, like fireflies. Although she could not hear what Ralph and Theo were saying, she was sure they were talking about her children. They had one interest in life and that was adolescent beauty. How much time could an educated person spend discussing the virtues of beardlessness, for God's sake? And didn't they know how bad they made her feel when they talked like that? She was, after all, a mother. Dear friends though they were, she sometimes felt like shooting them.

Aspasia was waiting at the door. She was looking better than usual tonight, with her frosted hair, her best black dress, and her garish jewelry. "So you've decided not to wait for Hector," Amy said.

"If he's not here, he may never come."

I'll call you a taxi, if you like."

"No. I'm not dead yet. I'll walk."

It was nine o'clock when they started down the rocky path to the Ashes', and the air rang with ferocious barking.

"*Vah, vah, vah,* look at that. It's a shame, it's a shame for the fatherland." The gatekeeper left his chair outside the Hisar Gate to chase the dogs away from the two ladies,

Professor Cabot's wife and the woman who was said to be his mother.

A taxi was coming through the gate, on its way down to Bebek, so the gateman asked Madame Cabot if she would like to go down with them. But she said no, she was not going all the way to Bebek. She thanked him for chasing away the dogs. He told her to be careful of the Aşiyan Road, which was dark and full of bad men. Madame Cabot smiled and agreed, but she did not seem worried.

The gateman liked Professor Cabot. Professor Cabot was a good man. He had given his life to the fatherland. This was why the gateman was puzzled by the sight of his wife in a sleeveless dress, the kind of dress the *consommatrices* wore at the *gazino* at the foot of the hill) walking down the dark hill without a male escort. He knew that the ways of the West were different, but this was shameful. He did not know what to think. And so he did not think. It was the best course of action. As he closed the gate behind the taxi, he closed his mind to all doubts that might have weakened his esteem for the worthy Professor Cabot.

Riding in the taxi were three women, all unmarried secretaries who worked at the college. One of them was Feza Hanim. Feza Hanim was Hector's secretary or, rather, the secretary for the entire mathematics department. She was a plump, cherub-faced woman in her midthirties. She was dressed, like her friends, in a simple cotton skirt and a short-sleeved orlon pullover. Draped over her shoulders was a cardigan. As with her friends, the most expensive part of her wardrobe was her shoes, navy-blue leather with sling-back heels and large gold buckles. They were the latest fashion from the finest shoe store on Istaklâl.

Feza Hanim and her friends were excited tonight because it was Feza's last night in town. The next morning she was leaving for Zurich, where she would check into a clinic to receive treatment for a kidney ailment. This trip was being paid for by her three benefactors. But that was another story, a story to which Feza never referred, a story which her true friends were careful not to repeat to careless gossips. It was enough to say that these men were fulfilling their obligations. No matter what anyone said, Feza and her friends knew that these men took their debts seriously, unlike so many of their compatriots.

As their taxi passed through the Hisar Gate, the headlights shone briefly on the glittering shawl of Professor Cabot's mother and the bare back of his wife.

"*Vah, vah, vah!*" said one of Feza Hanim's friends. "What are they doing on this road at this time of night?"

"It's pure stupidity," said the other.

"It is unsuitable clothing for such an expedition."

"Out of fashion, too."

"By five years or so."

"Where are they going?"

"To buy ice cream, maybe."

"In that clothing? Impossible. Feza dear, you must know where they are going, with your special connections."

"It is obvious. They are going to the party. There is a party at the Ashes' tonight. Look," she said, pointing up above the road toward the college terrace, beneath which was a house with so many lights shining in it that it sparkled like a galaxy.

"I hear they have orgies at those parties."

"You have been listening to careless gossips," Feza said. "Perhaps sometimes there are unsuitable occurrences at the homosexual parties. But not here. Professor and Mrs. Ashe are very religious. Do you know what the homosexuals call him? They call him 'the Priest.' "

"*Vah, vah, vah.* And what do they call that mother of Professor Cabot's? Someone told me she was Greek."

"She is Greek," said Feza. "But believe me, she is a wonderful woman. An excellent human being. *Vallahi billâhi.* I have spoken to her many times and she has a very good heart. How can I explain it? It is a pity she does not get along with Mrs. Cabot."

"Do they have unfriendly relations?" asked one of Feza's friends.

"The only thing I know is that she doesn't trust her. Last year she came to me with the instructions for her funeral and she asked me to keep them. She didn't want them at home because she was afraid Mrs. Cabot would find them."

"Ah, ah! What is this? Is this woman planning to die?"

"How should I know?" Feza said. "Perhaps it is a Greek custom."

Feza's friend shrugged her shoulders and popped her bubble gum disdainfully. She came from Ankara and knew nothing about Greeks.

By now the taxi had rattled its way down to the bottom of the Aşiyan Road. At the foot of the steps that led to the Aşiyan Gazino was an open-air ice cream store. A great excitement seized Feza and her friends at the sight of it.

"My most esteemed Hamdi *efendi,*" said Feza, her voice becoming quite shrill, "would you mind if we stopped here for a moment?"

Hamdi *efendi* bowed his head graciously, to show that he had no objection.

"Oh, I really shouldn't," exclaimed one of Feza Hanim's friends as she stepped out of the taxi.

"This is the third time today I have broken my diet."

"I had a banana chocolate at lunchtime."

"Shame, shame."

"Let me pay, big sister."

"No, it's my turn, I insist."

"Does everyone want chocolate? What about strawberry?"

"Hamdi *efendi,* you must allow us to buy you something. We insist."

Hamdi *efendi* raised his eyebrows in gracious refusal.

The women piled back into the taxi with their ice cream cones, still giggling like schoolgirls.

There was nothing like the Bosphorus on a summer night. The air was warm and fragrant with flowers. Along the shore, young and old walked arm in arm. There was a ferry sailing into Bebek bay, churning up its still waters, making them shimmer with reflected light from the yachts and restaurants, and the lanterns of the night-fishermen, who were casting for *lüfer.* Overcome by the beauty of her city, as she always was just before taking leave of it, Feza blurted out, "The only thing lacking now is the *mehtap,*" meaning, in Turkish, "the reflection of moonlight on water."

"Ah, ah! I didn't know we had a poet in our midst," said one of her girlfriends.

"It is fortunate that you will have time for leisure at your clinic this summer," said the other. "While we are wasting away at our offices, you will have the opportunity to advance your artistic career."

Nazmi's was an open-air café just outside Bebek, across the street from the Bosphorus. It was popular with artists and journalists, businessmen and fishermen, teachers and students. Tonight being Saturday night, it was full of students celebrating because they had finished their exams, students giddy with excitement because they were neglecting to study for their exams, even students trying to study.

There were animated groups of friends, sad-eyed couples holding hands, and here and there a young man sitting alone amid empty beer bottles, awash in sad thoughts—about a lost love? A shattered career? The prospect of two years in the military?—and sighing the attendant deep sighs that made the surrounding laughter even more poignant.

As Hamdi *efendi* drove Feza and her friends into Bebek, they caught a glimpse of Hector sitting at one of the front tables, next to the low wall that kept the café from spilling out onto the pavement. He was looking sad, they noticed, although perhaps only in contrast to the animated young man he was speaking to.

The young man was a former student of Hector's. He was back from the London School of Economics for what he called a "flying visit." It was impossible for Hector to carry on a normal conversation with him. Every time he looked away from the table, he spotted a dear friend. This would set into motion the loud exclamations of surprise, the warm embraces, the joyful laughter, the boisterous compliments without which no chance meeting among young Turkish men was complete. Much as Hector was usually touched by such performances, today it was too much for him. He felt weak at the joints and dizzy, and every time he opened his mouth to speak, he thought his voice was going to crack.

He was glad to see Emin Bey step off his yacht and approach the café.

The former student stiffened at the sight of Emin Bey, and the laughter among his long-lost friends died down. He greeted Emin Bey formally, and Emin Bey reciprocated with a stiff welcome, measured questions about the young man's academic progress, and best wishes for the future. The former student thanked him, and then meekly retreated to his friends' table, where he sat down and bowed his head like a child who has escaped with a lighter reprimand than he expected.

"My friend," Emin Bey said to Hector when all this was over, "how was your day?"

"Fine," said Hector. "And your day?"

"Extremely enjoyable," Emin Bey said.

They could each tell the other was lying.

"What did you do?" Hector asked.

"The normal tedious yachting expedition with a handful of my wife's indigent relations," Emin Bey said. Hector nodded in sympathy. "I sometimes think I ought to wear a captain's cap," Emin Bey went on. "That's how they make me feel, you know. I do wish sometimes that I had married into a smaller family."

Hector nodded in agreement. "I've had my fill of family today myself."

Emin Bey raised his eyebrows and put his hand on Hector's shoulder, betraying alarm. "You're not about to complain about your charming mother, are you?"

"No, not really. It's my father I was referring to."

"Your father?" Emin Bey asked.

"You didn't know I had a father, did you?" Hector said. "Well, I might as well not have one. I don't think we have very much in common. We do not even share a surname."

"My friend," said Emin Bey, "in my humble experience, it is very rare that one has something of value in common with relations. At least . . . at least this is how I feel today. Today, my friend, I discovered that my nephew is a fascist."

"How awful," said Hector.

"I suspected it, of course," Emin Bey went on. "But today I have had proof."

There was a silence. Emin Bey saw that this subtle hint had not registered with Hector. The poor man was too preoccupied with family concerns. Emin Bey searched his tired brain for another way to let his friend know that this nephew of his, whose name was Ismet, and who worked for the secret police, had been asking prying questions about Hector—not only about Hector but about Aspasia, that dreadful

Greek washerwoman Emin Bey could still not quite believe was Hector's mother.

Had it not been for Emin Bey's confounded wooden-headedness, Policeman Ismet and Hector's mother never would have met. The meeting had occurred a month earlier, during an ill-conceived luncheon at the Villa Rifat on Büyükada.

Emin Bey and his wife, Roksan, were in the habit of spending a weekend on that island sometime during the late spring—after the weather turned fine but before the dreaded season began. The purpose of the weekend was to enjoy the sparkling marine vistas and sweet pine forests in solitude.

This year, however, there had been no question of solitude. The unseasonably warm weather had attracted the city crowds in unprecidented numbers. Everywhere you went, there were dowdy, doe-eyed lovers holding hands in rented horse-drawn carriages, trying to negotiate creaky rented bicycles down rocky paths, stumbling through the shrubbery in unsuitable shoes, searching bashfully for a picnic spot so isolated that they would have no trouble making love after lunch.

The weather had also attracted those with closer ties to Emin Bey. Among them was his dear old schoolfriend, Moris.

Moris now figured as a member of the class that Emin Bey scorned above all other: the haute bourgeoisie. The heir to a small import-export concern, Moris had taken his spoiled, affected wife's millions and translated them into an unparalleled industrial fortune. He now had the life that every entrepreneur dreamed of: Parisian clothes, English schools for his children, Swiss bank accounts and ski vacations, ostentatious houses in all the right places. He spent his summers on Büyükada playing bridge with his dull, self-centered, mercenary peers, at the exclusive Anadolu Club. His boredom, his despair, were apparent in his every gesture. And yet Emin Bey held none of these things against him. They were friends, and all friends were exceptions to the rule.

They usually saw each other only once a year, in the autumn, when he and Moris would manage to shake off their wives for an evening and join their other two exroommates at their favorite *meyhane* in the Çiçek Pasaj. Here the four of them would sometimes recapture the spirit of their schooldays.

And what days they had been. Four foreign students, lost in London, always cold, never able to find even a pub where they felt at home. Four brothers—a Turk, a Greek, an Armenian, and a Turkish Jew—all with the same longing for the Istanbul sea air, for a warm plate of *köfte* and *pilâv*, for *beyaz peynir*, for a plate of really excellent *turşu*. Sometimes their longings had reduced them to tears.

And yet, when they had returned to their beloved city, that brotherly feeling that had existed among them in London had disappeared. He, Emin Bey, had taken up his teaching post. Moris had gone into business. The Armenian, who had been studying medicine, had set up his practice in Ankara. The Greek, who had been studying engineering, had gone into the textile business and made a killing, which he then lost during the troubles of 1964. He had never bothered to acquire Turkish citizenship, and so had been expelled with twenty thousand other Greeks. He now lived in Athens, where he was rich once again. He came to Istanbul every autumn to visit his wife's relatives, so that was when they had their reunion. Emin Bey was sure he had become a pederast. There was something shrill and girlish about his appearance which had not been there before.

That was all Emin Bey noticed now when they saw each other, the hundreds of tiny little ways in which his dear old roommates had changed over the years, the ways in which the Greek had become more Greek, the Armenian more Armenian, the Jew more Jewish. It was as if an honorable man had no choice but to blend into his surroundings as he grew older, no choice but to allow himself to be squeezed into the mold and become, in the eyes of younger men, a stereotype they could point to with disdain and say, "*I'll* never be like that."

Just as he and Moris and the others had said when they were young. *They* were never going to be like their fathers—henpecked, circumscribed, going through the motions, never seeing anyone socially who was not a member of their class or religion. *They* were friends for life. It was a new age, the age of Atatürk, in which the old barriers would crumble and all men would live together like brothers.

And yet it seemed that they were only brothers now when they managed to shake off their wives and escape to a *meyhane,* and, for a few hours, dream of all the discomforts they had once shared in London. Who among them would have believed then that one day they would be sitting at a table together, surrounded by all their favorite foods, remembering with tears in their eyes the shilling heater, the stuffy pubs that closed too early, the boiled food, the warm beer, the unending rain, and the strange aromas that had emanated from the bedsitter of the Nepalese gentleman who had lived across the hall from them in Queensway? It was a personal tragedy with national implications that they could be brothers only when they were abroad. It was a tragic flaw that did not speak well for the future of the nation.

But it was not a tragic flaw Emin Bey and his old schoolfriends would ever think to discuss openly. Whenever Emin Bey and Moris ran into one another by chance, they greeted each other with such warmth and joy that one would think no barriers existed. The chance meeting in Büyükada earlier that spring had been no exception.

They ran into each other on the *iskele.* After many embraces and shouts of surprise, they had arranged to meet for lunch with their respective wives (who hated each other) at the Villa Rifat, at one P.M. the following day, which happened to be Saturday.

Emin Bey knew all along that the antipathy between the wives would create difficulties during the luncheon, although he had absolute confidence that they would observe propriety as always. There would be the insincere exchange of compliments and much chatter about Paris and Rome fashions. It could be endured.

But when he awoke on Saturday morning, he found himself dreading the luncheon. He was therefore overjoyed to run into Hector and Amy when he went down to the *meydan* to buy cigarettes. They were accompanied by Hector's mother, whom Emin Bey had met once or twice but whose face he did not remember. "You've met Aspasia, of course," Hector said. Emin Bey nodded with assurance and smiled at her. A dark, solid woman dressed in black with a cheap orlon kerchief, he had mistaken her for the Cabots' Greek maid.

There had been instant inconsistencies, but he had not paid attention to them. For example,when Emin Bey had insisted that the Cabots join his party for lunch at the Villa Rifat, Hector had said, "It's up to Aspasia. It's a sentimental journey for her. As I may have mentioned, she spent some of her happiest years here" It was not the sort of thing one said about one's maid, Emin Bey had realized in retrospect. But at the time, he had been too preoccupied to make the connection.

Even this mismatched group would have been manageable, had there not been a third chance meeting. Or had it been planned? Emin Bey would never know for sure. His wife, Roksan, took her familial duties seriously, so she was perfectly capable of having arranged for Banu, her favorite niece, and Ismet, Banu's sneak policeman of a husband, to join them for the weekend on Büyükada, even though she knew very well that they had come to Büyükada for solitude.

But chance, mischance, what did it matter? The facts were as follows. When Emin Bey returned to the Villa Rifat with his new pack of cigarettes, Roksan said, "You'll never guess who I met coming off the ten o'clock ferry. Banu and Ismet! Imagine the coincidence. Of course I invited them to lunch. I didn't want to be rude."

"Of course, my dear," Emin Bey said evenly, but as the words left his lips, his heart sank.

And so, at one that afternoon, they had all convened at the Villa Rifat, where the owner, a friend, had arranged a beautiful table for them on his small terrace. Not even Emin Bey's worst fears had prepared him for the social ice that set in among his guests. he had been counting on Moris and Hector to help him keep the ball rolling, but they were curiously subdued. Emin Bey was forced to conjure up one anecdote after another so as to keep his guests from realizing that they had nothing to say to one another.

He had made free with the *raki* bottle, in the hope that *raki* would eventually loosen tongues, thus creating a more congenial atmosphere. This had proved to be a miscalculation. He had not taken into account the social deficiencies of

Policeman Ismet, whom he suspected of being at least half Kurdish, if not more than half.

Policeman Ismet hailed from Van, a city in the east of Turkey where many Kurds lived and which Emin Bey therefore considered uncivilized. He was university educated, this Ismet (it was at Istanbul University that his wife's niece, Banu, had fallen into his clutches), but his accent still had the telltale guttural edge to it. He looked like a fox, always sniffing for prey. He was oblique when asked questions about his line of work, but everyone in Roksan's family knew he worked for a certain government agency which kept dossiers on subversive elements.

Ismet had friends in high places, it was said. He was bright and he was going to go far. But there was one yawning gap in his education and that was languages. This hungry Eastern fox, in devouring knowledge from alien cultures, had neglected to arm himself with even a modest understanding of English, or French, or German. Many times, Emin Bey had watched him squirm with resentment when he was forced to listen to conversation in a European language. But not until this fiasco of a luncheon had Emin Bey deliberately tried to humiliate the man for his linguistic shortcomings.

It was possible, Emin Bey conceded, that he, too, had drunk too much *raki* and therefore had lost his normal caution.

He had insisted that Ismet sit next to him. Having insured that the conversation was primarily in English, with occasional forays into French and German, Emin Bey had then insinuated himself into the role of Ismet's interpreter. How he had enjoyed watching Ismet's face darken with each fresh glass of *raki*.

The more Emin Bey played with his mouse, the greater his pleasure. As a final jab to Ismet's primitive nationalism, Emin Bey turned to Aspasia and began to address her in Greek. His knowledge of the language was more than adequate, as his mother had always preferred Christian maids. In order to put her at ease, he treated her with exaggerated courtesy, as he always did when servants found themselves sitting at the same table as their employers.

"I understand that this is not your first visit to Büyükada," he said.

"I don't call it Büyükada," Aspasia replied in a gravelly voice. "I call it Prinkipo."

"Ah, Prinkipo, Prinkipo, of course!" said Emin Bey. "What a beautiful name. I had almost forgotten it. What a pity they had to change it. Prinkipo has such a magical ring. And Büyükada, it sounds like army boots. Büyükada. Listen to the sound of it. Clump, clump, clump. What a clumsy name. It is a pity that we Turks could not do better than Büyükada. Ah! But you must find it changed."

"It was so much nicer in the old days, before the Greeks left," said Moris' wife, also in flawless Greek.

"But we were among the first to leave," Aspasia said. "We left in 1923."

"In 1923?" Emin Bey said. "But you couldn't have been more than a child."

"A child only in years," Aspasia said. "Innocence does not last long if you've seen what I've seen."

"It is a shame how respectable people will put children to work in their homes," said Moris' wife, for she, too, thought Aspasia was the Cabots' maid. "My own best friend has done so. She says it is a better life for the child than she would have in the village. She says she'll marry her off when the time is right. But in my opinion, it is a form of slavery."

"They should have laws against it," Emin Bey agreed, and then he happened to glance at Hector, whose face was riddled with bewilderment. It was the first inkling Emin Bey had of his miscalculation. The second was the sight of Hector's arm around Aspasia's shoulder. Not the sort of gesture you expected on the part of an employer toward a maid. Not in public, in any case. The confirmation of Emin Bey's doubts came moments later, after Aspasia said, "I don't know what you're talking about. I didn't work as a maid until after Hector was born, and even then it wasn't because my family hadn't provided for me. I had a dowry, you know. At least I did until 1923. It's a shame what they made us leave behind, a shame."

Hector tried to silence her with a friendly pat on the back. "Let's just let sleeping dogs lie, shall we, Mother?"

At the word "mother," Emin Bey froze.

He looked at Hector, who had received the unintended insult with admirable calm. Emin Bey tried to think of a way to undo it. Since he could not, he continued in the same vein.

"Oh the Greeks, the Greeks," he said, recklessly pouring *raki* into as many glasses as he could reach. "What a loss to the nation that those Anatolians in Ankara had to send them packing to Athens. What a loss for us, what a gain for Athens. The joy is gone from the streets. Don't you think so, Moris, my ram? Don't you remember the sublime restaurants we used to go to in the old days? Such dancing, such singing. It is all gone now, all gone. Alas, the celebration has been moved to Athens, leaving us Turks to plod on joylessly in our inimitable fashion. What a shame. What restaurants they were."

"My family had a restaurant, on Prinkipo, as a matter of fact."

"No! You can't be saying this! Your family—a restaurant on Prinkipo? What a fortuitous coincidence. I came to Prinkipo myself as a child. You must tell me your father's name. Perhaps I remember him."

"His name was Manos," said Aspasia.

"Manos! Not Manos of Prinkipo?"

"You were too young to know him," said Aspasia.

"Yes, but my father knew him, I am certain. He often spoke with sighs of a restaurant on Prinkipo that had closed before my time, and I'm sure the name of the man was Manos. Yes, of course it was! Of course it was Manos! It is, after all, an unforgettable name. This is most extraordinary, Madame Aspasia. To think that you are the daughter of Manos about whom my dear father sang so many praises. Hector, my friend, why have you never told me? I seem to remember . . . a fondness, a fondness for music."

"His singing was famous," said Aspasia.

"Of course! Of course! His singing. Famous. My father spoke with nostalgia about his singing. I remember well now. Tell me, did he ever sing *kantades*?"

"He sang everything," said Aspasia.

"But *kantades*—*kantades* have no parallel. My heart melts at the sound of them. Moris, my friend, you must remember how our dear classmate Yannis, who shared digs with us in London, would melt our hearts with *kantades* on cold evenings. He had a voice like a nightingale, didn't he, Moris? He tried to teach us, but to no avail! I am tone-deaf, I'm afraid. But you're not, are you, Moris? Now I remember. You were not bad yourself. You must remember some of those *kantades*, Moris my child. Sing one for us."

Moris did not look entirely comfortable. "I'm afraid it's been too long since I last . . ."

"Nonsense! You are being modest. Now even I remember the words. The one about the eyes, 'Your beautiful eyes, my world is your eyes, without you I don't even want palaces. . . .' You know which one I mean. It starts like this: *'Ta matia, ta glika sou ta matia* . . . 'Look, even I am singing it, and I am tone-deaf. I insist that you help me out."

"Perhaps some other time," said Moris.

"Some other time I won't be in the mood," said Emin Bey.

Moris then switched to French. "I am afraid it will not be appreciated by the entire party," he said in a low voice.

It was at that exact moment that Policeman Ismet slammed his fist on the table.

"Enough of foreign languages!" he bellowed. His Turkish sounded more guttural than ever. "I said enough! Emin Bey, the time has come to remind these *gâvurs* where they are. They are in Turkey. When in Rome, even infidels must do as the Romans, and speak the language of the country."

Emin Bey felt his blood coming to a boil, but he remained outwardly calm. "The scope of your knowledge continues to surprise me, Ismet, my child," he said. " I had no idea that the directors of secondary education in your much-sung of city of Van had seen fit to instruct its diligent students in the ways of the Romans."

"I will take no such taunts from a man who makes light of his country's dignity," Ismet snarled.

"Ismet, my poor child!" Emin Bey continued, "I am so very sorry if I have offended you with my frivolous cosmopolitan ways. Alas, it is inevitable: we are a city of many cultures, as I am sure you have become aware. But you mustn't misunderstand my motives. Scratch the surface, and you shall find underneath the most ardent patriot, the most diligent disciple of our illustrious founding father."

"No true disciple of Atatürk wastes his afternoons warbling songs in the language of the enemy. Our founding father was a warrior, not a clown."

"Then I must infer that the honorable directors of secondary education of Van did not see fit to instruct you concerning the personal tastes of our beloved founding father. He was no Anatolian, my son. He was a cosmopolite. For your information, he considered our local whining and wailing to be fit only for dogs. His preference was for Western music. We are merely following his example."

"I will not tolerate such treacherous statements!" Ismet cried, slamming his fist on the table again.

"As I said," Emin Bey answered, "I am devastated to have offended your nationalist purity with unfit sounds."

"It is a disgrace, my uncle. A disgrace, I said. You should not act like this in front of foreign guests. It gives them unnecessary ideas. That one, for example," Ismet said, gesturing at Moris. "He should not put on airs. He should take care not to cross his benefactors. He should realize that his welcome in this country depends on the quality of his behavior."

"It depends on nothing of the sort," said Emin Bey sharply. "He is a Turk, just like you and I."

"What nonsense you are saying. He is not a Turk, he is a Jew."

Emin Bey's wife and her niece both gasped and looked at each other, mortified. Then there was silence. Emin Bey waited to see if Moris wished to respond to Ismet personally. But he did not. He looked shaken and so did his wife, who was suddenly bereft of her affectations. They looked as if they believed what Ismet had said, that their welcome in Turkey depended on the quality of their behavior.

And all thanks to Emin Bey's careless baiting of a dangerous man. He felt like kicking himself in the head, as the Greeks said. He had failed dismally as a host, and now he had to find a way to settle accounts. There was only one course open to him. He bided his time, waiting for the perfect moment.

"Enough political discussions," he said. "We're here to enjoy ourselves."

He had fruit brought to the table, and after they were finished with the fruit, he had the waiter take orders for coffee. Then, as soon as the waiter had gone inside, he gave Ismet the most ingratiating smile in his repertoire, and suggested that the two of them step into the street for a moment. "There is a proposition I would like to put to you in private," Emin Bey said.

As soon as they were out of sight, Emin Bey punched Ismet in the jaw. He knocked him out cold and left him lying in the gutter. He then returned to the table to enjoy his coffee.

He made no mention of the incident. When his wife's niece inquired feebly as to the whereabouts of her husband, Emin Bey said he thought he had gone for a walk.

For the rest of the weekend, even after his wife and her confounded niece had discovered Ismet in the street, even after his wife had reproached him tearfully for his uncivilized behavior, Emin Bey gloated over his victory. Over and over, he recalled the happy moment when his fist plunged into the bony Kurdish jaw of Policeman Ismet. It was only when he and his wife, Roksan, returned to Istanbul on Sunday evening that he began to pay attention to his wife's reasoning.

Think of the possible repercussions, she had said to him. It was unwise to have an enemy in the secret police. "Of course it is unwise!" Emin Bey had protested in the beginning. "It is unwise, but it is manly. The man is an ignorant fundamentalist, completely uncultured, not to be tolerated. Look at his eyes—typically Kurdish. They are so close together that they are practically on the slope of his nose."

But in the end Roksan had eroded his resolve. "Think of the next time the military authorities take power. Family members, offspring of dear friends will number among the unfortunates who fall afoul of the authorities. If Ismet is our ally we can help them. If he is our enemy we, too, could find ourselves among the victims. Especially if you continue to talk in your careless, childish manner." Roksan was right. It was important not to lose useful connections. And so he had telephoned the Kurdish fox of a policeman and apologized profusely for his drunken indiscretions, even though he knew that given a second chance he would punch Ismet even harder.

Ismet was not a stupid man, however backward his ideas. He knew why Emin Bey had been obliged to apologize to him, and he took advantage of it. He had now insinuated himself into the position of family confidant and constant yachting companion. He admired Emin Bey's yacht, and hinted that it was his ambition to own one like it one day. In the month that had passed since the Büyükada fiasco, there had not been a Saturday or a Sunday that had not been darkened by his sneering presence. Today had been no exception.

Today, Ismet had been asking questions. Casual questions, such as whether Emin Bey knew of any members of the Communist Party working at Woodrow College. Emin Bey said no. Ismet said he had heard that a certain TASS reporter made frequent visits to the houses of certain prominent professors. "And that man, for example," Ismet had continued. "Your friend. Professor Cabot. I understand that he is an anarchist."

"If he is an anarchist," Emin Bey had said, "I am the secret genius behind the Palestine Liberation Organization."

"This is not a laughing matter," Ismet had said sharply. "There are other facts to be considered. His mother, for example. How much do you know about her? You thought she was a cleaning woman."

"What can I say?" Emin Bey said, concealing his annoyance at Ismet for exposing a still painful wound. "Such is the price we Ottomans must pay for our snobbery."

"It is true. Your elaborate phrases have created an impermeable barrier between you and the daily reality. You do not realize, for example, that she is a wealthy woman."

"It is none of my business," said Emin Bey.

"But it is your business. It is the business of every patriot. How do you think your friend Professor Cabot became involved with anarchist concerns? Through his mother, of course. The woman is a prominent member of the underground anarchist movement of the United States. And now you must ask yourself what she is doing in this country."

"What nonsense," Emin Bey said. "There is no anarchist movement in the United States."

"We must not lose sight of the facts. This mother of Professor Cabot was a confidante of the Rosenbergs."

"The Rosenbergs were not anarchists."

"Anarchist, Communist, what does it matter? The important thing is that they are all traitors. My question is, what is this woman doing in the fatherland? What is she hoping to achieve?"

"Once a policeman, always a policeman," Emin Bey had said airily, as if the subject under discussion were boring to him. "No one can be innocent in your eyes. I tremble to think what you suspect your poor uncle of being up to in his free time. Perhaps you suspect me of conducting secret rendezvous with Russian submarines outside Anadolu Kavak?"

He had made light of Ismet's insinuations, but the fact was, they worried him. He did not like to hear about a dossier being compiled on his dear colleague, Hector Cabot, and he did not like to have that oily fox coming to him and asking him questions in order to fatten that dossier. As he sat now with Hector in Nazmi's, Emin Bey tried to think of how to warn his friend in a way he would take seriously— warn him so that he thought twice about talking to TASS reporters, warn him so that he might be aware of the dangers of spontaneity in a country where no *faux pas* was ever forgiven or forgotten.

But where would Hector be without his spontaneity, Emin Bey asked himself, as he looked at his friend across the table. It was the quality Emin Bey prized most in him. Hector was the only man with whom he could be sincere without unpleasant repercussions. Oh, the fights they had had over the years! They had argued about the Armenian question, they had argued about the riots of '55, they had argued about capitalism and socialism and the price of modernization. They had called each other names. They had insulted each other's intelligence. Hector had called him a typical Turk and Emin Bey had called him a typical American. And yet, the next day they were always brothers again, with none of the tensions and insincerities that marred his other friendships.

Looking at his watch, Emin Bey saw that it was ten o'clock. The Bosphorus road was crowded now with the expensive cars of the nouveau riche returning from the restaurants of Tarabya, but beyond them was the water, the deep, lustrous blue of peaceful dreams. Gazing at the lights of fishing boats and Asian villages, Emin Bey willed himself to put politics out of his mind. The night was too beautiful. His friend was already too sad for serious discussion. There would be plenty of other times to pass on the necessary warnings. He ordered a bottle of *raki* and insisted that Hector join him.

"To your health," he said, lifting up his glass. After a day of artificiality, it did his heart good to say something and mean it.

"And to yours," said Hector, smiling wanly.

Emin Bey settled back into his chair. "And so," he said, determined to get to the bottom of his friend's depression. "Your father's not up to scratch, is he?"

"Not really."

'You Americans have a shocking lack of indebtedness to your parents, you know."

"I know. But in my case it's partly justified. I never knew him."

"And it seems you'd prefer to continue not knowing him. Well, who am I to pass judgment? How long is he here for?"

"Indefinitely. He's the new Anglican priest. You may have even met him. Phillip Best."

"Phillip Best? The new priest? How can this be? I thought priests were meant to be celibate."

"That's Catholics."

"Of course. Excuse me. Christianity is sometimes confusing to us Moslems."

"He hasn't been a priest very long," Hector continued. "In fact, I don't know whether to take him seriously or not. He used to just knock about from country to country doing nothing in particular. Perhaps he was a spy. Perhaps he still is—how should I know? But don't you think that's an abrupt change, to go from part-time journalist-spy, or whatever he was, to being an Anglican priest? I didn't think they let people like him into the clergy. Unless the M15 twisted someone's arm, I suppose."

Emin Bey put his hand on Hector's shoulder as if to silence him. "My friend, you must not tell me such things. I am saying this to you for your own good. As I said, my nephew is a fascist. He works for the Secret Intelligence Service. Unlike some of our young students, I am under no illusion about how I would act under torture."

Once again, Hector paid no attention to his warning. "You see," he continued, "I met my father before, six or seven years ago. But I didn't realize it was he. It was at Nikolai Kadinsky's. Do you know him?"

"Of course I know him. Who does not know this man?"

"I didn't. Not well enough to remember his name, anyway. Thank God. We were trying to leave a party of his, you see, and when we went into the bedroom to retrieve our coats, there he was—my father, I mean—with Nikolai's houseboy."

"And you are sure this man was your father?"

"Of course I am."

"But you cannot be sure. It was a long time ago, as you said. It would be better, perhaps, to give the man the benefit of the doubt."

"But I can't. I always remember faces. I know it was him. I remember the scene clearly. My father had the houseboy pinned down, right on top of our coats."

"Pinned down, you say?" Emin Bey asked. Hector nodded. "Then the mystery is solved. You may stop worrying."

"Stop worrying? What do you mean?" Hector cried—a bit too loud, Emin Bey thought, if you considered how many students were sitting within earshot.

"It is elementary, my dear boy. I assume that if you were attending one of Nikolai's infamous orgies and came and went without ever learning the rascal's name, you were already one over the eight when you arrived and even more inebriated by the time you left."

"Perhaps."

"Most definitely. And so, when you saw this scene in the bedroom, you were viewing it with impaired faculties. It never happened, my friend. Your father could never have had Nikolai's houseboy pinned down. If it had really happened, the houseboy would have been on the top and not on the bottom."

"How can you be so certain?" Hector asked.

"It is Nikolai who plays the woman. His houseboys have always played the man."

"How do you know?" Hector asked.

Emin Bey's eyes hooded over. "Such things are known," he said.

"Well, maybe he usually played the man, but on this occasion I happen to know he was playing the woman."

"Anything is possible," Emin Bey said. "But I doubt it."

"Why?"

"A Turk never plays the woman. He only plays the man."

"Oh, come now," Hector said, raising his voice. "You don't believe that crap, do you?"

"It is not crap, as you call it. It is the truth. Why do you think there are so many foreign homosexuals in our country? It is because they are willing to play the part of the woman."

"If that were so," Hector protested, "there would have to be a posse of foreign homosexuals posted in every village in Anatolia."

"I cannot speak for Anatolia," said Emin Bey, trying not to appear annoyed. "All I know is that a true Turk only plays the part of a man."

"You're beginning to sound like that nephew of yours," Hector said.

That was when Emin Bey's temper snapped. The indignity of it, after the day he had endured!

"How dare you equate me with that cross-eyed peasant!" he cried. "I demand an apology!"

All over Nazmi's, heads turned at the sound of Emin Bey's raised voice. "*Vah, vah, vah,*" Emin Bey heard a former student of his murmur. "The sages appear to be divided." Not for the first time that day, Emin Bey cursed his headstrong nature. Here was his friend in the midst of a family crisis, and instead of helping him he had begun a pointless argument about sexual mores. He longed to let his friend know of his remorse, but he did not want to reveal further weakness while so many people were watching.

So he sat back, sighing like a man of the world, and looked sardonically at Hector.

"I'm sorry I ever brought the subject up," Hector said finally. "Perhaps you're right. Perhaps there *is* something wrong with my memory. God knows there's something wrong with every other facet of my personality."

"I asked for an apology, not abject groveling," Emin Bey said sharply. "Remember where you are, dear boy, and who is watching."

"I don't care who's watching."

"You Americans never do, do you? You act like children, and then you are surprised when people refuse to treat you like adults. It is an appalling trait in an imperialist power. No wonder there are effigies of Nixon being burned on the steps of every university in the western world. Why is nothing done about this problem? Because Americans do not demand respect."

"Why should I demand respect if I don't deserve it?" Hector asked.

"That is a secondary question. The real issue is: why don't you deserve the respect?"

"Do you really want me to answer that question after the kind of day I've had?" Hector said in a shaky voice.

"I was not considering the matter from an individual viewpoint," Emin Bey said," but rather from the national. Or, to be correct, the international, because that is what . . ." Emin Bey's voice trailed off, as he glanced at Hector and saw that he was sobbing.

Once again, heads turned. *"Vah, vah, vah,* look at that," one young man murmured. Another whispered, "What does this mean?" "Probably nothing," a third said, laughing softly. "Nothing serious, just a normal lovers' quarrel." Emin Bey's hair stood on end at that one. The boy had been in his class three years before. He remembered distinctly giving him a C when he deserved a D. Now he wished he had given him an F.

He was tempted to put the boy smartly in his place, but then the situation grew graver as Hector's sobs grew more audible. He cursed himself for bringing up politics at such an inopportune moment. What had become of his discretion? Flustered, Emin Bey jumped to his feet, determined to salvage what was left of his and his colleague's social standing.

"Come, my friend. It is time for an evening stroll." He took Hector firmly by the arm and led him into the street.

They headed for the college gate, because the road was darker in this direction. Once they were out of sight of Nazmi's, Emin Bey handed Hector a handkerchief. "Please, try not to be so upset," he said. "It has been a long day for you, and I now see that I have been carelessly adding insult to injury. You are depressed, I can see, and furthermore you are a bit taken aback. Please, follow my advice and go home now. Get a good night's sleep. Then tomorrow everything will look normal again."

"I can't go home now," Hector said. " I've got to go to a party."

"Forget the party. Go home and go to bed."

"But they're all waiting for me."

"They would give you the same advice as I if they could see your condition."

"No, they wouldn't," Hector said.

"You are underestimating your friends," Emin Bey said, "Go home, go to sleep, and leave the explanations for tomorrow. Let us go back to Bebek. I shall find you a taxi."

"I don't need a taxi. I can walk."

"Nonsense," Emin Bay said. "I insist on a taxi."

"But by the time we get back to Bebek—" Hector said.

"Fortunately," Emin Bey said, his eyes on the oncoming traffic, "there will be no need to go back to Bebek. Here is Hamdi *efendi*."

"Don't make him stop," Hector said. "He already has a passenger."

But Emin Bey had already hailed the taxi, and it was now coming to a stop.

"Hello, my teacher," Hamdi *efendi* said to Emin Bey.

"Good evening, Hamdi *efendi*. Would it be a great inconvenience for you to take my friend Professor Cabot home?"

"It would be a pleasure, my teacher."

"You are very kind," said Emin Bey. "Put it on my account."

"As you wish."

"Thank you very much." As Emin Bey opened the back door of the taxi for his reluctant friend, he smiled at the passenger, an elderly man dressed in black, with a clerical collar, and said, in English, "I hope you don't mind, old chap."

"Not at all, not at all. Plenty of room back here, plenty of room."

Emin Bey patted Hector on the back as he got into the back seat. "We shall speak tomorrow," he said. Smiling, he shut the door. He waved as the taxi set off down the shore road.

Hector smiled at his fellow passenger. "Well!" he said, smiling lamely.

"Well, indeed!" said the man.

"You're going to the Ashes', I take it."

"Yes, do you know them? Nikolai left me a note. I'm to meet him there. Do you know where we're going? I was beginning to worry about our driver's intentions."

"You needn't," said Hector. "He's scrupulously honest."

"That's good to know! Well, then. What can you tell me about the Ashes?"

"They're friends," said Hector. "It's a big party. They give it every year. I'm on my way there, too. In fact, I'm late."

"Oh, dear," said Hector's father.

The taxi left the main road and began to climb the Aşiyan. "You see," Hector said, pointing to a house high on the hill above them that was shimmering with light. "That's the house."

"Splendid!"

"But I feel I should warn you that my mother will be there."

"Oh, good. I was hoping she would be."

"Are you sure?" Hector said.

"You can't think I have ill feelings toward her after—what is it now? Thirty-five years? Come, come, now."

Hector shrugged his shoulders and gazed gloomily out the window. A moody sort of chap, his son, thought Phillip Best.

* * *

They entered through the kitchen, where the Ashes' maid and her family were seated around the punchbowl brandishing glasses full of wine-stained orange segments and shouting at each other in Armenian. One of the men—the maid's brother?—jumped to his feet at the sight of Hector and Phillip and offered them drinks.

Upstairs, the party was in full swing. As Hector led his politely beaming father up the narrow winding staircase, they ran into Margaret on her way down. "You at last!" she said. "People were beginning to worry!" She was carrying an empty hors d'oeuvres tray, which she lifted above her head so as to give them enough room to pass. She smiled her most charming smile, but Hector was not fooled. He knew her well. Her smile was an alibi, a way of distracting her victims while she took everything in. She had registered the alcohol on his breath, the tension between him and his companion, the vague resemblance, the clerical collar, the accent, the condition of Phillip's teeth, the little piece of gauze at the top left corner of his forehead, which Hector had also noticed, though only after an hour or so, and which had led him to believe that his father was wearing a toupé. She noticed everything but the soul. She was merciless. Hector had never felt comfortable in her presence, not since the day she had told the papers he was dead.

He had earned his death sentence, he knew that. He had acted badly. He had barged into the Ashes' house one Sunday evening, when Thomas was out drinking with the maid's husband, and tried to convince Stella to elope with him. It was a few weeks after Beatrice's birth, and he hadn't seen her yet, although he had given much drunken thought to his new status as illegitimate father.

He had been in the living room with Stella and Margaret, both tight-lipped, when the baby started to cry. Stella headed upstairs, and Hector followed her, saying he wanted to see his child. "She is *not* your child," Stella had said to him. "She's Thomas'." She had slammed the door to the baby's room in his face. Repulsed, he had staggered downstairs to the living room, where Margaret stood primly with crossed arms, waiting to deal with him. She had been dealing with drunken family friends all her life. He found himself admiring her.

He had never thought of her as anything other than his daughter's playmate, but here she was a young woman overnight. And what a young woman. An Amazon, in character if not in size. So like her mother, yet without her hardness. This one would never slam doors in his face. Overcome with emotion, he had taken her gently into his arms and offered to elope with her instead of her mother.

He could still remember his shock at the harshness of her voice as she pushed him out the door and slammed it in his face, a chip off the old block, just like her mother. He had just managed to stagger down to the bottom of the steps. It was here Thomas had found him, sobbing, when he returned from his own drinking expedition several hours later.

Not knowing of Hector's treachery, he had invited him inside and they had drunk till dawn. When Margaret came downstairs for breakfast, they had admired her better qualities together, Thomas still unaware of the fact that earlier in the evening Hector had once again stepped over the line.

Hector had left the Ashes feeling vulnerable to the beauty of the world. He had driven down the hill crying tears of painful joy, and when at the bottom of the hill, he had seen the fiery ball that was the sun emerge in all its glory above the Asian hills, he had gasped and taken his hands off the wheel, and driven smack into the Bosphorus. He remembered the water but not his escape. He came to in a hotel just off Taksim. He read about his death in a tabloid which a student brought to class on Tuesday morning.

It was a front-page article with a color photograph of his poor old Peugeot being lifted from the water. The caption read: LOVESICK AMERICAN PROFESSOR DEVOURED BY SHARKS. Underneath was a photograph of Margaret eating an ice cream cone, with the caption: HE LOVED MY MOTHER AND WAS HEARTBROKEN WHEN SHE WOULD NOT ELOPE WITH HIM. The accompanying article contained a dramatic tale about how Margaret had gone down the hill to catch a bus for school on Monday morning and found Hector's car poking out of the water. She claimed to have seen the tail of a shark circling around the wreck. She told the whole story of Hector and Stella's affair, mixing fact with fantastic lies, which was fortunate for Hector in a way, because Thomas had refused to believe a word of it. Thomas had punished

Margaret by grounding her for a week, but he had never succeeded in getting her to apologize. She stuck to her story with vehemence, claiming that she had, in fact, seen a shark circling the wreck. "Which means that what I said could have been true, couldn't it?"

It had occurred to Hector at the time, and many times since, that perhaps he and his friends had been raising their expatriated children the wrong way. That perhaps it might have been better had they pretended to be adults. A little bit of church might have gone a long way. A little unreasonable authoritarianism, a touch of moral inflexibility here and there, might have given them a chance to find out what they really believed in and allowed them to escape from their obsession with surface, their casual, infinitely adaptable attitude toward the truth, which could change, in their opinion, from moment to moment, in order to fit in with their most recent observations. Did they ever think about love, or God, or death? Hector thought not. That was why, when his father turned to look down the stairs and said, "What a charming girl! Does she come with the house?" Hector could not help but disagree.

"She's charming, yes, but she's also a bit of a shark."

"A bit of a shark? Come come now."

"She once told the papers I was dead," Hector explained.

"Told the papers you were dead? Goodness! Have you any idea why?"

"I suppose because I was having an affair with her mother."

"Oh?" said Phillip Best.

"I had asked her to elope with me and then I drove my car into the water."

"Ah."

"I also asked Margaret to elope with me that night. I was drunk."

"Aha." Phillip Best looked with regret into the living room, which was filled wall-to-wall with people. For a moment he was at a loss for words, and then he brightened. "Well, then! I think you've cleared up the mystery quite nicely, don't you?"

"I said too much," said Hector. "I've embarrassed you."

"Nonsense! Enough gloomy talk for a Saturday night. Shall we enter the fray?" Phillip Best gestured toward the living room. "After you."

"I luf you, my darlink," Avram whispered from the darkness of the furnace room. "Come here, my darlink. Geef me a kees."

His eyes glowed in the shadows like little moons. Margaret paid him no more attention than she would a cricket.

She lingered at the foot of the stairs until she heard Hector and the English minister leave the hallway. She did not want to have to speak to Hector again. She had not felt comfortable around him since the day she had told the papers he was dead. Even two years later, she felt pangs of guilt at the sight of him, guilt which Chloe said was typically Catholic, although Margaret thought this could not be. She only went to church when she stayed with her grandmother.

The thing that made her feel the worst in retrospect was the joy, the boundless joy she had felt that morning at the sight of the Peugeot sticking up out of the water, and the moving black object she had been so sure was the tail of a shark. The exhilarating interview with the journalist (whom she knew from some art exhibition or another) who had bought her a large ice cream cone and then tea at the Aşiyan Gazino, when she should have been on a bus for school. The pleasure she had taken in embellishing the facts. It had seemed such an appropriate way for Hector to die that it had not occurred to her that perhaps it had not happened.

Although she now regretted the glee with which she had jumped to conclusions, she still remembered running up the hill to the Girls' College later that morning, her arms spread to either side, free as a bird, though not for long.

The living room, when Margaret ventured up with a replenished tray of olives and nuts, was fuller than ever. A Theodorakis song—"Make Your Bed for Two"—was playing on the record player. No one was dancing yet. It was still early. The guests were locked in conversation. Most of them were just beginning to forget how many drinks they had

had. Their voices grew louder as their conversation grew less reasonable.

Margaret knew all of them and almost all about them, though she was always happy to find out more. As she made her way through the room with the tray of olives and nuts, she listened with interest to the conversations going on around her.

Jozefin Dalman was talking about the last caliph again. Leslie Lacey was sitting next to her, hanging onto every word. Instead of wearing his normal expression—eyes weary and mocking, mouth clamped shut as if to take in as little as possible of an unpleasant smell—he was starry-eyed, like a boy on his first trip to the Empire State Building. Like everyone else, Leslie treated Jozefin like a monument.

Jozefin was in her seventies. The daughter of a pasha, she had scandalized her family by becoming a singer. In her time, people said, she had been the Edith Piaf of Istanbul, which Margaret thought strange, because Jozefin predated Edith Piaf. But, as Jozefin herself would have said, what was time?

She had had scores of lovers, one of whom she had tried to stab in a justified fit of jealousy, and three illegitimate children who had now become respectable and deplored her bohemian life. She lived in a run-down apartment, once grand, that was cluttered with family heirlooms and cats. When she drank, she was in the habit of listening to her old recordings.

Once, years before, she had heard Margaret sing, and had, with great excitement, proclaimed her a diva in the making. She had spent the rest of the evening discussing what was to be done about it. There were lessons to think of (kindness of Jozefin, gratis), there were the great conservatories of Europe to review, there were words of advice from a retired professional to a future one. There were vague, though emphatic, invitations to her apartment for tea. "Any time," she had said. "Any day you happen to be in my neighborhood."

When Margaret's father, who was in awe of Jozefin, finally summoned the courage to take Margaret downtown and drop by, several months had passed, and Jozefin had forgotten ever meeting Margaret, although she was as warm as ever and served Thomas and Margaret a splendid tea. Thomas had awkwardly tried to bring the subject around to the promised voice lessons. "Oh! Do you sing?" Jozefin had said to Margaret. "How charming."

On that occasion, she had told them the same story about the last Caliph. "A scaredy cat," she had called him. "Good riddance to bad rubbish," she had said, and now she was repeating the same words to Leslie. "Good riddance to bad rubbish, that's what I say, or have I mixed my metaphors?"

"Oh, no," said Leslie. "It was well put," he assured her with a boyish smile, even though Margaret knew that he took ten points off any paper in which one of his unfortunate students used a cliché.

Scanning the bookshelves behind them was Ömer, a former movie director who now made his living translating into Turkish foreign novels that he stole from the collections of his friends. He was a dour man, whom everyone loved for the originality of his methods. He found the Ashes' books particularly interesting. Sometimes Thomas would even advise him on what to steal. Tonight he had recommended *The Ginger Man*, but Ömer was seriously considering the autobiography of Sean O'Casey. The friends Ömer had come with were teasing him. They were, respectively, a modest, gifted actor, said by many to be the most accomplished in Turkey, and a man who, entirely ignored by critics, called himself Turkey's foremost poet.

"Ömer, my child," said the poet, "in order to make your living you are sacrificing political objectives. You must leave behind the works of the petty bourgeoisie and turn your skills to widening the readership of Soviet realism."

The poet was a Maoist, while Ömer was said to have remained faithful to the Kremlin. "*Ha siktir,*" Ömer said testily. "Leave me alone."

"But I am only trying to help you. This book in your hand will only promote unsuitable thoughts."

"On the contrary, " said Ömer. "Excuse me if I am exposing your ignorance concerning the oppression of the Irish peoples, but all Irish authors are enemies of imperialism."

"Nonsense! And now you are going to tell me that William Butler Yeats was a revolutionary."

At the word "revolutionary," both Miss Flannery Carr (a

six-foot-six-inch Canadian journalist who had once written a very bad three-act play about the Shah's love life) and her Russian lover (a TASS correspondent) looked around sharply, to see who the speaker was. When they saw it was Ömer, they lost interest. They were standing in a group with Hector and his minister friend. The fifth member of the group was a young and attractive Girls' College teacher who was active in amateur theatricals and was said to be athletic in bed.

The TASS reporter was inviting the others to join him at the Russian Consulate the following Saturday for vodka and caviar. He was always trying to get people down to the consulate. He had been trying to infiltrate the college for years. Almost every house on the Hill contained an unabridged edition of *And Quiet Flows the Don,* donated by the TASS correspondent in his effort to ingratiate himself. (The Ashes' copy had long since been stolen by Ömer.) The only person he had had any success with was Calvin Root, who had accepted first the novel, then the vodka and caviar. He had drunk the TASS correspondent under the table and been carried out of the consulate singing the Internationale.

Calvin Root was the son of a Colorado Wobbly. He had once taught at the Academy and now worked on and off for the Peace Corps. An engineer, he specialized in building roads to isolated villages and so was a hero in many forgotten corners of Anatolia. His wife, a missionary manquée, played the organ at the American Protestant church downtown. She had been at the party earlier but had left (saying silent prayers) after Calvin had passed out under the dining room table and she had been unable to revive him.

He had revived only moments after her departure, and now he was on the balcony embracing his lover, the elegant, wall-eyed, bejeweled American widow of a Turkish chromium magnate.

They were sharing the balcony with two stringers, one young, one old, the first with AP, the second with Reuters, who were trying to convince each other that they were spies. A Russian naval vessel had just sailed by and they were competing to see which of them knew more about it. One knew the name, the other knew its tonnage. "En route to Odessa," said the first. His companion lit a cigarette.

"And then back through here on the twenty-ninth," he said as he waved his burning match. "Destination Mogadishu."

"Certainly not Mogadishu!" cried the first. "I'd heard it was on its way up to the Baltic."

"Ah, yes," said the second, looking very pleased with himself. "But plans do change. I have it on the highest authority."

" 'I have it on the highest authority,' " mimicked Noel, a young, bright, birdlike Englishman who was standing just inside the balcony door. He was in Istanbul for a year to work in the archives. His wife, Tash, whom he had met at Oxford, was teaching German at the Girls' College. Tash came from a better family than Noel did and was annoyed by his nervous joking. "Do try and restrain yourself," she said sharply. "I think he heard you."

"Oh, did he? Did he? So sorry, dearest. Sorry for living."

"You're drunk again," she hissed.

"Drunk? Again? Hardly, Tash, my beauty. I've only just begun. You wouldn't say I was drunk, would you, Roy, my boy?" Noel said, turning to the man standing next to him. Roy was a Byzantine scholar who came to Istanbul every summer. He was engaged in conversation with a fellow historian, also American, and his very Leftist, very independent, very ugly and yet at the same time very sexy Turkish wife, who was raking him over the coals about the iniquitous role of the Sixth Fleet. "How would you feel if *our* navy were constantly sailing into *your* seaports?" she asked. The Byzantine scholar ignored her question, just as he had ignored Noel's. He was staring over the heads of the other guests, looking at his wife.

His wife, a Dane, was now discussing the peace movement with Ömer and his actor friend. She had learned Turkish the previous summer; no one knew quite how. As she dazzled Ömer and his friend with her impressive grasp of it, they trained their eyes on her breasts, her hips, her flat stomach, her low neckline, her reddish curls, and, from time to time, with trembling lips and smoldering looks, her eyes. Whenever their eyes met, she interrupted her monologue to suck in deeply on an ivory cigarette holder. She would allow her own eyes to travel down their bodies with

Nordic cool. Then, as abruptly as she had stopped speaking, she would begin again.

They paid no attention to the once nearly famous American novelist at their feet. He was now washed up and passed out. Meredith's friend, Ginger, was trying to revive him. The bottle of Drambuie he had brought to the party with him had now passed into the hands of two middle-aged bachelors who taught at the Academy. One was a poet who had recently flushed his life's work down the toilet. The other was a former child actor who had torched a novel it had taken him nine years to complete. He was planning to spend the summer writing children's books. The two men were discussing the sorry career of the washed-up, passed-out American novelist with such equanimity that you would never have known they had ever suffered artistic defeat themselves. "It's drink that did him in," said the poet, sipping his waterglass of Drambuie. "Oh, yes, it certainly is," said the former child actor. "Even three novels ago I detected cirrhosis of the mind."

"Do you really think it was that?" said Cyril, a hearty middle-aged Englishman who had been listening to their conversation. Cyril did calisthenics every morning at six, and it showed. "I would rather tend to think not. I would say that he simply ran out of steam. It does happen, you know. God knows I've had my troubles." He fingered his foulard with the satisfaction of someone who believes he has fought off disease with pure willpower. He had the puffed-up chest of a weight-lifter, which his foulard accentuated. He worked for a small British firm downtown, but his true love was painting. His paintings were dreadful. He had a weakness for shocking pink. He gave away his paintings, and one of them hung faithfully on the library wall, next to another painting that would come down the next day, after all the guests were gone, to be replaced by works of better local artists who were not at the party.

The other painting that was up only for the night was the work of Sadik, a gentle, bug-eyed man who had infinite patience with children, but who got on a plane for Europe, it was said, every time his wife went into labor. His wife was not at the party. He never took her out. Tonight he was being wooed by Mary Ellen, the new wife of the headmaster of the Academy. She was a Radcliffe graduate. She had an infant upstairs whom she had been breastfeeding every half hour since her arrival and she looked desperate. There were two unbuttoned buttons on her blouse. Sadik kept looking at them.

"Goodness gracious, I must help that woman with her blouse!" Meredith cried. "You will excuse me, won't you? I'll be right back." She was trying to get rid of an Irish-American consular official. His name was Rory. He had been asking prying questions about her son Eric's drug habit. He was drunker than usual tonight because his wife was back in Philadelphia attending a funeral.

"Rory! Rory! Maybe you can convince her!" Margaret's father cried. His eyes were glassy, his face flushed. "I'm trying to get Stella to sing."

"Sing, Stella, sing! You heard what your husband said, you . . . saucy Irish—"

Stella tossed back her hair and stamped her foot. "Buzz off, both of you!" Margaret could tell from her deepened voice that she was already drunk.

"But darling," Thomas protested.

"Don't you darling me, you bastard."

"Okay! Okay!" Thomas made a backward pirouette and fell into the clutches of another man Margaret was careful to steer clear of: a teacher who had been fired the year before after announcing that he had become a witch. Rory, meanwhile, turned to two former students of Thomas' who had emigrated to the U.S. and were back in town for the weekend. One, a physicist, had married into Denver society. The other owned a small midwestern airline. Quickly tiring of their company, Rory moved over toward the dining room, where Blake, the Peace Corps worker who was engaged to the *muhtar's* daughter, was busy baiting Willy Wakefield.

Willy Wakefield was a colleague of Rory's at the consulate. His title was political attaché, but Chloe and Margaret had been friends with his daughter briefly, before she went away to prep school, and once when they went to Willy Wakefield's office with her, they had seen that the walls were covered with sophisticated radio equipment. That was how it had become common knowledge that Willy was a spy.

"Come on, admit it," Blake was saying to him now. "Admit you're a spy. What's wrong with checking up on the Russians? I'm on your side. We're all on the same side. Who has a kind word for the Russians these days?"

"You do," growled Rory.

"*I* do?" said Blake with mock surprise.

"Yes, *you* do," said Rory. "You're a fucking Communist."

Chloe, who was standing next to Blake, suppressed a giggle. She squeezed his hand, then traced a circle on the palm. She did not realize that her mother, who was standing next to Margaret popping olives into her mouth with the precision of a machine on an assembly line, was watching.

Amy looked miserable. She was also watching her son, Neil, who was watching Winifred Lacey and Winifred Lacey's boyfriend, a young American teacher who had a yellow Fiat sports car and was said to take opium. She sighed, as if to say, Is this what I get after all the work I've done? Seeing Margaret's eyes upon her, she collected herself as much as she could. "Oops!" she said, still flustered. "I think I ate all the olives."

"Don't worry. I'll get some more."

Downstairs, Avram was waiting for her, his moony eyes shining from the shadows of the coal cellar. "Geef me a kees. Geef me a kees, my darlink" She ignored him, but Michael and Selena, who were having one of their conspiratorial tête-à-têtes near the door, did not.

Michael and Selena wanted everyone to believe that they thought sex was the biggest joke ever invented. They had an inflated banana hanging over their one-year-old daughter's crib, and played Ravel's Bolero whenever people came to dinner. When they had younger people as guests—or older people who were known to "hang loose"—they tried to get everyone to take their clothes off. Men who refused were assumed to have shamefully small penises.

For a few years now, they had been watching Margaret with interest.

"So what do you think?" Selena asked Michael as they followed her up the stairs at what they thought was a safe distance. "Has she or hasn't she?"

"I'm not sure," said Michael. "I'll have to have another look."

"I think she has," said Selena. "Something has changed."

"What?" asked Michael.

"Her eyes," said Selena.

The little landing outside the living room was crowded with people in search of privacy. Sitting on the stairs was a woman who had come to the party with a bottle of champagne to celebrate her divorce. She was now sobbing pathetically. She always cried when she drank. Just below her, leaning against the flimsy telephone table, was Theo. He had his arm around a Frenchwoman who was threatening to kill herself if he didn't make love to her. Theo looked solemn, appearing to think it over, although Margaret knew that sooner or later he would skip out with Bob and Louie, a freelance photographer-journalist team who were watching the romantic scene with barely suppressed laughter from the safety of the living room.

Margaret was offering olives to Bob and Louie when Michael and Selena came up to her and looked her straight in the eyes.

"Oh, yes," she heard Michael say to Selena. "Her eyes."

"They're different, aren't they?" Selena said.

"They are."

"So what do you think? Has she or hasn't she?"

"She has," said Michael. "I think she finally has."

"She has," Selena repeated. Glancing at Margaret once again, she took her husband's hand. "She has! Oh, Michael, I think you're right! She has!"

"Now, the only thing you don't want to do when you're one-hundred-odd feet underwater is panic,"said Charlie Jordan. He was standing in the library next to the record player, having just turned down the volume. He taught engineering. His wife had recently left him for another woman. The man he was talking to taught chemistry. The year before, he had suffered a similar fate when his wife ran off with the Turkish lab technician.

Ralph and Aspasia were sitting on the windowseat. Ralph was pumping Aspasia for stories about Hector's childhood which he could use one day to embarrass Hector. Margaret had seen him do this before, with other mothers. With hands clasped, he was listening to Aspasia talk about Hector's first swear words, when suddenly the English minister entered the room. Both Ralph and Aspasia stopped short.

Aspasia remained composed, but her mouth twitched and her hands tensed. That was how Margaret knew that she had met the minister before. Ralph was less restrained.

"No!" he bellowed. "Phillip, you old bugger you! That has *got* to be a costume you are wearing! You can*not* hope to convince me that that white . . . *thing* around your neck is the genuine article! What *has* come over you, my dear? What *is* this nonsense? I will just not stand for it. It is sacrilege."

The English minister smiled, unruffled, as if he were accustomed to such outbursts. He weathered the rest of Ralph's attack gracefully, and when Thomas came in to turn up the music, he did not betray any relief.

The dancing began soon afterward, so few people saw the minister leading Aspasia out of the library. They sat down on the living room sofa and proceeded to have an earnest talk, which Margaret could not hear because of the music.

When they stood up to leave the party, it was Hector who was dancing in the library. He was surrounded by politely smiling spectators. When he saw the minister drape Aspasia's shawl over her shoulders and guide her to the door, he froze in the midst of his badly executed Irish jig and, putting his hand to his heart, let out a strange croak. Then his knees buckled. Everyone rushed to his aid, thinking he had had a heart attack. By the time it was clear that nothing was the matter, that it had just been another of Hector's jokes, Aspasia and the minister were gone.

Then the dancing resumed. Hector was joined by a handful of dancers who knew even less about Irish jigs than he did. Drink had given them false confidence. As they bounced around the library, the library floor bounced with them. Books came sailing out of bookcases, lamps swayed, tables trembled, the record player skipped. It looked to Margaret as if the floor were going to fall through again. The last time it had fallen through, a throw rug and a large chunk of plaster had fallen into the kitchen below, and had landed on the maid's husband's chest. He had been lying on the floor at the time, snoring happily. He had been in charge of making the punch that evening and had passed out.

The gaping hole had been the source of much drunken laughter. No one seemed to know or care how close they had come to a terrible tragedy. Only Margaret had been upset. She did not like standing in the library and seeing the black and white tiles of the kitchen floor, nor did she like standing in the kitchen and looking at their bookcases. She did not like thinking about the accidents that had almost happened. Not then, and not now. She went out onto the balcony so that she didn't have to look at the swaying floor anymore. The music was too loud for her to hear any of the familiar night sounds, but she had a good memory. She could imagine them.

Watching the searchlights of the ferry boats as they circled around and around, sometimes shining straight into her eyes, she imagined the sound of foghorns. Watching the dimly lit portholes of a tanker rounding the point, she imagined the vibrating window panes. Watching a pair of headlights crawling down the Aşiyan Road, she imagined the rattling of a 1956 Chevrolet as it rolled over rough cobblestones, and the howling of dogs whose territory had been violated. Spotting the amber lights of cigarettes here and there among the bushes, she could imagine couples giggling. Only one voice rose loud and clear above the music and the laughter, and that was Avram's.

He was sitting on the park bench in front of the pond, looking as moony-eyed as ever. Gazing up at the balcony, he repeated the usual lines.

"Come here, my darlink. Geef me a kees."

She wondered if he thought he looked romantic. She wondered if he knew how short he was, or if he realized that the plaid fisherman's cap he had been wearing so proudly for the past few weeks made the top of his head look flat. She wondered what she looked like to him, if he saw her faults or was blind to them, if his hackneyed desires made it possible for him to see the soul within, or perhaps imagine a soul where none existed. Margaret could not be sure, because there were things other people could see that she could not.

When they had first moved into this house, when Margaret

was eight, she had been fascinated by the story of the angel—the angel who had visited the poetess' son in his sleep and warned him about the curse, and told him to leave the house at once. She had wondered if the angel still existed. She had asked her father about it, being not yet old enough to understand how irate he became at the mention of the supernatural. "How big is the angel?" she had asked. "Is it male or female?" "Does it have wings and what language does it speak?" Her father had answered that it was neither male nor female, and it spoke no languages, and it did not have wings. "It does not exist," he had concluded. "Then how did the poetess' son see the angel?" Margaret had asked.

"Hardening of the arteries," he had explained. "When you are old and overweight and have a diseased heart, you begin to see things that no one else does."

"But not till then?" she had asked.

"Not till then," he had said, with a smile, as if it were a joke. He did not realize how many nights she would spend with her elbows propped on her windowsill, staring into the darkness, waiting for a sign—a voice speaking any language, an ethereal glow in the trees, a flapping of wings—and feeling desperately sorry for herself because her arteries were not hard enough for her to see angels.

She had been a literal-minded child, exaggerating the importance of trees because she knew so well she could not see the forest. She remembered little things. She remembered the day her father had come home, depressed, from a faculty meeting, and said that the Hill and everyone who lived on it were going to the dogs. She had taken him seriously, and prepared herself for a nomadic life on lonely, windswept, rabies-infested hills. How they had laughed when they discovered the misunderstanding. They were always laughing.

She remembered how they would joke with their friends about how uncomfortable they had felt when they first moved into their Ottoman villa. It had seemed too beautiful, they would say. They had half expected someone to step forward with a clapboard and say, "Cut!" and tell them they were trespassing. But Margaret had felt comfortable in the house immediately, her mother would say to her friends.

She would laugh and say that it was one of the first ways it became clear to her that her daughter belonged to another generation. She would laugh, but at other times she did not think it was funny.

One day, when Margaret was sulking after an argument (there had not been enough eggs in the house for meringues), her mother had turned against her. She had said it was criminal how Margaret took her good fortune for granted, how she had the gall, the brazen confidence, to call this paradise on earth home.

It was one of the many arguments Stella had forgotten and Margaret hadn't. She went on to tell Margaret how most children would give their eyeteeth to grow up in an Ottoman villa. "Look at that enchanted scene outside your window," she cried, gesturing at it with a clenched fist. "Any other child standing in your shoes would thank me for it!" Although Margaret had a gift for foreign languages, her own tongue remained a source of horror for her, and the image of a crowd of angry, gap-toothed children pouring into her room to take possession of her shoes was one that haunted her throughout her childhood.

It was this fear that one false move might cost her everything, this uncomfortable sensation of feeling comfortable in shoes that were not rightfully hers, that enabled her to see one thing that no one else could see, and that was the day when their tenure in paradise would come to an end. She could see her house empty, and her bags packed, and Beatrice sitting on the floor in her snowsuit, while her parents looked anxiously out the window as they waited for the taxi. She could see her whole world crumbling in her dreams: the walls of the tower coming apart in a cloud of dust, and the hills of Asia dissolving into dunes of shifting sand that rolled over the Bosphorus one by one like waves breaking against the shore, and the dogs howling all around them, as the angry, gap-toothed children gathered at the gate to tell them that their time was up.

IV

A Hair of the Dog

Sunday, June 15, 1969

THE party ended as all parties at the Ashes' ended, with Hector leading the last stragglers down the hill at dawn for a swim in the Bosphorus. Usually Amy went down with them, although she did not actually go in. She disliked swimming nude in icy water. Instead, she would stand on the shore guarding clothes, towels, and valuables. While the others splashed about and tried to swim against the current, she would admire the glorious dawn scenery and try at the same time to ignore the lewd comments of taxi drivers as they slowed down and opened the doors of their 1956 Chevrolets to welcome her.

This morning, however, Amy decided she could better appreciate the dawn from the Ashes' balcony. As long as no one left any valuables on shore, there was no need for her services. She collected their watches and jewelry, which she put into her large handbag. It was large precisely for this reason. She was constantly having to pick up the pieces of other people's lives.

Standing on the balcony, she watched her husband lead his little band of admirers down the road, and then, when they had disappeared, she sat down and lit a cigarette, happy to see the last of Captain Yorgo.

Captain Yorgo was the man Hector became when he drank too much. Although she had once found him charming, over the years Amy had come to dislike Captain Yorgo intensely. She had had it to the limit with his fake Greek mannerisms and his fondness for rolling his cigarettes between his teeth instead of smoking them.

Captain Yorgo was a complete fraud. Although he was always interesting himself in other peoples' problems, Amy found him overbearing and insensitive. He said the same things to everyone. Everyone was the greatest, or the best, or the finest. Listening to him carry on party after party, Amy was always surprised to see how receptive people were to his (in her opinion) overblown reassurances.

Captain Yorgo had come into his own tonight, during a scuffle between the Ashes' maid and her husband. The maid had gone into hysterics after her husband did a suggestive belly dance with Meredith's friend, Ginger. She had been threatening to tear his hair out, or stab him, or both, when Hector had stepped in.

Having quelled the fight, Hector, or rather, Captain Yorgo, had decided it was his turn to do a suggestive belly dance with Ginger. To make the show more interesting, Ginger had begun to remove her outer garments one by one. Hector had followed suit, until he was in his underpants. He had then picked her up and carried her off into the bushes. How Amy detested that woman. And how she hated Hector for humiliating her in front of so many people. All she asked of him was that he make his conquests behind her back.

The thing that made it so unbearable was the weight of everyone's pity—especially Stella's. Stella immediately came over to her and offered her some brandy. She put her hand on Amy's shoulder, as if to say she knew how Amy felt. Now that he had moved on to new challenges, Stella seemed to say, she and Amy were in the same boat.

Sometimes Amy thought all Catholics were alike. They thought all they had to do was wait for the right moment to say they were sorry. One well-timed brandy and the slate was wiped clean. Amy felt like telling Stella, "Like hell

I'm going to forgive you,'' but instead she smiled and told her she was not in a brandy mood.

It was while Hector was outside with Ginger that Amy noticed that her daughter was also missing. So was Blake. So was Winifred and her opium-smoking boyfriend. Her son, Neil, who as everyone knew, had a crush on Winifred, was looking miserable in his chair in the corner. He was drinking something green. She remembered wondering if it was green because it contained Turkish *Krem de Mant*. She remembered feeling furious at the very thought of it. Neil was fourteen and he had no business drinking *Krem de Mant*. She had been about to go over and scold him when Hector returned from the bushes and announced the start of the bicycle race.

The bicycle race was another tradition. It went back to the early sixties, and it was always between Hector and Jozefin Dalman. Jozefin always rode the tricycle and Hector the English racer. Jozefin always won, because when Hector tried to overtake her in the English racer, she would lift up her dress and let him see she wasn't wearing any underpants. This would send him crashing into the furniture.

Hector had broken quite a few chairs, lamps, and tables over the years, but nothing anyone would ever miss—Amy made sure of this. Before the race began, she removed all articles of sentimental value from his path. She prided herself on her tact. She would just drop the porcelain figurines, slender crystal vases, and memento ashtrays into her handbag and then put them back when no one was looking.

Tonight, in keeping with his new recklessness, Hector (still in his underpants, which were covered with brambles from his rendezvous with Ginger in the bushes) took the bicycle race just a bit too far. Instead of just going off course, he threw himself into Jozefin's path and knocked the poor woman over. Everyone was aghast. Jozefin looked rattled, and her brother, who had accompanied her to the party and who thought she did far too much for a woman her age, took her home at once.

Hector had knocked his head against a marble tabletop. He had a small gash above his left eyebrow. Amy had to take him to the bathroom to wash it off. After that, she had lost track of Neil. Later, Chloe (stoned and also covered with brambles) told her that Neil had gone home.

The party, which had not been particularly enjoyable for Amy during its opening hours, became impossibly boring after midnight, because all the people she usually talked to had become incoherent.

Amy sometimes felt she was the only person on the Hill who drank in moderation. She always stopped herself when she felt she was becoming tipsy. She did not like to lose control, but even so, it was difficult, in the present company, to keep it. Tonight, from midnight until dawn, she had limited herself to one drink per hour and grown increasingly sour as everyone around her drank to their heart's content.

She had spent much of her time scooping up Hector's cigarette ashes as he strolled from room to room helping everyone out with their problems.

At one point, Hector had appeared in the living room with a box full of Thomas Ashe's love poems. Apparently, he had found them in a desk drawer. Thomas had always been secretive about his writing. He had never shown his work to anyone. The only reason Amy knew about it at all was because she had overheard her daughter and Margaret discussing his poems one day. Apparently, Margaret had also gone through her father's desk drawers. She was upset because some of the poems were obscene. She couldn't imagine her father thinking such thoughts. Actually, now that Hector was reading these poems out loud for one and all to hear, Amy decided that they were not so much obscene as embarrassing. They were full of references to the author's "trembling member" and a "lady love" who fit Meredith's description far better than she did Stella's. Hector, of course, proclaimed them masterpieces. Thomas began to pass them out to everyone in the room, a mad glint in his dark brown eyes.

Amy tried to gather them up again, as tactfully as she could. Hector got angry at her for this, but then he decided it was a good idea. "You give me the whole fucking bundle," he said to Thomas. "You give me the works, and then I'll pick out the best ones and send them to my friend at the *New Yorker.* Did I ever tell you about my friend at the *New Yorker?* We were roommates in college. He's quite a guy. He has more power than the two of us put together. When he sees these poems they're going to knock him flat on his face. Flat on his face. If these poems don't knock him flat on his face, he's not worth the shit that comes out of his asshole."

He gave the box of poems to Amy, who put it under her shawl in the spare bedroom. She considered putting them back where they belonged, but her curiosity, the voyeur side of her character, encouraged by years in a community that fought off boredom by manufacturing intrigues, got the better of her. She could not pass up the delicious pleasure of reading a family friend's abominable love poems. She decided she would simply do as she was told and take them home with her. No one would ever know that she had done so for ulterior motives.

After this, there was a rough stretch when Hector became a broken record on the subject of his friend at the *New Yorker.* "Did I tell you about my friend at the *New Yorker?* He knew Thurber. . . . He used to write 'Talk of the Town.' . . . He refuses to set foot in the Algonquin anymore. . . . He goes to another place on the same block that has better hors d'oeuvres. . . . He and Thurber used to take the train together. Did I tell you he knew him? He used to take Thurber's cartoons down to the *New Yorker* for him on the train. They were six feet high, some of them. . . ."

It was while Hector free-associated on the subject of Thurber that Amy overheard an infuriating conversation between two people she did not know well—a younger woman married to a teacher at the Girls' College, and a man about her age who had been teaching at the Academy for a year, who was invited to most of the big parties even though most people found him quite dull.

The younger woman was asking this man if Hector always acted so offensively. She was upset by what Hector had done to poor old Jozefin, and she was also offended, she said, because at one point, Hector had pinched her. The man said yes, Hector did often act offensively. It was a shame, he said. His students claimed Hector was a great teacher, but he himself could not see any signs that this was so. As far as he could see, Hector was a hopeless alcoholic.

"Why doesn't his wife make him stop?" the younger woman asked, wide-eyed and smug.

"Oh, Amy's one of those types who likes to play the martyr," said the man. "You know what I mean—passive-aggressive. Hector is her weapon. She lets him do the damage while she walks around spreading sweetness and light. But you can tell how much she hates everybody. Don't look now, but if you look at her mouth, you'll see what I mean—those tight little creases at the corners. I like to look at mouths—they can tell you a lot. Actually, her lips are full, but she's so tense and angry most of the time that they look tight and thin."

Amy was as startled by that conversation as if she had suddenly woken up to find herself naked on an operating table, bathed in fluorescent light. Was that how she looked to other people? It was so unfair. She *had* tried to get Hector to give up drinking. What these people didn't understand was that when things didn't work out the way you wanted them to, you had to be a good sport. They dismissed her as a martyr. They were so goddamn smug.

It was at times like this that she wished she had never met Hector, and had married one of the dull men her parents would have liked her to marry. Then there would have been no opportunities for martyrdom.

Amy watched angrily as Hector stood on the balcony lecturing to a group of admirers. All women. Young women. She watched them stare with awe as Hector directed their attention to the most interesting colors in the sea and the sky, using grand gestures that sent sparks from his cigarette flying in all directions.

They all thought he was so wonderful. Well, she invited any of them to take her place and see how they liked it. She welcomed any suggestions as to how she could better handle the daily frustrations of life with Hector and his goddamn mother. She invited any of those young women to see how they liked opening their homes to the likes of Aspasia. What they didn't see was that Amy had no choice but to be passive-aggressive. What they didn't see was how hard it was to be passive-aggressive when you really would prefer to be something else.

When had she stopped having fun?

* * *

Alone on the balcony after the others had gone off for their dawn swim, Amy finished her second cigarette and lingered for a few moments more to admire the morning: the yellow light on the castle walls and the leaves of the two palm trees that framed the view, the sharp gray row of turbaned tombstones in the cemetery, the brilliant blue water of the Bosphorus, and beyond it the mottled hills of Asia and the sun itself.

She had grown spoiled during her years here—now the only time she could enjoy a view was when she was alone. It was only then that she could recall how things had looked to her the first time. The hills and the water had looked so fresh and full of possibilities. Later on, the view had acquired landmarks: the restaurant where they had had that famous meal, the playground where they had had that disastrous picnic, the ferry station where they saw that man get crushed to death between the ferry and the landing stage.

She set off for home. She forced herself to enjoy the scenery, the silence, the empty paths and tennis courts, the judas blossoms, the cobblestone streets of Rumeli Hisar with their lovely rickety houses. She had to stop several times to catch her breath. (Perhaps she was anemic, she thought; perhaps she ought to take iron pills. Or had she—despite all her efforts—had too much to drink?) She sidestepped the occasional pile of donkey manure, smiling affectionately at the dogs and puppies that were yapping (playfully, she hoped) at her heels.

Normally, she would not have taken the footpath that went between the Duxburys' and the Laceys'. It was more direct to take the cobblestone road up from the *meydan*. But it was just next to the footpath that she saw a rabid dog lurching blindly toward her.

It was small and black and frothing at the mouth and trying to shake itself free of its body. Amy paused for a moment before escaping up the footpath, suspending fear as she thought for the first time how miserable it must be to be a rabid dog. She had never thought before about what it was to be on the other side of the gurgling and frothing mouth, to be thirsty and afraid of water at the same time, to want to bite everything in sight, to lose all peripheral vision. Forgetting her own safety, she suddenly saw how selfish it was of her to dismiss rabid dogs as a public nuisance.

She had allowed the dog to get much too close. It was only when he'd lunged toward her leg that she had jumped out of the way. She'd had to run for her life. The footpath was paved with large, uneven stones—not the best surface for high heels. Just as she reached the corner of the Duxburys' garden, one of her heels snapped off.

The Duxburys were seated at their new picnic table, eating breakfast.

Donald and Susan Duxbury were missionaries. They had been living in Istanbul since before the war. They were known to their bohemian neighbors as the Donald Ducks.

"You're up early!" Donald Duxbury said to Amy as she limped past them. His wife Susan pursed her lips. Amy was wearing cultured pearls and a backless cocktail dress, so it was clear, to Susan at least, that Amy had not been to bed yet.

"Care for some coffee?" Susan Duxbury asked, trying hard to sound Christian. Amy accepted the invitation. She did not like to be rude to the Duxburys, if only because everyone else was. She hobbled up to their garden, trying to conceal her broken heel in her hand, and sat down at the far end of the picnic table, because she realized that she might reek of alcohol or cigarettes. These were two of the many vices the Duxburys did not indulge in.

Since rabid dogs were one of the few things besides the weather that Amy and the Duxburys shared an interest in, Amy mentioned that she had almost been bitten by one a moment earlier.

"Yes, it's the season for rabid dogs," said Susan.

"I really think we should get an immunization program going," said Donald. Donald had a crusty breadbasket-of-America voice. It was so loud you might have thought he was deaf. Amy liked Donald. His twinkling—almost unseeing—blue eyes, his boxlike smile—the same boxlike smile for every occasion—and his thin, almost emaciated frame reminded Amy of her own father, who was dead now.

She had more difficulty with Donald's wife, Susan, perpetually stern and well rested, careful never to ask her

Moslem maid to cook pork, and forever making pies out of disgusting things like carrot peelings. Once, in August, Chloe had gone over to play with the Duxburys' niece and been conned into licking envelopes for their Christmas letter. The Duxburys always sent out their Christmas letter in August—seamail, to cut down on the expense. She had brought home a copy: "Kenny has taken a breather from his studies at Johns Hopkins to travel to Nepal, where he hopes to gain a deeper understanding of Eastern ways of understanding God. Mom and Dad had their qualms about it, but after a fruitful discussion with him at Granny Jen's last June . . ." and so on and so on. "On the lighter side, Steve and wife Betsy, now happily stationed in Georgia, report that five-year-old Rebecca is turning into a regular little Picasso. . . ."

Susan Duxbury poured Amy a second cup of her dreadful coffee, which she mixed with barley or something to make it last longer.

"Thank you," said Amy. As she lifted her cup, it clattered noisily against the saucer. This surprised her. She was so sure she had not had too much to drink.

"Your hands are trembling," said Susan suspiciously. "Are you cold? Should I bring you out a sweater? That dress doesn't look too warm."

"No, thank you," said Amy. "I'm fine."

"Isn't it a beautiful morning?" Donald said, failing as usual to perceive the tension between the two women.

"Yes, isn't it?" Amy said.

"Is Hector up and about?" Donald asked. "I wanted to discuss the chorus with him. We're planning to perform some Bach cantatas in July and we sure could use a baritone."

"With any luck, Hector's asleep in bed by now," Amy said. "How about popping over this afternoon? I'm sure he'll have recovered by then."

"Recovered?" Donald asked, looking surprised.

Amy toyed with the idea of making up an illness, but her better half won. She decided to tell Donald the truth. "Oh, no, it's not what you think," she said firmly, as if she had nothing to be embarrassed about. "We were at a party last night."

"So I see," said Susan.

"Well, if you get home and find he's woken up..." Donald said.

Amy shook her head, proud to have held her ground in the face of Susan's disapproval. "Don't count on it. He had a busy day yesterday, and I'm sure he's exhausted."

Just then, there was the sound of raucous laughter coming up the footpath. Hector, Leslie Lacey, and Ginger went racing by, stark naked. Hector was waving his undershirt like a flag. As they passed under the Duxburys' garden, Ginger stepped on something sharp—a piece of glass, perhaps, or a pointed stone. She squealed and bent over to examine her foot, giving Amy and the Duxburys a full view of her anus.

The Duxburys gasped. Susan grabbed hold of her husband's arm. Amy wrapped her hand around her coffee cup and gritted her teeth.

Then she saw Meredith Lacey crawling up the cobblestone path on all fours, dressed in a man's shirt, her eyes darting from side to side like a wild animal's, her hair wet and tangled. Amy's cup began to clatter violently against the saucer.

They watched Meredith crawl up her front steps like a spider. She grabbed hold of the doorknob and pulled herself to her feet. She rang the doorbell, but no one answered, so she hurled herself against the door, moaning, "Let me in, you cocksuckers! Let me in or I'll fuck your balls off!"

Amy couldn't stand it anymore. She jumped to her feet so abruptly that she knocked over the bench. "Oh, dear me, look what I've done," she exclaimed in her cheerful "good morning, children!" voice. "I'll just run inside and get a towel to clean up all this coffee."

She bounded across the lawn, forgetting that one of her shoes had no heel. Before she knew it, she had twisted her ankle and fallen flat on her face. The contents of her handbag went flying all over the grass: the broken heel; Thomas' poems, with all their references to trembling members; Meredith's necklace, which she had found next to the soap dish in the Ashes' bathroom; someone's glasses, which she had found on the windowsill; a porcelain statuette and a slender crystal vase that she had forgotten to put back after the bicycle race; and five wristwatches.

While Susan Duxbury cleaned up the coffee with pursed lips and chased after Thomas' poems, which were flying everywhere, and retrieved the necklace and wristwatches she so very clearly suspected Amy of stealing, Donald Duxbury lifted Amy to her feet. He patted her on the back and gazed into her eyes like a sad St. Bernard. "Tell me honestly," he said. "Would you like me to go back there with you?" His expession reminded Amy of her father's expression the day he found out she liked boys.

"Oh, no, no, thank you," Amy said. "If it's Hector you're worried about, don't be. I can manage him."

"Are you sure, now? I would consider it my duty to protect you."

"Oh, don't worry," Amy said. "He'll be no problem."

"How about you?" Donald asked. "Can you make it back without falling?"

"Of course I can!" Amy cried indignantly. "It's nothing, nothing at all. I'm sure what happened was that someone stole their clothes." This distressed Donald even further.

Amy hobbled home in Susan's red galoshes (they had insisted on her wearing them). She found Hector snoring and sprawled diagonally on their bed. It took her a few minutes to shift him over to his side.

She already had a headache, so she threw an old robe over her cocktail dress and went downstairs to take some vitamin C, some vitamin B_{12}, and two aspirins to head off any undeserved hangover.

The kitchen was a wreck. One of the children had made him or herself scrambled eggs, and had left the pan on the stove, the dishes on the table, and three eggshells on the floor. The dining room was a wreck, too. One of the children had been drinking out of the crystal glasses she had carted all the way back from Ireland, and one glass was lying on the table, broken. When Amy saw that glass she swore out loud. Didn't those children have any respect for things of value? Would they go through life never cleaning up after themselves, expecting to be waited on hand and foot by an army of maids? She took the broken glass, went outside, and threw it into the garbage can. Then she went upstairs.

As she was climbing the stairs, she caught a glimpse of herself in the mirror. She paused to examine her lips, to see if that awful smug man was right about the little creases at the corners of her mouth. Then she smiled, to see if her smile was tight and angry. It was. The bastard was right. She was going to have to practice and come up with a new smile. But how could she help having a tight and angry smile? It was remarkable that she could smile at all these days. She smiled at the mirror again, just to prove to herself that she could. When had she stopped having fun? Clinging to the banister, staring through the posts, she closed her eyes and opened them again to see if she could still look provocative. Before she knew it, she had fallen asleep.

She came to about noon, feeling dizzy and not really remembering why she had chosen to sleep on the stairs. The house was silent. She wondered what had awoken her. It was a few moments before she heard someone clearing his throat at the door.

It was Ralph, his face pressed against the glass.

You could tell that he had not been drinking the night before. He looked well rested, freshly showered, and self-satisfied.

"And a very good morning to you!" he exclaimed when she opened the door. "My goodness, Amy. What dreadful galoshes. They look like the things Mrs. Donald Duck wears when she's gardening."

"They are," Amy said.

"How awful for you," he said. "You must take them back to her at once. They don't suit you. The color brings out your varicose veins."

"I will," said Amy. "Don't worry."

"I was rather hoping you'd invite me in for a cup of coffee," Ralph said. "Or have I come too early? Perhaps you are hung over and need a bit more sleep."

"I am not hung over," Amy snapped. "Come in." She led him into the kitchen, which was still a wreck. While she got the coffee ready, Ralph tidied up. He was good that way. She regretted snapping at him, especially since he was right:

she did have a hangover. While Ralph was sponging off the tabletop, she surreptitiously took another two aspirins. Then, when the coffee was ready, she sat down across from him at the table, determined to make a fresh start, determined to forget yesterday and enjoy today, determined, for once, to have a friendly conversation with Ralph instead of a sparring match.

Ralph had opened the windows. Tempering the warm June sun was a light breeze from the Black Sea that swayed the branches of the trees in the garden and lifted Amy's spirits. Nothing could be so bad on a day like this. Looking at Ralph, she smiled her new, warm, happy, life-celebrating smile.

"Good God!" Ralph exclaimed. "What's happened to your mouth?"

"Nothing's happened to my mouth. I was just smiling."

"I thought for a moment that you had lost muscular control of your face. Goodness! What a turn you gave me. It's one of the first signs of multiple sclerosis, you know. I suppose I've told you about my aunt."

"Yes," said Amy wearily. She was determined not to be provoked today, no matter what. "You have told me about her."

"And your hands are shaky. That's another sign, you know. Although in this case I'm sure we can blame it on that lethal brandy you were drinking."

"You've got me mixed up with Stella," Amy said patiently. "Stella was the one who was drinking the brandy."

"Oh, I know, I know," Ralph said. He shook his head. "That woman is headed for disaster, you know. She should see a doctor."

"Nonsense," Amy said. "She just had a bit too much to drink."

"I'm surprised to hear *you* jumping to that woman's defense. You must have an extraordinarily forgiving nature."

"My nature has nothing to do with it," Amy said.

"Well, she shouldn't be drinking at all, that Stella, if you want my opinion," Ralph continued. "She's an alcoholic. Do you think it was Hector who pushed her over the edge? It's an interesting thought. Hector does have a way of pushing his friends and lovers over the edge, doesn't he?

But I suppose it would be unfair to blame the whole thing on him. She obviously had an inclination in that direction. She has a passion for chocolate. There's a link, you know. Something to do with the level of blood sugar. But that's just hypothetical."

"It certainly is," Amy said. Amy loved chocolate herself.

He picked up the piece of toast Amy had made for him and bit into it with obvious enjoyment. He loved toast, and he loved doing post-mortems on parties. Sometimes Amy thought that was the only reason he went to them. "Do you notice how Stella's beginning to walk now?" Ralph continued. "Little mincing steps. Mince, mince, mince, as if she had Chinese lotus feet. She used to be so beautiful when she first came out here. It's a terrible shame what this place has done to her. What's more, she has suicidal tendencies."

"So do lots of people," Amy said.

"You *are* feeling magnanimous this morning, aren't you? What happened last night? Did you fall in love? Who would have thought that you'd be defending Stella from vicious gossips like myself? I suppose you even have a kind word for your mother-in-law this morning."

"I'm not feeling quite *that* kind," said Amy.

"Not *that* kind, you say. It must be a drain having her breathing down your neck all the time. I'm sure that's why Hector's been drinking too much. You know what I was thinking the other day? It was a terrible thought, really. I was thinking that mothers should be abolished."

Amy said nothing. Ralph looked at her like a fox. "So. You're not going to jump to her defense," he said. "That's interesting. I don't think mothers should be abolished, of course. I was just testing. So! You really do detest her. You'd like to see her go. Well! Perhaps there's hope. Perhaps that wolf in sheep's clothing, Phillip Best, will knock her into shape."

"No one can knock that woman into shape."

"Aha! Oho! You don't know our Phillip. You saw him, I presume. The rascal! How dare he appear in public wearing that collar! He must be after her money. Did they spend the night together?"

"How should I know?"

"I didn't hear them come home. Did you?"

"I wasn't here," said Amy.

"I'll bet he took her back to his place," Ralph said. "What a cad. Hector must be a nervous wreck."

"I'm sure he hasn't given the slightest thought to the problem, if indeed it is a problem. He's still sound asleep."

"I'll bet he is, after all the drink *he* went through last night. What has come over this man? Can we possibly blame it all on his mother? His drinking is completely out of control these days. That episode with Jozefin was preposterous. He was drunk when he arrived, you know. Have you any idea where he was all day?"

Amy stiffened. "I don't know and I don't care. I am not in the mood to gossip about my husband."

"But, Amy, my dear woman, you must understand that I only wish to help."

"We're doing very nicely without your help, thank you very much."

"I hate to be argumentative on such a beautiful morning, but I must point out that you are not doing so nicely, not nicely at all. Your family is falling apart! Look at Chloe, goddamn it. What is she doing gallivanting with that mushroom-faced Peace Corps worker, who is, in any event, supposed to be engaged to that peasant girl?"

"She's not gallivanting with him. They're merely friends."

"That shows how much you know. She brought him home with her."

"I refuse to believe that."

"You would, wouldn't you? You're completely blind sometimes. Those rifles, for example. It has never even occurred to you that perhaps you should not have them hanging on the wall all the time. It's really not very wise, not with all the drink you people go through."

"Since when have you been my family's moral guardian?" Amy cried. "For God's sake! The only reason *you* aren't drinking is because you had hepatitis!"

"True, true. But you know, I'm beginning to think it was a blessing in disguise. I enjoy sobriety. I may never drink again. I like waking up in the morning with a clear head. But goodness! Sobriety does cast the rest of you in a dreadful light."

"Is that what you came here for this morning?" Amy shrieked. "To lecture me on my drinking?"

Ralph sat back, quietly triumphant. "I knew you'd lose your temper sooner or later," he said. "Don't think a little cup of coffee and a piece of toast can fool me. And no, to set the record straight, I did not come here to lecture you. I came here this morning to talk about your son. Did you know he was serenading me last night? Don't you dare make that face at me. He really was."

Five minutes later, they were both standing in Ralph's bedroom, watching Neil snoring quietly in Ralph's double bed. Despite the warmth of the day, he was entirely wrapped up in Ralph's down quilt, and he was wearing a pair of Ralph's black satin pajamas.

"He was so drunk he could hardly walk," Ralph explained. "He was reeling around with an armful of LPs and singing at the top of his lungs. Terrible voice. It kept cracking. The LPs were all falling out of their jackets. I tried to pick up as many as I could, but as I was sure I'd missed a few in the darkness, I went out again this morning. That was when I found this." He handed Amy a rifle. It was one of the three that hung on her living room wall. "So you see, I was not speaking off the cuff, as they say, when I cautioned you about guns."

"I'm sorry," said Amy.

"*De nada*, my dear. I was glad to be of assistance, although you probably think I spent all night trying to seduce him."

"Of course I don't!" Amy protested.

"Of course you do, but never mind. The question now is, what shall we do? Do you think the two of us equal to the task of carrying him across the street? Or shall we awaken his despicable father?"

"I'm sure if Theo helps us, we'll do fine," said Amy.

"Theo," said Ralph sharply, "is not here."

"Oh, I see," said Amy.

"Theo," he went on in the same tone, "did not come home last night."

"Oh, dear."

"Theo," Ralph concluded, "may not be back for days."

"I'm sorry. I didn't realize."

"You realized."

"I beg your pardon?"

"You knew," said Ralph. "You were at the party. You saw him skip off with those friends of his. You saw him. I saw him. Don't pretend."

"I'm not pretending," Amy said.

"But you're glad," Ralph said.

"Why should I be glad?" Amy asked.

"Because that means you have only one pederast to worry about instead of two. The amount of time you spend worrying about whether we are going to seduce your son! What a laugh! You seem to think he's just what we're after, when in fact, my dear Amy, in actual fact this pimply little son of yours is simply past his prime."

"How dare you talk about my son like that?" Amy shouted.

"I'm not lying. Look at him."

"*You* look at him!" Amy shouted as she stormed toward the kitchen door. "I've had enough of you! Enough! I'm going to get Hector. You wouldn't dare talk to him the way you talk to me. You know what the problem is?" she called from the kitchen door. "The problem with you is that you hate women!"

"Go to hell, Amy!" Ralph called back.

"*You* go to hell!" she shouted, slamming the door. "I mean it."

She was so angry she forgot to take the front gate instead of the side gate. Before she knew it, she had thrust herself into full view of the Duxburys, remembering only when it was too late what she must look like, in her old robe and wrinkled cocktail dress and Susan's galoshes, with her hair uncombed and a rifle in her hands.

They were seated once again at the picnic table—Donald, Susan, and a handful of boarders, all looking disgustingly healthy. Donald Duxbury was helping himself to some macaroni salad, while Susan Duxbury poured out one of her health drinks that were the butt of so many jokes. Donald looked down with disappointment, Susan with disapproval, as Amy scuttled past.

Hector woke up with a splitting headache to the sight of his wife standing over him with a rifle. She really looked as if she were thinking of killing him, although he could not think why. He could not remember much of the previous evening.

"What did I do this time?" he asked wearily.

"You almost hospitalized Jozefin Dalman, for a start."

"Oh no. How did I do that?"

"You attacked her. And before that you carried Ginger off to the bushes."

"Ginger?" he asked. His voice cracked. Not even in his wildest dreams had he ever felt attracted to Ginger. "Are you sure?"

"If you don't believe me, you can ask any of the hundred-odd other people who were watching."

Hector put his head under the pillow. "What else?" he asked hoarsely.

"You made a complete fool of yourself."

"Is that all?"

"No. Then you ran through Rumeli Hisar stark naked with a few of your friends. I was sitting with the Donald Ducks when you went past. They were having breakfast and had invited me up for coffee. I was mortified."

"God. I'm sorry."

"You're going to have to go over there and apologize."

"All right," said Hector.

"Now."

"I don't have to go over there this very minute," Hector said.

"Maybe not, but there's something else you have to do this very minute."

"What's that?"

"You have to go get your son."

"Where is he?"

"At Ralph's."

"At Ralph's? That's only across the street. Why do I have to go and get him?"

"He's asleep."

"He'll wake up sooner or later," Hector said. "I really can't get up right now. I have a splitting headache."

"I want you to go over there and get him *now!*" Amy screamed.

"Would you stop waving that rifle at me?" Hector said. He shaded his eyes. "What are you doing with it in the first place?"

"I am holding this rifle," Amy said in a trembling voice, "because Ralph gave it to me."

"What was *he* doing with it? It belongs to us."

That was when Amy sat down on the bed and began to cry. It was hard to get a straight story out of her. He had never seen her so distraught. He made her undress and get into bed.

Then, after he and Ralph had moved Neil to the safety of his own bed, he got back into bed himself and tried to caress Amy to sleep. But she was too upset to sleep. She wanted to talk. And so he talked. He was ready to agree to anything, so long as she calmed down.

There was another reason for this. On his way to Ralph's, he had peeked into his mother's bedroom. The bed had not been slept in. This meant that his mother had spent the night with his father. The time had come to tell Amy who Phillip Best was. But he had to calm her down first.

So he let her repeat to him in fuller detail all the things he had done the night before, until she had replaced all the shady areas in his memory with a nightmarish vision of a green and purple monster with red fangs, who had wrecked households of furniture with his clumsy dancing and endangered the entire tree population of the Hill with burning ashes from his cigarettes.

"How can I make it up to you?" he asked, and he meant it, even though he knew what she was going to say.

What she wanted was the same thing she wanted the morning after almost every party they had attended in the past ten years. She wanted to give up drink for a few weeks. "The social whirlwind has become too much for us," she said. "We're not young anymore. And we're ignoring the children."

"I agree," he said.

"Do you think you're capable of giving up drink?" Amy asked.

"Of course I am. I can take it or leave it."

"The older you get, the harder it is to stop."

"Not if you really want to," Hector said. "And I really

do want to. I've got a good idea. Let's spend the day in bed." He snuggled up next to her, hoping she might be in the mood to make love. But she wasn't. She was too tense. She moved out of his reach without even giving the unspoken invitation any thought.

"What I want more than anything," she said, "is a quiet evening." She knew exactly how to make it happen. They would eat early, she said, so as to avoid the trauma of cocktail hour. Their meal would be simple—something, like lambchops, that went well with soda water. After supper, they would retire *en famille* to the living room, where they could play Scrabble. After the game, Hector could have that long-overdue conversation with Neil about prep schools. He could also try and find out what the hell Neil had been doing at Ralph's. If they needed privacy, Amy would be happy to take Chloe and Aspasia into the kitchen. They could make fudge.

The mention of his mother's name sent a shiver down his spine. Seeing that their quiet evening was already in danger, he tried to lower Amy's expectations. "That's no way to plan an evening. If the slightest thing goes wrong, you'll be upset. Let's just try and have as quiet an evening as possible. And if it proves impossible, we'll just try again tomorrow."

"So you think your mother won't go along with it," Amy said.

"No, no, no, that thought never crossed my mind! She'll be fine," Hector said.

"I certainly hope so."

"You haven't seen her, by the way, have you?"

"No," said Amy, "I haven't."

"I think she may not have come home last night."

"That's what Ralph said. He said she went off with that unspeakable Phillip Best."

"You know him?" Hector asked.

"Of course I do. So do you. You remember—the man in the bedroom with the houseboy."

"I didn't think he'd introduced himself."

"But you know him now," Amy cried.

"How do you know that?" Hector cried, alarmed.

"You came in with him last night."

"Oh, yes, of course. We shared a taxi from Bebek."

"So you saw the clerical collar," said Amy. Hector nodded. "What a hypocrite! I can't stand hypocrites like that."

"Well, please try and be polite to him if my mother brings him home with her," Hector said.

"Of course I'll be polite to him."

"We'll have to invite him in."

"Yes, but not for a drink. And there's no reason either why he has to stay to dinner."

"Promise me you won't get angry if it turns out we have to invite him for dinner," Hector pleaded. "There's something I should explain to you. You see, my mother—"

"Your mother has the right to her own social life. I know, I know, you've said that a thousand times. There's no reason why she should have to enjoy it in our living room. She has legs. She can go out."

"But, you see—" Hector tried again.

"Bore me another time. I'm just glad she's out of the house. I'd prefer not to think about her until I have to. I'm going to go make lunch. I want to eat lunch before she gets back. That would be a nice change, wouldn't it, to have lunch—just the four of us?"

But lunch did not turn out to be just the four of them. Neither Neil nor Chloe responded to their mother's calls. Hector had to physically drag poor Neil out of bed. Hector felt sorry for him, because the boy looked the way Hector felt. There was no rousing Chloe. The door to her bedroom was bolted.

Then, as soon as he and Amy and Neil had seated themselves at the wrought-iron table underneath the yew tree, the stream of visitors began.

First it was Meredith. She was looking for a necklace she had mislaid the night before, which the Ashes couldn't locate. She wanted to know if Amy had seen it. To Hector's surprise, she had. For some reason, it was in her handbag.

Meredith was somewhat taken aback. "I was only picking up things I found," Amy explained defensively. "I always do. I'm so glad you asked me. I didn't know whose it was."

"I'm glad I asked you, too. It's extremely valuable."

Meredith sounded miffed. Amy put her hand on Meredith's shoulder.

"Stay for lunch. We have plenty. I insist."

"Are you sure?"

"I'm sure. Here, have this sandwich."

"But that's yours."

"I have another one here."

But then Willy Wakefield appeared. He pulled up a chair and helped himself to Amy's other sandwich. "I'm not making anyone go hungry, am I?" he asked, after he had sunk his teeth into it.

"No, of course not," Amy hissed. Only Willy failed to catch the sarcasm.

Willy was the only consular official who lived in the immediate neighborhood. He lived at the other end of the *meydan,* in a beautiful pink villa known as the Pasha's Library. It was surrounded by a walled-in pine forest and had an incomparable view, which Willy took advantage of through powerful telescopes and binoculars. He insisted he was bird-watching. Willy seemed to have a crush on Amy. He was always contriving to visit the Cabots when Hector was out. Willy's own wife was in Chicago studying law. Hector felt sorry for him. The others barely tolerated him. He had a better way of ingratiating himself than his nemesis, the TASS correspondent. Instead of handing out copies of *And Quiet Flows the Don,* he handed out bottles of expensive Scotch whiskey.

He looked as if he were there for the duration. Not until Amy yawned loudly and announced she was going to take a nap did he realize he was not welcome.

He was just getting up from his chair when Chloe appeared. She was looking sheepish but at the same time defiant. She came outside holding hands with Blake.

Although he could not be completely sure, Hector realized it was possible that Blake had spent the night in Chloe's room. That would account for the bolted door. The same thought crossed Amy's mind at the same moment. She glared at Hector, as if it were somehow his fault.

"Any lunch left?" Chloe asked.

"Not unless you're in the mood for eating plates," Amy snapped.

"What can we do, then?" Chloe said. There was a childish whine in her voice.

"Make yourself some eggs."

"I'm fed up with eggs. I already had some last night," Chloe grumbled, as she and Blake went back inside.

The adults watched the door slam. Then Willy opened the garden gate. Pausing, he said to Hector, "That was the guy who kept trying to get me to say something bad about the Soviets last night. I don't hate the Soviets. They have one goddamn impressive navy. I'm telling you, I have to take my hat off to them. It's strange sometimes what people think you think. Especially in a job like mine. What's he doing with your daughter, anyhow? I thought he was engaged to some village type."

"Well, you know how it is," Hector said.

Willy slapped him on the back. "Tell it to me, baby. People living in glass houses shouldn't throw stones, right? You devil, you. I don't know how you do it. I really don't." He laughed, and then he stopped laughing as he looked back up the stairs to the Cabots' front door. "What was his name, did you say?"

"Blake."

"Blake what?"

"Blake Moffet."

"Blake Moffet, huh? He thinks I'm a spy."

"Oh, well, I mean, really now—" Meredith began with a scornful laugh, but Hector shut her up with a look.

"So how about a nap, then?" Hector said to Amy when they were alone again.

"You must be joking," she said.

"Why would I be joking? My head feels like a split coconut."

"Which means that you don't give a damn what happens to your daughter, is that it? Which means that you want *me* to deal with her, while you get a few hours more sleep? *I'm* the one who needs a nap, goddamn it! I didn't get a wink of sleep all night."

"Then why don't you take a nap?" Hector asked.

"Because I have too much to do!" she cried. "I'm a mother. I happen to care about my children. I happen to think it's important for me to be around. They have to have at least one parent who cares about them. You ignore them completely."

"Oh, Amy, you know that's not true."

"When was the last time you played basketball with your son? Or tennis? Or volleyball?"

"You want me to play volleyball with Neil? If you wanted me to play volleyball with Neil, why didn't you just ask me?"

"What I'd like to know is why it never occurs to you unless I ask you. You're like a third child. You don't even pick up after yourself."

"Amy, Amy, Amy, calm down. Let's just go upstairs and take that nap. You'll feel better after a rest."

"I don't have time for a rest. I have to get dinner started."

"But it's only three o'clock."

"We're eating early, remember? I don't have time to lie around in bed all day. Neither do you. You still have to talk to Neil, you know."

"I said I'd do that after dinner."

"And you still have to go and apologize to the Donald Ducks."

"Believe me, I haven't forgotten. I'm just waiting for the right moment."

"And sometime today, you're going to have to find time to read Thomas' poems."

"What poems?" Hector asked, aghast. But she was already inside. She always did this. She always saved the worst thing for last. He was about to follow her in to find out more about the poems, but he changed his mind. Let her come to me, he thought. He turned his attention to Neil, who was standing at the other end of the garden next to the fishpond.

"How about a game of volleyball?" Hector called.

Neil nodded shyly and went inside, to get the equipment, he supposed. His demeanor was very much like that of their dog, Lazarus, who followed him closely. Despite the warm weather, Neil was wearing an army jacket—inside out. He had turned into a closet patriot lately. According to Amy, he had an American flag hidden underneath his bed. It was hard to tell why he felt he had to hide it. It was hard to talk to him about anything these days. Hector did not have the faintest idea how he was supposed to get the boy to open up about Ralph.

Amy seemed to think that something had happened over there, although she wouldn't admit it. Hector didn't think so, knowing Ralph, but the facts were not important to him. What Hector didn't want was for Neil to feel ashamed. He wanted to let Neil know that he had had homosexual experiences at Neil's age, and that these experiences had not kept him from enjoying sex wih women when the opportunity finally arose. He wanted Neil to know this, even though it was a pack of lies.

Hector's adolescent homosexual encounters had almost driven him to suicide. They had involved a sadistic cousin of his who had blackmailed him into giving him sexual favors, and the last thing he wanted was for his son to undergo that same kind of misery. And Ralph, of all people! If Neil was going to be a homosexual, couldn't he at least have the pleasure of a more youthful partner?

While Neil set up the volleyball net, Hector tortured himself with thoughts of how Ralph must look naked. He had succeeded in putting him out of his mind when Ralph appeared in person at the garden gate.

Ralph was a wreck. It seemed that Theo had not come home yet. He had assumed that Theo had run off to a *hamam* or whatever with Bob and Louie, but now that he was still not home, Ralph was beginning to wonder if the Frenchwoman hadn't gotten her claws into him. Ralph detested the Frenchwoman. She had been after Theo for years; she just wouldn't give up. Ralph referred to her as "the other woman."

"I'm sure he's run off with the other woman," he kept saying. "I'm getting surer of it every minute."

"Don't jump to conclusions," Hector said. "He's probably off on a binge. And if he's on a binge, he's not coming back until he comes to. Who knows? He may have flown to Beirut to visit what's-his-name like he did last year, in which case he'll be back on the first plane what's-his-name can find for him."

By the time Amy came out with the tea, Ralph had

calmed down. Hector had done his job and prepared Ralph for the possiblity that Theo would be away for two or three days, and would then come back bruised with no wallet and no idea where he had been since the Ashes' party. "So long as he doesn't come back with a taxi driver," Ralph said. "I don't think I can live through another taxi driver."

Then Amy ruined everything by saying, "Well, with any luck, Theo will hail a heterosexual taxi driver. I can't believe that *all* taxi drivers in the city are male prostitutes."

"I hate to disillusion you, Amy, but they are."

"I can believe that *some* of them are, but not *all* of them."

"Believe it or not, all of them are."

"Even Hamdi *efendi* in Bebek?"

"Even Hamdi *efendi* in Bebek."

"Horseshit!" They were all shocked. Amy did not usually use that word.

Ralph slammed his teacup on the table. "Amy, you know nothing about homosexuals. You know nothing about Turkish culture. You're a puritan, that's what you are. You can't accept that every last man in this country is bisexual."

"Don't come to me as an expert on Turkish culture," Amy said. "You don't even know enough Turkish to order food in a restaurant."

This went on and on. Twice Hector tried to make them stop. They would try a neutral topic but then Ralph would start needling Amy again and Amy would lose her temper. Finally, Ralph got up and left. Hector was upset, because he knew how fragile Ralph was whenever Theo was missing.

"Why were you so mean to him?" he asked Amy.

"It's not just Ralph, it's everyone. This place has turned into Grand Central Station."

"Why don't you go take a rest? I'll make sure no one disturbs you."

"I told you. I can't. I have to make dinner."

"But it's only four o'clock."

"It's only four o'clock and you still haven't apologized to the Donald Ducks."

"I thought you wanted me to play volleyball with Neil."

"You can do that afterward. The volleyball net isn't going away on vacation, you know."

"Oh, for God's sake. All right," Hector said. He decided to get it over with. He gritted his teeth, hoping that Susan Duxbury was out singing hymns somewhere so that he wouldn't have to see her.

Donald Duxbury was alone, as Hector had hoped, but it turned out to be a disadvantage, because Donald insisted on bringing out two beers that he had hidden behind the lettuce in the refrigerator. He loved drinking a secret beer from time to time with Hector in his garden, especially when Susan was out singing hymns somewhere.

It was almost half past four, the time Hector would have been enjoying his first drink of the day if he hadn't agreed to go on the wagon. All of Amy's torture methods put together were not as bad as having to sit in front of the icy mug of beer without being able to touch it.

Donald thought Hector had come by to discuss the choir. When Hector apologized for running past the house naked that morning, Donald shrugged his shoulders and said, "Oh, that. You sure were having one heck of a time." Donald then went on to describe his single drunken escapade in college, a tale Hector had heard many times before.

It was hard for him to sit still. His hand kept inching across the table toward the frosted mug of beer, and then he would get control of himself and pull it back. When Donald, looking rather hurt, asked him why he hadn't touched the beer, he told him he had stomach trouble. Donald nodded. "Amy mentioned you were recovering from something."

"Why don't you have my beer, too?" Hector said, trying to keep his voice from shaking. "It would be a shame to see it go to waste."

"Oh, no, I couldn't," Donald said.

"Go ahead."

"Oh, all right," Donald said. Hector then had to sit there and watch Donald drink a second beer. By the time he had finished it, Donald was looped. He tried to convince Hector to stay and help him finish off a bottle of sherry he had hidden in the cellar. Hector had to help him inside. The man could barely walk.

When Hector got home, he was feeling very proud of himself for not having buckled under pressure. He expected Amy to be pleased with him, but she wasn't. "Did you have a good time?'' she asked, her voice harsh with sarcasm. Her lips were stretched tight across her face. At first he couldn't figure out what was wrong.

Then he saw Blake and Chloe standing over the stove.

''Hi,'' said Blake. ''We're making fudge.'' Despite his jaunty smile, he looked uncomfortable. It was Chloe who was calling the shots. In spite of himself, Hector felt proud of her.

''Why fudge?'' he asked.

''We just felt like it,'' Chloe explained.

''I thought you were going to make fudge after dinner,'' Hector said.

''Who told you that?'' Chloe asked.

''It was part of your mother's game plan,'' Hector explained.

''Oh,'' said Chloe. She shrugged her shoulders.

''So, Blake,'' Hector said. ''I haven't had a chance to talk to you today. What are you up to?''

''Nothing much,'' he said.

''Are you staying for dinner?''

''No, he's not,'' Amy snarled from the sink. ''I've already taken care of that. He's going to the Ashes, no thanks to you.''

''What did I do wrong this time?'' Hector asked.

''Nothing,'' she said, as she hacked at a cucumber.

''Then why are you snarling at me?''

''I didn't know I was.''

He racked his brain for some reason for her hostility. Then a terrible thought hit him. Perhaps his mother had called while he was out and told Amy everything.

''Did anyone call while I was out?'' he asked.

''Yes.''

''Who?'' His voice was no more than a whisper.

''Your friend the budding poet.''

''Thomas?''

''Yes, Thomas.''

''No one else?''

''No one else. Why? You aren't worried about your mother, are you?''

''I am, a little.

''She can take care of herself. She always has,'' Amy said. ''Just put her out of your mind. And stop looking over my shoulder. It gets on my nerves. Why don't you go sit down in the library? Your soda water is waiting for you on the ledge—if you can bear the thought of soda water."

"Of course I can," Hector said. "Stop going after me."

"I'm sorry," Amy said, as she tore at a head of lettuce.

"I think I'll take my soda water outside, if you don't mind."

"You can't," Amy said.

"Why not?"

"Because there's not enough light out there to read by."

"What do I have to read?"

"Thomas' poems. The reason he called was because he wanted to come over and pick them up. But I said you wanted to read them first. I told him you'd read them tonight and he could pick them up tomorrow at your office."

"Why did you say that?" Hector asked.

"First of all, because I didn't want him coming over here tonight. We've had enough visitors. The second reason is that last night you promised him you'd read them and help him get them published, and I know you don't like to go back on your promises."

"But we were both drunk," Hector protested.

"You certainly were."

"Why are you punishing me like this?"

"I'm not punishing you," Amy said, throwing the lettuce leaves into a basin of water. "You enjoyed the poems last night. Perhaps you'll enjoy them again tonight."

"Oh, God."

"You know you're supposed to be selecting the best ones to send to the *New Yorker*," Amy continued.

"Oh, God."

The time usually reserved for cocktails was to have been short, but ended up being two hours long because the gas was too low for Amy to broil the lambchops. This was unfortunate because it gave Hector enough time to read through Thomas' poems.

They were terrible. They were lewd, they were far-fetched, they were full of metaphors that even Hector, with his abysmal personal record, found in bad taste. He could not believe that they had been written by the same man he had known for so many years. Clear-eyed, loyal Thomas, always harder on himself than on his friends—was this what went on inside his head?

There was about two hundred poems, addressed to four or five different mistresses. Hector hadn't even known that Thomas had mistresses. Where had he hidden them? With a sinking heart, he leafed through poem after poem, looking for one that was salvageable, that would restore his faith in his friend. At the bottom of the box he came across a ten-page story.

It had a clean if somewhat self-conscious style—more what Hector would expect of Thomas. It took place in Istanbul, and the protagonist was very much in the mold of Thomas, with the exception of hair color, height, and academic discipline. The story was about this man's friendship with an obnoxious life-of-the-party type, the kind of man Hector really couldn't stand, who was always interrupting other people's conversations with the same tired lines, always breaking things, always confident that his so-called charm would open every door for him.

The story began with the hero's discovery that the obnoxious life-of-the-party type had been having an affair with his wife. At first he felt betrayed and remembered all the other bad things his friend had done to him over the years. He had finally decided to have it out with him, but the obnoxious life of the party cleverly chose that night to come to his house. Drunk, of course. He had dragged Thomas out on a binge with him, but not until he had insulted the wife. Before the binge was through, the hero and his brute of a friend had made friends again. It was supposed to be a happy ending. Hector was halfway through the story before he realized that the story was autobiograpical, and that the obnoxious life-of-the-party type was himself.

He felt like crying. Was this what he looked like to other people? Why did his friends put up with him? He had always assumed that Amy was exaggerating when she told him how horrible he was when he drank. It was as if he became a different person. With trembling hands, he lifted his soda water to his lips, pausing for a moment to examine it, to make absolutely sure there was no alcohol in it. After reading that story, he didn't know whether he would ever be able to drink again.

The Laceys were entertaining a large group on their balcony, and from the Cabots' library it sounded as if they did nothing but laugh. You could hear one thin little voice saying something, and then it was drowned out by a chorus of ho-ho-hos. No one could possibly be that funny. They had to be plastered. Hector's theory was proven when the electricity went out. They laughed and laughed as if the sudden, unexpected darkness were the funniest joke they had ever heard.

Meanwhile, Thomas Ashe walked up and down, up and down the cobblestone street. He had his hands in his pockets. His head was bowed and his shoulders stooped. Despite the fact that he had been drinking all day, he still had a hangover.

He was thankful for the power failure. When he passed under the Cabots' library window, he slowed down and tried to make sense of the voices inside: Hector and Amy calling out to each other, fumbling for candles. "So!" he heard Amy say. "Did you get a chance to look at the poems?" Thomas could not quite hear Hector's response, although he could imagine it.

How could Hector possibly like those odious, odious poems? He had written them in the army, to a succession of German prostitutes. He ought to have thrown them out years ago. Well, now he was paying for his sentimentality. Now they were public property. Who could tell how many people had taken his poems home with them to read and ridicule? For all he knew, that was what the Laceys were doing on that balcony of theirs: reading his poems to their snooty friends, laughing at his adolescent metaphors, laughing at *him*. He could almost hear them: "I always thought he was a hopeless sap. I mean, really, imagine putting a pun like that into a love poem! 'Trembling member' indeed! And to think he calls himself an English professor."

Leslie and Meredith Lacey were responsible for the Ashes' having been ostracized by all but the dullest Woodrow College professors during their first three years in Istanbul. They were also the ones who had nicknamed Thomas "the Priest." They had given him this nickname because of the way he had acted at his first dinner party. The dinner party had been at the Laceys'.

Meredith considered herself the Hill's most accomplished hostess. She made a point of entertaining new arrivals, whom she categorized rather ruthlessly into "dullards" and "promising talent" after a single meeting. Because the Ashes' social life until their arrival in Istanbul had been confined to babysitting pools and holiday meals at the homes of relatives, Thomas and Stella had felt uncomfortable at the Laceys' dinner table, in the company of so many witty, sophisticated, amoral people. Since they were not quite sure what you were supposed to talk about at dinner parties, they hardly spoke at all. They ate too fast, with their heads bent shyly over their plates. Then they rose to leave before Meredith had even offered coffee and brandy.

Doing her best not to let them know what a terrible gaffe they had made, Meredith urged them to stay for coffee. But they said no, coffee would keep them awake, and it was already past their bedtime. (It was only ten o'clock.) This was another count against them, and secured them a place on Meredith's dullard list. But the next thing that happened earned them an even lower place in Meredith's hierarchy—a place among the people Meredith hated so much that she grouped them, rather implausibly, with Nazis—those "clean-living, so-called pillars of society who never pass up an opportunity to jam morality down your throat."

What happened was that as Thomas and Stella descended the Laceys' front steps, they heard manificient piano music pouring out of the flat below. On the spur of the moment, they decided to go see who was playing. Having entered the garden, they soon found themselves standing outside a living room, which was ablaze with light. The curtains were wide open. Inside they saw three men standing in line with no clothes on—one of whom Thomas later identifed as Ralph. Theo was kneeling in front of him committing fellatio, while in the corner, a pregnant woman—a *pregnant woman*—played the piano.

Years later when greater exposure to such perversions made him numb to them and even tolerant of their perpetrators, he discovered that the activity he and Stella had witnessed was known locally as "playing the French horn."

But at the time it was a nameless horror. He was so shocked at the sight of the pregnant woman that he did not allow himself to look at her face—out of respect for her privacy, out of consideration for the unborn child. But he grew to be sorry, because there were three or four pregnant women on campus that year, and he suspected them all equally. For years the question plagued him at night—which one had it been?

For a few moments, he and Stella stood there staring, paralyzed. Then Stella fainted. She had not known that homosexuality even existed. Without thinking, Thomas picked her up in his arms and ran up the Laceys' back steps and into the lion's den, so to speak, where the Laceys and their other dinner guests were having an uproarious time over coffee and brandy.

At the sight of Thomas and Stella they stopped laughing.

"Well, speak of the devil," said Leslie.

"Goodness gracious, what happened?" asked Meredith.

"We had quite a shock downstairs in the garden," Thomas said, and he blushed.

"A shock? What kind of shock?" Leslie asked. He was in one of his nasty moods—he often became nasty when he drank—and now he went after Thomas like a cat after a mouse. He backed his prey farther and farther into the corner. "In the garden? Where in the garden?" Leslie asked Thomas. "Oh, so it was not in the garden, but in the garden flat. . . . In the living room of the garden flat, was it? . . . And you say the curtains were open. . . . How many men? . . . Three, you say? Dear me, this *is* shocking. And one of them on his knees? What on earth could he be doing on his knees? Please try and be more specific. . . . What do you mean, you prefer not to say in mixed company? We are all big boys and girls here. I assure you there will be no more fainting spells. . . . Ah, I see. So they were naked. And a pregnant woman at the piano, was there? Tell me, was *she* naked, too? No? What a pity."

Finally, one of the dinner guests—a Turk, a former student of Leslie's—took pity on poor Thomas and offered him and Stella a lift home.

Leslie and Meredith turned this episode into an amusing anecdote. With time, as the story became second, third, and fourth hand, Thomas' embarrassment turned into a self-righteous condemnation of homosexuality. Therefore, none of the bohemian set would have anything to do with him for years.

Even now, eons after it had been decreed that he threw the best parties, they still excluded him. For example, the Laceys had never again invited him and Stella to their house for drinks.

He stood in the cobblestone street and looked up at the Laceys' balcony, which was dark except for the glowing embers of cigarettes, and quiet except for a single well-modulated voice telling a story. The dark house towered above him, mocking his pretensions: the citadel.

He was never going to let them know how he felt.

The lights went on, causing more paroxysms of laughter on the Laceys' balcony.

"Yoohoo! Yoohoo down there!" Meredith's voice floated across the street. "Yoohoo, Thomas! That *is* you, isn't it? What are you doing down there? Don't tell me you've come to serenade us!"

"Come on up for a drink!" Ralph shouted.

"Yes, do!" Meredith chimed in. "And while you're at it, write me a poem." More laughter. "Thomas? Thomas? Where did you go? Can anyone see where he went? Good God, he's run out on us."

"Thomas! Tho-o-o-ma-a-as!"

"Come back here, you bastard!"

"What could have come over him?" Meredith asked.

There was the sound of running feet.

Hector tried to get up from the dinner table but Amy clamped her hand down on his shoulder.

"Don't go out there," she said. "It's just not worth it."

"Who do you think you are, my jailer?"

"No, of course not. Hector, please. Don't look at it that way. Here. Have some more soda water."

She poured him another glass. Hector stared at it without appetite. He was already sick of soda water. Every time he tasted those soapy little bubbles, he had the same hollow feeling he had had the first time he ate out in Paris, when, after five days on a train, he forgot to order vegetables with the main course, and all he got for dinner was a huge white plate with a little piece of meat on it that looked like a mouse.

"You're tired of it already, aren't you?" Amy said, staring into his eyes. "I can tell. I was afraid of this. How about some lemonade?"

"Darling, just relax. I'm not going to the Laceys'."

"I know, I know. I just thought lemonade might make it easier."

"Lemonade is not going to make it any easier," Hector said.

"We still have that rum extract we bought in Athens. Why don't I make some lemonade and put some rum extract into it?"

"Amy!" he shouted. "For Christ's sake! Stop it!"

"I'll go get dessert," she said. "I made something very sweet." They ate dessert in silence.

What Hector would really have liked to have done after dinner was soak in a hot bath and then go to bed, but he knew Amy was counting on him to play Scrabble with the children. So he went into the library and set up the card table. He closed the windows so that they wouldn't have to listen to the Laceys anymore. He hoped that if they settled into a Scrabble game right away, Amy might forget he had promised to discuss prep schools with Neil. He had been avoiding this topic for months, because he was afraid his son might tell him he wanted to go to a military academy.

It was one of their more tedious Scrabble games. Hector started out with an X, a Y, a J, and four I's. Every time he found a triple-word score for his valuable letters, Amy loused it up with some word like DIN or RAIN. Neil was even worse. A few years back, he had made the word HOGPLUM, just as a joke, just so everyone would see how bad his letters were, only to discover that the Oxford English Dictionary defined it as a West Indian fruit. His game had never recovered from this stroke of luck. All he wanted to do was make up words like FISFUS and DILKOBE, and look them up in the dictionary.

Usually he could depend on Chloe for some interesting competition, but not tonight.

She was sulking because Amy had kicked Blake out of

the house. Every gesture she made seemed designed to annoy her mother. She also kept going into the kitchen and coming back with pieces of fudge.

"Are you planning to eat the whole tray?" Amy finally asked.

"If I feel like it," said Chloe. "If I'm bored enough."

"Well, at least you could try and eat with your mouth closed."

Chloe continued to chew with her mouth open.

"I though you were on a diet," Amy said to her.

"You know, if you'd let Blake stay for dinner," Chloe said, her voice ever so slightly slurred, "there would have been no problem. He was the one who wanted this fudge in the first place. I'm just eating it because I'm so bored."

"You're going to see him tormorrow morning, for God's sake," Amy said. "Though *what* you see in him is another question."

"If you bothered to be nice to him, you'd see why I like him," Chloe said.

"So you like him, do you?" Amy said. "And may I ask if you intend to bring everyone you like home for the night?"

"He slept on the floor," Chloe snapped.

"You seem to forget he's engaged," Amy said.

"Oh, that. That may be over," Chloe said, licking the fudge off her fingers.

Now it was Hector's turn to be outraged. "Over? What do you mean, over?"

"He's changed his mind," Chloe explained.

"You can't just change your mind in a situation like that! The poor girl will be in disgrace!"

"She'll weather it," Chloe said. "They would probably have been miserable together, anyway."

"It doesn't matter. He gave his word. Goddamn it, he's a selfish little bastard. No wonder Americans are discredited all over the world. It's thanks to people like him."

"You'd better watch what you say. You're no saint yourself," Chloe said.

"I may be bad, but I've never dragged an innocent peasant girl through the dirt just for the fun of it!" Hector said, his face flushing. It was at this atypical moment of moral outrage that the telephone finally chose to ring.

Amy answered it. She spoke for a long time. While she was speaking, Chloe retired from the Scrabble game and went up to bed. Hector was so worried about the phone call that he did not think twice about the fact that she was staggering.

"That was your mother," Amy announced when she returned. "She's in Bebek. But don't worry. I told her not to come home."

"What?" Hector gasped.

"Oh, don't act so high and mighty," Amy said. "I *did* give her a choice, you know! I said she could either come home alone or stay out with Phillip Best. That's who she's with, you see. I was right. God! What *can* she see in him?"

"Why do you insist on calling. . . . Why do you. . . ." Hector's voice trailed off under Amy's defiant state. He let his eyes fall to his letters. He began to shuffle them with trembling fingrs. He sighed.

Just then Chloe screamed.

"Oh my God!" Amy cried. "What's happened now?" They all rushed upstairs, where they found Chloe crouching in the corner of her bedroom. She was shaking violently.

"What's wrong, Chloe? What's wrong?"

She answered with a low, anguished moan. She pointed at the closet.

"Neil! Go check the closet! What did you see, Chloe baby? A rat? A bug? Talk to me, Chloe, talk to me." Amy was clutching her daughter by the shoulders and shaking her gently. "Talk to me, Chloe! Please! Don't just sit there! Are you in pain? Should I call the doctor? What do you think is wrong with her?" Amy asked, turning to Hector. "She's as pale as a ghost."

"She's hallucinating," Neil said.

"Don't be facetious," Amy snapped.

"But she *is,*" Neil insisted. "She is completely stoned. She and her asinine boyfriend put a hunk of hash this big into the fudge, and then she ate every last bit of it, so what do you expect? What a pig she is. She's so stupid. But I wouldn't worry about it. Eric made the same mistake a year or two ago with some brownies. He was fine afterward, after he had hallucinated for three days.''

''How *can* you children be so stupid? And why didn't you tell me?''

Neil shrugged his shoulders. ''I'm surprised you didn't smell it,'' he said.

Then the doorbell rang.

''*Goddamn it!*'' Amy screeched. ''This is just the limit. Who do you think *this* is?'' She marched downstairs and threw open the door so roughly that the glass almost broke.

It was Thomas Ashe. Hector cringed, and hesitated at the door to Chloe's room.

''Do you make a habit of calling on your friends at half past ten Sunday evening?'' Amy said to Thomas. ''Or have you arranged your teaching schedule so that you don't have anything on Monday morning that might interfere with your weekend program?''

''I'm sorry if I disturbed you,'' Thomas said. ''I didn't realize. . . . I just wanted to tell Hector not to bother. . . . I wanted to have a brief word with him so that I could explain. . . .''

''I'm afraid any brief words will have to wait until tomorrow,'' Amy said.

''Amy! For God's sake!'' Hector cried. ''Let the man in!'' But she must not have heard him, because the next thing he heard was Amy slamming the door.

He could hear Lazarus' ferocious barking in the front garden. It sounded as if he had taken Thomas hostage. That was the limit. Hector was going to have to go out there and call Lazarus off, no matter what nonsense Amy gave him.

But by the time he had put on his shoes, the barking had become nothing more than an intermittent strangled gurgle. Thomas had obviously gotten away. He was about to take his shoes off again when it occurred to him that if that had been Lazarus barking, there was something very wrong with him. He decided to go out and check. And before he did so, he was going to have it out with Amy for being so cruel to Thomas.

But when he got downstairs, he could see neither Amy nor Neil. All he could hear was heavy breathing. Then he saw Neil crouching under the dining room table. ''What are you doing down there?'' he asked, when suddenly he heard Amy. ''Quick!'' she hissed. Scanning the room, he found her feet sticking out from underneath the living room drapes. Looking up from the feet, he saw her hands pop out from behind the drapes and beckon him.

''What is going on?'' he cried. Then he saw them: two people climbing the stairs to the front porch. His mother and father.

Without thinking, he threw himself onto the floor, as if to avoid crossfire.

They stood at the door for at least five minutes, patiently ringing the bell. This gave Hector time to regret his evasive action. But how could he just get up off the floor and let them in? How could he explain it? I'm sorry to keep you waiting. I was hiding, but I changed my mind. Do sit down. How nice to see you. That's my wife, Amy, behind the drapes. And that fellow under the dining room table is my son.

''That was awful,'' he said to Amy, after his parents had given up on them. He watched them climb the hill toward the Laceys'. ''It's not fair to my mother. She's too old to be wandering outside at this time of night.''

''She looks fine. She's the least of our worries,'' Amy said. Just then, Chloe emitted a deathly moan. Amy ran upstairs to attend to her. She sent Hector to the kitchen to make some coffee.

Lazarus was curled up next to the stove, looking gloomy. He had probably been looking forward to a game of fetch that afternoon, and was depressed after a day of being completely ignored. It was even possible that he was depressed because of some unspeakable thing Hector might have done to him the night before, which Hector, thank God, did not remember, and which Lazarus—dear, loyal Lazarus—had no way of reminding him about. That was what he loved about dogs. They couldn't talk.

''Are you miserable, Lazarus?'' Hector said to the dog, nudging him gently with his foot. ''Would you like to take a little walk? Are you tired of being inside?'' Lazarus listened patiently, his eyes showing hope. ''How about if you and I just slip out for a walk now? We can drop by the Laceys' for a moment. I can introduce you to my father. I think you'll like him. He'll like you. He's English. Englishmen always like dogs. I think you two will get along fine. How about it?" he said. He knelt down to put on Lazarus' leash.

"And where do you think you're going?" Amy said. She was standing in the doorway staring at him, her arms akimbo.

"I'm going to take Lazarus out for a walk."

"And I suppose you'll stop off at the Laceys' while you're at it."

"Well, I thought it might be a good idea. I want to make sure my mother's all right."

"You're not going over there to see how your mother is," Amy said. "You're going over there because you want to pick up Thomas and go out for a drink. I know you. You've been planning it all along."

"Planning it all along?" Hector cried.

"You probably phoned him and asked him to come over to bail you out so you could go somewhere and have another beer."

"What do you mean, *another* beer?"

"It's convenient I've fallen apart like this," Amy said with ice in her voice. "Because now you can blame it all on me. You can tell them all that I made life so unbearable for you that I practically chased you out of the house. No wonder they call me Pollyanna."

"'Amy, what are you talking about?"

"I saw you at the Donald Ducks' with that beer. That was very clever."

"I didn't touch that beer. I swear to you."

"Oh, yes, you did. Don't think you can fool me. You drank it, all right. Well, I've tried to help you, but you're hopeless. You're a hopeless alcoholic. You can go out and drink all you like and pass out on the curb, for all I care," she said.

"All right," said Hector, "I will."

He waited until Lazarus' tail was safely out the door and then he slammed it as hard as he could.

He was halfway down the steps when he heard Thomas calling to him in a half whisper.

He found Thomas crouching in the little space underneath the stairs. He was shaking.

"There's a rabid dog in the garden somewhere," Thomas said. "He almost got me."

"Where?" Hector asked. "I don't see anything."

"He's back there, in the bushes." Hector went to look, but there was nothing there.

"Are you sure it wasn't Lazarus who chased you in there? He does that sometimes, you know. He may not have recognized you."

"You're probably right," Thomas said. "It was awfully dark."

"I'm sure it was Lazarus," Hector said, completely forgetting that Lazarus had been inside all evening. "Let's go over to the Laceys'. I'm dying for a drink."

They had not gone far when Hector remembered that if they went to the Laceys', he might have to tell Thomas—and everyone else—that this hypocritical minister they all had such contempt for was actually his father. And to endure this embarrassment stone sober! Maybe it would be better if they went down the hill to Osman's first.

Thomas, being his usual agreeable self, said he was up for anything, and so off they went down to Osman's, Lazarus straining at the leash all the way. They were almost there when Hector remembered that Thomas was waiting for him to say something about his poems. This was going to be tricky. He didn't want to discourage him, but he also didn't want to be dishonest. He decided to have a beer or two before venturing anything.

After three beers, he decided to say that they were powerful poems, but that they needed some work. If Thomas fixed them up, he would say, then he would be happy to send them to his friend at the *New Yorker*.

What a relief. It was the perfect way out. It was mild enough not to jeopardize their friendship, and at the same time it was not a lie. He would have one more beer and then they could get down to business.

But then Hagop decided to join them with a bottle of *raki*.

Hagop was the Ashes' maid's husband. He had a black eye from his argument of the night before and he seemed proud of it. They had a repetitive and disparaging coversation about wives. They were all in agreement about them. They toasted freedom with their first round of *raki*, and again with their second, and their third, and their fourth. That was why Hector could not remember afterward if they had gotten around to discussing Thomas' poems.

In fact, they had discussed them over the second bottle of *raki*, when Hector blurted out, "I read your poems. They're horseshit."

"Yes, aren't they the worst things ever written?" Thomas had agreed. "I'm so glad you had the courage to be honest."

But Hector did not remember a word of this conversation. Since Thomas never brought up the poems again, he was forced to come to his own conclusions. Clearly he had said something cruel to Thomas. Clearly he had done something to break whatever bond existed between them, had broken it beyond repair. Because although Thomas continued to be friendly after that evening, it seemed to Hector as if Thomas no longer trusted him.

Amy went to bed at midnight, but she was still awake at half past one, when Hector and Thomas came staggering up the hill singing army songs. She was relieved to hear them decide to join the crowd at the Laceys'. She didn't care what kind of hangover Hector had in the morning, so long as he left her alone.

She tossed and turned, trying to think of sheep jumping over a fence instead of chocolate. She could have killed for a Toblerone.

She usually kept a secret bag of Toblerones behind the record albums, but today they were missing. Today of all days! The thought she couldn't get out of her head was how it tasted when you sank your teeth into it, how soft, how delicious as it melted into the roof of your mouth, and then how thrilling when your teeth hit a nut and had to crunch through it. That was how she finally coaxed herself to sleep at half past two in the morning, by pretending she was eating a Toblerone. There were many noises in the night—the mindless laughter drifting over from the Laceys', Chloe's snores, the sound of foghorns, snarling dogs—but when she pulled the covers over her head, she couldn't hear anything but her own breathing. She comforted herself with the thought of how guilty Hector would feel in the morning.

* * *

At half past three in the morning, Neil awoke to the sound of drunken brawling in the street below his window. Looking out, he saw his father, his grandmother, and the English minister his mother claimed to have seen fornicating with a houseboy at a party. His grandmother was wringing her hands and screaming. His father, meanwhile, was pushing the Englishman down the hill, his forefinger firmly planted in the Englishmen's chest. He was calling him a motherfucker.

"I say, Hector," said the Englishman. "Don't you think you're being a bit ridiculous?"

"Don't you ever say that to me," Hector growled. "Don't you *dare* say that to me *ever* again." At that there was a struggle between the two men, which ended when Hector knocked the Englishman out with a punch in the jaw. The Englishman crumpled onto the cobblestones. Neil's grandmother screamed. Hector, looking pleased with himself, picked up Neil's grandmother, tucked her under his right arm, and carried her, protesting, into the garden.

After some commotion, there was silence. Neil's father came inside. He made an inside call. A few minutes later, Mr. Ashe, Mr. and Mrs. Lacey, Mrs. Lacey's friend Ginger, and Ralph came giggling down the road. They paused next to the fallen Englishman. After some discussion, they decided to carry him inside. This turned out to be harder than they had foreseen, and caused more giggling. Neil heard his father letting them into the house.

Moments later, Neil heard someone yodeling under his window. To his surprise, it turned out to be Mr. Duxbury. He was waving a bottle of something. Neil's father came out through the front gate and tried to pull him inside, but he wouldn't go. "Oh, come on, you American donkey's ass," said Neil's father, as his head bobbed like a doll with an iron coil neck. "Forget that wife of yours. She's nothing but a turd out of a donkey's ass. Let's get rid of her. Let's get rid of her for once and for all. Let's turn her over to the Russians."

"The Russians?" Mr. Duxbury said, lurching toward the front gate.

"She'll be happy as hell up there, believe me. Plenty of

donkey turds for her care packages. It's perfect for her. I should know. She'll have her work cut out for her. Let's get this piece of shit out of your life. Let's call up TASS right now and tell them to ship her off tonight. You can't let that donkey turd order you around."

"You think so?" Donald said.

"Yeah, let's call up TASS and tell them to come right over. They can have my mother, too."

"You have the number?" Mr. Duxbury asked.

"Sure I have the number," said Neil's father. "What do you think I am, a sheep's brain? What do you say, you donkey, you?"

"I say we call," said Mr. Duxbury.

They disappeared through the gate.

"Who's this on the floor here?" Mr. Duxbury asked, when they had come inside.

"Some bastard my mother used to know," said Neil's father. "He works for the CIA."

Less than a minute later by his watch (which was the kind frogmen wore), Neil could hear them in the hallway dialing for the operator. "Hello, operator? Get me TASS." They were laughing and falling against the banister.

Neil got back under the covers, deep in shock. There was no more evading the issue. For months now, he had been trying to laugh off his father's anti-American remarks, trying to ignore the way his father would shrug his shoulders when someone mentioned the Domino Theory and say, "Who cares if all of Southeast Asia goes over to the Chinese? That's their decision." Neil had been trying not to notice the way his father grimaced when Neil hinted to him that he was thinking of a career in the United States Armed Forces. But now the facts were in and he had to face them.

His father was a Communist.

On Saturday evening, before he left for the Ashes' party, Neil had been looking through the books on the shelves in the library and had come across a copy of *The Communist Manifesto*. Further examination of the shelves had turned up books by Lenin, Trotsky, and Gogol.

At the time he had told himself that mere possession of *The Communist Manifesto* was not enough to prove that someone was a Communist. It was possible that his father was just interested in the subject, or that he had flirted with the ideology as a youth, and eventually turned into a cultural imperialist with the approach of middle age. But now he had proof from his father's own lips. All those things he had said to Mr. Duxbury on the street. The fact that he even had their phone number. The fact that he didn't think twice about waking them up in the middle of the night. The fact that he knew Russia would be perfect for Susan Duxbury. "It's perfect for her," he had said. "I should know." The fact that he hated the English minister because he worked for the CIA.

All day long, Neil's father had been acting strange. Neil had thought it was because his father was angry at him for getting drunk and wandering over to the Laceys' garden, and worried, as Neil was himself, about what might have transpired at Ralph's.

Now he saw that what worried his father was something far more important.

It was Neil's flag. His father had found the flag under Neil's mattress and this had upset him. Any Communist who discovered that his son was a patriot would feel the same.

He wondered what it was that had turned his father into a traitor. Blackmail? A drunken promise? A Swiss bank account?

Neil went out to the landing to see if they had gotten through to TASS. He saw his father sitting on the floor with Mr. Lacey. Mr. Lacey looked stern, Neil's father distraught.

"You can't keep your mother in the shed all night," Mr. Lacey was saying. "If you don't give me the key, I'll have to kick in the door.

"No," Hector said. "I can't. I just can't. Believe me."

He gave Mr. Lacey a tragic look. Neil went back into his bedroom, once again in deep shock.

It was all clear now. It was Mr. Lacey who was the leader of the cadre. It was Mr. Lacey who had turned his father into a Communist. He was making his father pay the price now. He wanted him to turn his mother over, and the strain was killing him—Neil could see it as plain as day.

Neil got out of bed as quietly as he could. He put on his slippers and his robe and stuffed his precious American flag inside his pajama shirt. He tiptoed to the stairs. He was going to have to hide in the pine forest until morning, at which time he would go alert the relevant authorities.

They were playing Greek music now. Neil could hear them dancing. He was just outside Chloe's room when suddenly they all danced out of the living room in a line, holding hands, his father in the lead, waving a handkerchief. Stepping over the English minister's body, he led the dancers up the stairs. Neil dashed back up to his bedroom before they could notice him. He threw himself into bed and buried his head under the covers, clutching his flag to his heart. "Think straight," he told himself. "Don't panic." This was the crisis he had been waiting for for so many years.

His first taste of unhappiness had been political. He had been in first grade at the time. He was sitting on the terrace of the Mehtap Restaurant in Bebek, eating a plate of potato croquettes, when a Russian ship carrying missiles to Cuba had rumbled past them. It sent huge waves crashing against the stilts that supported the terrace, causing it to rock so violently you would have thought there had been an earthquake. Looking through the gaps between the floorboards, Neil had noticed for the first time how flimsy the stilts were, how easily they could buckle and send the entire terrace and everyone on it into the sea. Looking up, he had seen his parents' faces crumple into worried wrinkles. He could not understand everything they said to one another. All he could tell was that there was going to be a war, that this war was inevitable, that the missiles they had just seen were capable of ending civilization as his parents knew it, perhaps even capable of ending life on earth.

That night, he came down with a fever and was out of school for a week. Every night, when he went to bed, he said goodbye to life, and all his toys, and prayed that he would be allowed to go to heaven with his parents. When he woke up in the morning to find that the war had been postponed, he would be filled with joy, but as the day continued, the joy would turn to sorrow as he prepared himself and his possessions for the end of the world. Until one day, when his father came out of the bathroom with half his face still lathered and said to Neil's mother, "Let's move to southern Chile. I think we'd survive there." His mother said, "Do you really think so?" and his father said, "I do."

Neil had started packing at once. Having found southern Chile on the map, he had realized that if civilization were to survive with them, they would have to take it with them in their luggage. But what parts of civilization to take, and how to pack them? Neil's suitcase was not large enough for all the things he wanted to put into it. For months, he agonized over what was more vital, a baseball glove or Webster's Dictionary, as if the entire burden of preserving his parents and the civilization they knew rested on his shoulders. It was during this period that he had acquired his flag.

Then one day he was walking with his father along the Bosphorus and they saw the same Russian ship carrying missiles back to Russia. The end of the world had been averted. Everyone went back to the old life. Everyone, that is, but Neil. He had never taken things for granted after that, never relaxed. There were too many signs of another emergency just around the corner.

He had thought that when the time came, he would be the only one on the Hill prepared for crisis. But now the time had come and instead of taking command he was here in bed, with his mind blank and his heart pounding. He had been checkmated before his first move. As he listened to his father and the others dancing up the stairs, he clutched his flag with both hands and recited what he remembered of the Lord's Prayer.

Amy was still in a fog of sleep when the door to her bedroom flew open and the room filled with the reedy blare of Greek dance music. She opened her eyes to see Hector and his friends prancing into the bedroom, bringing with them the fumes of Kanyak, wine, and stale cigarettes, to dance a crooked chain dance around her bed.

They were all panting with laughter—Leslie, Meredith, Ginger, Ralph, Thomas, and, of all people, Donald Duxbury, who was stumbling over his big feet because he didn't know the steps. Hector led the dance. He had changed, once again, into Captain Yorgo. He had a cigarette hanging out his mouth. His eyes were blank, staring straight ahead—

rather like a rabid dog's, Amy thought—as he leaped over chairs and bed and knocked rugs and lamps out of the way. He was waving a handkerchief in his free hand, and crying, "Hopa! Hopa!"

Downstairs, the Greek record began to repeat itself. Perhaps it was drunk, too. "Mrs. Yorgina," it screeched, "where is your Yorgo going? Mrs. Yorgina, where is your Yorgo going?" Hector did not seem to notice that the record was scratched. Crying "Hopa!" he led the chain of dancers out of the master bedroom and into Neil's bedroom, where there was much commotion as Hector roused his son. "Dad! Dad! Please! Not my flag! For God's sake, Dad!" Neil cried. By the time Amy had thrown on her robe and reached the door, the chain of dancers was emerging from Neil's room. Hector was snapping his fingers as he did some elaborate dip steps. Draped around his neck was Neil's flag.

"Oh, my God," said Amy.

She ran after Hector and tried to take the flag off his neck, but he pushed her away, sending her crashing into the trunk in the hallway. He continued down to the first landing, from which he led the dancers into Chloe's room.

Amy watched aghast as they came out of Chloe's room with a barely conscious Chloe in tow. Halfway down the stairs, Chloe lost her balance and disappeared from view. Amy and Neil rushed downstairs to find her groaning on the floor. Lying next to her was Phillip Best, who was unconscious.

While the dancers proceeded, giggling, through the dining room to the kitchen, and the record player continued to ask Mrs. Yorgina where her Yorgo was going (which was something Amy would have liked to know, too) Amy and Neil carried first Chloe, then Phillip Best, upstairs to safety.

They put Phillip into the master bedroom because they couldn't figure out what else to do with him.

What Amy really felt like doing was getting on a plane and leaving Istanbul forever. That would show that man who thought she enjoyed being a good sport, who thought she took pleasure in being passive-agressive. But then she reminded herself that she was not being practical. She was stuck. She was a mother. She had two children. She was doomed to continue being passive-aggressive whether she liked it or not.

There was only one course open to her, and that was to pretend that the ruckus downstairs was not happening. They were just going to have to go back to sleep and pretend that nothing out of the ordinary had occurred. When they woke up in the morning, it would be all over. So she sent Neil to bed, reminding him (a bit too sternly, she thought later) that it was a schoolnight.

She had trouble falling asleep next to the unconscious Mr. Best. What was wrong with him? There was a bump on his forehead. She had almost dropped off, almost forgotten he was there, when she opened her eyes and mistook him for Hector.

But what an aged and ravaged Hector! What on earth had he done to himself? She stifled a scream.

Once she had calmed herself down and convinced herself that if was fatigue that was making her see things, she decided to transfer him to the floor. That way she would get some sleep. If he was still unconscious in the morning, she would get someone to take him to the infirmary.

But the sight of him lying helplessly on the floor made Amy feel guilty. To make up for her callousness, she gave him one of her pillows. It was while she was adjusting the pillow that she saw Neil come out of his room.

"And where do you think you're going, young man?"

"To get my flag," he said.

"Oh, no, you're not," Amy said. "You're going straight back to bed."

"Mom, please. I've got to. What if they're defiling it?"

"All right," said Amy. "If you insist. We'll go down there and get the flag, but then we have to come right back up."

The dancers had retired to the kitchen. Neil's flag was on the floor, covered with footprints. Neil grabbed the flag and began to fold it, glancing up nervously all the while, as if he were surrounded by Communists.

Hector was pouring drinks for everyone, spilling *Krem de Mant* on the table and the floor. Amy found a damp rag and tried to clean up the puddles before people tracked them all over the house. What would Kleoniki think when she came to clean in the morning, if she found green footprints all over the house? Kleoniki was a superstitious woman. Morning was only a few hours away.

Although she knew that it was pointless to reason with Hector when he was in this condition, the sight of his face drained of all intelligence made her too angry to care whether or not she got her point across. She did not think she could stand acting passive-aggressive for one more second. "Hector," she said, "I think the time has come for you to apologize to your son."

"For what?" Hector asked blankly.

"For taking his flag."

"Did I take his flag?"

"You certainly did. You know, Hector, it's about time you started taking your son seriously. Your son is not a joke."

"What are you talking about, you piece-of-shit sow? You're trying to take my son away from me! Not in a million years, sow. I'm wise to your tricks."

Hector went over to Neil, pulled the folded flag off his lap, and threw it on the floor. He then enveloped Neil in a bear hug.

"Oh, my son! I'll do anything for you! I worship you! Don't listen to that frigid cow manure of a mother." He smiled and kissed Neil's forehead, and then turned angrily to Ralph.

"If you ever try and bugger my son again, I'll knock your head off, you cocksucking bastard!"

Before Amy could get up from her chair, Neil had bolted through the door into the garden. She went out to look for him but could not see him anywhere.

Ralph was in tears when she returned to the kitchen. "How could you say such a thing to me?" Ralph was saying. "Do you really think I would bugger the son of my best friend? Do the same thing to him as was done to me? Send him down a long road of lifelong misery? You know what, Hector? In my entire life, I could count the number of happy days I've had on one hand. Do you know how long it's been since I had a boy? Seven years! Seven goddamn years! How could you think I would want to ruin your son's life? I thought it would be kind to take him in out of the cold."

Hector went to sit next to Ralph. He put his arm around him. "Poor bastard," he said. He patted Ralph on the back and rolled his cigarette between his teeth, looking pleased.

Amy was overjoyed. So! she thought madly. There was nothing to worry about after all. She ran outside to find Neil, crying, "Neil! Come back! Don't worry! Hector was wrong! Ralph didn't do it!" She realized she was shouting louder than she intended when the lights went on in the Duxbury house.

As she ran past the woodshed, she heard someone moaning inside. Opening the padlock, which still had the key in it, she found Aspasia tied and gagged. For one wicked moment, she thought she might just leave her there. But her better side won. She untied the rope around her hands.

"He's trying to kill me!" Aspasia said in a stage whisper as soon as she had taken the gag out of her mouth. "My own son!"

"Oh, stop being so melodramatic," Amy said. "He's just been drinking again."

"Something terrible is going to happen if he keeps on drinking like this," Aspasia insisted.

"He's been drinking like this his entire adult life, and nothing has happened yet," Amy said.

Still, Aspasia was too afraid to go into the kitchen where Hector would see her, so Amy smuggled her through the front door. Then she continued her search for Neil. She went to look for him in the Laceys' garden. Instead she found her Toblerones. They were lying in the flower beds underneath Ralph's window. Her Toblerones! There were eight of them left. She couldn't believe her luck. She gathered them up in her arms and rushed across the street to the house.

At the gate to her own house, she stopped and savagely tore one of them open. Just then she saw Susan Duxbury coming down the road, looking furious and self-righteous. Amy tried to pick up the seven remaining Toblerones with one hand, but a few of them fell, so she had to put the Toblerone she was eating into her mouth so as to have two hands for carrying the others. Then she had trouble opening the gate. She had to put the Toblerones into her arms again. She looked with panic up the road to see if Susan Duxbury had seen her. Susan Duxbury was standing right next to her.

Amy screamed. The chocolate nearly fell out of her mouth. She ran into her garden, slamming the gate in Susan's face. When she had taken refuge under the steps, she realized that she had done the wrong thing.

Susan Duxbury opened the gate, marched up the stairs to the front door, and rang the bell. For a long time, no one answered. Finally, Aspasia opened the door.

"What do you want?" she asked in her stage whisper. She was obviously enjoying playing cloak and dagger.

"I've come to take my husband home," said Susan.

"*Ssssshhhhh!* They're in the kitchen. But you better not go in there. My son's on the loose. He tried to kill me."

"Oh, my goodness!" said Susan Duxbury.

"Never mind, never mind. We're safe so long as I have this rifle. Come on in. I'll see if I can reach the other one. It's on the wall. Maybe if I stand on a chair."

After Aspasia closed the door, there was a silence. The next thing Amy heard was Hector shouting, "Charge!" Following this there were stampeding footsteps, women's screams, and laughter. Then it sounded as if they were all upstairs. Amy sneaked into the kitchen, her mouth still full of chocolate. Then she saw them coming back into the kitchen. She ran outside.

It was then that she heard the rabid gurgling in the pine forest, and her son's screams. She dropped her Toblerones and ran up to find him. He met her halfway.

"It bit me! It bit me!" he cried. "It just hung onto my leg. I couldn't get it off!"

She helped him back into the kitchen, trying hard to finish off the chocolate in her mouth before they got inside. There was still some left. She tried to store it in her left cheek. When she began to talk, it sounded as if she had cotton in her mouth.

"Now look what you've done!" she said to Hector. She pointed at the blood running down Neil's leg. His pajamas were ripped, and there was a deep gash.

"What?" Hector said.

"I said, now look what you've done to your son. And who's going to take us down to the rabies hospital, that's what I'd like to know. *You* can't. You'd drive the car right into the Bosphorus. It's enough to make me scream! It's the same old story. You play the life of the party and leave *me* to do the dirty work."

Hector turned to his friends. "What's she talking about?"

"Amy, do you have cotton in your mouth?" Meredith asked. "We can't hear you."

Amy angrily swallowed the last melting chunk of Toblerone. A nut caught in her throat. Everyone watched, puzzled, as she had a coughing fit. No one seemed to notice Neil's leg. That was some measure of how drunk they were.

"You people!" Amy said, when her coughing was under control. "I've had enough of your antics. I really have! Neil, you sit down and hold this rag on your leg. I'll go get the dressings from the bathroom."

But the bathroom door was locked. Susan Duxbury and Aspasia were inside. "Let us out!" Aspasia shouted. "If you don't let us out, we'll write a letter to the trustees!"

Usually the key was in the lock, but now it was missing. Amy went back into the kitchen. On her way in, she tripped over a rifle. Hector had the other one on his knees.

"Give me that rifle," Amy snapped. She took it and put it on top of the refrigerator. "You shouldn't be playing with rifles in your condition. And you shouldn't have taken the key to the bathroom, either. Hand it over." Hector looked at her blankly. "The key," Amy explained.

"What key?" Hector asked, completely bewildered.

"The key to the bathroom, where you locked up Aspasia and Susan."

"What are they doing in the bathroom?" Hector asked.

"You locked them in there."

Hector paused, as if he found this news upsetting. Then Donald laughed, and everyone else joined in.

"Now, where's the key?" Amy asked.

"They threw it out the window," Meredith said wearily. Everyone laughed. Hector looked around with a childish smile, delighted at the mirth he had caused. "How lucky I am," he said. "I have so many friends."

"Now, why did you lock those women in there?" Amy asked.

"You want to know why?" Hector asked. He grabbed

Amy by the collar of her robe. "Because they're both piece-of-shit donkey-turd sows."

"And how long do you plan to keep them in there?"

"I don't know," Hector said. He looked puzzled. "It depends on what their fate hangs on."

"And what does their fate hang on, may I ask?"

"A pubic hair," Hector said. He thought this was very funny, and so did the others. He rolled his cigarette between his teeth, dropping more ash. "A pubic hair sticking out of some underpants with a smile on the front."

He turned around abruptly, forgetting once again what he had just been talking about. Amy went through the kitchen drawers trying to find something to dress Neil's leg with. When she looked up, Hector was embracing Ralph. "How you doing, blueballs?" Hector said. He gave his audience a lopsided smile. His head bobbed back and forth. "It's amazing," he said. "I feel so proud. Amy, look. Look how many friends we have. Did you ever think we'd have so many friends?" Smiling proudly, he set his drink on the table, right on top of Neil's carefully folded flag. The drink tipped and spilled all over it. Neil jumped up. Sobbing, he limped over to the table to rescue his flag. When Hector saw he was crying, he looked surprised. "What's wrong?" he asked. "What happened to your leg?"

"There's a rabid dog out there that bit him, for God's sake," Amy said.

"A rabid dog?" Hector said. "In *my* garden? Why didn't you tell me? I can't let a piece-of-shit rabid dog in here! Something's got to be done about this." He got up, went over to the refrigerator, picked up the rifle, and headed toward the door. Amy got there before him and barred the way.

"You're not going out there with that rifle."

"Oh, yes, I am. Get out of my way.

"Oh, no you're not. You're too drunk. You might hurt yourself."

"I'm not drunk, you piece-of-shit frigid sow."

He turned to his friends. Leslie was falling asleep and Thomas and Donald were already snoring. Ralph was still sobbing. "You see this woman?" Hector said to them.

"You wouldn't know it unless I told you, but she's as frigid as a monkey's anus."

He tried to push Amy from the door. Amy struggled to hold her ground.

This was not the first time she had stood between him and one of his harebrained plans. Dealing with Hector at times like this was almost an art—saying the right thing at the right time, holding your tongue, being unobtrusive, always tactful and sensible, and, most important, trying to look at things as they would look the next day, keeping your sense of humor, laughing quietly to yourself, and remembering details to torture Hector with when he was hung over. If this was what that man called passive-aggressive behavior, Amy had one thing to say to him, and that was that it required great finesse.

But maybe he was right. Maybe she had been protecting him too much. Maybe she should just let him shoot his foot off, and then he'd learn his lesson. Why should she protect him when he treated her so badly? She allowed him to push her away from the door.

She watched him tramp off into the pine forest. What did he think he was, a big-game hunter? For all she cared, he could kill himself.

She went over to the kitchen table and sat across from Meredith, who was yawning. Meredith rubbed her eyes, and then pointed toward the kitchen sink. "There's your key, by the way."

"What key?" Amy asked.

"The key to the bathroom. It's lying on the dish rack. I guess they missed the window."

"Oh, that," said Amy, glancing over her shoulder. There it was.

"Aren't you going to let them out?"

"I suppose I'd better," Amy said. "And then I'm going to have to get Neil to the rabies hospital somehow. You don't happen to remember what time it opens, do you?"

"Oh, God, no," said Meredith. "It's been years since I was bitten."

What Amy remembered best about rescuing Aspasia and Susan from the bathroom was the one thing she had not seen: her face. What people must have thought of her, with her pinched, twisted lips, her unbrushed hair, her wild eyes. So this was sweet little Amy, long-suffering martyr. She had finally snapped and revealed her true nature.

She had told Aspasia where Hector was and why. When Aspasia had expressed concern, Amy had laughed at her. "Hah!" she had said. "He can blow his foot off for all I care.

"It's your fault, you know," Amy had continued, as she followed Aspasia down the stairs. (How had Aspasia felt at that moment? Amy remembered seeing her lips trembling.) "It's all your fault," she had repeated. "It's the way you brought him up. I hope you know that."

Aspasia had not answered. Amy later wondered why. Perhaps, she thought hopefully, she had not been listening. As soon as they were downstairs, Aspasia had gone straight for the rifles.

"Oh, for God's sake," Amy had said, as Aspasia headed for the door. "Don't you go out there, too. One lunatic in the pine forest is enough." But she had let her go out there anyway, because she didn't care what happened to her. She had watched her disappear into the half light, and listened to the sound of her feet thrashing through the underbrush. "You'd think they were stalking a deadly tiger," she had said to Meredith.

She was just biting into a new Toblerone when the gunshot sounded. She had just finished telling Meredith, who had not known she loved chocolate, that she loved it more than anything else in the whole world. She had not been concerned by the gunshot until she heard Hector wailing.

How had her face looked then? Later, she remembered it clearly, even though she had never actually seen it. Her eyes had dilated, her breathing had stopped, her mouth had untwisted as she opened it to scream.

She had rushed up to the pine forest to save him. He was the only one she was worried about. On the way up, she had tripped and fallen, and felt the earth caving away beneath her. A suitable punishment, she decided later, for a woman who had gambled everything in a fit of pique, and then lost.

V

Requiem

ASPASIA'S funeral was not the one she had planned, because the woman she had left the instructions with (Feza Akyol, the math department secretary) was away on vacation. Not away on vacation, strictly speaking, but away at a clinic in Switzerland, receiving treatment for a kidney problem at the expense of her three benefactors. But that was another story.

No one except Feza Akyol knew of the elaborate arrangements Aspasia had made with the Greek Orthodox Patriarchate, with Mr. Pistoff the undertaker, with Kirios Papastratou the choirmaster. So instead of being driven through the city in state, blessed and sung to by her own kind, and buried in the plot in Balikli—only a stone's throw from the shrine where Aspasia's mother had once given the Virgin Mary good silver in order that Aspasia might be placed under her protection—instead of receiving the honors that were her due, Aspasia received nothing more than a simple burial service at the little chapel in the Şişli Protestant Cemetery, at the end of which service two gruesome-looking Laz gravediggers burst into the chapel and dragged her coffin off to the cemetery, where they hurled it into the open grave. They placed her between a Mr. Hamilton Brown and a Mr. John Fish Eliot, both of whom had taught at Woodrow College in the twenties.

The whole thing was a farce. Donald Duxbury officiated. He didn't even pronounce her name right, and no one bothered to correct him. Meredith Lacey gave an elegy that betrayed how little she knew about the woman. The Turks in the congregation, most of whom did not know Aspasia well but who had come to give their dear friend Hector support in his hour of need, were appalled by the ungraciousness of the proceedings. They went away from the funeral feeling as if the deceased woman had not been given respect. They did not blame this on their dear friend Hector—they did not blame anything on Hector. Those who had heard rumors about Hector's involvement in the tragedy dismissed them out of hand. Rather than blame their dear friend Hector, who was, as always, beyond reproach, they blamed his wife and the minister, Donald Duxbury, who was, they all agreed, a typical missionary.

As they filed past Hector on that sad June afternoon, they assumed that his air of unconcern was a mask, behind which hid a truly grief-stricken son. They predicted that his would be a long period of mourning.

But the truth was that he hardly had a thought for Aspasia during that first half of the summer. Or so it seemed to Amy. This was not to say that his life continued as normal, for he kept to the house, avoided his friends, and refused, without explanation, to touch a drink. But within these new boundaries, his days were as carefree as a child's. Sometimes Amy felt she was doing the mourning for both of them.

Even before the funeral, there were clear signs that Hector was abdicating his responsibilities. When the lawyers called from Hartford to discuss the terms of Aspasia's will, he refused to be awoken, and so Amy had to do the talking. He also refused, on that first awful afternoon following the accident, to drive Neil and Amy to the rabies hospital. Not only did he refuse: he was indignant that Amy should have the gall to ask him. Couldn't she see that he was reading? Amy had no choice but to call a taxi.

The rabies hospital was a Dickensian monstrosity in the

old city, not far from the Blue Mosque. It was one of two places in the country where you could get the injections. If the idea of going all the way down there every other day for six weeks seemed a bore to you, and you told the nurse that you'd rather take your chances, they took you upstairs to see the wards where they kept the people who had not made it to the hospital in time. They were chained to their beds, these hopeless cases, screaming for mercy and frothing at the mouth, their eyes revolving in their sockets out of control. Or so Amy had been told. She and Neil could hear the wails of these unlucky victims from time to time as they stood in line with the lucky ones (some of whom were bandaged from head to foot), waiting for the nurses to prepare the serum.

They waited in a huge, vaulted ballroom that was painted a sickening green. The nurses' station was in the corner, hidden behind curtains. Even if you were at the very back of the line, you could hear everything. It was always the same. "What side?" the nurse would bark. "This side," the patient would answer. Then he would cry out, as if someone had punched him. He would emerge clutching his stomach.

"Next!" the nurse would say.

As Neil's turn approached, Amy would ask herself, Why me? What did I do to deserve this? In a just world, it would be Hector standing here, not me.

She would return home hot, shaken, and nauseous, to find Hector stretched out on the chaise longue with *The Mask of Demetrios*, or *The Five Red Herrings*, or *The Steam Pig*. "Hello," he would say pleasantly. "Did you remember to pick up the paper? Any interesting mail? What time is dinner? I'm famished. Why don't you send Kleoniki up with a snack." More than once, Amy had considered picking up a lamp and smashing him over the head with it. While she went through hell, never able to forget the things she might have done to save Aspasia but had not done out of spite, Hector had no thought for anyone but himself.

He refused to do anything unpleasant. He relegated letters of condolence to a desk drawer, sometimes without even reading them, and he ignored the increasingly frantic letters from Aspasia's lawyers, who needed his signature on various documents in order to proceed with probate. He stood to inherit three hundred thousand dollars, in addition to the Woodstock estate, but this was not incentive enough, it seemed. All he could think about was what game he would play next, and which child he could rope into playing with him.

What would it be? Vollyball? Badminton? A hand of bridge? If there was no one to play with, he resorted to brainteasers and crossword puzzles. When he ran out of these, he played solitaire. He would go on solitaire binges, playing nothing else for days on end. It was the solitaire that bothered Amy most—especially in the early hours of the morning, when the dealing and shuffling had reached a frantic speed and Hector took to cursing under his breath. No matter what approach Amy tried (sympathetic, rude, authoritarian, reaonable), Hector would refuse to come to bed. "Just a minute," he would say. "Just one more game." But he would still be at his desk when Amy woke up in the morning.

Hector was in the midst of one such binge on the morning Kleoniki made her discovery.

It was early August, about forty days after the funeral. Kleoniki had gone into Aspasia's bedroom to clean it out. While removing Aspasia' clothes from the closet, she stumbled onto the tombstone Aspasia had purchased and stored in her closet. It was shiny new marble, with a flattering photograph of the deceased inserted into a plastic-covered recess.

Summoned by her bloodcurdling scream, Hector had been nonplussed. After examining the tombstone with a detachment that verged on boredom, he wandered off to his study again to continue his game. He left Amy with the impossible job of calming down Kleoniki, who had rushed down to the kitchen and was sitting at the table muttering strange things under her breath and crossing herself repeatedly.

Being Greek herself, Kleoniki wanted Amy to go to the Patriarchate and get a priest who would exhume Aspasia's body and see if it had dissolved. Kleoniki was sure it had not dissolved. Aspasia had not received a proper burial, and if you did not receive a proper burial, your body did not dissolve. If she was right, Kleoniki said to Amy, it would be necessary to burn the remaining flesh off the bones. If they didn't do that, she said, Aspasia was going to come back to them as a *vrikolakas*, and they were all going to die.

Amy dismissed this as superstitious gobbledygook. The last thing she intended to do was exhume Aspasia's body. She wasn't even sure it wasn't against the law. Suicide was against the law in Turkey—perhaps exhumation was, too. When Kleoniki saw that Amy was going to do nothing to prevent Aspasia from coming back and haunting them, and dragging them one by one to the underworld, she showered her with curses. "When I tell your husband about this, he will beat you to a pulp," she said.

"Oh, he will, will he?" Amy retorted. "We'll see about that." Together they marched upstairs, only to find that Hector had fled his study. Terrified by the thought that Aspasia had already taken him off to the underworld, Kleoniki gathered up her things and left.

Was it cruel of Amy to subject Hector to the full venom of her frustrations when he reappeared toward noon (red-cheeked, bouncing a basketball) and asked her what she was making for lunch? Hindsight told her that she ought to have realized that the sight of the tombstone had been too much for him. But at the time all she could see was a selfish, lazy bastard where a knight in shining armor should have been, and all she could think was that she never wanted to see him again.

It was unfortunate that Leslie and Meredith were lunching on their balcony when Amy chased Hector out of the house. Blind to Amy's fear and pain, what they saw was a fishwife lacking only the proverbial rolling pin, hurling insults after a man she had already reduced to tears, who was begging her to stop as he stumbled down the cobblestone street with his hands over his ears.

He stayed away three days—no wonder, everyone said. When Theo found him wandering around Bebek on the fourth morning—feverish and coughing, his clothes torn and smelling like a bar, his eyes as blank as his memory—there was talk about keeping a close eye on Amy, lest she vent her wrath on the poor man again. But there was no need. Amy was contrite, so contrite that she could hardly find the strength to take care of him. Just the sight of him shivering pathetically under his bedcovers was enough to make her knees buckle. It was lucky, in a way, that Hector's fever worsened, because it was Dr. Ibrahim who rescued Amy from her remorse and showed her how to be strong again.

Dr. Ibrahim was a strange-looking man. Short, with luminous green eyes and an oversized head, he wore a child's windbreaker with the hood tightly tied beneath his chin. When he appeared for the first time at the Cabots' door, clutching his imitation-leather briefcase, Chloe mistook him for one of those deaf mutes who came around every so often to solicit charitable donations. She told him (rudely) that her mothr was out and that she herself had no money to give him. Amy was mortified.

He brushed aside her apologies gracefully, although his eyes betrayed a flicker of pain. This was the first thing that impressed Amy: she saw in him a kindred spirit, a man who suffered ridicule with dignity. Since she had a weakness for doctors anyway, it was inevitable that she came to have a crush on him, even if this crush proved short-lived. He became, for a few hours, the hero she longed for. This was why she broke down and told him everything.

How cruel the children were during the interview. While she and Dr. Ibrahim sat in the living room, they eavesdropped from the piano room, doubled over with silent laughter and occasional not-so-silent guffaws. This was on account of Dr. Ibrahim's stilted English. (He had trained in France.) He pronounced the word invalid as if he were talking about an expired driver's license. He said nourish instead of nurse, chock instead of shock, griff instead of grief, pillules instead of pills. "First a programme of slipping pillules and obscurity in the bedroom," he said, "supplemented by generous alimentation. We shall follow this programme until the chock and griff have abated to acceptable nivels. *Ensuite* . . . how are you saying it in English . . . no matter, it makes nothing . . . *ensuite*, we shall permit occasional ambulation and simple domestic amusements in bed. As his nourish, you shall be charged with the tasks of guiding and perhaps overpowering him if he is too naughty. I should add that I am always ready to lend you a helping hand. Please remember that I am eternally your faithful servant. Your wish is my commandment.

"Consider yourself an illusionist. Utilize your female

wiles to create an ambiance of everyday life. A routine that is simple and cheerful will coax your husband out of his depressment."

Amy followed Dr. Ibrahim's advice as meticulously as if she herself were an invalid. She overfed and pampered her husband, turned away guests, and talked to him like a child. Her dearest wish was that he return to the pastimes that had once aggravated her so. She was overjoyed, therefore, when he got out of bed one day and went into his study to play solitaire. This, she thought, was a step in the right direction. How times had changed!

Reassured by Hector's progress, Amy set about looking for a new maid. This proved difficult, because Kleoniki had been terrifying all Rumeli Hisar with stories about the return of Aspasia in the form of a *vrikolakas*. Having heard that Amy (born on a Saturday) was herself a *vrikolakas* and that she had murdered Aspasia for her money (which amounted to no less than a million dollars), the women of Rumeli Hisar were reluctant to walk past the Cabot house, let alone work in it. In the end, the only woman who would agree to come was a peasant woman fresh out of the Anatolian heartland, who had just moved into the shantytown in the hills behind the college. Since the Rumeli Hisar women looked down on the shantytown women, this new maid, whose name was Meliha, had not heard about the scandal.

Meliha was a good woman, although she had her faults. Being fresh out of the Anatolian heartland, she was not accustomed to the conveniences of modern living, and every time she came into contact with one of them, she broke something. Amy could not even remember how many toilet seats they went through that August. Meliha insisted on standing on them. And every time the doorbell rang, Meliha cried out in alarm and dropped one of Amy's crystal glasses, until finally there were no more crystal glasses left.

Meliha was a diligent worker. There was nothing she loved more than getting down on her hands and knees with a bucket of soapy water. But she took it too far. No matter how Amy pleaded with her, she insisted on washing the armchairs every day, so that they were never dry, and she scrubbed the hardwood floors so hard that soon they were warped and waxless. She also made yogurt, which she would wrap in blankets and store overnight in closets and every so often forget there. But Amy did not hold these things against her, because she knew it was Meliha's innocence that made the house feel like a normal one.

Meliha found nothing disturbing in the fact that Hector spent the day in his robe and slippers, his hair uncombed, his skin as white as alabaster, his eyes never straying from the brainteasers, crossword puzzles, and card games on his desk. She assumed that this was how all American men acted. She accepted him with the same puzzled smile with which she accepted the inexplicable purring of the refrigerator, the howling of the vacuum cleaner, and the galloping horse inside the washing machine.

Because Hector never looked up when she entered the study, she assumed he was asleep in his chair. She would squat next to the desk in that peculiarly Anatolian way and scrub the floor around his feet, pausing every so often to look up at him, her face transformed by awe. She was equally respectful of Amy, but once again this was because she was unable to interpret what she saw. She did not know, for example, that the water bottle in the door of the refrigerator that Amy took frequent, hurried swigs from actually contained vodka.

Such was the state of affairs when Feza Akyol, the math department secretary, returned from her Swiss clinic.

When she discovered that Aspasia had died and been buried by the wrong people in the wrong place, she was hysterical. She blamed herself for the misunderstanding, although of course she had had no idea when she left that Aspasia would die in her absence. She went straight to the Cabots' house to break the news to Hector, but she, like so many visitors before her (Thomas, Leslie, Ralph, Theo, Phillip Best), was refused entry.

"Why don't you tell *me,*" Amy said. And so she did.

When Feza finished her story, Amy sighed, as if the whole thing was a big nuisance. Feza never failed to be surprised at how often Americans dismissed important family obligations as nuisances. There were some things you had to do, no matter what the personal cost, and this included honoring the wishes of the dead. Exactly how these particular wishes were to be honored was something Feza could not say, but she had hoped that Amy would provide helpful suggestions, that she would at least hire a priest to say a prayer over the grave. Feza was not well acquainted with Christian customs, but she was sure that some ritual existed that was appropriate for the circumstances.

Amy, however, said that she did not want to do a thing until Hector "recovered." "And I'm sure that when that time comes, he will agree with me that it is better, in the end, just to let the dead rest in peace," she told Feza. "In the meantime, I would be grateful if you did not mention this unfortunate problem to anyone else. Hector is having a hard enough time as it is." She had taken the envelope and put it into one of Hector's desk drawers.

Feza had done her best to honor Amy's wishes, but it was too upsetting a secret to keep bottled up inside forever. Before long, she had told the whole story to her nearest and dearest friends, both of whom were also unmarried secretaries working on campus. The friends proceeded to tell their nearest and dearest, who went on to repeat the story to their not so nearest and dearest, until there was hardly a student or a secretary who was not aware of the tragic misunderstanding.

Feza's story only made them feel sorrier for Hector than before. They pitied him for having such an insensitive wife, and they pitied him because they did not think he deserved the additional suffering he would have to endure when he discovered the true story. They were happy, at least, that he would emerge from this tragedy a multimillionaire.

And so the summer came to an end without Hector showing his face. Everyone agreed that life without him was exceedingly dull. They all despaired at not being able to help him through the difficult mourning period. They all looked forward to the day when he would emerge from mourning and once again be himself.

VI

Storm Without A Center

Autumn 1969

THE first repercussions of Hector's failure to be himself were felt at the office.

That September, a young man name Halûk Yildizoğlu —a former student of Hector's—returned from America to take up an associate professorship in Hector's department. He arrived in Istanbul completely unaware of the events of the summer. His last letter from Hector had been the one in which Hector had congratulated him on his wise decision to return to Woodrow College and expressed enthusiasm about the prospect of having Halûk as his colleague. This letter had reached Halûk in May.

Hector Cabot was such an important figure in Halûk life that Halûk sometimes forgot he did not hold an equally important position in Hector's. He sometimes allowed his imagination to get carried away, and this was what happened on the airplane. He arrived in Istanbul half expecting to see Hector waiting for him in the airport lobby with a bottle of champagne. When he did not see Hector, Halûk was not so much disappointed as returned to earth. It had been silly of him to expect a man with so many responsibilities to travel all the way out to Yeşilköy when they were going to be living practically next door to one another.

Hector was probably waiting to greet them at their new home, Halûk decided, but he was not. There was no bowl of fruit, no bouquet of flowers, no message, no sign that Hector had even remembered that this was the day Halûk was to move in. In the days that followed, there was not even a visit from Hector's wife. It slowly became clear to Halûk that something terrible had happened over the summer.

Halûk made discreet inquiries. He soon discovered that Hector's mother had died over the summer—in unusual circumstances, someone said, but that someone refused to go into any detail out of respect for Hector's privacy. Halûk also discovered that Hector had been in seclusion since the tragedy. That was all he could find out for sure. There were stories, needless to say—stories about a rifle, stories about an improper burial, stories about a fistfight in the street— but Halûk discounted them as the idle concoctions of servants.

There was one rumor about a wicked dogcatcher taking his revenge on Hector by planting a rabid dog in his garden—apparently, Hector had once humiliated the man in public. There was another, even more preposterous story about Hector's mother being attacked by a rabid dog while meeting secretly in the garden with her lover. The Yildizoğlus' own maid, who lived within earshot of the Cabots, had the worst story of all, and after she told it to Halûk for the first time, he scolded her and instructed her never to speak that way about Hector Cabot again.

What the maid said was that one night in June, Hector had been possessed by an evil spirit. He had torn off his clothes and run through the streets of Rumeli Hisar naked. Then, the following midnight, he had danced in and out of his house like a crazy person. He was defiling an American flag, the maid said, and when he heard the sound of a rabid dog in the garden, he had hailed him as a brother and gone out to embrace him. His mother had gone out with a rifle to save him. But he was so crazed that he had turned the rifle against her. She had died on the spot.

The maid explained Hector's bizarre behavior the same

way she explained the ever-growing rudeness of taxi drivers and the declining quality of bread. *Vah, vah, vah,* she would say, shaking her head, things have never been the same since the man landed on the moon.

Whatever truth there was in these stories, and Halûk was sure there was not very much, it was clear that a rabid dog had been involved. Each story, no matter how far-fetched, referred in one way or another to a rabid dog in Hector's garden. This made Halûk ashamed for his country. In what Western nation were rabid dogs allowed to roam the streets unchecked? That a distinguished professor, a brilliant man who could have risen to uncharted heights in his own country but who had chosen instead to devote his life to Turkey, that a man of this caliber should have been left open to an attack by a rabid dog, purely because of municipal negligence—this made Halûk furious. If he had been able to find out exactly what had happened, and therefore been sure of not causing further embarrassment, Halûk would have gone to Hector and apologized himself.

Halûk Yildizoğlu was a man in his early thirties. His family was from Mardin, in the east of Turkey, where they owned a number of mines, but Halûk himself had been brought up in Ankara, where his father had practiced as a lawyer. Halûk was tall for a Mardinli. Unfortunately for him, because he had never harmed anyone, he looked like a European's idea of a Barbary pirate. He had curly, jet black hair, fierce brown eyes, a hooked nose, an engaging smile, and an aristocratic bearing that had become somewhat less pronounced after seven years in Cambridge, Massachusetts.

He had been in Cambridge studying for his doctorate in mathematics at MIT, while his wife, Yasemin, studied for her doctorate in psychology at Harvard. It was on Hector's advice that he had decided to continue his studies in America after completing his military service. (His family had wanted him to go into business with his uncle, who owned several factories.)

And it was at Hector's invitation that he had decided to return to Turkey once they had earned their degrees. It had been a difficult decision, because both Halûk and Yasemin had been offered lucrative positions in America. But once they had made up their minds, they were both certain they had done the right thing. They had never seen their education in America simply as a furthering of their own careers, but also as a way of bringing foreign expertise back to Turkey.

And so they had returned to Istanbul in September 1969, Halûk to take up an associate professorship in Hector's own department, and Yasemin to teach psychology at her alma mater, the American College for Girls.

Wishing to make their return as pleasant as possible, Yasemin's family bought them an apartment in Rumeli Hisar that had a beautiful view of the Bosphorus. When Halûk first heard how close this apartment was to the Cabots', his imagination went wild with idyllic visions—visions of walking to and from classes with Hector, visions of leaving the office together on Friday afternoons and going down to Nazmi's for a beer, and on the way discussing all the new ideas that had come Halûk's way during his seven-year absence (during which time Halûk had had many imaginary conversations with Hector, whose responses to Halûk's dilemmas had been, without fail, wise, measured, and reassuring). He had imagined other simple pleasures: spur-of-the-moment trips to the seaside, afternoons when Hector happened to have something on his mind and dropped by for some *raki* and pistachio nuts. And other days, when they were less thoughtful and both had *keyif*, Halûk imagined the two of them jumping into a *dolmuş* and going downtown to drink at the Pasaj for a few hours. They would sit across from each other at a table next to the window, slowly sipping their enormous *Arjantins*, two men taking a break from the pressures of work and family, sharing plates of *börek* and fried mussels and white goat's cheese and stuffed grape leaves and all the other succulent foods Halûk had dreamt of so often during his cold, lonely years in Cambridge.

But apparently, this was not to be.

A few days before registration, Emin Bey, who was also a former teacher of Halûk's, and who was now, as head of the mathematics department, to be his boss, invited Halûk and his wife to dinner. He told Halûk that he had invited everyone in the department, and so it was at this gathering that Halûk hoped to finally see Hector.

Although he had felt very much the foreigner while in America, his long stay there had changed him in ways that he was only becoming aware of now that he was back in Turkey. One of these changes could be described as an increased preference for informality. Because of this, Halûk had grown deaf to certain social nuances. When Emin Bey had assure him that the dinner was to be "small and informal," Halûk had failed to recognize that Emin Bey had said this out of polite self-deprecation. He was, as Halûk remembered later, said to be a gracious and extremely generous host. But for some reason, Halûk had forgotten what people had told him about Emin Bey and his wife, and so he did what he would never have done before going to America: he took Emin Bey at face value. He dressed for the dinner party the same way he would have dressed for a Sunday afternoon barbecue in one of his MIT professors' backyards. A pair of jeans—his new ones, thank God—and loafers, and the first T-shirt that came to hand when he opened his drawer. What a fool he had been. The only thing he was thankful for was that he had let Yasemin talk him out of wearing his high-top sneakers. She had been right all along—she had wanted to wear a lovely silk dress and her new burgundy high-heeled shoes that matched her purse, but he had stupidly forced her to change into jeans like him. It was simply that he had forgotten what thought and care his compatriots gave to their dress.

But there was so much he had forgotten. Almost every experience included a rude awakening, and the Sunday of Emin Bey's dinner party was no exception. Because it was a beautiful afternoon, they decided to walk down through Rumeli Hisar and then along the Bosphorus to Bebek. The road down to the shore was cobblestoned. They had forgotten how difficult it was to walk on cobblestones, and how dirty these cobblestone roads could be. They remembered the fresh breeze that met them when they reached the shore, but not the pungent smell of donkey manure that accompanied them down the hill.

The pavement along the Bosphorus was teeming with young urchins clothed in scanty rags, sunbathing, swimming, and shouting obscenities at Yasemin. He tried to protest their rudeness, but he ended up making a fool of himself. He was outnumbered. "Did it used to be like this?" he asked Yasemin. She shook her head sadly. Like her husband, all week long she had been regretting their decision to return to Istanbul. Like her husband, she felt duty-bound not to admit it.

Emin Bey lived in a spectacular apartment tucked away in the hills outside the town of Bebek, on a meandering road known as Ayşesultan Sokaği. It was Emin Bey's wife's money that had bought them the apartment house (for they owned the entire building), as well as the expensive foreign cars parked in the garage, not to mention the thirty-five-foot yacht that was moored at the foot of the hill.

This wife, whose name was Roksan, was known to be spoiled. Because she had spent her early childhood in Paris, she did not really consider herself Turkish. She spoke all languages—Turkish, English, German—with a French accent, and she regarded her two annual trips to Paris as necessary to maintain her sanity. While their two daughters were at home, it was said that the only reason Emin Bey stayed with Roksan was because of the children. Now that they were married with children of their own, it was said that he only stayed with Roksan because of her money. And this was why, they said, she was able to twist him around her finger.

But when he ushered Halûk and Yasemin into his apartment that Sunday evening, Emin Bey gave every indication of being a man whose mastery over his destiny had never once been challenged.

He was dressed, as Halûk noticed with a sinking heart, in a perfectly cut black suit, the likes of which Halûk had not seen during his entire stay in America. His wife, Roksan, stood behind him elegant in a dress of violet silk, her bleached-blonde hair piled up on her head in a bun of well-sprayed curls. Halûk was mortified and quickly blurted out an apology for his casual appearance, which Emin Bey brushed aside with a frozen smile. He ushered them into the living room, where Professor and Mrs. Edison, as well as Betül Hanim, were already seated.

Professor Edison was an ungainly man in his midforties. He came from Montana and walked as if he had been brought up on a horse. He was tall with hunched shoulders. His pants were always too short, and his socks unlikely colors such as yellow and green and red. His chest was reputed to be hairless, but his legs, as every student saw when he sat down on his desk during lectures, were hairy beyond expectation. There was a story, passed down to Halûk by upperclassmen, that Mrs. Edison had once made him shave them.

Halûk remembered Mrs. Edison as being equally ungainly. She was tall and gaunt, with feet so big she looked like Popeye's wife. She set her own hair and it was full of bobby-pin marks. But today, Halûk noticed with a shock, neither she nor her husband looked that different from the people he had worked with at MIT.

It was an even worse shock to see Betül Hanim. Until now, his imagination had dwelt on the more pleasant aspects of his new job, namely, proximity to Hector, rather than on the drawbacks. Now memories came flooding back to him, not only of Professor Edison, with whom Halûk had always been on correct terms, but also of Betül Hanim, with whom Halûk's relations had been of a more childish nature.

Betül Hanim was an extraordinarily ugly woman. Thin and wiry, without an ounce of soft flesh on her, her face and arms were covered with moles, which was why her students called her "the leopard" behind her back. She was a brittle woman who did not take kindly to practical jokes, to the perpetual delight of her students. Halûk himself had once put a live mouse into her desk drawer. It had almost given her a heart attack. He had also once put a joke cushion on her chair, one that farted when she sat down on it, and another time he had suspended a toy spider from the ceiling with a thread. She had not suspected Halûk of being the perpetrator: in fact, the poor woman had almost seemed to have a crush on him. Like many spinsters, Betül Hanim was gullible. Halûk remembered in particular the afternoon when he had convinced her, with the help of two friends, that his grandfather was Chinese.

And now this woman was to be his colleague.

He greeted her with warmth and sat down in the straightbacked chair next to her, but she was not very friendly. First Halûk thought it was because she had discovered the truth about his grandfather, the mouse, the joke cushion, and the spider. Then he gathered from her remarks that she was distressed by his clothing. But what Halûk could not understand was why she kept peering with alarm into the mirror that hung on the wall behind their chairs. Curiosity made Halûk look around himself to see what was the matter, but he could not find anything out of the ordinary. So he continued with their polite conversation, which he hoped would set the tone for their future relationship.

First Halûk made the required speech about how happy he was to have the privilege to teach at his alma mater.

"Well, it *is* a pleasure to welcome you back into the fold," said Betül Hanim, in her loud British accent—she had trained in England during the thirties. "But I do hope you won't be using the podium as a pulpit from which to preach revolution."

"But of course not!" he protested. "It would be a shame to use the classroom for political discussions, and anyway, my ideas are far from revolutionary."

"Well, *that's* good," Betül Hanim said. She did not sound convinced. "Because, you know, we've had far too much trouble already with the likes of you. The situation is volatile to begin with. I am glad to hear you intend to keep your politics to yourself."

"As I said, this goes without saying," said Halûk. "And additionally, I doubt my ideas would be of much interest to my students."

"I'm sure," Betül Hanim said dubiously, and she gazed once again into the mirror behind Halûk's back. It was at this point that it suddenly dawned on him what she was looking at. He felt like kicking himself in the head for dressing so carelessly.

While Halûk sat, perplexed, trying to think of some polite way to explain his *faux pas* without drawing undue attention to it, Emin Bey listened for the sound of Hector's Citroen and tried not to glance at his watch. Where could Hector be? When they had spoken the previous week, Hector had seemed happy to accept Emin Bey's invitation. But Emin Bey was the first to admit that appearances could sometimes be deceptive.

Emin Bey and Hector had not spoken since their argument about Nikolai Kadinsky's houseboy. Emin Bey now wanted to kick himself for his tactlessness. He had tried to make amends. When he had heard of Hector's mother's untimely death, he had written a letter of condolence, but to this he had received no answer. He took Hector's silence to mean that he had still not forgiven Emin Bey for his rudeness. And it was true. Emin Bey had not behaved in a correct fashion.

All summer, Emin Bey had waited for some sign from Hector to show that his anger had cooled, but to no avail. Now it was almost time for the new school year to start, and it was essential that the senior members of the department set a good example. Furthermore, Emin Bey felt genuinely sorry for his behavior, and he sorely missed Hector's company. And so it was to bring about a reconciliation that he had thought up the pretext of a departmental dinner.

Of course, he had been equally sincere in his stated intention for the dinner party. That was to welcome young Halûk into the department. Emin Bey had always liked Halûk. As a student, Halûk had been quick, cooperative, and respectful. A nice boy who came from a good family, even if it was true that they originated from Mardin. It did not matter. When Halûk had married Yasemin—who happened to be Emin Bey's niece—Emin Bey had been one of the few family members to applaud the union. Now he wished to do everything in his power to help Halûk make the difficult transition from student to colleague.

But the moment he saw Halûk and Yasemin standing on his doorstep dressed in blue jeans, he knew he had made a miscalculation. Something had happened to this boy in America. He had changed. Although his apologies for his appearance had seemed sincere, his behavior ever since had been shifty. He had refused, for example, to get out of his seat, even when that meant that his wife was left standing. At another point he had mystified everybody by asking his wife for her cardigan and wrapping it around his shoulders, when in fact it was a very warm evening. Although Emin Bey had tried to direct the conversation to topics that might be of interest to him, Halûk had not paid much attention. His thoughts were elsewhere. Once or twice, he had seemed on the verge of making some statement, only to withdraw into his thoughts again. He had asked, several times, if Emin Bey was sure Hector was coming, as if he had received information to the contrary. Hector and Halûk were, after all, practically next-door neighbors. Emin Bey asked himself, therefore, if there might have been a special reason why Halûk had come to his dinner party improperly dressed.

It was not that Emin Bey himself enjoyed formal occasions. He would have preferred to live like a fisherman, protecting himself from the elements with nothing more than a rugged pullover, eating fish so fresh that they were still jumping when they fell into the pan, passing his evenings in coffee houses playing backgammon. Although he loved their garden, especially in the spring, when it became a sea of graceful tulips, and although he was sustained by their view of the Bosphorus, Emin Bey hated the apartment itself. This was his wife's domain. The furniture was luxurious but uncomfortable. The light from the imitation *Dolmabahçe* chandelier was harsh. The coffee tables and bookcases were cluttered with porcelain figurines, and ashtrays from famous Swiss and Parisian restaurants. It was impossible to make a grand gesture in this room without breaking something. Were it not for his concern for his wife's precarious social standing (it was not easy to be a middle-aged woman in Turkey these days—almost all her friends had been abandoned by their husbands for young girls), Emin Bey would have moved out in a second and happily taken up residence on his yacht.

But despite his love of sincerity and spontaneity, despite his flair for the generous gesture, despite the allowances he made for people he regarded as his equals, Emin Bey had narrower ideas when it came to younger men, especially younger men who he suspected of being more knowledgeable, or at least more up to the moment, in his own field of mathematics. His first thought had been to question what Halûk meant to say to him by wearing blue jeans to such an occasion. Was it simply a personal gesture of contempt, or did it have more far-reaching implications? Perhaps Halûk was intending to dress in this manner in order to make a political statement.

Like almost everywhere else in the world, the students at Woodrow College had become increasingly rebellious during the past few years. They had been insisting lately that they should have a voice in the administration of the college. Being for the most past Leftist and anti-American, they wished the college to sever its ties with the U.S. There were frequent political forums in the college auditorium, at which all shades of Leftist ideology were represented. There were Maoists and Stalinists and Socialists and Trotskyites and Guevarists. There were those who favored a program of political education and those who advocated direct political action. Despite their many differences, these groups had recently formed a coalition known as *Dev Genç,* for which group some of the younger faculty had shown sympathy, if not actual support. So far, Emin Bey had not had this trouble in his own department, but now he foresaw that he might start having problems of this nature with Halûk.

The irony was that Emin Bey shared many of the students' anti-imperialist, anti-capitalist beliefs. He did not like the way his country, once great, had become the pawn of the superpowers. He did not think Turkey had been adequately rewarded for its loyalty to Washington. Like any good Socialist, he dreamed of the day when there would be one hundred percent literacy, thriving universities in even the most backward provinces, and an elimination of the differences between rich and poor. Most of all, he longed for the day when the angry hordes would break into his father-in-law's ivory tower and throw him to the dogs. But these were ideas he kept to himself, except for the occasional evening when the turn of events became too painful for him and he shared his private thoughts with Hector.

The rest of the time he kept them to himself because, unlike his students, he understood the contradictions of his position. How could he continue to work at an American institution if he were to make public his anti-American ideas? How could he continue to take money from his wife if he were to preach the demise of capitalism? And even if he left his job and his wife tomorrow, it would still be impossible for him to be frank about his beliefs, out of loyalty to the people who had innocently supported an ingrate for so many years. It was an unbearable predicament, and the source of unending tension, tension that only went away when he and Hector escaped down to the Pasaj for a few hours, or when he untied his mooring ropes, pulled up anchor, and pointed his yacht in the direction of the Marmara Sea.

Every summer until this summer, he and Hector had gone away on a fishing trip to the Marmara Islands. Now it seemed that such pleasures were things of the past. Although he continued to play the perfect host, apologizing for the delay in serving dinner, insisting that his guests partake of the pretentious hors d'oeuvres his wife had put out on the coffee table, Emin Bey's head was full of sad memories. Who would have guessed that it would all be over so soon? he asked himself. For with each minute that passed, it became more obvious that Hector had decided never to forgive him.

When the phone call came, Emin Bey was not at all surprised.

It was not Hector at the other end of the line, but Amy. This fact alone was significant. She told Emin Bay a half-baked story about laryngitis. The fact that the story was so transparent, together with the fact that the call could have been made hours earlier, were further indications to Emin Bey of the strength of Hector's reluctance to make peace.

Emin Bey remained collected, assuring Amy that she had not called too late, and asked her to extend his best wishes to her husband. But as soon as he put down the receiver, he was overwhelmed with shame. If they had only made the phone call earlier, Emin Bey could have glossed things over. Now it was going to be clear to everyone that there was a serious rift.

He returned to the living room and cast a miserable eye over his guests. He felt as desolate as if he had been standing on a tower surrounded by lifeless marshes. What did he have in common with these people? Who, besides Hector, was a friend? Not Betül Hanim, certainly. He had inherited her, unwillingly, with the department. She reminded him of a gargoyle, and whenever he talked with her he felt the impatience of a young man who has been forced to abbreviate his social schedule in order to pay his respects to a maiden aunt. Toward Joe Edison and his wife, Emin Bey felt pure contempt. They were the worst kind of Americans—clumsy, raw-boned, oblivious to social nuances, and so unattractive that the idea of the two of them making love sent shivers down Emin Bey's spine.

The only eyes in which he detected the faintest sympathy were Halûk's. When he saw this, Emin Bey's heart warmed to the poor fellow. He saw that he had been judging the boy too harshly. Of course. The poor boy was merely disoriented after his studies in America. It would take him time to adjust. Emin Bey understood completely, because he himself had once been in an identical position.

As soon as Emin Bey had said what needed to be said to his wife, he pulled up a chair next to Halûk, put his arm around his shoulder, and said, "I see that you are still feeling uncomfortable. I insist that you put the matter of your clothing out of your mind."

"Oh, you are very kind," said Halûk, "because I honestly . . ."

Emin Bey put up his hand. "There is no need for any discussion. Everything is understood. The important thing is to relax and enjoy the evening. I insist."

Halûk looked relieved.

"I am afraid I have some bad news, however. It seems that our friend Hector will not be joining us. A case of laryngitis, it seems."

At this Emin Bey sighed, and to Halûk it was a sigh that seemed laden with hidden significance, a sigh that confirmed his worst suspicions. Obviously, in some unknown way, Halûk had offended Hector, and that was why he had been avoiding him, and why he had decided not to attend Emin Bey's dinner party. The laryngitis was merely a pretext—this much was clear.

Since Emin Bey was being so friendly, Halûk decided to inquire about Hector's mother. Perhaps Emin Bey knew the true story. Struggling to keep his voice from trembling, Halûk said, "I understand that there have been unpleasant situations this summer, and that because of them our friend has been under the weather."

"Unpleasant, yes, but for whom, I should ask," said Betül Hanim. "As I understand it, the entire affair was Hector's fault from start to finish. I shouldn't wonder that he's feeling thoroughly ashamed of himself now. Americans are always so surprising, don't you think? I'd no idea, for example, that his mother was Greek. Not just Greek, mind you, but one of *our* Greeks. A Phanariot. Her father had a taverna on the islands, someone said. I take it you knew about this?" she said, turning to Halûk. "You don't seem surprised."

Halûk, who had not heard this, bowed his head to indicate that he was familiar with the story. "Yes," he said. "And I understand that she was also involved in the unfortunate occurrences last spring.

"Well, she died," Betül Hanim said, "if that's what you mean."

"There was a story. . . ." Halûk said vaguely. He gave Emin Bey an anxious look, hoping that Emin Bey would take this opportunity to tell him what he knew.

But Emin Bey misunderstood his intentions. Emin Bey took Halûk's words to be an insinuation about Emin Bey's failure to be a good host to Hector's mother.

So . . . said Emin Bey to himself. So. Halûk understood the problem in its entirety. He had heard the story from the horse's mouth. He had probably known all along that Hector had never intended to join them this evening.

Emin Bey felt ashamed. Because it was true: he had acted without forethought and deserved to be treated shabbily as a consequence. He was thankful that Halûk had been kind enough to explain the situation to him in an oblique manner so as to spare him further humiliation in front of his guests. He chided himself for judging the boy so harshly. Halûk had changed in appearance, perhaps, but his heart was still in its place.

Then something happened that made Emin Bey realize that he had made another gross miscalculation.

"To be very frank," Halûk said to Emin Bey, "I have heard so many stories about Hector's mother's unpleasant experiences last spring that I cannot make head nor tail of them. I was wondering if I could ask you to give me a reliable version. I am sure that you are in a position to know more than anyone."

Halûk, who was closer to tears than he had been in years, mustered a smile. Like many insincere smiles, it was toothy and stiff. His eyes were glistening with tears.

Emin Bey was shocked when he heard Halûk's words. Halûk was not trying to help him after all. No, now he was taunting him, trying to cause him additional humiliation.

Once again, Emin Bey had foolishly laid himself open to ridicule. He looked up, hoping to be proven wrong by Halûk's expression, but there he was, hunched over in his chair, his hands clasped in false concern, his mouth stretched into an insolent smile, his eyes glistening with contempt.

It was at this point that Emin Bey's wife rose from her chair and invited the guests into the dining room. She had made French food, against his will. The table was laid with her finest silver and china.

Halûk jumped to his feet and took Betül Hanim's arm to escort her through. Emin Bey was thus saved from Halûk's insolent questions. But he followed his guests into the dining room with the distinct impression that this had only been the first round. For some reason, Halûk had decided to destroy his position, to ruin his reputation, to crush him. Was it ambition, Emin Bey asked himself, or was it something more far-reaching? Seeing for the first time what was printed on the back of Halûk's T-shirt, Emin Bey had an answer to this question.

Although it was partially concealed under the cardigan that Halûk had draped over his shoulders, Emin Bey could make out a crudely designed clenched fist. The slogan printed beneath the fist was smudged but still legible: POWER TO THE PEOPLE. As Emin Bey took his place at the head of the table, he was barely able to contain his rage.

Meanwhile, Hector was at home in bed, sipping weak tea and staring at the lump in the covers created by his feet. He looked deathly pale, as if he had just seen a ghost. And in a way, he had.

It had been a bad day. From the moment he had woken up that morning, he had been dreading the dinner at Emin

Bey's: an obstacle course he did not feel ready for. To calm his nerves, he had kept to his invalid's routine of card games and crossword puzzles, under the annoyingly watchful eye of Amy. Between games, he would remember, with dread, the piles of unanswered letters and unsigned legal documents in his study. He would remind himself that he had yet to make up his mind about the blood money coming to him from his mother's estate. He would wonder about his father. Was he still in Istanbul? If he was, why hadn't he gotten in touch? Then Hector would remember, with rising panic, the envelope he had discovered in his desk drawer.

This envelope contained his mother's funeral instructions, and they had confirmed what had been worrying him all along. He had buried his mother in the wrong place and now he had no idea what to do about it.

Amy said not to do a thing. It was too late, she said. Still, Hector knew that his mother would have appreciated some small token of her true faith at her graveside—a candle at the very least. And he had not even taken her any flowers.

And here it was, the middle of September. The school year (that storm cloud looming on the horizon) was less than a week away. Time was running out. Glancing at his watch, he had counted silently: only five, four, three, two, one more hour left until the showdown at Emin Bey's.

It was not the company Hector dreaded. It was the presence of alcohol, and the unbending view of the host. Emin Bey had no time for teetotalers, who he dismissed as effeminate missionaries. A true man, he thought, should be equal to the challenge of alchohol, without having to resort to what he called "ridiculous health measures." He would insist on Hector having one small *raki*. "Just one, for the sake of hospitality." "Just one, for your good friend." "Just one, to keep me company." But Hector couldn't risk even that. He had only one memory of his most recent binge, and that was going into the Divan Bar for "one small *raki*."

God only knew how much *raki* he had ended up having there, or where he had spent the next three days. If he wanted to stay alive, if he cared about his family and his friends and his work, he could never drink again. But he despaired of making Emin Bey understand this. The only way he was going to get out of a drink at Emin Bey's was by inventing a liver condition.

Why did Emin Bey have to be so imperious, so overbearing? The prospect of having to lie to his friend depressed Hector. If he had to lie to him, could he even call the man his friend? A friend was someone you could relax with, someone who accepted you as you were. And this—he could see it already—was turning into a masquerade. Disgusted, Hector abandoned his card game and went out onto the balcony. The view, which he usually found so inspiring, today seemed to be closing in on him like prison walls. He longed to step onto a plane and leave all this behind him, start all over again somewhere else.

He sat down on the lawn chair and picked up the *International Herald Tribune*, which was open to the crossword page. Unfolding it, he glanced at the opposite page and noticed a short article about a journalist who had been killed in Vietnam while researching a feature story on the Ho Chi Minh Trail. The journalist was almost exactly his age, and the picture looked familiar, even though the name did not.

Where had he seen this face before? After reviewing the various chapters of his life, Hector came up with an answer that satisfied him: they had been at college together. He was not quite sure if they had lived in the same dormitory or merely taken a course together. But he did remember dismissing the fellow as a nothing.

How wrong he had been, as this article proved. The man's death at thirty-nine was the culmination of a long and distinguished career as a war correspondent. He had spent his life in the center of things. He had died while pursuing the truth. It was Hector who had turned out to be a nothing.

He threw down the newspaper. He had never felt so useless, so insignificant, so jealous of those lucky men and women who, by virtue of being in the right place at the right time, shaped the course of history. What had *he* done to shape the course of history? Not one thing. And yet, he knew he was as bright as the best of them. If he had stayed in America, if he hadn't been sidetracked, if he had planned for the future, who knows what might have become of him?

It was too late now.

He had dashed his chances and was condemned to a life of insignificance. He was like a man in a wheelchair watching the world go by. What could he do when Nixon or General Westmoreland or Brezhnev or the Ku Klux Klan committed some atrocity but shake his fist in futile anger?

The answer, when it came to him, seemed to illuminate the world like a flash of lightning.

He had trouble getting the letter started. He was on his fifth draft when Amy interrupted him with the news that it was time to get dressed for Emin Bey's. She peered over his shoulder to see what he was writing.

"Dear Ho," she read. "Who's Ho?"

"Ho Chi Minh," Hector explained.

She looked at him sharply.

"I thought I'd write and offer my services. Don't get the wrong idea. I'm not a Communist. It's just I think the war is immoral. The Pentagon's gone mad and we've got to stop them."

She signed and went inside.

"My idea was that he might be able to use a mathematician," Hector continued, following her through the door.

She sat down at her makeup table and looked at herself in the mirror.

"I guess you think I'm crazy to write to him," Hector said.

She shook her head, sighed, picked up her comb, and started fixing the part in her hair.

"Is it that you think I should answer all those other letters before I write to a stranger?" Hector asked.

Amy cleared her throat. "Listen," she said. "I don't want to have an argument."

"Why not? Because you're afraid it might 'upset' me? Because you're afraid that if I get 'upset' I might 'lose it' again?"

"No! No! Of course not! You're doing so well," she said dubiously.

"You think I'm crazy," Hector said, his voice growing louder. "Admit it." Amy looked away. He could see her frightened eyes in the mirror. "Well, let me tell you this, my dear woman. I don't think I'm crazy at all. I don't think it's crazy to want to shape your destiny!"

"No, of course not, darling." He could see her hand shake as she applied her mascara.

"I didn't think he would answer me, for God's sake! It was just a pipe dream. The idea of being a folk hero after sitting on my backside all these years achieving nothing is, I admit to you, very appealing!"

Amy put down her mascara brush and looked at herself in the mirror long and hard. Finally she said, "He's dead."

"Who's dead?"

"Ho Chi Minh."

Hector sat down on the bed, suddenly feeling weak. "Oh."

They stared at each other. "When did this happen?" Hector asked after a long pause.

"Last week. I believe there's a picture of him lying in state in today's paper. I mean the one I brought home today. Didn't you see it?" Amy asked in a small, scared voice.

His hands trembling, Hector opened the paper he was holding to the front page. "Yes. Here he is. Well, what do you know. I must have skipped the headlines today."

"It's been in the headlines all week."

"It has?" He picked up the pile of papers lying next to the bed on the floor. All of them were folded open to the crossword page. One by one, he unfolded them and turned to the front page. HO CHI MINH GRAVELY ILL. HO CHI MINH DEAD AT 79. NORTH VIETNAM EXPECTED TO HOLD WAR POLICIES. A SILENT HANOI BEGINS MOURNING. VIETCONG DECREES THREE-DAY TRUCE IN MEMORY OF HO. HO'S DEATH TO TEST EFFECTIVENESS OF HANOI'S COLLECTIVE LEADERSHIP.

How could he have missed it? Had he become so provincial (so . . . ?) that he didn't even read the headlines anymore? Feeling Amy's eyes on him, he went out onto the balcony to collect himself. It was at this precise moment that he saw his mother.

She was lumbering down the hill, weighed down by two overstuffed shopping bags. Hector's first thought was to run down and scold her for overtaxing herself. Where could she be going at such an hour? It looked as if she were taking supplies to her latest charity case. She was like that—always serving others. Hector shook his head affectionately as he told himself that his mother's generosity would be her undoing. Then he remembered she was already dead.

His mother was dead. Therefore, this woman was a hallucination. Which meant that he had lost his mind. How strange! He had always thought hallucinations were indistinct, like figures in dreams. But this one was so fully realized, from the paisley kerchief and the navy blue housedress he remembered so well, to the espadrilles and the uneven seams in her stockings. What did it mean when you hallucinated with such attention to detail?

And what next? As his eyes followed the apparition down the hill, he pictured himself at Emin Bey's table, smiling at guests who were not there, answering questions that had not been asked. He pictured his colleagues giving each other looks. First they were polite, giving Hector the benefit of the doubt. Then they were confused, alarmed, appalled, pitiful. He saw Amy's frightened eyes as she stuttered her excuses: "He just isn't himself yet . . . must get him home . . . please don't worry . . . nothing a good night's sleep can't mend. . . ."

No. It was out of the question. He couldn't risk going to Emin Bey's. Emin Bey must never know, and the same went for Amy. He panicked, trying to think of a way to get out of the dinner party without arousing her suspicions. But he needn't have worried, because when he went inside to confront her, he discovered he had lost his voice.

Amy rose to the occasion with an eagerness that Hector found suspect. She insisted that he retire to bed at once, going so far as to help him into into his pajamas. "I'll call and tell Emin Bey not to expect us," she said. "Don't you worry. I'll take care of everything." She was true to her word, rushing up and down the stairs with tranquilizers, ice packs, food, warm drinks, and all the while keeping up her cheery, mindless, and very grating head-nurse chatter. Why, he wondered, was she never this affectionate when he was well?

He avoided the obvious conclusion. He closed his eyes and tried to count sheep. But even as the tranquilizers blurred their contours, turning them into shapeless balls of fur, his horror returned. So he had started to hallucinate. What next? Voices?

He fell asleep holding the pillow over his head. This proved to be insufficient protection.

At four in the morning, Hector had a dream in which he woke up to hear his mother calling him from the street. Her voice—deep, coarse, menacing—was not at all like her real voice, which Hector remembered as melodic. Even so, in the dream he had known right away that it was his mother who was calling him, and that she had risen from the grave to settle accounts.

He had also known, with absolute certainty, that he was safe so long as he did not answer her. And so he had stayed in bed, still as a corpse, while she stood underneath the window reciting her woes: "Release me. . . . Set me free. . . . What did you expect? My legs are crossed . . . not even one candle . . . call father . . . call father . . . the candle is extinguished . . . Virgin Mary, have mercy on my soul, it is trapped. . . ."

Her voice grew louder and harsher as the lament continued. Before long, Amy (who in the dream as in real life was lying in bed next to him) began to stir. Fearing that she might wake up and write both their death sentences by answering his mother's call, he put his hand over her ears. She began to struggle. He tightened his hold on her. But it was no use. She opened her eyes and stared at him as if she didn't know who he was. Then she pushed him away with surprising strength, stood up, and moved toward the balcony, as if in a trance.

At the door she screamed and crumpled to the floor. Hector was picking her up when his mother called his name from the balcony. Her voice was harsh and urgent, as if he were a small boy who had run into the street. Involuntarily, Hector looked over his shoulder. And there, standing on the railing, defying gravity, was . . . not his mother, but the devil.

His face was in shadow, though the shadow did not conceal his smirk. He was drinking out of a flask. His back was arched, and he was waving his free arm as if he were trying to regain his balance. He was wearing street clothes, which confused Hector when he thought about it after he woke up.

Why, in the dream, had he been so sure this man was the devil? There had been no horns, no red cape, no pitchfork. What was more, his face had been disturbingly familiar. Who had the devil reminded him of?

The answer came to him toward dawn, as he sat in his study, waiting, for the second time in twelve hours, for transquilizers to calm his nerves.

Hanging on the wall opposite his easy chair was a framed photograph Thomas had taken of him years ago. Not of *him,* strictly speaking, but of Captain Yorgo. (He had been very drunk at the time.) He was standing behind a huddled, windblown group of friends in the bow of a caique, drinking out of a flask. His face was in shadow, though the shadow did not conceal his smirk. His back was arched, and he was waving his free arm as if he were trying to regain his balance.

Hector remembered the day well, not only because he had fallen into the sea shortly after the picture was taken, but because of the pain he had been in, on account of an impacted wisdom tooth. He was to have gone to the dentist that day, but Thomas and Leslie had talked him out of it, saying that the boat trip would be a flop without him. He had taken along the flask of brandy for medicinal purposes. He had gotten drunk to kill the pain.

What a fraud he was! For all his kingly gestures, he was the pawn of all the friends he couldn't say no to.

He thought about the night of the accident. He wondered if his mother might still be alive if he had pleased himself and gone to bed early that night, instead of letting Amy and all the others talk him into doing things he didn't want to do.

He thought about his mother. He wondered why her voice had been so harsh in the dream. He closed his eyes and tried to remember her voice as it had really been. After some concentration, it came back to him.

They were sitting together in the garden in Connecticut. His mother was spinning yarn and he was holding one of the spools for her. It was springtime. He was looking at the tops of the trees. Her deep, soft, musical voice wafted to him through a cloud of daydreams. "Cut the thread, Hector. Cut the thread, my boy." "With what?" he asked. "With the scissors in your hand." He looked at them. They were glistening in the sun. He lifted his hand and did what his mother had asked.

He shuddered. He opened his eyes so as not to remember or imagine or hallucinate anymore. He tried to calm himself by breathing in deeply. Although the tranquilizers soon made him drowsy, he was not able to fall asleep until he had promised himself to seek professional counsel.

But when he woke up toward noon the next day, he was not so sure. The sunshine streaming through the half-opened shutters onto his cluttered desk made the horror of the previous night seem unreal. That half-remembered afternoon in the garden, the eerie visitation in his nightmare, that hallucination—perhaps he had only imagined them.

He had been wallowing in the past. He had to stop this. He had to put the accident behind him. What was done was done. Today was the day, he told himself. Today he was going to give up crossword puzzles, card games, brainteasers, hallucinations, recriminations, and nightmares, and move forward. Today he was going to get organized.

The first thing he did when he sat down at his desk was to take the letter to Ho Chi Minh and tear it up. He didn't dare pause for a moment to ask himself what had possessed him to write such a thing. The reason was too skewed for comfort, and to dwell on it might shatter his newfound resolve. He moved on instead to the piles of letters and legal documents that had been awaiting his attention all summer. He was putting them into chronological order when he heard a noise behind him. He looked over his shoulder.

It was his mother again.

She was wearing the same paisley kerchief, the same navy blue housedress Hector knew so well. She was so close that he could even see the crooked seams in her support hose, the protruding veins on the back of her hand. She was crouching in the corner with her back to him, running a damp cloth over the lowest bookshelf.

She was washing the books.

Dear God, Hector thought, what does it mean when you have a hallucination of your mother washing your books?

Dear God, help me! He turned back to his work, trying to will the hallucination away. But as he plowed on through his correspondence, discarding envelopes and subdividing piles, his panic grew.

What if the hallucinations kept coming? Was there a doctor here who was qualified to treat him? Perhaps he should take the first plane to Connecticut and seek help there. He didn't want to run the risk of being committed to a Turkish institution. But what to tell Emin Bey? And Amy? And Thomas, and Leslie? How would the children take it? How long would he have to stay in the hospital? Was there a cure at all? Would he have to undergo shock treatment? Shuddering at the thought, he glanced down to see that he had just doodled on an important legal document. He tried to erase it, and then realized that he had been doodling with a pen. He groaned.

He glanced over his shoulder to see if his mother had gone, but she was still there, busily destroying his books. Despair made the damp cloth sound like a cat-o'-nine-tails as it flapped against the bindings. So. This was it. He was insane. He could not deny her presence any longer. She wanted something, and she wasn't going away until she got it. He buried his head in his hands. He closed his eyes and surrendered to her.

"Mother," he said wearily. "Just tell me what you want."

There was no sound other than the flapping of the damp cloth.

"Just tell me," he repeated. "I'll do anything you want. I'll go light a candle for you if that's what's bothering you."

Still no answer.

"I can arrange a memorial service. How about that? I'll go down to the Patriarchate this morning and set the ball rolling. Would that satisfy you? Please, Mother, answer me!" Losing all shame he turned around to see that she was still bent over the bookshelf. "You can't leave me in the dark like this, Mother! You've got to help me!"

She looked up with a blank smile that was one of the most terrifying things he had ever seen.

Her face was all wrong. It was as if a cartoonist had stretched it out of shape, crushing the nose, pushing the eyes closer together, lowering the hairline and elevating the eyebrows so that the forehead was a narrow strip of rubbery creases. Even the gold tooth was in the wrong place. How could his imagination do this to him—distorting the only thing he had left of his mother, which was his memory of her kind face?

He stared at her, trying to will the distortions away. It was only slowly that he realized that this woman was not his mother, but someone else wearing her clothes. It was Meliha, the new maid.

Of course. It made perfect sense. In Turkey, you never threw things away. You gave them to the servants.

So. It was all a mistake. He was not insane after all. He was not going to have shock treatments, and he could skip the Patriarchate. Rejuvenated by the thought, he threw open the window and looked outside. Was it true that it had been here all along, waiting for him to get better—this emerald garden, this sunshine, this sea breeze? He took in a deep breath, as if it were his first. He felt like singing and dancing. He had a strange urge, which he had not felt since the darkest days of adolescence, to fall to his knees and pray.

He made it a silent prayer, so as not to frighten the maid any further. When he was through, he remained at the window, still thankful and surprised that life had continued in all its splendor without him.

Looking beyond the garden wall, he could just see a young man walking down the road.

Halûk!

Hector had completely forgotten about him. Now it all came back. He rushed into his bedroom to get dressed, thinking how fortuitous it was that Halûk had chosen this moment to drop by.

As he rummaged through his closet, he pictured the scene downstairs: Halûk sitting in the living room with Amy and the children, his hands clasped, an expectant smile on his face. Halûk jumping to his feet at the sight of Hector, and running toward him with his arms outstretched. "Professor Cabot!" he would say. "What a pleasure to see you looking so well! I must confess I was worried about you, but I see my fears are unfounded!"

Hector would smile and remind him that they were colleagues now, so it was no longer "Professor Cabot" but "Hector." He would go over to Amy and put his arm around her. Amy would smile, the tension disappearing from her face. She would look young again. She would whisper in his ear that she was happy to see him back on his feet.

The children would be sitting on the sofa looking worried, and so he would go over and pat them on the shoulder. "Stop looking like the end of the world," he would say. "Your father's somehow managed to resurrect himself." Chloe would throw her arms around him. Neil would hang back, looking shy but proud.

That was the welcome he envisaged as he walked downstairs. He was therefore confused to find the living room and the library empty. He went out into the garden. Halûk was not there either. He went out to the street and looked in both directions. Still no sign of the man.

He reviewed the possibilities. Perhaps Halûk had been intending to pay him a visit but had changed his mind at the last moment. (Why? Because of something someone said?) Or: he had never been intending to visit, and had simply been passing by. (Passing by? How could he pass by his old professor's house without stopping for a moment to say hello?) Or: he had forgotten that this was where Hector lived.

How could he forget that I lived here? Hector thought angrily. Then he reminded himself that Halûk had many more important matters on his mind—his wife, his relatives, his friends, his work. . . .

The world is perfectly capable of revolving without your help, old boy, Hector told himself. You are not quite as essential as you think you are. Despondent, he returned to the garden, closing the gate with considerable difficulty. (When was the last time it had been oiled?)

He looked up at the house. It wasn't white anymore: it was gray and the paint was chipping. He looked at the garden. It didn't look so emerald from down here. It looked overgrown. How could Amy have allowed the grass to get so high? Didn't they have a gardener anymore?

He walked along the flowerbeds, inspecting them. There

were weeds everywhere, encircling, smothering, strangling the plants. How could Amy have permitted this? He bent down and started pulling them out with his bare hands, then gave up in disgust after he was stung by a nettle.

He walked up the brick path to the kitchen door. The dog was lying next to it, his fur matted, his tongue hanging out, his eyes silly with thirst. His water bowl had been empty so long that it was half filled with dirt. Hector bent down to pick it up. He looked into the kitchen and saw his family sitting at the table eating lunch.

His family? He had to pinch himself, because at first glance his wife and children all looked the same age: Amy with her short shorts and her hair in pigtails, like Judy Garland in *The Wizard of Oz*. Neil, with his insolently hunched shoulders and his pimply nose. Chloe, who looked . . . what was the word? Vulgar. Her face was caked with makeup, bright blue eyeshadow, heavy black eyeliner, cheap pink lips. Something had happened to her over the summer.

They were laughing. This surprised him. He couldn't understand how they could laugh in a room where he still felt his mother's presence so strongly.

"You children don't miss a thing, do you?" Amy was saying. Her face was flushed.

"Then admit it," Chloe said. "You have a crush on him."

"How could I have a crush on him?" Amy protested. "He looks like a gnome."

"You blush every time you see him. Even on the phone your voice changes. And your laugh! God! It's so fake!"

"It is not!" Amy cried. She put her hand over her mouth and giggled like a teenager.

"You should have married a doctor. You're always having crushes on them."

"Oh, do hush up, Chloe."

"Let's see. There was Dr. Bozbağ, and Dr. Selimoğlu, and Dr. Yilmaz, and—"

"Don't forget the dentists," Neil added.

His voice had cracked.

"Oh, you two are impossible!" Amy cried. Laughing, she leaned back, opened the refrigerator, and took out a water bottle. She threw her head back and took a long drink. It surprised him to see her drinking right out of the bottle. She was normally so concerned about hygiene. It occurred to him, as he backed away from the door, that he no longer loved her.

Halûk arrived at work on registration day to find that his desk, which had previously been in the same room as Hector's, had been moved into the foyer where Feza Hanim, the department secretary, had her desk. Thinking that there had been a mistake, he went in to talk it over with Emin Bey, who was, to his surprise, remarkably unfriendly. The last time Halûk had seen him was at the dinner party, and they had parted on what Halûk had thought were highly cordial terms—almost too cordial, with Emin Bey draping his arm around Halûk's shoulder in a fatherly fashion and giving his guests an embarrassing speech on the onerous tasks awaiting Turkey's youth.

Now he would not even look Halûk in the eye. For Halûk, there could be only one explanation for Emin Bey's change of attitude. This was that in the interim, Emin Bey had spoken with Hector, who had told Emin Bey the reason why he had been avoiding Halûk.

Halûk longed to ask Emin Bey directly: what had he done to offend Hector? But etiquette made this impossible, and for the hundredth time since his return, Halûk longed to be back in America, where life was not so complicated.

So instead of referring to his true worries, Halûk confined himself to the matter of the desk. He tried to appear reasonable. "This is the problem we are facing," he said. "When Feza Hanim is sitting at her desk, it is impossible for me to get through to mine."

"This is not our problem, my child," Emin Bey answered in a mocking voice. "It is your problem. Because this is the way things must be."

"I hope I am not overstepping my position," Halûk said, trying to sound apologetic. "But I had no complaints about the former position of my desk. The idea of sharing an office with Hector was completely suitable."

"I am sure it was suitable from your point of view,"

Emin Bey said, "but I am sorry to inform you that it was not for all parties concerned."

"Then, excuse me, but perhaps we could find another corner for my desk, because—"

"I am afraid there are no other corners that would be suitable for this purpose."

"I see," said Halûk. "Then in this case I would like to ask your permission to change the position of the filing cabinet. If I moved it closer to the door, I would be able to come and go more easily."

Emin Bey opened his drawer and took out a toothpick, with which he then proceeded to pick his teeth. He gave Halûk a long, hard look. "So you would like to change the position of the filing cabinet. But this is only the first item on your agenda, I suspect. It seems that there are many changes you are planning to make."

"Perhaps I have not been able to explain clearly," Halûk said. "I was only trying to make the office more comfortable for all concerned."

"Of course," said Emin Bey. "Of course. However, I am afraid there can be no possibility of moving the filing cabinet. Feza Hanim, who has been with us for many years, would be extremely upset. Excuse me, but the filing cabinet must remain in its place." Emin Bey gave Halûk a hostile and victorious smile. Making his apologies, Halûk retired to his desk in the foyer.

Halûk's first lecture was to be the following day, and he was nervous about it. He had hoped to spend registration day reviewing his lecture notes as well as casting an eye over the textbook he would be using. But this proved impossible, because for some reason there were no copies of this textbook available in the office. Further, Feza Hanim made so much noise at the desk in front of him that it proved impossible to think. In addition to the pounding on the typewriter and the constant flow of students with special problems, there were the telephone calls, many of which were from Feza Hanim's personal friends.

It seemed she was in poor health. Her conversations with these friends consisted mostly of hopelessly demoralized complaints. She was wearing a strong perfume which made Halûk feel ill. Worst of all, when she was not chainsmoking foul-smelling cigarettes, she was chewing gum. Halûk had always hated the sound of women chewing gum.

And so, in order to contain himself, he took this opportunity to go to the college bookstore and buy supplies.

It was strange to walk on the campus again, and to be a teacher instead of a student. Still, the walk brought back pleasant memories. He returned to his office refreshed, but his light-hearted mood did not last long, because when he tried to open his desk drawer, he found that it was stuck.

"How is this drawer supposed to be opened?" he asked Feza Hanim.

"How should I know?" she said, chewing as loudly as ever.

This is impossible, he said to himself. If he was going to be pushed into a corner, fine, but at least he deserved a desk in good condition. Once again, he found himself knocking on Emin Bey's door.

Emin Bey received him graciously. "How may I be of assistance?" he asked.

"I have two small problems," Halûk said. "First, I have somehow misplaced the teacher's copy of my textbook."

"What a shame," said Emin Bey.

"I was wondering if you might possibly have in your possession a spare copy which I could borrow in the meantime."

Emin Bey got up slowly and perused the bookshelf. He picked out the textbook in question and handed it to Halûk.

"Thank you," said Halûk.

"There is no need to thank me."

Now came time for Halûk to mention the desk. "My teacher, I am sorry if I am disturbing you . . ."

"Please. Do not call me 'teacher,'" Emin Bey said. "We are colleagues. You said you have two small problems. Please let me know what your other problem is."

"My other problem is, I'm afraid, my desk. Unfortunately, it is not possible to open the drawers. For some reason they are stuck. There is a dent in the side which leads me to believe that the damage was done when it was moved. With your permission, I would like to exchange my desk for another one in better condition."

"My dear boy, I am afraid you have become accustomed

to impossible standards during your stay in America. Unfortunately, we cannot ever hope to attain the level of your Harvards and MITs. We are a backward country. Our resources are limited. My dear boy, how can I explain myself? You are fortunate to have a desk at all."

It was becoming difficult for Halûk to remain polite. "Why am I fortunate?" he asked, his voice cracking.

"Because," said Emin Bey, "there are said to be shortages."

"Shortages?" Halûk asked.

"Yes," said Emin Bey. "I am afraid the demand for desks is greater than our existing supply. It is an unfortunate situation, but it must be endured."

By now it was lunchtime. Rather than go to the faculty dining room, where Halûk did not feel he belonged, he decided to have a toasted sandwich at his old stomping ground, the student snack bar.

After a moment of hesitation, the man working behind the counter recognized Halûk and embraced him warmly. Remembering Halûk's former passion for banana chocolates, he gave him an entire box of them as a present.

Even though they looked much the same as his old classmates, the students eating in the snack bar seemed to recognize that he was not one of them—did he look that old?—and so they left him to himself. He felt so uncomfortable sitting alone among their gossiping cliques that he took his toasted sandwich, his apple, and his box of banana chocolates back with him to the office.

Emin Bey was not back from lunch yet, but the door to Hector's office, which had previously been open, was closed. Peering through the little window, Halûk could see Hector bent over his desk with his face in his hands.

"When did Professor Cabot arrive?" he asked Feza Hanim.

"About ten minutes ago," she said.

"Was he in a good mood or did he seem upset?"

"Upset," she said.

"Did he give you any idea why?" Halûk asked.

"Why should he tell me if he's upset?" she said, shrugging her shoulders.

Halûk knocked on Hector's door but there was no sign that the hunched-over figure at the desk had heard him. It was possible that the man was asleep, though not probable. Bearing this in mind, Halûk returned to his desk and gave the outward appearance of being unconcerned. He would wait for Hector to come to him.

He decided to kill some time by double-checking his lecture notes and first-week assignments. Opening up the textbook that Emin Bey had lent to him, he soon discovered that it was a different edition from the one he had been using all summer while making his preparations. If this was the edition the students were using, his lecture notes were worthless. He panicked.

"Feza Hanim!" he cried. "Do you happen to know what edition they are using these days in one-oh-one?"

She stopped typing and looked at him quizzically. She put out her cigarette and popped another piece of gum into her mouth. "Why should I know what edition they are using?" she said, chewing noisily. "What difference would it make to me?"

Halûk felt like knocking her head against the wall, but instead he remained at his desk with a calm expression. His heart beating wildly, he marked his lecture notes in pencil to fit with Emin Bey's edition of the textbook—just in case that happened to be the one they were using. He was halfway through when Hector's door opened. Looking up, he saw Hector peering through the crack in the door.

Halûk jumped to his feet. "My friend!" he cried, rushing toward him with open arms. Hector jumped back a few inches in surprise. He cut short Halûk's embrace with a nervous handshake and then headed for the door. "Wonderful to see you, Halûk," he said. "We must talk soon. Got to run now, though. Late for an appointment." He raced into the corridor, leaving Halûk stranded, with his arms flapping uselessly at his side.

"He must have seen a mouse." said Feza.

"Apparently," said Halûk, trying to hide his true feelings. "Has he been acting his way for a long time?"

"My son, I am not the Delphic Oracle," said Feza. "I am in the dark about this man's complexes just like you. Perhaps you do not realize that I spent this summer in a clinic outside Zurich."

"A clinic?" said Halûk. "What for?"

"Kidney problems," Feza said.

"Serious problems?"

"No," Feza said. "Not serious. Bothersome."

"And couldn't you have found a suitable kidney specialist closer to home?" Halûk asked.

"I could," she said, taking her gum out of her mouth to examine it, "but I didn't."

"Why not?" Halûk asked.

"Because. The kidney specialists in this country are *boktan,*" by which she meant "made from shit."

"That's not true!" Halûk said.

"How could you know?" Feza said. "You are a recent arrival."

Halûk let this slur pass. "My uncle is a kidney specialist," he said. "He is highly regarded both in Turkey and abroad. He works in Ankara."

"He works in Ankara?" said Feza. "My condolences."

"Why do you say that?" Halûk asked, his anger growing.

"Because Ankara is *boktan.*" Having examined her wad of gum, she put it back into her mouth.

"Aman!" Halûk cried. This woman's snobbery was unbearable enough, but, in addition to have to listen to her noisy chewing! "I implore you! Take that disgusting thing out of your mouth. It is an insult to your womanhood. It makes you look like a cow!"

"Ah, ah! What is this, now?" she snapped. "To whom do I have the honor of speaking, a five-star general?"

"There is no need for this argument to continue," Halûk said.

"Yes, sir! Anything you say, sir! On the double, sir!"

She burst out crying and rushed out of the room. She returned two minutes later with her face blotched and her eyes red. Halûk felt terrible. In order to make peace with her, he offered her the bowl into which he had put his apple and his banana chocolates. "Please. Have something."

"No, thank you," she said, and she blew her nose.

"I insist. Have a banana chocolate."

"Banana chocolates are not good for cows."

"You are making me ashamed," Halûk said. "I did not

mean that I thought you looked like a cow. Please accept this chocolate. I am going to have one, too. Please," he said again, and she finally accepted.

Emin Bey arrived back at the office just as Halûk and Feza Hanim were peeling the wrappers off their banana chocolates.

Emin Bey was feeling very upset because of the humiliating event that had just occurred on the playing field. He had been coming out of the building that housed the faculty dining room when he had seen Hector rushing down the Washburn Hall ramp. Emin Bey had waved and called to him, but Hector had appeared not to notice. And so Emin Bey had run after him, finally catching up with him outside the Academy Gate.

"My friend!" Emin Bey had cried. "How are you?"

Hector had stopped and smiled, but Emin Bey was aware of a certain inward shudder, not unlike Emin Bey's wife's inward shudder when she wanted to give the impression that intimacy had been forced on her. "I'm fine," he said in a hoarse voice. "The laryngitis is almost gone. But I have to run now. I have an appointment. I'm sorry about the dinner party," he added, as an afterthought.

"Don't worry about it," Emin Bey said. "It was extremely dull. You and I must do something more interesting in the near future. Perhaps one of these Friday nights we could nip downtown for a few drinks."

This suggestion made Hector blanch. He rushed off through the Academy Gate, shouting over his shoulder that they would have to talk soon. Since it was clear that Hector had been to the office, Emin Bey was left with the impression that Hector had spoken with Halûk, who had succeeded in winning him over to his side.

How dare he? Emin Bey said to himself as he walked up the Washburn Hall ramp. How dare this young upstart seek to poison a friendship that had begun when he was still a boy in *orta* school? How dare he try to influence Hector with his political ideas? Adding insult to injury was Halûk's insolent behavior when he returned to the office.

Not only did Halûk fail to say hello to Emin Bey, but he made a point of not offering Emin Bey any of his banana chocolates, even though Emin Bey could see that there were at least twenty more banana chocolates in the bowl.

This was, for Emin Bey, the straw that broke the camel's back. How dare this boy offer a banana chocolate to his secretary and then fail to offer one to him? It was a tacit declaration of war.

But revenge, as the French said, was a dish best eaten cold. He decided to bide his time. When Halûk came into his office to resolve the confusion surrounding Math 101 textbook, Emin Bey gave every appearance of good will. He sent Halûk on his way having reassured him that he would look into the matter.

But the problems had not been resolved by the time Halûk was due to walk in front of his first class the next morning. The bookstore had both editions in stock, and it was not clear which one they had been selling to the students. Emin Bey, though giving the outward appearance of concern, was not helpful. He seemed to enjoy the string of small mishaps that befell Halûk that morning.

First there was the affair of the missing supplies. Because he had been forced to leave his supplies on his desk top (since his drawers would not open), some unknown party had seen fit to borrow his pencils. And so Halûk had been forced to do the rest of his lecture note corrections in ink. Then, when it came time to staple them together, he discovered that his stapler was also missing. No one seemed to know where it was. Furthermore, no one seemed to care. It was as if they had all turned against him. When he walked in front of his hundred-odd students at ten that morning, he was already so rattled that the sight of so many eyes resting on him unnerved him completely.

It would have been a strange moment even without the earlier aggravations. How many years had he sat in those seats where his students now sat? How many exams had he taken there, and there, and there? He remembered how mercilessly he and his classmates had judged their teachers, taking note of every nervous tic, every weakness that their teachers revealed, giving them cruel nicknames . . . and now he was exposing himself to the same dangers. Now he was paying the price.

And yet, while he wondered what nickname they would end up giving him, he also understood them perfectly. He understood their hopes and joys and foresaw the disappointments that awaited them. As Turks suspended halfway between East and West, they would have to betray many of their parents' beliefs, just as he had. They would feel the same shame when they became too Americanized, and the same isolation. When they went abroad to complete their studies, they would spend just as much time as he had searching for an Armenian delicatessen where they could buy stuffed vine leaves and white goat's cheese. And, having trained themselves adequately, they would encounter the same frustrations when older, narrower minds stood in the way of progress.

Was it worth it? he asked himself as he stared back at the sea of unfriendly eyes. Was the knowledge he was about to impart going to give them anything but unhappiness? Even though their gazes were arrogant, his heart went out to them. He longed to break the ice, shatter this artificial barrier separating student and teacher, let them know that he had once been one of them—and still was one of them in his heart. On the spur of the moment, he decided to share his thoughts with them, and it was this unguarded speech that earned him the nickname of "the Janitor."

"My friends," he said, "I do not feel I belong at this podium. I have spent so many years sitting where you are sitting that it seems unnatural for me to be standing in front of you. Is there anyone," he said, hoping to cause laughter, "who would like to trade places with me?"

But instead of laughter, there was an unfriendly silence.

"In that case," Halûk continued lamely, "let us turn to the question of the textbook." Having made a false start, he found it impossible to regain his balance. Thoroughly unnerved by the discovery that half his students had the 1967 edition of the textbook, while the other half had the 1969, he soon gave up referring to the textbook at all, deciding instead to rely on his lecture notes and the blackboard. But since he had been unable to staple his lecture notes, they were all out of order.

It was when he turned to the blackboard that nervousness turned into paranoia.

There was no chalk. Well, Halûk said to himself, it was fortunate that he had planned for such an emergency. He delved into his briefcase and retrieved a small piece of pink chalk. So, he said to himself, whoever had sought to trip him up had been outwitted. He filled the board with calculations, writing large. Then, when he had run out of space, he reached for the blackboard eraser.

There was no blackboard eraser.

"Fuck!" he muttered. At this there was scattered laughter. He delved into his briefcase, and when he was unable to find an eraser there, he hit his forehead with the palm of his hand in frustration. His undignified gesture caused additional mirth.

"Does anyone have a blackboard eraser?" he finally asked.

One student raised his hand. "I do, sir," he said.

"Then please bring it up to me. And do not feel obliged to call me sir."

The student walked up to the front of the lecture hall and offered Halûk his shoe. Halûk looked at it in shock. He was at once angry at having been made the object of ridicule, and ashamed by memories of having done the same type of thing in his own time. How cruel he had been. His poor, beleaguered teachers!

He had been speaking in English, but now he broke into Turkish. "My son, I must inform you that we are here to study mathematics and not to audition for the vaudeville."

A girl in the back of the class screeched with laughter, and the rest of the students followed suit.

"Go back to your seat," he said. "And everybody stop laughing," he said, reverting to English. "This is a serious matter, as I said." And, as the laughter turned to barely audible giggles, he erased his calculations with his handkerchief.

When the class was over, he slammed his briefcase shut and left the lecture hall in a rage. First the textbook, he said to himself. Then the pencils, and the stapler, and the chalk and eraser. Someone was trying to sabotage him. And he knew who it was. It was Emin Bey. He returned to the office determined to confront him.

He found Emin Bey sitting as his desk looking very

pleased with himself. He was eating a succulent-looking apple, and savoring each bite. There were a few more apples in a basket next to the phone, and also a banana. Next to the basket of fruit was a box from the Haci Bekir Pastry Shop. Emin Bey's lack of good will for Halûk was emphasized by the fact that he neglected to offer him anything.

"And so," he said to Halûk between bites, "you have emerged from your first lecture in one piece."

"I did, but with difficulty," Halûk said. "Not only was there no chalk, but there was also no blackboard eraser."

"Ah," said Emin Bey, "what a pity." But as he sank his teeth into the brilliant red skin of the apple, he did not appear to think it was a pity at all.

"You don't find it strange that the chalk and eraser had been removed?" Halûk asked.

"As I said a moment ago, I find it a pity," said Emin Bey. "However, I do not find it at all strange. As I mentioned yesterday, we are a nation plagued by shortages. We do not have the unlimited funds of your Harvards and MITs. We must make do with what we have."

"Excuse me," Halûk said, "but I do not find this explanation satisfactory."

"So be it," said Emin Bey. Opening his drawer, he took out a pair of scissors, which he used to cut the string around the box from the Haci Bekir Pastry Shop. Inside was baklava, the most succulent baklava Halûk had seen in years. It glistened with honey. It was rich with nuts. Emin Bey gingerly extracted a piece for himself and proceeded to eat it, savoring each bite. He neglected to offer the box to Halûk.

Halûk left Emin Bey's office in exasperation and returned to his own desk behind Feza's desk. He proceeded to devote himself to the futile task of trying to get his desk drawers open. A few minutes later, Emin Bey came out of his office.

"Feza Hanim, you must try a piece of this baklava. It is wonderful. You, too," he said to Betül Hanim, who had just walked through the door. "And take this piece for Joe." Having offered pieces to everyone by Halûk, Emin Bey knocked on Hector's door.

"Come in!" Hector said.

"My friend," Emin Bey said, as he went into Hector's office, "you must try this baklava. It is wonderful." The door closed, and Halûk thought he heard congenial laughter. Suddenly it was all clear to him.

It was not Hector who had been prejudicing Emin Bey against him, but Emin Bey who had been prejudicing Hector. Emin Bey was out to destroy their friendship. He was jealous of the intimacy they enjoyed. He suspected that Halûk intended to subvert his position with new ideas. Like everyone in his generation, Emin Bey was a typical member of the old guard. He was, to state things clearly, a fascist.

But he was also Halûk's boss. A contract had been signed, and Halûk was bound to honor it, even if it caused him extreme misery. So he bowed his head over his desk and tried to pay no attention to his colleagues as they exclaimed about the excellence of the baklava. When Feza Hanim offered him a bit of hers, he nearly bit her head off. "I'm on a diet!" he snapped. But when Emin Bey came around with the baklava box for the second time that morning, Halûk was able to give the impression of being completely unaffected by Emin Bey's rudeness.

Emin Bey was out to break him, so he did not finish with the baklava.

After lunch, which for Halûk had been nothing more than a dry toasted cheese sandwich, Emin Bey made his rounds of the mathematics department again, this time with his basket of succulent fruits. Every time someone came into the office, Emin Bey came out and said, "You must try one of these apples. They are wonderful." Or, "You must try this pear. I insist."

While he would not take no for an answer from Feza or Betül Hanim, not once did he offer a piece of fruit to Halûk. The sound of his colleagues enjoying the succulent apples and pears became unbearable. Why was he being singled out in this fashion? Halûk asked himself. What had he done to deserve such torture?

But the exclamations subsided as the pear and apple cores landed in the wastepaper baskets. As the office returned to normal, Halûk calmed down.

It was at this point that Emin Bey appeared in the door of his office with the banana.

It was the most beautiful banana Halûk had ever seen. Its skin was golden and speckled. It looked soft and ripe. It was sitting all by itself in the middle of the basket, like a seductress. As Emin Bey came into the office, it looked for a moment as if he had regretted his rudeness to Halûk and was going to offer him this banana as an apology.

But instead he said, "Feza Hanim, it is a shame to let this banana go to waste. I am too full to eat it myself, so I insist that you take it."

"Ah, sir, you are very kind," Feza said. "But really, I am very full. Too full. And I have already broken my diet."

"What a pity," Emin Bey said. Sighing, he knocked on Hector's door, and Joe Edison's door, and Betül Hanim's door, but they were all too full, too. "Are you sure you don't want this banana?" he said to Feza Hanim.

"I'm sure," she said. "*Vallahi.*"

"Ah, what a pity," he said, and he returned to his office.

As soon as he had closed the door, Halûk jumped to his feet and said, "This is unbearable!" He pushed Feza aside as he squeezed past her desk. He threw open Emin Bey's door without knocking.

"Emin Bey," he said, "the time has come to be frank."

"Of course," he said. He put down his pen and looked up from his papers with the self-possession of a grand vizier.

There was a silence, as Halûk waited for Emin Bey to state his case. But he did not. When he finally spoke, it was to say, with the vague politeness of a municipal official who has not been adequately bribed, "Please. How may I be of assistance?"

"I would like you to explain what it is I have done to deserve such treatment," Halûk said.

"What treatment?" Emin Bey asked.

"I am talking specifically about efforts to exclude me from the department."

"Efforts to exclude you from the department?" Emin Bey said. "I was not aware of this problem."

"Furthermore," Halûk said, "there have been a number of items which have disappeared from my desk."

"Hmmmmm," said Emin Bey. "What you have told me just now upsets me. But it does not surprise me. As I said, we are a poor country. We are plagued with shortages. And unfortunately, there are those among us who have reacted to these shortages by taking what does not belong to them. It is deplorable behavior. Our people still have a long road ahead of them before they are to attain the high level of personal honor of your Harvards and MITs. But what can we do?" Emin Bey sighed, and he gazed mournfully at his fruit basket, where the solitary banana still reposed. Sighing, he picked the banana up and gazed at it lovingly. Then, sighing the more fulfilled sigh of a man who had decided to allow desire to overcome conscience, he began to peel it.

The meat of the banana was so soft and rich that it looked as if it had been bathed in honey. Emin Bey unpeeled it as slowly and carefully as if he had been undressing a virgin. He paused for a moment, and then, smiling triumphantly at Halûk, he let his teeth sink slowly in.

Halûk could bear this presecution no longer.

"*Şeytan!*" Halûk cried, shaking his forefinger. "*Şeytan!* You're a devil! You're a devil! I'll get you for this! I'll make you pay!" He backed into the foyer, where his colleagues had gathered to find out what was the matter.

"He's a devil!" Halûk said to them, point at Emin Bey's door. He was pale and his voice was trembling. They looked at him in bewilderment. He backed out into the corridor without pausing to collect his briefcase. War had been declared.

All this while, Hector was sitting in his office, gazing thoughtfully out the window and smoking cigarette after cigarette. He heard the raised voices and slamming doors but paid little attention to them.

Spread out before him on his desk was a newspaper, an English-language daily published in Ankara. It was open to the society page, at the top of which was a photograph, taken the previous week, of the British ambassador greeting guests at an Embassy reception. From time to time, Hector would pick up the paper for a closer look at the man in the dog collar who was shaking the ambassador's hand. It was not the best of pictures—sharp contrasts, together with the fact that the man's head was turned away from the camera, made positive identification impossible. But the more he examined it, the more Hector was certain that the man was his father.

He looked well. There were no signs that the concussion had done him any lasting harm. He looked kind: the sort who would forgive a son his trespasses.

When Hector walked into the chapel, he would open his arms in welcome. "I've been wondering when you'd turn up," he would say. "Well, better late than never." They would embrace and Hector would apologize. His father would say, "Never mind, my boy. We all make mistakes." And Hector would tell him, "I'm making a fresh start, just like you did." His father would smile and put his hand on his shoulder, and guide him down the aisle like a shepherd. "On that happy note . . ." he would say. He would open the door, flooding the chapel with light.

The vision of the two of them standing in the chapel door, their faces upturned to accept the sun, was what gave Hector the courage he had been hoping, almost praying, for. He stood up and prepared to go.

There was to be no more avoiding people. When Halûk greeted him, he would not run off with his tail between his legs as he had done yesterday. Instead, he would say, "How are you doing, old sport?" and slap him on the back. There were to be no more shameless lies. When Emin Bey asked him, as he had done for three days running, if they could meet at Nazmi's for some *raki,* he would simply say, "I'd be happy to, although I should warn you that I won't be very good company. You see, I've given up drinking. And as for that story I told you about Amy the other day—well, I was lying. There is nothing wrong with her, really. I simply needed an excuse not to go drinking with you." There would be no apologies, no pointless lingering. Having greeted all his colleagues in the proper manner, he would leave the office and stride manfully across the campus. He would not stop to watch the soccer match. He would not—and this was essential—he would not allow himself to entertain the slightest suspicion that the students who were standing on the sidelines, ostensibly watching the match, were actually staring at him out of the corners of their eyes, and discussing him, exchanging vicious rumors, even making up new ones. No, he couldn't allow himself to think like that. It was insane. No, he had to keep his paranoia in check and stride manfully across the campus, and hail a taxi, and go downtown, and present himself to his father.

There was just one problem, he realized, and that was his jacket.

He had it draped over his right arm. Perhaps he should be wearing it. If he had it draped over his arm, where was he going to put it when he slapped Halûk on the back? He would be carrying his briefcase in his left hand, so if he transferred his jacket to his left hand—in order to slap Halûk on the back with his right hand—he would have to put his briefcase on the floor. If he put his briefcase on the floor, he ran the risk of forgetting it. He didn't want to forget it. His lecture notes were inside. If he lost his lecture notes, he would never find the courage to face his first class, which met the next morning. And if he missed his first class . . . and if . . . and if. . . . His head spun with hypothetical nightmares. Gripping the icy doorknob, he tried to regain control of himself. Slowly the ifs swirled away into the darkness, to be replaced by a single, undeniable fact.

It was a weekday afternoon. His father would not be at the chapel—he would be at home, wherever that was. The entire plan was based on a false premise. There was no point in going through with it.

As Hector walked into the foyer, he felt like a traveler who has arrived at the airport only to be told that the flight he is booked on does not exist. He looked around him. The room was empty. There was no one to slap on the back, no one to explain himself to, no one to avoid. Where to now? The clock on the wall said half past four. That meant seven and a half more hours to kill until tomorrow.

"So, my friend. You have emerged from hibernation. How nice. We have missed you." It was Emin Bey, who had come out of his office. He was eating—and Hector thought this was strange, too—a banana.

His manner was calm, his smile studied, his eyes furious. It was an expression Hector had seen, and laughed off, many times before. Today, however, it did not seem so funny. He shuddered, and wondered what he had done to cross him. His first thought was that Emin Bey had caught him out in his lie about Amy, although he could not be sure which lie. In his zeal to avoid social engagements, he had told so many lies about Amy's health he could no longer keep track of them.

But Emin Bey did not give any indication that he had caught Hector out in his lie. His questions about Amy's health showed genuine concern. He even went so far as to recommend a good osteopath, from which Hector deduced that he had gotten out of going to Nazmi's the day before by saying Amy had broken a bone.

No, it was not Amy he was concerned about. And it was not Hector's failure to join him at Nazmi's for a *raki*. It was some other failing of Hector's that was irking him (a vicious rumor? an exaggeraton? a half truth?). Because after they had exhausted the subject of osteopaths, Emin Bey looked him straight in the eyes and sighed, like a kindly uncle whose favorite nephew has failed him.

Hector wondered what the rumor had been about—his mother, his father, some lover who had decided to tell all, some gross exaggeration of the accident. . . . The list of possibilities was enormous. There were so many things he had done wrong, so many things that were wrong with him. It could be almost anything. When Emin Bey opened his mouth to speak, Hector was almost relieved: any accusation was better than this cloud of apprehension. But Emin Bey's words only served to mystify him further.

"So," he said in an ominous voice, "the hens have finally come home to roost."

He strolled to the window, where he sighed again and began to chew his nails. Hector's heart began to pound. What could they have told the man? That he was a murderer? A spy? An agent provocateur? He followed Emin Bey to the window, painfully conscious of the way his shoes scuffed the floor as he crossed the room with small, tentative steps. He wondered if Emin Bey could also hear his heart. He looked out the window.

It was a typical late afternoon scene: a soccer match, with a hundred or more students standing on the sidelines, some watching, some talking among themselves. At the bottom of the ramp that led from Washburn Hall to the campus, Hector could see Halûk conversing in a rather animated manner with a group of young men. Before Hector could even consider the possibility that had been foremost in his mind for days now—every time he saw people talking—he stopped himself.

No, they were not talking about him. They had other, more important things to discuss. No, they were not gesturing in his direction, or glancing angrily up at the window where he and Emin Bey stood. They were looking up beyond them, at the sky and the clouds that were racing across it. They were not angry at him, but worried about a change in the weather.

Then he had to be honest with himself. There was no room for doubt: Halûk had turned now and was staring straight up at him. He was smiling, but even a fool could see the mockery in it. He was giving him a mock military salute. Hector gasped. What had he done to deserve such contempt? Whatever the rumor was, it was clearly monstrous—something on a par with the war crimes of Goebbels. Only yesterday, Halûk had been greeting him with open arms. Now he was making a spectacle of his hatred. It was as if he wanted to let everyone know where he stood.

He felt the weight of a hundred pairs of eyes on him. Even the soccer players seemed to be watching him out of the corners of their eyes and exchanging nasty jokes at his expense as they chased the ball. He could almost read their lips. *He's a murderer,* they were saying. *He didn't even bury his mother in the right place. He gave his father a concussion. You should hear the things his father says about him now. He's a womanizer, a drunk, a* gâvur, *an infidel. All foreigners are alike. It's a shame to the motherland. . . .*

Hector tried to shut his mind off. He tried to look at the soccer players' lips until it was clear as clear could be that they weren't even moving. But even the sight of their unmoving lips was too much for him. It was the thought that their lips could move at will, the thought that the rumor might already have been planted in their minds. . . .

Seeing Emin Bey's quizzical gaze, he attempted a smile. He took out his handkerchief and wiped the sweat off his forehead.

"Oh, for goodness' sake," said Emin Bey. "There is no need to go to such lengths. Go ahead and have some."

"I beg your pardon?" Hector whispered. His voice was almost gone.

"The baklava." He pointed at a box on his desk. "Go ahead and have some. I can tell you're dying for it."

Hector stared at the box, unable to move.

"Don't play games. I beg of you! You know we don't stand on ceremony, you and I. You must not read anything into my actions. I simply forgot to offer it. Now, please. Take a piece before I become angry."

His hands shaking, Hector opened the box and took a piece. He bit into it. It tasted like wet cement.

Emin Bey smiled, or rather, bared his teeth. "So," he said. "The farce has begun." He sighed and looked out of the window. "The world is falling apart, my friend. Just look at those idiots. We have created, I fear, a nation of Neanderthals. It is a fitting metaphor, is it not?"

"I beg your pardon?" Hector whispered.

"I was referring to the soccer match, of course."

"I'm afraid I don't follow you."

Emin Bey gave Hector a contemptuous look. "How trying you Americans can be at times. Must I spell everything out for you? The human condition, don't you know. Two opposing teams, ready to fight to the death... uninvolved spectators, taking sides. . . . Surely you follow my drift."

Hector shook his head.

"Must I assume the subtlety of a jackhammer in order to warn you? Are you Americans incapable of understanding allusions? Did you never study poetry in school?"

Hector bowed his head so that Emin Bey would not see his shame. "I did, I did," he said.

"Then surely you know the timeless verse of your very own Robert Frost: 'The road not taken,' and so on. Because that is where you stand, my friend: at a crossroads. Allow me to suggest that you are in danger of taking a wrong turning."

Hector's mind raced over the possibilities: someone had told Emin Bey a rumor about an affair with a married woman. Or: the parents of a student had seen him during that binge. Or: the telephone operator had been repeating and misstating conversations he had overheard between Hector and the lawyer in Connecticut.

"You should have come to me right away," Emin Bey continued. "We could have talked it over. But I would like you to know I hold nothing against you. We shall always be friends. All I ask is to be treated fairly.

"They are using you, of course. Forgive me for saying so, but you are really better off out of it."

Emin Bey paused to offer Hector a cigarette, and light his own.

"My advice is the following," Emin Bey went on. "Stay on the sidelines, as you always have. It is all anyone ever expected of you. Let them confide in you: this is fine. But do not let them force you into a false position. Remember what kind of people you are dealing with. They may feign friendship, but they are not your friends. Americans are an anathema to them. They cannot distinguish between a man and his nationality. They could slit your throat and dismiss it as a symbolic gesture. They are ruthless as only robots can be. Let others call them the flower of our youth," Emin Bey said in a low and trembling voice. "To me they are the pawns of Mao!"

Emin Bey shook his fist at the window. Hector stared at him, the blood draining from his face. "Who are you talking about?" he asked in a hoarse whisper. "Who exactly?"

"Halûk, of course. Halûk and his bolshy friends."

"What have they been saying about me?"

"I am hardly in a position to know that, my dear boy. But *you* are, and all I ask is that you be careful."

It was an interesting question—what was a man suffering from paranoia to do—how was he to cure himself—if his worst fears turned out to be true? As Hector walked across the campus on his way home, struggling to keep his head high, he told himself again and again that he had done nothing to earn Emin Bey's contempt, or Halûk's vicious mockery. No, it was a rumor that had turned them against him.

He wondered what the rumor was. Monstrous possibilities marched through his mind. Someone had linked him with the KGB. Or: someone had decided he was working with the Greeks and Armenians to overthrow the Turkish state. Or: someone had linked him with a gun-smuggling ring, or a subversive organization that supported the Kurds. God only knew what they had dreamed up. In a city where a man standing on a beach looking at a map could be arrested for spying, anything was possible. For all he knew, they could have linked him with the Rosenbergs.

By the time he reached home, he was ready to cry. All these years, all the time and love he had given those two, and now, when he needed their friendship the most, they had turned him into an enemy. He was glad to find Amy sitting at the kitchen table, even though she was wearing that new hard and brassy expression on her face, even though he knew that the drink sitting in front of her was not soda water, as she claimed, but vodka and tonic. It was not a time to quibble about details. At least she was not Turkish. She was American and not susceptible to conspiracy theories. She was his wife, and he needed her. Her face would soften when she found out what was wrong. He imagined her running her fingers through his hair, and asking him if he would like some camomile tea. But Amy had other plans.

While Hector told her what had happened at the office she just sat there and stared at him, blowing smoke in his face. After he was through, she offered him no words of comfort. She just kept staring at him. Then, after a good ten minutes, she announced out of the blue, "Meredith invited herself to lunch today."

"What does that have to do with it?" he asked.

She ignored him. "It was, without a doubt, one of the strangest lunches of my life." She paused to light a cigarette. "First it was the pitying looks. And the way she insisted that I stay in my seat. And the compliments—things like, 'My, you're remarkably courageous to attempt such an elaborate spread.' 'What are you talking about?' I said. 'It's just a couple of cheese sandwiches.' 'But the knife,' she said. And then, when I got up to make coffee, she was jumping around like a jackrabbit, guiding me past tables, finding spoons and cups for me. I must say I got rather annoyed. 'I was only trying to help,' she said. 'I didn't want you pouring boiling water over yourself.' Imagine how I felt! And then, when I asked her if I could pick anything up for her when I drove down to Bebek, she got positively huffy. 'Now, that's just going too far,' she said. 'I'm just not going to allow it.' 'For God's sake, Meredith,' I said, 'what the hell makes you think you can run my life?' And that was when she told me.''

Amy leaned forward. ''You told Thomas and Leslie you couldn't go out with them because *I* had lost my glasses!'' she shrieked. ''You told them that I couldn't even get out of bed without them because I was *legally blind!*''

For a moment, Hector thought she was going to spit at him. Her face, contorted with rage, reminded Hector of a gorgon. ''You take advantage of me. You make me look like a fool. You concoct vicious rumors about me, and then you come to me with some cock-and-bull story about how they're all mad at you at the office and you expect me to sympathize. Well, let me tell you this: if they're mad at you at the office, I'm betting ten to one you did something to earn it. You're a good-for-nothing selfish bastard. I know you too well. But I wouldn't worry my little head about it too much. You'll find a way to make it up to them. One night of carousing on the town and they'll all forget why they were angry at you. You'll fool them, all right, just like you always do.''

''But I can't,'' Hector said. ''I'm not drinking anymore.''

''Hah! I've heard that before. By nine tonight you'll be drinking with the fishermen down at Osman's.''

''But I've changed!''

''You haven't changed. You'll never change.'' She knew how to hurt him. ''You're too weak.''

At nine o'clock that night, Hector was not sitting inside Osman's. He was testing his strength by standing across the street and staring at the happy people inside—waiters carrying trays of *mezes* above their heads, students swaying back and forth as they sang together, fishermen lost behind a haze of smoke, and, at the corner table, Ralph, Thomas, and Leslie drinking beer after beer, their faces flushed, their eyes so bright they looked electrified. From time to time they would throw back their heads in laughter. More than any other group in the restaurant they were bathed in golden light. And yet Hector was able to resist the temptation to join them. He was cold and he was alone but at least he could take pride in the fact that his wife was wrong about him: he was strong.

He stared through the plate glass window until it seemed to detach itself from the building and shimmer in midair, like a mirage. He did not close his eyes because he wanted to feel the temptation in his bones. *Come inside*, the window said. *Leave your troubles behind. Have a* raki. *Have two. Have as many as you like. You're not man enough to go on like this, abstaining and spoiling the fun.*

He felt himself weaken. He felt a force that was almost magnetic pull at him, tugging him into the street that separated him from the golden window. He closed his eyes and almost gave in to it. As effortlessly as a man falling asleep, he imagined what would happen if he gave in entirely and allowed himself to be pulled across.

He imagined gliding through the door into the smoky room. He imagined Ralph and Leslie and Thomas waving at him from their corner table. He imagined their effusive embraces. He imagined their faces growing blurrier as the *raki* bottles piled up. He imagined walking down the street arm in arm with them, laughing at the blurry lights that were the oncoming traffic. He imagined a devil beckoning him. He imagined laughing as he pushed Ralph under the wheels of a bus, as he kicked Leslie through the air like a soccer ball, as he took Thomas by the collar and tossed him into the sea without effort. He imagined swimming through the sea, way way down, and looking up, and seeing flames. He imagined the devil smiling down on him and saying, "So you've proved to me you're strong. Well, what of it? Do you think people will like you better for it? Do you think it will make you happy?"

"Of course it won't make me happy."

"Then why bother?"

Why bother? Why bother? Hector opened his eyes and shuddered. He looked at his friends. The waiter had just arrived at their table with a plate of fried mussels. He could almost smell them. He shivered. The evening was growing cold and his hunger made him feel like an empty shell. He was strong but he found no comfort in his strength. He could think of no reason not to weaken, no reason to resist the warmth and happiness he would find at this friends' table. He didn't care that in the long run it would kill him. He didn't care if he lived or died. All he wanted was to stop thinking, feeling, and fighting.

He stepped into the street, and at that moment something happened that was so extraordinary he had difficulty assigning it to chance.

On the surface, it was commonplace. A bus came barreling around the corner, nearly running him over. He jumped back with a gasp, shocked out of his black mood, suddenly grateful to be alive. He watched the bus screech to a stop, admiring its powerful brakes like a child on his first trip to the city. The doors opened and discharged one passenger—a well-dressed woman with silver blonde hair who was carrying a high pile of books. She was frowning as she stepped onto the pavement, but when she saw Hector, her face lit up. And in a curious way he knew—even before he remembered her name—that she had been heavensent, to save him.

"I see you have had visitors," Halûk said to his wife as he emptied the contents of his pockets onto his bedside table. It was a few minutes after midnight. Halûk had just gotten home.

"How did you know?" Yasemin asked.

"There are two coffee cups in the sink."

"You are right. I did have a visitor. A colleague of yours, in fact."

"A colleague? What colleague?" Halûk asked. His face darkened.

"You are not still harboring grudges against my uncle Emin, are you? Allah, allah, allah. It's pathological. Really it is. You are incapable of trusting older men. No, it was not my uncle who was here. It was Hector Cabot. I happened to meet him at the bus stop."

"And so you invited him in for coffee?"

"I had hoped you would be home sooner. He had said he wanted to talk to you."

"There was no need to invite him in for coffee, nevertheless."

"But Hector is your mentor! I thought you would be angry with me if I did not show him courtesy."

"There is no need to invite men in for coffee at such an

hour of the night, especially if I'm not at home. It will only create misunderstandings."

"Allah, Allah, who will misunderstand such a visit? Here we are surrounded by Americans."

"Please. Let's not have this discussion again. I have nothing new to say."

"Well, I'm sorry you weren't here, in any case. We had a very pleasant conversation."

And it had been. As she snuggled under her covers, Yasemin remembered Hector's kindly, intellectual face and smiled. She had invited him up to the apartment out of politeness. Hence her joy when she had discovered that, despite his very different academic credentials, he shared her passion for her own field, which was psychology.

How wonderful it had been to speak with someone who did not mistake her for a witch doctor. After a month in Turkey, Yasemin had begun to despair of ever again finding anyone who shared her interests.

She had begun to despair of many things lately. One of these things was her marriage. Halûk had changed since their return to Istanbul. Once a genial partner, he had turned gruff and imperious. This demanding a full accounting of her every waking minute, while he himself felt no obligation to explain to her where he had spent his own evening, was typical of his new personality.

She did not want to press him on this point today. For once, she was glad he had stayed out late. If he had arrived home at the expected hour, he would have berated her for coming home after dark. He had grown excessively protective since their return. Only that morning, they had had a disagreement about her running.

Ever since classes had begun, Yasemin had been getting up an hour earlier than Halûk for calisthenics and running. It was the same routine she had followed in Cambridge, without comment or interference from her husband. Except that in Cambridge, she had run two miles. Here, with the hills, her run amounted to less than a mile. Even so, Halûk was unhappy with her routine.

He did not want her wearing running shorts. People would misunderstand, he said. He insisted that she wear her warmup suit, even on warm mornings. He didn't want her running through the campus, because people would misunderstand. He didn't want her running through Rumeli Hisar either, because people would get ideas.

He was right, in a way—people did get ideas. Everywhere she went, she was followed by a jeering band of street urchins who called her "big sister." Grown men called out rude invitations from doorways and automobiles. Grown women clucked their tongues.

But it had become a crusade. If she continued to run every morning, sooner or later they would grow accustomed to it. In this way, she was paving the way for some younger emancipated woman who found herself in a similar cage. This was how attitudes changed, she told herself. If you wanted to change attitudes, you had to swim against the current.

And what a formidable current it was. In addition to Halûk, all her friends and relatives ridiculed her. They were, for the most part, people whose knowledge of foreign countries was limited to couturiers, hairdressers, and hotel clerks; restaurants, casinos, and ski slopes. Despite their soigné appearances, they were out of touch with Western thought. They thought Yasemin was crazy to want to run up and down hills before breakfast. They also pointed out that running would ruin the shape of her legs—when these same people had encouraged her to be active in sports as a schoolgirl! It seemed that in Turkey the shape of your legs became important only after marriage.

In addition, they had an unenlightened view of psychologists. They thought she could take one look at them and swiftly learn their deepest and most frightening secrets. And so they would not confide in her, not even her dearest friends and cousins.

Whereas Hector—he trusted her. He respected her professional opinion. The things he had confided to her! She was glad that he had, because she had then been able to give him good advice.

About his problems at work, for example. Such a complicated web of anger and mistrust, and yet she had been able to see at once the misunderstanding that had started it. It was startlingly simple: Hector had failed to explain to his colleagues the true reason for his absences and changes in behavior (this reason being his battle with alcoholism). And so they had sought to explain these things with paranoid conspiracy theories. What Hector had to do to dispel these theories was simply to be frank with them. "You must go to Emin Bey tomorrow morning and tell him: 'This is who I am now, and this is what I plan to do. My reasons are a, b, and c.' My uncle Emin is a reasonable man. He will see then that there are no conspiracies. As for Halûk, I assure you that he has not become a revolutionary. I shall speak to him tonight about these misunderstadings, and tomorrow at the office you can make sure that he and my uncle speak frankly. The only way to quell these suspicions is through communication."

Communication. When she had been advising Hector, it had seemed so easy to achieve, but now, as she watched Halûk emerge from the bathroom flushed and angry, she felt her optimism dissipating. Oh, well, she thought. I must at least give it a try. When Halûk had gotten into bed, overpowering her with the combined fumes of toothpaste and *raki,* she turned to him with a smile and said, "Did you realize that Hector has given up drinking?"

"No, I didn't realize this. And I don't see what it has to do with anything."

"On the contrary, it is highly relevant. It is the reason why we have not seen him socially. You see, he still feels uncomfortable in social situations. He has not gotten over the longing for alcohol."

"Why did he stop?" Halûk asked. "Health reasons?"

"Not exactly health reasons," Yasemin said. "Mental health reasons."

"You think everyone does everything for mental health reasons."

"That's not fair, Halûk. It's not fair for you to malign my profession."

"But it's true. You see the whole world through the same pair of glasses. According to you, everyone has mental health problems. You probably think I have mental health problems, too."

"Of course you have mental health problems," Yasemin said. "Everyone has mental health problems. It is normal."

"So what is your analysis of Hector Cabot's mental health problems?"

"He blames himself for his mother's death."

"Ah, how insightful," Halûk said. "What a succinct analysis. My hat goes off to you, Yasemin. With your extraordinary powers of insight, I advise you to open up a mental health clinic. It would be a real service to our fatherland."

"If you insist on ridiculing me, then I refuse to talk with you," Yasemin said. She turned her back on her husband and turned off the light.

When Hector woke up the next morning, he felt like a new man. Thanks to Yasemin, he now saw his life clearly. Everything was going to be fine, so long as he stood firm and communicated his resolve to all who knew him.

He made a list of all the things he had to do and then proceeded to do them. He called up Nikolai Kadinsky and asked after his father. He told Amy who his father was. He apologized to Emin Bey, to Halûk, to Leslie, to Thomas, to his children, and announced to them all that he was giving up drink forever. He even told Neil he wanted to sit down and discuss prep schools. To his dismay, he discovered that no one believed him.

"What a joke," Neil said. That was everyone else's reaction, too. Later he decided that he had done it all wrong.

What he had done was get up from the breakfast table and say, "I guess I'll go try and call my father."

"That's a good one," Amy had said as she buttered her toast.

"How can you call your father?" Neil had asked. "I thought he was dead."

"Actually, he's not dead," Hector had said. "He's alive. You may even have met him. His name is Phillip Best."

"That's a good one," Amy had said again.

"Actually, it's not a joke," Hector had protested. "It's true. He really is my father."

"And the moon's made of blue cheese," Amy had said. She had then gone on to explain to the children who Phillip Best was in highly uncomplimentary terms. She dwelt in particular on his hypocrisy. Someone with his past had no business going into the Church, she said. It was such a cruel indictment that tears formed in Hector's eyes. When the children saw the expression on his face, they burst out laughing. "Look at him!" Neil said. And Chloe said, "What a relief to see you clowning around for a change. You've been so gloomy all summer. You'd think this place was a mausoleum."

"Don't talk with your mouth open, Chloe," Neil said.

"What do you mean, don't talk with you mouth open? How else am I supposed to talk?"

"I mean, don't talk with your mouth full."

"That's better," Chloe said. They both giggled. Even Amy smiled, and that was rare these days. Hector did not have the heart to insist that he had not been joking about his father.

After breakfast, he gathered up what was left of his courage and called up Nikolai Kadinsky, remembering too late that Nikolai was the sort of man who might sleep until noon. His fears were confirmed: Nikolai sounded testy. It was possible, Hector thought, that he had interrupted his love-making to some wretched street urchin. "Did you say Hector Cabot?" Nikolai bellowed in his exaggerated Oxbridge voice, when Hector had explained who he was and why he had called.

"Yes, I did," said Hector.

"Aren't you the chap who swung at poor old Phillip last June?"

"If you want to put it that way, yes."

"And now you say you wish to see him," Nikolai said.

"Yes, if he's still in town."

"Oh, he's still in town, all right. But you won't find him here. He has his own flat now."

"Then would you mind telling me where I could reach him?"

"Would I mind telling you where you could reach him?" Nikolai repeated, like an English teacher trying to improve a foreign student's accent. "Yes, actually, I *would* mind."

"Would you mind tell me why you mind?"

"Would I mind telling you *why I mind?*" Nikolai repeated. "No, I don't think I *would* mind telling you *why I mind*."

"Then tell me why."

"Why," Nikolai echoed. "Why. It's awfully simple, really. It's just that *you're* not *our* sort of *chap*."

"Why am I not your sort of chap?" Hector asked.

"You're too rough."

"Too rough?"

"Yes, too rough," said Nikolai. "*We* don't *like* putting ourselves at the mercy of chaps like you, who swing at us and give us concussions and then let someone else foot the bill. It's just not on, you know."

"I can't tell you how sorry I am about that," Hector said.

"You're sorry, are you? Well, you certainly took your time to tell us, didn't you? How long has it been now? Three, four months?"

"I'm sorry about that, too."

"You're an awfully *sorry* sort of chap, aren't you?"

"This is ridiculous," Hector said. "Just tell me where I can reach him."

"I'm sorry, my dear fellow, but I promised him I wouldn't."

Hector sighed. "You say there were bills," he said after some moments of silence. "Well, I'd be happy to reimburse whoever paid them."

"How sporting of you."

"So if you could just tell me how I could get in touch with him."

"No . . . no . . . I don't think I shall, actually."

"Why not?" Hector asked.

"I don't think he'd like it, to tell you the truth. He doesn't need the money, you know. That was all seen to months ago. He's still rather fragile, and, do you know, I think he'd have a terrible fright if he had to see you again. He thinks you're monstrous."

"He thinks I'm what?"

"Monstrous. I said monstrous. That's the word he's most likely to use when your name comes up."

"Well, I don't blame him if he calls me monstrous. I *was* monstrous last time I saw him. I was dead drunk. But please, assure him for me that it's never going to happen again. If you're not going to tell me where he is, could you at least tell him that for me? Tell him I've given up drink. Tell him I've given up drink forever."

"Given up drink forever?" Nikolai said. "Oh, ducky!"

Hector slammed down the phone in frustration. "You goddamn queen!" he yelled at the receiver. Five minutes later, when he had composed himself and prepared a haughty speech, he tried to call Nikolai back.

To make an outside call, you had to go through the college operator. When Hector gave him the number for the second time, the operator said, "But sir, I have already put you through to the number five minutes ago."

"Yes," Hector said. "But the party on the other end hung up."

"The party on the other end?" repeated the operator. "Allah, allah, allah," Hector heard the operator say to his companion in Turkish. "These professors do nothing but go to parties. Don't they ever get tired?" Hector put down the receiver in despair.

The rest of the morning was in the same vein, with Thomas laughing outright when Hector told him he had given up drink, and Leslie snorting in disbelief. "I've heard that one before," Leslie said. Hector supposed he had. For thirteen years, every time he had a hangover, Hector had been saying things like, "I want to spend the next Christmas frozen in a block of ice." Or, "Please, next time I want a drink, could someone remind me of what happened yesterday?" Or, "This has got to stop. Every time I drink, it gets worse." His friends had been listening to him say things like this for years, and watching him indulge himself once again come cocktail hour. No wonder they didn't take him seriously.

By the time he arrived at the office, his confidence in his own words had reached such a low that he felt like an actor reciting lines. "Now, you two apologize to each other," he said to Halûk and Emin Bey. He made them shake hands. He was not sure if his act was convincing, if they would take his apologies and kindly reprimands seriously.

But they did take him seriously, very seriously indeed.

It was not that they believed him when he said he had given up drink. They did not believe him for a second. A man did not do such things. A man did not change so easily.

A man was someone who remained consistent. Especially a man like Hector. No, said Emin Bey to himself. No, said Halûk to himself. Hector was telling them that he was giving up drink because he no longer wished to spend any time with them. Halûk concluded that he had sided permanently with Emin Bey. Emin Bey concluded that he had sided permanently with Halûk. They did not blame this on Hector. They did not want to blame anything on Hector, because each suspected the other of having poisoned Hector's mind with lies. Instead, Halûk and Emin Bey sharpened their swords to use against each other. They watched each other's movements like eagles. Cloaking their intentions behind a façade of forgiveness and peace, they waited for the right moment. They lived and breathed revenge—so much so that Emin Bey's first move was almost an afterthought.

The opportunity arose during a telephone conversation with Policeman Ismet in mid-October.

Ismet had called up on behalf of a friend of a friend whose son had been involved in a cheating incident. It had been a sordid affair, involving not only Ismet's protégé—an empty-headed womanizer—but also the mathematics department's most gifted student in a decade, an Armenian. Emin Bey had been troubled by the disciplinary action he had been forced to impose. It had been hard enough to put a black mark on the academic record of a genius and thus jeopardize his future. But then, on top of everything, to have the oily Ismet insinuating himself into the debacle—this had been too much for Emin Bey to bear. At the sound of Ismet's voice on the telephone, Emi Bey had almost lost his calm.

Ismet did not understand the administrative process at Woodrow College. He did not realize that once a disciplinary committee had recommended suspension, there was no going back. And so, in his devious, roundabout way, he had called to ask Emin Bey to bend the rules for this worthless son of a friend of a friend of his. And how was he putting pressure on Emin Bey? By giving Emin Bey the impression that Hector Cabot was under investigation by the secret police, and by hinting that Ismet was in a position to curtail this investigation should Emin Bey grant certain favors.

Ismet had begun by asking Emin Bey to extend his condolences to Hector on account of the tragic death of his mother. He then tried to find out more about the circumstances of the death. When Emin Bey was not forthcoming, Ismet had gone on to share some disturbing allegations with him.

It was a pack of lies from start to finish, and afterward Emin Bey asked himself why he had even bothered to listen. They were a disgrace, these secret police, fabricating conspiracies where none existed. They were fascists. Their ultimate aim was to crush all national opposition.

Although he did not put it so bluntly, what Ismet was hinting at was this: that Hector Cabot was in the pay of either one or two governments. There were puzzling friendships which led Ismet's colleagues to this conclusion, notably Hector's intimate relations with a certain William Wakefield, a known CIA operative, and his less intimate but longstanding friendship with a certain TASS reporter who went under the name of Aleksei Kokalov. Then there was the recent opening of communications with a certain Nikolai Kadinsky, a Cambridge-educated White Russian who had once worked for Radio Liberty. Although he masqueraded as a stringer for the *Daily Telegraph,* he was a known double agent, as well as a homosexual, which raised still other questions. Finally, there had been a secret meeting last summer with a certain Phillip Best, who was masquerading as a priest but who was known to be a gunrunner. Emin Bey was so angry when he heard this last rumor that he almost lost his temper and told Ismet that this Phillip Best was none other than Hector's father. But then he realized it was unwise to give such a man any more information than he already possessed. He held his tongue, only to loosen it a moment later.

Emin Bey waited until Ismet had exhausted his supply of rumors. "There is an expression in English," he said. "It is," and here Emin Bey switched from Turkish to English, " 'You are barking up the wrong tree.' Do you know this expression? No, of course you do not. Excuse me. I had forgotten that you do not speak English. How rude of me. Let me translate it for you." After he had done so, he continued. "Please do not misunderstand me, my dear

Ismet. You are not to infer that I think you are a dog. I mean, rather, that you are, as I said, barking up the wrong tree. The danger to our national security does not come from the social engagements of my colleague, Hector Cabot. On the contrary, the threat is much closer to home."

Ismet asked for names. Of course, Emin Bey did not supply any. He could not resist provoking Ismet further. "This is a test I am giving you," he said. "Let us assume you are a bloodhound. I wish to determine your sense of smell."

He later saw that this had been going too far. He had given Ismet a challenge, and now he ran the risk not only of involving Halûk, about whom he cared little, but also his niece, Yasemine, about whom he cared very much.

He foresaw that Ismet would begin to harass either one or both of them. He also foresaw the family tempest that would ensue. The phone calls from Yasemin's mother. The reproaches from his wife, Roksan. He braced himself for the worst, and when nothing happened, he was puzzled. Could it be, he asked himself, that Ismet was not as consummate a bloodhound as he had taken him for?

He at least expected insolence from his niece's husband, but Halûk remained distant and outwardly courteous. It was "Good morning, my uncle! How fit you look today!" And "My uncle, I am dashing off to the snack bar. Tell me what your soul desires and I shall obtain it for you." Emin Bey was not a stupid man. He was aware of the sarcasm lurking behind these courteous phrases. And yet . . . and yet . . . he could not put his finger on it. Just as he could not connect Halûk with the whispering campaign that he could detect around him.

A senseless array of vicious rumors began to reach his ears. First it was a young American chemistry professor who came to him one day and asked him if it was true that his grandmother had been an Arab concubine. A second colleague asked him for his advice on whorehouses. Where, this simple-minded engineering instructor had asked him, was one least likely to pick up a disease? "I was told you were something of an expert in this area," he said. Still another American colleague—this one old enough to know better—asked him for the name of someone to bribe in the police department. "A friend of mine hit a pedestrian in Beşiktaş," he explained. "They're taking him to court. I've been told you're well connected in police circles. So perhaps you can point me in the right direction." It was all Emin Bey could do to keep from boxing the man on the ears.

It was from this last "police connection" rumor that Emin Bey deduced that Policeman Ismet had taken action again Halûk, and that Halûk was now planning a revenge. Where would the arena be? Emin Bey received his first clue in late October, at a reception at Kennedy Lodge.

Kennedy Lodge was the large, stone presidential residence at the edge of the college terrace. All important functions took place here. The guest of honor on this occasion was a visiting trustee, a slightly palsied American stockbroker.

Almost everyone was in attendance. The Turkish faculty were dressed in flawless dark suits, while their wives and female colleagues looked equally presentable with their chic hairstyles, their unobtrusive makeup, their tasteful accessories, and their graceful silk and linen ensembles, which fell, without exception, to below their knees. There was less uniformity among the Americans. Some wives wore outrageously short skirts. Those who did not wore dresses long out of fashion. While some men were dressed in suits (suits from the forties and fifties, with narrow ties from the early sixties), others had been content to arrive in corduroy trousers and tweed sports jackets. One elderly professor, soon to retire, was wearing a parrot-green velvet suit and a Carnaby Street tie. Another American professor—a dean—a fool—had turned up in a mountain climbing jacket.

When the weather was fine, receptions at Kennedy Lodge took place on the front lawn. But today, with the weather turning nasty, it was inside. The refreshments were laid out on long tables covered with stiff white linen. In one room were the hors d'oeuvres: deviled eggs, zucchini cheese boats, Danish sandwiches, *böreks*. In the other room was the punch—a dreadful concoction Emin Bey refused to touch. He had a secret and long-standing arrangement with a certain waiter—good old Ramazen *efendi*—who served him the president's whiskey on the sly.

Today, as always, Emin Bey had invited the other members of his department—and their wives—to enjoy this privilege with him. It was while they were waiting for the contraband that Halûk played his first card.

"My uncle," he said, "there is something I have been meaning to ask you. May I do so now?"

"Of course, my son."

"I have been thinking about Kirkor," he continued.

Kirkor was the gifted Armenian student whom Emin Bey had been forced to suspend. "And so," Emin Bey said, "you have been thinking about Kirkor. What have you decided?"

"I have been worrying about the effect any mention of the disciplinary action he has suffered would have on his chances with graduate schools. I was wondering if, perhaps, you mind find a way . . . not to mention this unfortunate episode in your letters of recommendation."

"My son," Emin Bey answered, "I, too, wish the very best for our misguided genius. But I shall not tarnish my integrity by lying for him."

"Of course, my uncle. I understand." He flashed that toothy pirate's smile of his, as if to say, "I've got you now."

By the time the whiskeys arrived, Halûk and Yasemin had moved away. Emin Bey was left with two extra glasses—a humiliating experience. He tried to get Hector to take one—just for appearances—but Hector, who was drinking lemonade like a missionary man, would not oblige.

Soon he, too, had moved away. Emin Bey was left in the company of three middle-aged women—his wife, Amy, and Betül Hanim. He glanced over his shoulder and saw Halûk standing with a group of friends, among whom numbered Tevfik Erzincan, an engineering professor with known radical connections. They were all looking in Emin Bey's direction with mocking smiles.

They were whispering to each other. What were they saying about him? What vicious lies where those shameless anarchists, those unscrupulous stool pigeons, those puppets of Stalin and Mao, inventing in order to undermine his position?

As she finished off her first glass of whiskey and reached for her second, Betül Hanim provided the answer.

"You really have put your foot in it with young Kirkor, haven't you? If you'd had your ear to the ground, you would have known that our younger colleagues are up in arms about that suspension. They say you did it for political reasons! I'm afraid, old boy, that you've given them the excuse they were looking for."

By this point in the reception, the Turkish faculty had divided itself into two groups, with the old guard standing next to the windows and the younger faculty standing near the punch. Tevfik Erzincan, with his heightened sense of political irony, had already commented on this phenomenon to Halûk and Yasemin. "Isn't it interesting," he now said for the second time, "how the fascists have remained to the right of this room, while we have remained to the left?"

"I am sure they are not all fascists," said Yasemin. She was looking especially beautiful this evening. "It is not fair to make generalizations about a group on the basis of the actions of a few of its members. Furthermore, it depends on the point of view of the observer. If we were looking from the opposite direction, these people you have labeled as fascists would be standing on the left."

"But we are not looking from the opposite direction," Tevfik said with an unpleasant smile. "We are looking from this one. And it is not just a few of them. They are all pro-American. In other words, they all support continuation of oppression."

"Not all Americans wish for continuation of oppression. This is a ridiculous statement," Yasemine said angrily. "It is our own countrymen who are furthering the objective of oppression. In America, the forces of liberation are strong—especially concerning the rights of women."

At the mention of the word "women," Tevfik's eyes glazed over, as did the eyes of his wife, Nilüfer. They had had to listen to far too many speeches on the subject of women lately. They were bored with it. Nilüfer had also suffered from this problem during their first year back from

America. But it had worn off, and the same thing would happen to Yasemin. In the meantime, she was in need of considerate treatment, due to an unfortunate occurrence, which they had just been discussing.

It had happened the previous evening, when Yasemin had, on account of pressing academic duties, left the Girls' College after dark. Having taken a *dolmuş* as far as the Woodrow College gate, she had then waited for a lift up the hill.

Everyone did this. It was one of the few things Yasemin did that Halûk did not disapprove of. The gatekeepers knew Yasemin well. When it was cold out—and it *had* been cold out—they invited her into the gatehouse to warm her hands by the stove.

The gatekeepers had to check every vehicle before they opened the gates. They never allowed Yasemin into a private car unless they were acquainted with the driver. And so, when a dark man wearing sunglasses pulled up in a green Anadol, and the gatekeeper greeted him not only with respect but with warmth, Yasemin assumed the man had a long-standing connection with Woodrow College. She thought nothing of getting into the front seat next to him.

Once inside, her doubts about the man began to grow. For one thing, he had the mannerisms of a peasant. There was a pink stuffed poodle perched above the back seat, and a large *maşallah* bead with tassles dangling from the rearview mirror. Clipped to the sun visor was a photograph of a buxom singer in a low-cut negligee. There was a Zeki Müren song playing at an unbearable volume on the tape deck, which the driver sang along with—"Without You I Can't Get Drunk Anymore." It was not the behavior Yasemin expected of an enlightened man.

He did not speak until they were near the top of the hill, when he pulled off the road at a curve.

"Why are you stopping here?" she asked in a shrill voice. He took off his glasses and smiled.

"You do not recognize me," he said. "But I am not offended. It was a long time ago. Before you went abroad. I am the infamous husband of your cousin, Banu." As soon as he said that, Yasemin remembered him. She had been present at the wedding, and as appalled as the rest of her family at her headstrong cousin's choice of a marriage partner. They had predicted marital strife for the couple. Yasemin remembered people saying that the groom—was his name Ismet?—worked for the secret police.

"Excuse me," she had said. ("What excellent manners you have for a feminist!" Nilüfer had exclaimed when she heard this.) "I don't have good vision in the dark." Embarrassed, she had accepted his invitation to drive her all the way home.

After they had passed through the Hisar Gate, Yasemin had instructed him to turn left at the tower.

"There is no need to give me directions," he retorted. "I know where you live. I also know where your office is and who your favorite students are. I know what your illustrious husband eats for lunch, and where, and with whom. I know everything."

"And why do you know everything?" she snapped back.

"I make it my business," he answered. "I make it my business to learn about the comings and goings of my beloved relations."

His sarcasm was evident.

"Can't you find a more fruitful way to spend your time?" she asked.

"Believe me," he answered, "my work is fruitful—in more ways than one."

When he pulled up in front of her apartment house, he peered up at the floor where she lived. Seeing it was dark, he turned to Yasemin and smiled at her ironically. This time he did not take off his glasses.

"You husband is not at home yet. Perhaps you would like to invite me up."

"I have work to do," she said sharply.

"What a pity," he said. "I would have enjoyed a tranquil interlude."

"There are more important things in life than tranquil interludes."

"It is a pity. All this reading will ruin your eyes. And that would be a shame, I think. Just as it will be a shame if you allow your legs to be deformed by this ridiculous habit of yours of running before breakfast. It is worse than riding a bicycle. Before long—excuse me—you will look like a man."

"How do you know I run before breakfast? Who told you this?"

Ismet paid no attention to her question. "If you were my wife," he continued, "I would not allow it. But of course I am old-fashioned. Your husband with his new political ideas must think differently."

"What are you insinuating?" Yasemin cried. "My husband is not involved in politics. Furthermore, his ideas are moderate."

"That is what he tells you, perhaps," said Ismet. "But there are those with close relations to him at his place of work who think otherwise. Those who think his motives are—how shall I put it?—subversive. But I would not worry about it, my dear Yasemin. There are ways. . . ."

"Ways of what?" Yasemin cried.

"Ways to insure that your husband comes to no harm." He reached over and put his hand on her leg, first softly, and then squeezing it with an iron grip.

"Take your hand off my leg!" she shouted. "Remove your hand or I shall scream so loud the entire neighborhood will be alerted."

"Please," said Ismet, not showing surprise at her reactions. "Stay calm. I am not a forceful man. I do not need to be. Look." He took his hand away. "You see? I don't need you. There are other places I can go. But frankly, I am surprised by your excellent modesty. I was under the impression that the members of our underground Left believed in sharing their women."

Later, when Yasemin, still hysterical, related the incident to her husband, she did not repeat this remark to him, even though it was the thing that had upset her most. In fact, she did not mention that Ismet had touched her or attempted sexual blackmail, because she was afraid of what Halûk might do in retaliation. Instead, she limited herself to an account of the insinuations Ismet had made about Halûk's political affiliations. "This man could hurt us," she said. "You must watch whom you talk to and what you say." She also repeated Ismet's parting words. "Give my regards to our uncle," he had said. He had been referring, of course, to Emin Bey.

This was the remark that upset Halûk the most. It confirmed his suspicion that Emin Bey was trying to undermine his position. And now he was going so far as to spread malicious rumors to the secret police! "We don't know for sure," said Yasemin. "We have no proof. Perhaps you could confront Uncle Emin directly. I'm sure he would be appalled to hear of Ismet's actions."

"You do not know what this uncle of yours can be like!" Halûk answered hotly. "He will simply deny everything. He knows no shame, this man. I am sorry, but it is the truth."

"There are other ways of dealing with this problem," Halûk had said. Tevfik and Nilüfer, when they heard an abbreviated version of the story at Kennedy Lodge, agreed.

"We shall let the matter rest for a while. And then we shall let the students do the dirty work for us. It will be impossible to trace the mischief back to us. As they say in France," Tevfik murmured, stroking the napkin he had wrapped around his glass of punch, "*'La vengeance, c'est un plat qui se mange froid.'*" Looking at his calculating smile, Yasemin thought how much he had changed.

Tevfik and Nilüfer had been back in Turkey since 1966. Two of these years Tevfik had spent in the military, and the third here at Woodrow College. Something had hardened in him during these years—or was it simply the regression she had noticed also in Halûk, a reversion to type, a return to attitudes and idea he had held before going to study at Columbia?

When Halûk and Yasemin were in Cambridge and Tevfik and Nilüfer in New York, they had visited each other frequently and become the closest of friends. In those days, Tevfik had been a good-natured sort of fellow, almost a buffoon at times. He had been eager—too eager—to sample every aspect of American culture. He had been the first to buy blue jeans, the first to try marijuana, the first to subscribe to the *Village Voice*. His enthusiasm had been infectious. "Would you mind," she remembered him saying with his eyes shining, as if he were about to propose something truly revolutionary, "would you mind very much if I *took off my shoes?* I am in an informal mood tonight."

She remembered how his socks were always as white as snow, and fragrant with detergent. He had never gone so far as to foresake his high standards of hygiene.

Nilüfer in those days had been studying anthropology. Now she had given it up. She had two children. She was an attractive woman, fine-boned, with angry brown eyes and smooth, shoulder-length hair that had been expertly cut in such a way that she was constantly having to brush it out of her face. It was a gesture she performed with sexual assurance. Like her husband, she had hardened in three years. From her description of her circumscribed existence, it was clear that she was not content with it, and yet she had contempt for anyone who dared to think conditions could be better. "You shall soon have the legs of a man," she had told Yasemin in a mocking voice when she heard about Yasemin's running. "It is stupid to continue such nonsense." And when Yasemin had complained about Halûk's reaction to her coming home after dark, she had laughed bitterly. "But of course he'll be upset. He is right." Watching her flutter her perfectly adjusted false eyelashes as Tevfik lit her black-market cigarette, Yasemin wondered if three years in Turkey would make her equally cynical.

Now their whole life was politics. They had been doing their best to convert Halûk and Yasemin to their new opinions. They acted as if they knew more, as if they were the ones who really knew how the world turned. Yasemin remembered one of their first evenings together, in September, when Tevfik had explained to Halûk how he and his younger colleagues were working toward the goal of the nationalization of Woodrow College. "But that would be a pity!" Halûk had exclaimed. "Education is sacred. It should not be dragged into the political arena."

Tevfik had smiled sadly. "My friend," he had answered, "how naive you are. We are all in the political arena, from the moment we are born. Everything is political. Even this glass in my hand is political." Yasemin remembered looking through Tevfik's raised *raki* glass and being almost frightened by the sight of his distorted eye shining through it.

"Everything is political." It was one of his favorite slogans. He had another favorite slogan, and it came up again now, as the Kennedy Lodge reception drew to a close, and the crowds began to thin, and there were fewer and fewer people standing between their group and Emin Bey's.

Yasemin, fearing mischief, pleaded once again with Halûk and Tevfik not to take the Ismet incident too seriously.

"We haven't any proof," she insisted. "And until he has proof, it is wrong of you to be plotting a revenge. There may be conditions we do not even know about. The situation is complicated."

At that, Tevfik smiled slowly. His eyes, as he allowed them to travel across the room in the direction of Emin Bey, contained, for a moment or two, the old sparkle. Then he turned to Yasemin, like a kindly hunter observing an animal in a trap. "So," he said, "you say the situation is complicated. You quote Stalin. When he was massacring his opponents by the hundreds or thousands, he used those same words."

"You must try to be open-minded," Yasemin pleaded. "If everyone thinks in this rigid manner, we shall soon be in the midst of a civil war."

"It is too late," Tevfik said. "The lines are drawn. Just look around you. See who is standing with whom."

Yasemin looked around her. Tight cliques everywhere, staring at each other with mistrust. There was only one man who was circulating, and that was Hector. Failing to see that it was a simple exercise in social graces (he had stood in front of the mirror that morning and said to himself, "You are going to that reception today. You are going to drink lemonade and you are going to be gregarious.") she, too, read greater significance into his movements, and allowed herself to hope.

During the next fortnight, the mood on campus turned from ominous to ugly. A bomb was discovered behind the basketball net in the main gym. The vice-president received an anonymous death threat. A skirmish broke out at a faculty meeting after a fistfight between two Turkish professors—once friends, now sworn enemies because of their difference of opinion on nationalization.

Nationalization, student representation, self-determination, autonomy, cultural purity, cultural imperialism—these were just a few of the terms that began to take on a life of their own during the first half of that ugly November. AMERICAN MURDERERS GO HOME. DEATH TO THE DOGS OF CAPITALISM. GOD DAMN CULTURAL IMPERIALISM. These were just a few of the slogans that were splashed over every stone wall, every concrete pavement, every asphalt road.

On the second Thursday of the month, the students held a forum at which they drafted a petition demanding Emin Bey's resignation. It denounced him as a fascist, a collaborator, and a capitalist stool pigeon. It accused him of suspending Kirkor for political reasons, and of attempting to ruin his chances with the top graduate schools of America and Europe by writing unfavorable letters of recommendation. In addition to calling for Emin Bey's resignation, it also demanded that the suspension be removed from Kirkor's record, and that any letters of recommendation Emin Bey had already written on Kirkor's behalf be reviewed by a specially appointed student committee which reserved the right to revise the letters as it saw fit. Unless these demands were met, the students were going to call a boycott.

The forum at which this petition was drafted lasted until the early hours of the morning. It was rumored that a contingent of trouble-makers from Istanbul University attended, and therefore generally believed that they were the ones who had blown up the two cars during the night. Actually, they tried to blow up three. On Friday morning, Thomas Ashe found a singed, gasoline-soaked rope hanging out of his gas tank. The tank was empty—this was what had saved his car.

Thomas had taken it badly. He had taken the gasoline-soaked rope to school with him (he regretted this later, when he regained his equilibrium) and presented it to the students who were lining up outside Hamlin Hall to sign the petition. "Why did you do this to me?" he asked them, his lips trembling with emotion. "What did I do to you to deserve it?" A few had shown genuine abhorrence and concern. The others had turned away with embarrassed giggles. "He's lost his mind," they said to each other.

Hector was only mildly curious when he walked across the campus that morning and saw Thomas arguing with a crowd of students outside Hamlin Hall. He noticed Thomas was holding a rope in his hand, but he was too well now to waste much thought on other people. He thought little of it. He thought little, also, of the fact that the math department had the atmosphere of a funeral parlor.

All day, Emin Bey stood at his window, sighing, examining his nails, so absorbed in whatever it was that was depressing him that when he lit up the occasional cigarette, he almost forgot to exhale. The smoke would come out, suddenly and too late, with a wheeze.

Hector didn't bother to ask him what was wrong, just as he did not bother to ask Halûk, who spent the day sitting stiffly at his desk, eyes downcast, shuffling papers. Hector assumed that the two had been quarreling again. He didn't want to know the details. It was all too tiring to watch others repeat the same ugly patterns when his own progress proved that it was possible to leave one's ugly patterns behind and start afresh. He was not saying he was perfect. He was not saying there weren't still things he was too weak to do, and no duties he had shirked, and no people he had avoided so long he couldn't even bring himself to mention their names. But he was on the right track. Every morning, he woke up feeling stronger, and he slept well now, without the aid of tranquilizers. He had no more nightmares, no more visitations, no more attacks of paranoia. He had conquered his ghosts. And as for dreams, he had only one.

Yasemin. Every night at five o'clock he would drive down to Bebek to pick up the paper, and when he drove back through the College Gate, there she would be, waiting for a lift up the hill. Seeing him, she would smile her brilliant smile, and Hector would blush. He would lean over to open the passenger door, his heart pounding. As she sat down beside him, he would wonder if this was the day when she would tell him, "Hector, there is something I must confess. I am in love with you." Because certainly she felt the same way he did—he could tell from her own high coloring and those longing glances that propriety forced her to cut short. Every day he was disappointed. She would continue the pretense. "What a pleasant surprise!" she would say. "How lucky I am that you are always picking up the paper at the same time!"

But by the time he had dropped her off in front of her apartment house, he would be almost glad they were friends instead of lovers. Lovers, he told himself, were hemmed in by jealousy, and with Yasemin, he felt free. Lovers were plagued by that constant urge to escape from one another, whereas all Hector dreamed of was the day when Yasemin would plant a kiss on his forehead and ask him never to leave her. Lovers only talked about love, while *they* discussed politics, work, ideas, the world.

And the most wonderful thing, he would tell himself, was that they had betrayed no one in order to have this joy. *They had no shame*. And yet it was Yasemin who shamed him out of his complacency on that Friday in November. She was the one who told him about the petition and the threatened boycott.

It was the first time Hector had seen Yasemin upset. "My husband, my uncle, they are all involved, and I can do nothing," she said. As he watched her dab her eyes with a handkerchief, he remembered how he had swept in and out of his office that day as blithely as a tourist. He remembered Halûk's stiff posture and uncomfortable downward gaze—he had looked up at Hector once like a scared child, but Hector had ignored the silent plea. He remembered Emin Bey's painful wheezing—he had been in need of comfort and Hector had just walked by. Not once that day had he asked himself what the problem was and what he could do to remedy it.

"You are the only one they all trust," Yasemin told him. "Couldn't you think of a way to guide them out of this terrible mess they have created?"

It was to restore himself in her eyes that Hector did what he had always vowed he would never do.

The following Wednesday, when it became clear that their petition had been ignored, the students gathered in Albert Hall to vote on a boycott. The student president had not yet finished his opening remarks when Hector threw open the doors of the auditorium, bounded up onto the stage, and delivered his personal plea to the six hundred men and women assembled before him.

His message was simple: the fighting had to stop. They were all making fools of themselves. And for what? God-damn it, *he* would write Kirkor's letters of recommendation, and, for the sake of peace, he would write any goddamn thing they wanted him to. The important thing was for them all to start acting like civilized adults:

"Political ideals are all very well, but you *cannot let them poison your lives*. The day you forget that your enemies are made of the same flesh and blood as you are *is the day you lose your humanity*."

When Hector invited questions from the audience, there was silence. It was as if they were all stunned by the brilliant simplicity of his ideas. So this is what it's like, he thought, to be in charge of your own destiny. And to think that only two months earlier, he had been hiding in his study, afraid to face the world. As he looked down upon that sea of eyes, he felt like a conductor who, having silenced the orchestra with a flick of his wrist, opens his arms to receive his applause.

But the silence continued, a few moments longer than he had expected.

Finally, a student at the back of the auditorium stood up. Hector recognized him. He had once given him a D.

"Sir, I would like to ask you a question. Why do you live in this country?"

"Because I like the life here."

"Do you like Turkey more than America?"

"Yes. I suppose I do."

"Then why are you wanting to send Kirkor Bardak to America?"

"Because it's the best place for him."

"Thank you, sir."

A second student stood up. "Sir, may I also ask a question, sir?"

"Of course you may."

"There is a word that I have been hearing which I do not understand. I cannot find it in the dictionary. But I think it is a machine. I am told that all American families possess two of these machines. Tell me, sir, what is a 'pigmobile'?"

There was a smattering of laugher in the crowd.

"Pigmobile is slang for car," Hector said.

"A car for pigs?"

More laughter, with a few cries of *"Ayip! Ayip!* Shame! Shame!"

"We are here to discuss a serious problem. Let's keep to the subject."

"I am sorry, sir." The student sat down.

"Is there anyone with a serious question?" Hector asked.

A student in the front row raised his hand.

"Sir," he said, "I have a serious question."

"Go ahead," said Hector.

"Why do Americans wear red socks?" More laughter.

"I do not consider that a serious question. Someone else, please. You in the corner. What do you have to say?"

"Yes, sir. I was wondering, sir."

"Yes?"

"Why do American women not shave their legs?"

"That is *not* a serious question!"

"I am sorry, sir. If you wish only serious questions, then let me ask you this. It is true, sir, that the children of certain faculty members sleep with their dogs?"

At this the hall exploded with laughter. Hector shook his head. "I don't understand you people, I really don't. Why are you treating me this way? You know me. I've taught most of you at one time or another. You know I love you and you know I want to help. So why the disrespect?"

A student at the front stood up. "Because, sir, your motives have been incorrect. You should not have been teaching us at all. We are Turks. We should be taught by Turks. There is no place in our fatherland for cultural imperialists."

"I am not a cultural imperialist. I am Hector Cabot."

"Sir, in that case I have another question. What is your true nationality?"

"American. U.S., I mean."

"And do you love your country?"

"In a way. I suppose so. Yes."

"In other words, you condone the illegal invasion of North Vietnam and the merciless oppression of twenty million black brothers who endure inhuman conditions in your own crumbling citadels of capitalism?"

"I'm sorry, but there is more to America than that."

"Yes, you are right. I have not mentioned the large population of psychopaths who fire shots from belltowers, killing countless innocents, or the police academies where fascist youths from Africa and South America are instructed in the arts of torture and murder."

"Have you ever been to America?" Hector asked him.

"I would not wish to go to such a place.

"If you haven't been there, then don't pretend to be an expert. Really, now, I expect more of you people. Of course I love my country. But not enough to condone all her policies."

"You *should* condone her policies!" a student shouted from the back. He was red in the face. "Sir! Do not let these shameless Communists pervert your patriotic beliefs!" The other students tried to boo him down. "They are scum, these people!" he shrieked. "They are scum!"

"Let's calm down, shall we?" Hector pleaded. "We've had enough name-calling already. As I said in the beginning, I have come to you as a friend. Let us leave my nationality out of it."

"You will gain nothing by talking to these scum! Nothing!"

"Please," Hector said. "Sit down."

But as soon as he sat down, another student rose to his feet. Turning to face his peers, he said, "I would like just to say to you one thing! It is important to remember that this man is not a true American! We must not take his opinions seriously. His mother was a Greek!"

"You leave my mother out of it. She was not a country. She was a woman."

The first student stood up again, "But, sir," he said. He waited for the auditorium to fall silent. "Sir, you say that people are not like their countries. But you, sir, you are like your country in many ways. There are significant parallels."

"Oh, really?" Hector snapped without thinking. "Like what?"

"Your country denies its links to the mother nations that fed and nourished it. Instead it seeks to crush them using inhuman methods. Your country has been involved in countless genocides. And you, sir, you killed your mother."

Hector did not remember jumping off the stage. He only remembered a cry rising from his throat, and his hands reaching out, reaching out but not touching the young man's face. He could see outraged mouths and heads thrown back in laughter, but he could hear nothing until they had pulled him to the side of the auditorium. And then the sound attacked him like an angry sea breaking through a wall. People came up at him like waves. "Are you all right, sir?" "Don't listen to what they say, sir." Their voices were drowned out by hoots and hisses and a chant.

One of the student leaders had taken the microphone. He was a Maoist, a senior, and an A-minus student. "Have you no shame?" he was saying. "Hector Cabot is a friend of our people. I will not permit for him to be kicked around like a dog." He could barely be heard above the hoots and whistles, the cries of "Death to America!" and "Let the man speak!" In the commotion, it was easy for Hector to slip out of the auditorium unnoticed.

They did not need him anymore. He had done his job. He had given them the excuse they needed to go after each other's throats.

He did not go to pick up the paper that night. He did not want to face Yasemin. He stayed up late reliving the nightmare, trying to pinpoint when it was he had laid himself open to ridicule, when it was that he had lost the upper hand.

The next morning he did not want to get out of bed. But he told himself to be brave. He had made so much progress. He could not let himself slip back into hell.

He went to school expecting to find it closed down, but there was no sign of a boycott. He gathered his papers and went to his first class.

The class was a small one. There were five students, one of whom was the now famous Kirkor. Looking at him, Hector could hardly believe that he had been the cause of so much uproar. Not a handsome boy at the best of times (skinny, with hunched shoulders and lank, mousy hair, a strand of which he was continually winding around his index finger), his looks were now further undermined by a red nose and a nervous tic. He and the others were in the midst of a discussion about discotheques. "What happened to the boycott?" Hector asked. "Oh," they said—casually, as if they were talking about a rescheduled soccer match, "it is not until tomorrow."

It was not until he turned to write a problem on the

blackboard that he saw the cartoon. It was a caricature of himself, standing on a castle wall waving a Greek flag. Underneath was written: "Society for the Advancement of Cultural Imperialist Donkeys."

"Who did this?" he asked.

They shrugged their shoulders. "It was here when we arrived."

"Why didn't you tell me about it?"

"We didn't wish to upset you, sir."

"Did it ever occur to you to erase it?"

They looked at each other, embarrassed. "We didn't have time."

He stared at the cartoon.

"Why would anyone do such a thing?" He turned around and faced his students: five pokerfaces. He ran his hands through his hair, searching for the right words to shatter the barrier between them. Why had he not just gone back to mathematics? he asked himself later. He knew the answer: it was because he wanted their sympathy.

"You people know me. You know I'm not a political animal. Why are you trying to force me into a corner? I'm not your flag-waving type. My patriotism—what there is of it—has never been so strong as to cloud my reason. I know what's good about my country. I know what's bad. And I just try to live my life. You have no idea how naive we all were, coming out here to teach. It seemed like the end of the world to us! We had no mission. We were just looking for adventure. We stayed here because we had a better life. We love it here. We all do. That's why we stayed. You have no idea how grateful we were to live in a place where there was history and tradition, where people still had neighborhoods and ate at outdoor restaurants, and bought their food in open-air markets, and still knew how to enjoy themselves. Don't you understand? We had never even heard the word 'imperialism.'

"And as for this Greek nonsense—I am not a Greek. I have no territorial claims. I am not 'land hungry.' I don't even own a house! I am American. Nominally, yes, I am that. But I am not an imperialist. I don't want to impose any ideas on you. Sure, I'd like to teach you what I know. Mathematics. The scientific method. Objectivity. Things like that. What we learn in this room. Everyone has a right to learning. But I didn't come here to teach Turks per se. I came here to teach you, and you, and you. Is that cultural imperialism?"

No one answered.

"Kirkor, you started all this. So I'll ask you: you're going to America to study next year. Is that wrong? Is that cultural imperialism?"

Kirkor shrugged his shoulders. He glanced nervously at the young man sitting next to him. "Perhaps he should not go," this student said.

"Why do you say that?" Hector asked.

"Perhaps he should prove his patriotic feelings by continuing his studies in Turkey."

"But that would be ridiculous! He would be wasting his talents if he stayed here."

"You are speaking as if we Turks have inferior resources. This is a cultural-imperialist attitude."

"But it's true," Hector insisted. "There *are* no resources for students of Kirkor's caliber. He would be wasting his life if he stayed here. Goddamn it, don't you people realize I wish the best for each of you? I'm not thinking about Turkey. I never think about Turkey. I'm thinking about you, and you, and you."

"It is this attitude that robs our country of its resources."

"Then so be it."

"Are you saying, sir, that we have no duty to our country?"

"You first duty is to yourselves."

"Then excuse me, sir. If this is what you believe, then you, sir, you are a cultural imperialist."

The student spoke gently, as if he did not wish to hurt Hector's feelings more than he had to. His smile was smug but also sad, and his large brown eyes had the inner glow of righteousness. Hector threw his chalk against the board. "Goddamn you people! Goddamn you to hell! When I think of the time I've wasted on you. I've taught you nothing! Nothing!" He gathered up his papers and left the room. But even as he slammed the door behind him, he knew that he had been wrong to shout at them.

He went into the bathroom. He looked down at his socks.

Red socks again. Only Americans wore red socks. He looked at his short-sleeved checked shirt, his Brooks Brothers pants. It was a uniform. He looked a his face—English eyes and Greek bones made bland by childish optimism. He had never felt so American.

Again that night he did not go to pick up the paper. He did not think he had the strength to talk to Yasemin and pretend there was nothing wrong. But she must have sensed something because she was waiting for him at the Academy Gate. She was pretending to examine a dead leaf.

When he saw her he wanted to put his head on her shoulder and cry like a child. He wanted to embrace her and feel her breasts against his chest. He wanted to put his hands through her lovely hair, and undress her, and feel her skin, and fall as in a dream into a bed, and lose himself in her.

He wanted to kiss her. He knew it was a risk but he didn't care. If she pushed him away, he would simply die, then and there, like a leaf falling from a tree. He stared at her. She was beyond his reach.

"You seem subdued today," she said. "Is there anything wrong?"

"No, not really," he said. His voice seemed far away, too.

"I hear there was an unpleasant scene during the forum," she said. He nodded. "What a pity. And you, of all people. It is a disgrace. Is that what is bothering you?"

He shook his head. "It's just that I'm . . . depressed," he said.

"And there is nothing in particular that is upsetting you?"

He thought for a moment before answering, "I feel no joy. I feel as if my life is over."

"Don't be so silly," she said. "Your best years are still ahead. You know, Hector, you must realize that all alcoholics undergo such depressions when they give up drink. It is not just you! It is everyone. You are not so different from others as you think." She put her hand on his shoulder. "Of course you feel empty. You have subtracted an element from your life without adding a new element to replace it. You should try a new interest or a new sport that would make your life full again.''

''What could possibly make my life full again?'' Hector said. He reached out for her. ''There is only one thing.''

She looked away from him and sighed. ''Only one thing? No. I think that is a pessimistic viewpoint.'' She turned to face him again, and for a moment he had hopes. But then she said, ''Why don't you try running? It's wonderful exercise. Not only is it good for the lungs and the cardiovascular system, it is also good for morale.''

It was advice Yasemin wished someone would give her, because recent events had given her friends and her husband their trump card. They had been able to talk her out of her daily exercise, saying it was too dangerous. ''No matter how fast you run,'' they had said to her, ''You will never be able to escape a man such as Policeman Ismet in his car. And it is politically incorrect. You cannot always run away from your problems. You must face them.'' She gazed across the Bowl at the tower and the Bosphorus and the Asian shore, and thought how much she would like to run there, and then beyond it, and beyond.

Hector did take up running. In fact, he took it up that same evening, because when he went home and saw Amy sitting at the kitchen table, waiting to ask him what was wrong, he knew he had to get out of the house right away—either that or die. So he found his old sweatsuit and his sneakers and set off down the cobblestone road.

And he ran and he ran and he ran, even though his smoker's lungs threatened to collapse on him. He ran uphill, downhill, through dogpacks, traffic, and crowds of jeering urchins. He ran across the Bowl, through the campus, around the playing field, down the Twisty Turny, around the castle walls, through Rumeli Hisar. But no matter how far he ran, he could not escape the feeling that the black sky was caving in on him, the windows were being shut and curtains drawn to exclude him, that there were people behind the curtains talking about him: the American, the imperialist, the infidel.

People who had known him for thirteen years were saying these things. People who did not know him at all. He ran and he ran, until he felt like a shell, a shell filled with hot air and other peoples' ideas about him. He ran until he felt like a ghost.

Phrases came back to him, reverberating in his hollow skull. *Is it true that all Americans have two pigmobiles? Is it true that American children sleep with their dogs?* Slogans jumped off the walls at him, slogans he had always dismissed: *American go home. Infidels go home. Death to the infidels.*

Why do American men wear red shocks? He was wearing red socks. And white sneakers, and blue sweatpants. He might as well have worn the flag. He might as well have paraded through the streets with a trumpet, reciting the pledge of allegiance. "I pledge allegiance to the flag . . ." He was back on the stage at Albert Hall. The students were jeering at him. ". . . and to the republic for which it stands. . . . One nation . . . indivisible . . . with liberty and justice. . . ." They were hurling tomatoes at him, and hissing, and hooting, and drowning out his words. "With liberty and justice . . . liberty and justice. . . ." They stood up and chanted. *Death! Death!* He couldn't go on any longer. His lungs hurt. He was coughing. He leaned against the wall. He looked at the black sky and moved his head back and forth, trying to shake off the billowing clouds of frozen breath.

A car came tearing down the hill, its headlights dancing as it rolled over the cobblestones. It stopped just in front of him, blinding him with its lights. For one brief, calm moment, Hector thought it was the car bombers, who had returned to execute him.

But then the car door opened, and Hector heard laughter. It was Leslie and Theo. They were drunk.

"Why, hello there," Leslie said, sticking his head out the window. "It's about time you fell off the wagon!"

"I haven't, actually," Hector said. It was hard for him to speak.

"Then what in God's name are you doing out here? It's late."

"I've been running."

"Running? At this time of night? You *must* be drunk. Hop in. We're going for a ride."

These are my friends, Hector thought. He tried to smile. "Where are you off to?"

"Where are we off to?" Leslie repeated. "Oh, I don't know. Nowhere in particular. Just wandering around looking for trouble."

They thought it was just an ordinary day.

"And don't think it's easy, either," Theo said. "You used to be the one with all the ideas. Life around here has become exceedingly dull since you went on the wagon."

"Oh, really?" Hector said. They were lost. He had led them astray. Now they were beyond his reach. "I'm sorry," he said.

"How long are you planning to keep this crap up?" Leslie asked. "You're not going to let us down at Christmas, are you?"

"Oh, of course not," Hector said. He smiled. The lies came hissing through his clenched teeth. "I may not be drinking, but you won't know the difference. By Christmas, I should be human again. Or inhuman, depending on how you look at it."

"It wouldn't be the same without you. Goosebuying Day, I mean."

"Oh, I'll come, all right. I might not join in the drinking, as I said, but I'll certainly join in the fun." I don't want to leave you in the lurch, he added silently. I'm your friend. I'm the one who made you what you are.

"You're beginning to sound like the Donald Ducks," Theo said.

"I guess I am," said Hector. "It's something of an occupational hazard when you spend your whole life sober."

"It must be awful," said Leslie.

"Sometimes it really is," said Hector.

"But not for much longer, eh? They say the liver regenerates in three months."

"My liver's fine," said Hector. "It's my brain I'm worried about."

They all laughed. For a moment it was like the old days. Remembering those days that were now lost forever, Hector felt deeply sorry. "Don't worry," he said, putting his hand on Leslie's shoulder. "I won't let you down on Goosebuying Day." It was the middle of November and the Christmas holidays seemed far away.

VII

Goosebuying Day

December 20, 1969

THE Saturday before Christmas was known on the Hill as Hector Cabot Memorial Goosebuying Day, in commemoration of Hector's famous binge in 1962, when he went downtown to buy a goose for Christmas dinner and returned three days later completely naked except for a Turkish flag which he had wrapped around his middle like a bath towel. It was the custom for Leslie, Thomas, and Hector to celebrate Goosebuying Day by going downtown and getting very drunk. They would begin at the Pasaj, just as Hector had done in 1962. Their wives usually drove down with them. Their excuse for accompanying their husbands was last-minute Christmas shopping, but their real purpose was to make sure the men didn't go missing, as this had been threatening to become part of the ritual.

After the women had dropped their husbands off at the Pasaj, they would go their separate ways, meeting up again at six o'clock at Markiz, a somber tearoom on Istiklâl which was one of the few places in the city where you could get Viennese coffee. Its tiled walls were adorned with turn-of-the-century murals depicting four garlanded women representing the seasons. However, it was not a cheerful place.

There had been some scandal during the fifties which had lost it much of its clientele. The owners, forever consulting each other behind glass cases of chocolate animals, looked as if the whole world were their enemy, and the waiter would totter to your table as if summoned from his deathbed. Still, the women would always manage to cheer themselves up by eating too many pastries.

At half past seven, they would make their way past the strip clubs, haberdashery shops, and fabric stores of Galata Saray and join their husbands at the Pasaj, usually with a following of disreputable-looking men who assumed they were either prostitutes or promiscuous airline stewardesses, because no respectable woman would be out unescorted after dark.

The Pasaj was an L-shaped alley lined with little drinking establishments known as *meyhanes*. It ran between the open-air flower market and Istiklâl Caddesi, once the grandest avenue of the European Quarter, and still one of the busiest. The Pasaj was known to be the most democratic corner of the country, because everyone—from the prime minister and the mayor and the distinguished graduates of the nearby Galata Saray Lycée, to porters and taxi drivers and the poorest beggars—drank there. Everyone, that is, except for respectable women.

However, Abdurrahman, the man who tended bar at the *meyhane* where Thomas, Leslie, and Hector drank, went out of his way to make things comfortable for the women when they appeared for their annual drink on the Saturday before Christmas. He would never have thought to bring his own wife to the Pasaj, and the fact that a party of distinguished professors would entrust their wives to his care moved him deeply. Abdurrahman was a fierce-looking man from Trabzon, a city on the Black Sea near the Russian border. He had enormous hands, hands intended for someone twice his size, and he himself was enormous. He guarded the women like an eagle, giving the evil eye to any beggar, prostitute, or condom salesman who dared approach them, any male customer who was foolish enough to glance in their direction. He would give the women beer but never spirits, and order plate after plate of *mezes* for them, which was the last thing the women needed after all those cakes, but which they ate and pretended to enjoy so as not to offend their self-appointed protector.

If only he had seen fit to protect them through their next adventure, which was to guide their husbands safely through the red-light district to Rejans. This was the trickiest part of the evening for the women—first waiting for a moment when all the men finished their drinks at the same time, and then suggesting brightly that they move on before Abdurrahman served them another round, and locking arms with them so that they didn't wander drunkenly into the street or fall into a ditch with the Christmas presents.

Rejans was a restaurant run by four elderly White Russian ladies who were said to have once been ballerinas with the Bolshoi. Like so many other establishments in Istanbul, Rejans was the last living link with another age—in this case, the period following the Russian Revolution, when the city became a port of entry for White Russian émigrés. You could still see how elegant the restaurant had once been, with its chandeliers, its wood paneling, and its gracefully curving balcony, which had once held an orchestra. But it required imagination, because over the years Rejans had grown quite seedy. The walls were painted mustard yellow, the lighting was dim, the former ballerinas were black and had hunched backs, and the once elegant balcony was now filled with broken chairs only partially concealed under a tarpaulin.

The restaurant's specialties were *piroshki,* chicken *kievski, stroganoff,* chocolate meringues, and lemon vodka, the last of which the old ladies would bring to the table only after throwing up their hands and exclaiming in their birdlike Levantine French that Messieurs would surely die if they continued drinking in this fashion. Their protests were just part of the ritual. It was never long before the lemon vodka arrived on a tray. This was when they would lift their glasses and say a formal toast to Hector's goose. Thomas would read a witty toast. And, if there were any newcomers among them, Thomas would tell them the whole story.

He told the story well, even if he was splattered with mud from having fallen headlong into puddles, even if his hair was singed and disheveled from his collision with the aged Rejans doorman and his electric bar heater. He could hold his liquor better than the others. Although he frequently lost his balance, he almost never became incoherent.

He would begin by painting a pathetic picture of himself and Stella ambling along Istiklâl Caddesi in the snow, friendless after three years in Istanbul, convinced that the doors to the city would remain forever closed to them, and virtually penniless. He did not explain why they had no friends in Istanbul, because it would not have reflected well on some of his dinner companions, nor did he attempt to explain why he happened to have so little money on him that day, because it did not reflect well on himself. In those days, Thomas had banked half his salary, and the way he had doled out the remaining half had been Scrooge-like. He was ashamed even to remember how he had been then. Hector had changed all that, of course. Now there was hardly anyone on the Hill who spent money as carelessly, as generously, as Thomas.

It was the Saturday before Christmas, Thomas would continue, and Istiklâl Caddesi had never looked so grim. Splattered with drizzle and slush, unable to wrest themselves free of the dark, hostile stares of the crowds of homeless men who gathered around the fires of the chestnut vendors to warm their hands, they had finally, after three lonely years, decided to give up on the expatriate life and return to America. This would probably mean living with their relatives in New Jersey until Thomas found another job. It would probably mean that Stella would have to support them for a year or two by working as a checker in a supermarket. Their relatives would be triumphant, because they had opposed Thomas and Stella's plans to live abroad. But what could you do when you have been proven wrong except swallow your pride and begin again? He did not mention that he had just received a letter from his former thesis advisor, now happily established at Mills College in Oakland, inviting him to come join his department as an associate professor.

He and Stella had hoped to spend a summer in Italy on their way back to America, Thomas said. The Italian vacation was to have been a sort of consolation prize. But when they did their accounts during a grim lunch at an Istiklâl

Caddesi cafeteria, they realized that they had only enough money for a week in Rome.

If the party contained any recently arrived Americans, Thomas made light of this part of the story. Once he had gotten into a fistfight with a man one year out of college who wanted to know why it was such a fucking tragedy to have to go back to America, and why it was so important to stop off in fucking Rome. "Who do you think you are," the man had asked, "a fucking Rothschild?" But if the party consisted only of hardcore expatriates, he made much of their disappointment at the abbreviated Rome vacation. He described how Stella burst into tears at the grim cafeteria, and how, fighting tears himself, he had tried to make her see the bright side of things. It was with heavy hearts, he said, that they returned to the muddy avenue.

Just then, they heard someone belting out a joyous Greek drinking song at the top of his lungs. Thomas and Stella gasped. Who could it possibly be? they asked each other. The crowds of shabbily dressed men parted and suddenly they saw Hector, larger than life in a bearskin coat, a green and red scarf, an Astrakhan hat, and fishing boots that went up to the middle of his thighs. He was swinging a freshly slaughtered goose above his head like a lasso.

Thomas had seen Hector on campus, where he had always appeared preoccupied and taciturn. Stella had once carried on a stilted conversation with him at one of those dreadful garden parties the president of the college gave for visiting trustees. From those encounters, they had formed a different impression of him. They had difficulty believing the stories people told about him, his generosity, his splendid parties, not one of which they had been invited to. They had come to dismiss him as the very worst the Hill had to offer—a typical example of the Hill crowd, whom they regarded as brittle, snobbish, fussy, and ingrown.

Now here was a different man, swooping down on them like an angel in search of lost souls. He embraced them both with such warmth and enthusiasm that you would have thought they were long-lost friends. He insisted that they join him for lunch at Rejans. When they pleaded poverty, he said it didn't matter. He would pay for everything.

Off they went to Rejans, which Thomas and Stella had

heard so much about but had never been able to find. Here they had the most joyous meal of their lives. Jozefin Dalman, the Edith Piaf of Istanbul, was there, and she was even more charming than they had been led to believe. She came from an old and eccentric Ottoman family and was full of stories about the last Caliph. It was clear that she was infatuated with Hector.

Amy was at home, waiting for the goose, although she said later that it was more like waiting for Godot.

Leslie and Meredith were both part of the group at Rejans. They were in excellent form. Sitting next to them was a wild artist who was half Irish and half Turkish and did translations for a living. Flannery Carr, the Canadian journalist who was said to be a double agent, was sitting at the next table with a man everyone said later was the head of the secret police. When he left, Flannery Carr joined their party. There was much singing—Greek, Turkish, French, Irish. Jozefin Dalman did a heartbreaking rendition of "Je ne regrette rien." At Thomas' behest, Stella overcame her shyness and sang "Honeysuckle Rose." Flannery Carr even sang an Appalachian ballad. They must have gone through eight or nine bottles of lemon vodka. Everyone treated Thomas and Stella as if they had been their friends for years. They could not believe their good fortune.

At four o'clock, the old ladies turned them out. Hector paid for everything, leaving an enormous tip. He was hardly able to rise from the table. When he collapsed on the way to the door, the old ladies brought him smelling salts, coffee, water. They fawned over him as if he were their own child. They made Thomas and Leslie promise to make sure he got home safely.

Off they went to the opera parking lot. Halfway there, Hector suddenly realized he had forgotten his goose. They all went back to Rejans to retrieve it, but the restaurant was locked tight. When Hector refused to go back to the parking lot, saying he could not return home without the goose he had promised Amy, Thomas and Leslie sent the ladies home in the car and accompanied Hector to the poultry shop.

They had to spend three quarters of an hour at the poultry shop, because the man was out of geese and had to send a boy out to find another. While they waited, the man served them cup after cup of tea. It was clear that the man adored Hector and was concerned about his condition. He, too, made Thomas and Leslie promise to see Hector home safely.

By the time they left the poultry shop with the second goose, it was pitch dark. Hector suggested that they stop at the Pasaj before heading home. Thomas had never been to the Pasaj either. He was completely entranced with the characters floating through: the four-hundred-pound prostitutes, the accordionists, the beggars, the young boys selling chocolates, black-market cigarettes, and lottery tickets, and the men sitting at the high tables inside, feeding each other *kokoreç* and fried mussels. Leslie translated some of the conversations at neighboring tables. The two men who looked as if they were having a heated political discussion were actually arguing about how many buttons belonged on a shirt. The group of distinguished-looking businessmen who Thomas thought were discussing important economic issues were actually debating water temperatures at various Istanbul beaches. They were out to enjoy themselves, which meant putting aside all serious matters.

Thomas had never seen such life. He was having such a good time that he forgot what time it was. Before he knew it, it was half past six and he was late for dinner. He forced Hector to drink up and hurried them to Taksim. They were sitting in the *dolmuş* that was to take them back to Bebek when Hector realized he had forgotten his second goose at the Pasaj.

They went back to find it, but it was nowhere to be seen. Someone claimed to have seen a one-legged beggar running away with it. Hector was shattered. He sat down on the curb and burst into tears. He had spent all his money on drink, he cried, punching his head in frustration. Now he had no money to buy another goose. Thomas' heart went out to the man. They went back to the poultry shop and had Hector's friend send out for a third goose, which Thomas paid for with the money earmarked for his daughter Margaret's Christmas presents.

On the way back to Taksim, they stopped at Kulis, a dark, wood-paneled bar favored by Turkish writers, artists, and journalists, all of whom seemed to be Hector's friends.

One of them, the owner of the newspaper, was worried about Hector's condition. He lent them the money for a taxi to take him home. Unfortunately, he lent them enough money for twenty taxis, being a generous man. Since Leslie and Thomas were also drunk by now, they were feeling just as irresponsible as the friend they were supposed to be looking after. Instead of using the money for a taxi, they used it to finance a tour of Istanbul by night.

Every time Thomas told the story, the list of places they had visited grew longer, until it included not only the Pasaj and Kulis, but also the Krepen Pasaj, and the Gypsy bar, and Thomas' favorite Greek taverna, the Boem, which was closed now, unfortunately, due to the Cyprus troubles of 1964. Here he had Hector joining the famous tenor, Todori Negroponti, at the microphone, and singing a Corphiot *kantada* that moved the entire restaurant to tears. Then he had him dancing out the door to Jozefin Dalman's apartment, and from there to Flannery Carr's apartment, to the Divan Bar, to the terrace of the Park Hotel, to restaurants and nightclubs on both sides of the Bosphorus. It was this expanding list of nightspots that annoyed Leslie whenever he heard the story, although he could not really remember which of them they had actually visited that night. The only thing he could remember was being kicked out of a place where they had belly dancers.

According to Thomas, Leslie had wandered off with a party of AP stringers, while Thomas and Hector had ended up in a Turkish bath. While this was indeed how the binge had ended, there was an entire twenty-four-hour period, an entire Sunday, which Thomas did not include in his story. It was early Monday morning when they parted company, and not Sunday morning as Thomas claimed. But this was one inaccuracy that neither Hector nor Leslie had ever felt the slightest urge to rectify.

Among themselves, the three men referred to the second day of their binge as "the lost Sunday," but this was wishful thinking. It was anything but lost. Seven years later, they were still paying the price for their disgraceful behavior.

It had started off with a visit to a whorehouse.

They had been on their way home late Saturday night when Hector decided that he needed a woman. It would have been wiser to go to a whorehouse with a more discreet location downtown, but Hector insisted on the green stucco whorehouse above the Aşiyan Gazino, only a stone's throw from Thomas Ashe's garden. It was not Hector's first visit to this establishment, as was made clear by the welcome they received: gaggles of voluptuous women in satin nightgowns tearing down the corridor, their voices shrill with excitement, and the plump, stern, heavily made-up madame breaking into a smile at the sight of Hector, and enveloping his then wiry frame in a muscular hug.

It was not Leslie Lacey's first visit to the whorehouse, either. He had gone along with Hector on several earlier binges, but this was the first time he had worked up the courage to participate in the debauchery. As for Thomas, it was the first time he had even gone near a whorehouse.

He later cursed himself for having allowed Hector to drag him into an establishment so very close to home. From then on, whenever Thomas passed the whorehouse, which was almost every day, he blushed and averted his gaze, for fear that the woman whose attentions he had purchased might stick her head out the window and wave to him.

It was also the last visit to a whorehouse for both Thomas and Leslie, and the beginning of a long vacation from organized debauchery for Hector, because a few weeks later, all three men discovered they had syphilis.

This caused numerous embarrassments and fierce arguments with spouses, due in no little part to revelations about the extramarital activities of said spouses. But it was nothing compared to the fallout from their next escapade, which was the abduction of Feza Akyol, who was later to be better known by the maidenly title of Feza Hanim, the math department secretary.

Feza was then in her midtwenties. She was a small, dark woman who would have been plain were it not for her large, almond-shaped, heavily lashed brown eyes. She had been working as a secretary in the engineering school for a year and a half. Feza was the daughter of a municipal official, and she was an alumna of both the American College for Girls and Woodrow College. Unlike the families of so many of her former classmates, Feza's family was not wealthy, but it was highly respectable. And like any daughter of a highly respectable Turkish family, Feza had grown up protected from every adversity. She was, in short, a woman who had no business accepting a lift from three men on a binge.

Because that was what had happened. They had found her standing at the bus stop in Bebek early Sunday morning, and offered her a lift. It was seven in the morning. Hector, Thomas, and Leslie were on their way back into town. After leaving the whorehouse, they had gone back to Leslie's house for money and breakfast. Their spirits dampened by Meredith's unwillingness to join in the fun, they had absconded with the Laceys' car. The weather had turned beautiful, and they had decided it would be a shame to spend such a fine day in the company of their embittered wives.

Feza was not the sort of woman who normally accepted lifts from men, not even men who had once been her professors. The only reason she accepted the lift that Sunday morning was because she felt her happiness had come to an end. Although she was secretly engaged to a former classmate, she was soon to marry a man of her parents' choice. Her official fiancé was of inferior education, but her family thought it a good match because he came from a respectable family. They thought she was lucky to find anyone to marry her. She was getting old, and her Western ideas made her doubly unattractive. Furthermore, there had been rumors that she was developing a bad character.

Feza had been trying to convince her secret fiancé to elope with her. She had spent that Saturday night at his apartment (having told her parents she was staying with a trusted girlfriend). They had spent the night arguing, because he had no intention of eloping with her. When she left him that Sunday morning, she had told him she never wanted to see him again. Usually a dutiful and well-behaved woman, that morning at the bus stop she was full of defiance for convention.

Even so, it was hard for both Feza and the men to understand the logic of what they had proceeded to do. Whose idea had it been? No one could quite remember. The terrifying question for the men, of course, was whether or not Feza had had a part in the decision or whether they had whisked her away against her will.

She had seemed up for anything when she got into the

car, but this was the subjective judgment of three men with impaired judgment. Still riding high on their whorehouse experience, it was possible that they had overestimated her joy at having run into them. Had she perhaps been too frightened to express her disgust at their drunkenness? Was she perhaps trying to find a polite way out when she said she could not join them for lunch because she was worried about being seen by her family? Certain that made it sound like she was doing something illicit, when all she was doing was riding downtown with three men in a car. For better or worse, her secretive behavior made the men think of her as a co-conspirator.

Leslie and Thomas both remembered Hector pooh-poohing her qualms about having lunch with them. "Is that all you're worried about, being seen?" he had said. "Don't worry. The place I'm going to take us, no one could possibly recognize us." What they didn't remember was whether Hector had bothered to inform her that the restaurant he had in mind was five hours away in the ultra-Moslem city of Bursa.

Still, she had had opportunity enough to voice an objection. It wasn't as if her only chance of escape was jumping out of a moving car. Twice they had taken car ferries. It would have been possible, on either of those ferries, to get out of the car and demand that they turn around. This, as far as they could remember, she had neglected to do.

Bursa was not the best place to go on a binge, as it was largely dry. But this did not occur to the men until after they had checked into their hotel.

Bursa was a small city at the foot of Mount Uludağ. At one time it had been the capital of the Ottoman Empire. It was famous for its monuments, its kebabs, its piety, and its hot springs. In the basement of the hotel where Feza and the three men checked in at two that afternoon, there were a number of private *hamams*. They consisted of two chambers: an anteroom with a hard bed, and a vaulted chamber containing a marble pool.

Hector reserved a private *hamam* for the afternoon, but they didn't end up having as good a time as they expected, because Feza, who was now frightened and having second thoughts, refused, to their confused and hung-over dismay, to join them in the *hamam*. She said she didn't want to have to face the attendant. The men took turns trying to console her, padding up from the basement in their thick white robes and clogs and trying to reason with her through the keyhole. Thomas had not made it through the door. Leslie had, but only for a brief interview. Hector had managed to gain entry for a longer period, and although he remembered little of his interview, it had been far from brief, because it was Feza who later told Hector that he had syphilis.

In Turkey a marriage license cannot be obtained unless both parties have had blood tests for venereal disease. Feza, of course, had not thought twice about it. When the results showed that Feza had syphilis, there was a terrible uproar, because Feza's official fiancé claimed not to have had sexual relations with her. It followed, therefore, that she had indulged in sexual relations with someone else. The wedding was canceled, and both Feza and her family were in disgrace.

A small amount of detective work led the family to Feza's secret fiancé. They suspected him of being the diseased party. Since his varied sex life gave him no reason to believe he did not have syphilis, he took their accusations seriously. They told him he was to marry their daughter, or else. So off he went to the doctor for his blood test. The discovery that he did not have the disease sent him into a self-righteous rage. He broke off the engagement and left the country. For the second time in less than a month, Feza and her family found themselves disgraced.

Her family cleared itself by disowning her. Feza was left penniless except for her small secretarial salary. It went without saying that her marriage prospects were dismal. Shunned by her society friends, she was sustained by a small group of old classmates (a few of whom had found themselves in similar straits) and also by the guilt-ridden attentions of the three men who had accidentally engineered her destruction.

There was no way they could ever make it up to her for ruining her life. That much they realized. But, as Hector said at the first secret meeting convened to discuss the problem, they had to pay the price for their reprehensible behavior. They decided it was their duty to support her.

A monthly sum was agreed upon, to which Hector contributed the least, because he had no savings. Thomas contributed a fair amount until his savings were depleted, and from then on, Leslie shouldered most of the burden, diverting practically all the money that came to him from his trust fund. Because Hector was contributing the least money, and because he felt he had done the most harm, he considered it his duty to suffer the most humiliation. And so it was Hector who went down to the Armenian moneylender every month to change dollars on the black market. It was Hector who arranged to have flowers sent on her birthday, and Hector who pulled the necessary strings for her to be given a comfortable little apartment on campus. It was Hector who convinced Emin Bey to hire her as the math department secretary. And it was Hector who, out of consideration for her self-esteem, offered his amorous attentions as long as it was humanly possible.

Feza let herself go after the scandal. In the first two years, she gained fifteen kilos. She had asthma attacks, suffered from shortness of breath when walking up stairs, and developed kidney problems. Twice—in 1967 and this past summer—Leslie had financed trips to Switzerland to see a kidney specialist. Now she was lobbying for a trip to England, to see another specialist who would perform an operation on her varicose veins. It was not that they begrudged her these trips—after all, they had committed themselves to supporting her. It was just that the commitment had turned out to be more expensive than they had thought. Leslie in particular looked forward to the day when Hector received his mother's money, so that he could begin to shoulder more of the burden.

There was one thing they were thankful for. That was that no one knew. Not even Emin Bey knew. The only part Stella, Amy, and Meredith knew about was the visit to the whorehouse, and whenever Thomas glossed over the lost Sunday, they smiled knowingly at one another. They assumed that the men had spent all Sunday in the company of prostitutes.

The lost Sunday came to a close with the men's decision to cut their losses and head back to Istanbul. Feza did not say one thing during the entire return journey. They arrived in Istanbul at about midnight and dropped her off at a girlfriend's house. From there they went downtown for some more barhopping. They ended up in yet another *hamam,* this one public.

This was where the official story took up again. By the time they reached the *hamam,* Thomas would say (smiling nervously lest one of the wives point out that he had omitted something), it was eight in the morning. Thomas was very tired, never having been on a binge before. But Hector was still full of zest. Thomas was silly enough to allow himself to doze off. He woke up just in time to see Hector tiptoeing out of the bath dressed only in his boots and his bearskin coat, with the famous goose, now in dreadful condition, slung over his shoulder. By the time Thomas had thrown on his clothes and run into the street, Hector was nowhere to be seen.

Thomas told about Hector's reappearance the following morning as vividly as if he had seen it with his own eyes. Amy had opened the door, Thomas said, to find Hector standing there dressed in the Turkish flag he had torn off the pole in front of the Bebek police station.

Thomas did not see Hector again himself until Christmas Day. There had been hell to pay when he got home on Monday morning. Stella was furious when he told her he had spent all the Christmas money on a goose that it now seemed no one would ever eat. He felt terribly guilty, not realizing that much of Stella's surliness stemmed from the fact that she, too, had fallen in love with Hector, and she did not know how she was going to live without him.

It was a hollow Christmas morning until Hector appeared at the door, laden down with flowers and gifts which he insisted on giving to Stella and Margaret, despite Thomas' protests.

This was the part of the story that annoyed Amy. It was a well-guarded secret that Hector had just grabbed those presents from under the Cabots' Christmas tree. To make matters worse, they were not any old presents—they were presents from the package her mother had sent them. It had cost Amy a fortune to get the package through customs.

It was also a shock for Amy when she discovered that Hector had asked the Ashes to join them for Christmas dinner—without bothering to tell her. She was completely unprepared when they arrived at the door, their faces freshly scrubbed, their eyes shining with hope, their breath still smelling of Ipana toothpaste. Amy had to scramble about trying to set three extra places at the table without being too obvious about it. Even so, she did agree with Thomas when he said it had been a wonderful dinner.

Everyone had been there. There had been no spats, no dull moments. Feuds were forgotten for the day. Stella had played the piano for them and sung the blues. Thomas, too, had sung for his supper by reading an amusing toast. They had played charades, they had laughed a lot, they had danced. Amy remembered that Christmas as if it had been yesterday. She had tried to recreate it each year since but had never succeeded.

This year, Thomas and Leslie were looking forward to Goosebuying Day more than ever, on account of Hector's promise to come out of hibernation. It had been such a depressing fall: what they needed to put the petitions and student forums and car bombings behind them was a smashing good time. They made elaborate plans. This year they would hire an orchestra. As for Hector's promise to stay on the wagon, that was a pile of horseshit. He wouldn't be able to hold out for long. They were all going to become as drunk as lords. They would also try and convince the women not to come, or else cook up some plan to send them home early.

They were crushed, therefore, when Hector went into hiding two days before the big event.

He had been acting strange for some time now, but never so strange as he had acted at the faculty meeting on Thursday afternoon. (This had been his last public appearance.) In keeping with his new image as health enthusiast, he had turned up in a track suit. The Turks had been shocked. Toward the end of the meeting, there had been an angry exchange between two other members of his department (Emin Bey and some new young fellow) which Hector had seen fit to interrupt with a pompous lecture that had made all the Americans' blood crawl.

He had said things you just weren't supposed to say—not

in public, anyway. Things like, "It is no accident that there are no Turkish words for 'self-righteous' and 'self-criticism.'" And "The tragedy of modern Turkey is that its citizens do not understand the spirit of democracy." And "It's very convenient, isn't it, to have America play the bogeyman." And "You people are your own worst enemies. You talk and dress like Westerners, but underneath you nurture a classically Ottoman mistrust of rational thought." It had been very embarrassing.

He had left the meeting before it was adjourned. When Leslie and Thomas got outside, they found him doing laps around the track. They had tried to talk him into going to Osman's with them, but he had turned down the invitation. "I have to get my five miles in," he had said through gritted teeth. He had bounded off in the direction of the Bowl, and that was the last they had seen of him.

Correction. Leslie glanced out of his bedroom window on Friday night and saw Hector returning from a run. On Saturday morning he saw him setting out on one. A few minutes after he had left, Amy called Leslie to say that Hector wasn't going to make it to Goosebuying Day this year because he had a "lingering cold."

She sounded pleased about it, so pleased that Leslie decided she was lying. He said as much to Thomas on the phone a few minutes later. "Pollyanna's won the day," he said. They had long since decided that Amy was the one who had forced Hector to go on the wagon.

At first they were not going to go at all, but then they decided to go through with it anyway, and drink to the memory of better times. They would take along some new people. They needed new blood anyway. Meredith's friend, Ginger, wanted to come—she had never been to the Pasaj, she said, and neither had the Pettigrews, who also wanted to come. The Pettigrews were that charming English couple who were living at the Pevners' while the Pevners were away on sabbatical. Noel was working in the archives, and his wife was teaching German at the Girls' College. Neither the Ashes nor the Laceys had been able to get to know them as well as they would have liked. They decided that Goosebuying Day was as good an opportunity as ever to do so.

They arranged for Thomas and Leslie to go downtown in Leslie's car at noon. The others would follow in the Pettigrews' little Hillman in the late afternoon. They would rendezvous at the Pasaj between six and seven.

Thomas arrived late at the Laceys' house because he had not been able to find his favorite corduroy jacket, and he and Stella had had a fight about it. Stella said she was positive she had picked it up at the cleaners the day before, but she was always telling lies like this to cover up for her domestic failures. Thomas didn't believe her for a second. He told her in no uncertain terms what he thought of her. Here she was, he said, with a full-time live-in maid who not only did all the cooking and cleaning but who was bringing up Beatrice almost single-handedly. The only thing Thomas asked of her was that she pick up the dry cleaning, and she couldn't even do that. Stella was so angered that she picked up a vase and threatened to smash it over his head. He then told her she was no-neck Irish, just like her father. That made her so mad she went ahead and smashed the vase against the banister. She immediately regretted it, because it was her favorite vase. When he left the house, she was in tears.

Out of the frying pan, into the fire. Another more serious scene of domestic turmoil awaited him at the Laceys'. Although it was one in the afternoon by the time Thomas arrived, the Laceys' son, Eric, was still asleep. His parents had been trying to wake him up for hours. Watching their fruitless efforts, Thomas found himself thinking, Thank God I don't have a son.

The Laceys had known since June that Eric was no longer welcome at his Massachusetts prep school, but they had told no one about it until September, when gradually it emerged that he would be staying home that year, doing correspondence courses. Thomas supposed they were ashamed. Meredith had been her typical positive self about the plan in the beginning, but lately even she had voiced misgivings. As everyone knew, Eric had let his correspondence courses slide. He had spent the entire autumn stoned. Now it looked as if he might never earn a high school diploma.

When Thomas arrived at the Laceys', Meredith was

standing outside Eric's door trying to sweet-talk him into coming out of his room. After Thomas had been twiddling his thumbs in the living room for ten minutes or so, Leslie threw his book against the wall and went upstairs to try his own brand of discipline. "Open up!" he yelled, "or I'll kick this door down!" When Eric obeyed, Leslie seized him by his forelock, marched him down to the study, and locked him in. He instructed Meredith that he was to remain in the study until he had completed the week's assignments.

It was humiliating for Leslie to have to do this in front of Thomas, but he had no choice. He could tell Thomas disapproved of his tactics, but it was unfair of Thomas to judge him at all. Thomas had no idea what it was like to be responsible for a delinquent son.

Leslie had been hoping to get out early enough to be spared the spectacle of his daughter's departure, but just as they got into the car, up around the corner came the Asshole in the Yellow Sportscar, which was how Leslie thought of him. He was, without doubt, the most obnoxious man on the Hill. Not only did he smoke opium, but he was mixed up in that encounter-group crap. He was one of the organizers. How many marriages had broken up after the last one? He was also good friends with that witch who nourished her child with nothing but herbs. She was a witch, literally. She and her friends would spend hours chanting in the moonlight. Leslie supposed his daughter was one of her friends now, too. He didn't know which was worse, a delinquent son or an undiscriminating daughter.

The Asshole in the Yellow Sportscar did not deign to ring the doorbell. Instead, he honked his horn until Winifred came out. Then, after Winifred emerged, they had to watch the two embrace and light each other's cigarettes. That was when Leslie lost patience. It was his turn to honk the horn.

"What's the hurry, man?" asked the Asshole.

And Leslie shouted, "Get out of my way!"

The thing that upset him most was that he had always seen himself as an understanding parent. His leniency had been based on the false premise that his children, who had spent so much time in adult company, were just as wise, if not wiser, than he was, that they had learned from his mistakes. That they were careening into adulthood with even less self-awareness or foresight than he had possessed at their age had been a great surprise.

He ought to have taught them to believe in something. But what?

Glancing to his right, he saw that Thomas was frowning. Not knowing that he was pondering the mystery of his missing corduroy jacket, he assumed that Thomas was frowning because he disapproved of Leslie's treatment of his children. He probably thought that Leslie's problems came from not being strict enough with the children. How could he be so damn self-righteous? Leslie felt so angry that he forgot he had been only guessing about Thomas' thoughts.

Halfway to Bebek, Winifred and the Asshole pulled up right behind them. The Asshole waited until there was a car coming in the opposite direction. Then he pulled out to pass them. As they passed, Winifred gave them a half wave, rather like the Queen.

"Don't you worry about his driving?" Thomas asked.

"Of course I worry about his driving, you fool," Leslie said between his teeth. The celebration of Hector Cabot Memorial Goosebuying Day was off to a bad start.

At Beşiktaş they had to sit in traffic for an hour because there was an anti-American demonstration going on in Taksim. During that time, Leslie didn't say one thing. Instead, he brooded. What a cold fish he was, Thomas thought. He was a typical WASP. Completely devoid of emotion. You never knew what was going on in his mind. Thomas tried to draw him into conversation a few times, but Leslie held back with a fishy smile. His magnified eyes swam behind his glasses as if under water. So Thomas was left stranded with his own thoughts: bitter memories of the way Leslie had humiliated him a decade ago, angry speculations about the fate of his favorite corduroy jacket, resentful thoughts about his wife's lack of domestic virtues, and then simple self-doubt, that followed him everywhere like a shadow. What was he doing here with these people? Perhaps it had all been a mistake. Perhaps he ought to have stayed with his own kind.

The Pasaj was not its charming self. The cobblestone alleyway was sprinkled with flecks of snow melting into mud puddles. The men sitting inside the *meyhanes* looked upset, the men milling around outside looked as if they were spoiling for a fight. A man went by with an effigy of Nixon. It was always like this after an anti-American rally.

They usually drank standing up at Abdurrahman's outside bar, but today he didn't want to serve them there. In a conspiratorial whisper he told them it was too dangerous out there today. Anarchists, he said. If they stood outside, he could not guarantee their safety.

Although he agreed to sit inside, Leslie was annoyed. He did not like to be bossed around by a bartender. He was even more annoyed when Abdurrahman decided what it was they were to eat and drink. Leslie knew as well as Thomas did that he did so to insure that his American friends had nothing but the best. But while Thomas was grateful for the attention, Leslie resented it.

"We're going to have to go somewhere else," Leslie said. "There's only so much of this Big Brother nonsense I can take."

"He's only trying to look after us," Thomas said.

"There's no need for him to look after us," Leslie said. "For God's sake, you'd think we were three-year-olds, or two idiots who arrived on the banana boat yesterday. I've been here for twenty years, goddamn it! I ought to be able to decide where it's safe for me to have a drink."

The longer they sat at the inside table, the testier Leslie got, until there was a real danger he might offend Abdurrahman outright. And so, while Thomas did not wish to offend the man by leaving early, he decided it would be better to go somewhere else until the rendezvous hour. They paid up and then Leslie went to the men's room.

As Thomas had feared, Abdurrahman was hurt that they were leaving so early, and Thomas' heart went out to him. In his broken Turkish, he told Abdurrahman that it was just not the same without Hector, and Abdurrahman agreed.

"I have been waiting for him for months," Abdurrahman said. "But he hasn't come."

"He's been ill," Thomas explained.

"Please send him my condolences. Tell him I am waiting for him."

"I will. I'm sorry he is not with us today. And I apologize for my friend, Leslie."

"The man in the bathroom?" Abdurrahman asked. "He has not eaten any food. Is he ill also?"

"No, he's not ill," Thomas said. "He's a bastard."

He had hoped to let Abdurrahman know in this way that he wished to disassociate himself from Leslie, that he was just as angry about Leslie's antisocial behavior as Abdurrahman must be. But Abdurrahman was puzzled. "A bastard?" he said. It was not the sort of thing a man said about a friend. Perhaps a bad man might say that, but not a good man like Thomas. Therefore, he assumed that Thomas was being literal.

But Thomas disabused him of this notion by what he said next. "He's a bad man. His heart is made of stone." Perhaps if his Turkish had been better, he would have been able to express his ambivalence less bluntly, but that was the best he could do. Abdurrahman did not know what to think. For no sooner had Thomas said this than Leslie returned. Thomas smiled at him as if they were close friends. But how could that be? Thomas had just said that Leslie's heart was made of stone. True men did not act in this womanly, two-faced fashion. But how could he even allow himself to think that thought? Abdurrahman chided himself. He had known Thomas for years, and he was a true man. Abdurrahman decided that Thomas was forced to act in this fashion because Leslie was his social superior. Even so, he could not understand why Thomas had chosen to tell him that Leslie was a bastard.

Thomas could tell he had puzzled Abdurrahman, but with his clumsy Turkish, he could think of no way to undo his words. Instead, he left Abdurrahman an extra-large tip.

"There was no reason for you to leave such a large tip," Leslie said, when they had closed the door of the *meyhane* behind them. "You'll spoil him that way."

"I'm not spoiling him," Thomas answered sharply. "All I wanted to do was make it up to him. Perhaps you didn't notice, but we offended him."

"Oh, for God's sake," said Leslie.

They continued in the direction of the flower market in silence. Just as they were about to leave the Pasaj, Thomas saw their maid's husband, Hagop, sitting at a table next to the window in the very last *meyhane*. He was with his son, Avram, who was the last person Thomas wanted to see.

He had had an overdose of Hagop and Avram lately. He knew that if they went in and joined them now, it would be Hagop and Avram for the rest of the afternoon. The conversation would be a strain, what with their only common language being that pidgin Turkish that locals called Tarzanian. It would swing back and forth from the subject of fish to the subject of women, all day long, without deviation, like a pendulum. There would be more hints about America, because in a weak moment the previous spring, Thomas had offered to help Avram emigrate. Thomas was tired. He wanted to relax. But he was so annoyed at Leslie that he insisted that they join Hagop and Avram for "just a few minutes," saying that if they didn't, they would injure their dignity.

"Oh, for God's sake," said Leslie, but he allowed himself to be dragged in.

They had been sitting with Avram and Hagop for about ten minutes (having temporarily exhausted the subject of fish and moved on to a discussion about the size of some prostitute's breasts) when Thomas noticed that Avram was wearing a corduroy jacket.

It couldn't be *the* corduroy jacket, it couldn't be. Not the jacket Stella had forgotten to pick up from the cleaners. No. It had to be his other corduroy jacket, the one he had never liked, the one that had ripped at the elbow, the one that Stella had passed on to the maid.

They always gave their old clothes to the maid, who did wonders with them. She had a cousin who did invisible weaving. There was little that Hagop and Avram were wearing this evening that had not once belonged to Thomas. Even the shoes had once been his. Looking at Hagop's trousers, looking at Avram's shirt, he asked himself if he had really given them to Stella to give to the maid. He wasn't sure.

Even as he lifted his glass to make a toast, he longed for escape. A tedious evening lay ahead. He thought how different things would have been if only Hector had come with them!

He tried to hide his feelings and was very successful.

As Leslie watched Thomas clink glasses with his maid's menfolk, he thought, How sentimental Thomas is about the working class. He doesn't even realize that all these fellows want is someone to pay for their drinks. They're making a fool out of him. They know he'd bend over backward to preserve their so-called dignity. He really is a priest after all, Leslie said to himself. I was right way back then when I pegged him at the dinner party. If only Hector had come, he could have kept this business from going too far.

At four o'clock that afternoon, Stella, Meredith, Ginger, and the Pettigrews set out for the city in the Pettigrews' little Hillman.

Noel Pettigrew did everything to make it a pleasant journey. Every time there was a near collision, every time a cement block fell off a truck and nearly smashed through the window, every time an oil truck backed into the road without warning, or their way was blocked by an old man placidly feeding his horse in the middle of the road, Noel tried to make a joke out of it. He was as lively as his wife, Tash, was serene. "Oh, Noel," she would say. "You *are* childish." Then she would return her gaze to the scene outside. It was disconcerting for Stella because Tash was sitting where the driver should have been. The Pettigrews' Hillman was right-hand drive.

Stella sat in back with Ginger and Meredith, who were practically holding hands. They were carrying on a desultory conversation about some article they had both read in the *New Yorker*. Stella, who did not read the *New Yorker*, did not join in. The only thing she did was laugh at Noel's jokes. She was the only one who did.

"Well, I'm glad I have *somebody* who appreciates me," Noel kept saying, but this was not sufficient encouragement to draw Stella into the conversation. She was terrified of speaking in his presence because he was English. She was even more terrified of Tash. It was clear from the way Tash held herself that she came from the best kind of family, the kind of family Stella's ancestors had served since time immemorial as housekeepers and scullery maids. Tash's voice was so crisp and melodious, her sentence structure so complex, her manners so graceful, that she made Stella feel like a fishwife. Her own voice sounded coarse in comparison, her tongue leaden, her reservoir of adjectives severely limited. She noticed that Meredith's voice had become more English, which affectation bothered her almost as much as the subliminal flirtation she was carrying on with that awful Ginger.

When they had parked the car in the old opera parking lot, it was decided that Stella (who had no shopping to do) would direct Noel to the Pasaj while the other three women did their last-minute shopping. They would meet at Markiz at six.

"Now, tell me more about Goosebuying Day," Noel said, as they made their way past the decrepit hotels and grimy nightclubs of the red-light district. He reminded Stella of some movie star, although she could not remember which. "Are we actually going to buy a goose?"

"Not unless you want one," Stella said. She noticed that her voice was unnaturally high, like a child trying to imitate a baby. "Do you want one?"

"Not really, but I *would* like to hear the story."

"We should really wait and let Thomas tell you. He tells the story so well," Stella said.

"My goodness, you *are* being mysterious. Well, if you refuse to tell me what Goosebuying Day is all about, perhaps you could tell me more about the Pasaj."

"Oh, it's marvelous," Stella said lamely.

"Marvelous, is it?"

"It's . . . it's hard to describe. You'll see what I mean when we get there."

"What sort of clientele does it attract?"

"Oh, men," Stella said. "Mostly men."

"I see. And I suppose there are enormous janissaries or eunuchs or what-have-you standing at the entrance to repulse the hordes of emancipated women who would drink there given half a chance?"

"Not exactly," Stella said. "We can drink there because Abdurrahman—the bartender—takes such good care of us. He's a marvelous man. Wait until you see his hands."

"His hands must be absolutely enormous," said Noel. "You are the fourth person today to tell me about Abdurrahman's hands."

The Pasaj was not looking its best when they reached it,

and Stella felt responsible. The crowd was a rowdy one. Abdurrahman looked surly. Thomas and Leslie were nowhere to be seen.

They went to the outside bar where the men always drank, but Abdurrahman made them go inside and sit at a table. Even if the atmosphere had been more congenial, he would not have permitted it. He did not think it was fitting for the wife of a dear friend to be seen standing up outside, drinking with a man who was not her husband.

Then Noel made the mistake of putting his arm around Stella as they walked through the doorway. Abdurrahman misunderstood this gesture to be Noel's attempt to let Abdurrahman know that he, Noel, was Stella's lover. As Abdurrahman saw it, his loyalty to his friend Professor Ashe was being put to the test. And even though Professor Ashe had injured his dignity a few hours earlier by leaving his *meyhane* and going to the neighboring one in plain view of all, Professor Ashe was still his friend.

So he instructed the waiter not to serve Stella and Noel anything. When Noel came up to the bar to demand service, Abdurrahman contrived for his eyes to flash. He intended in this way to let Noel know that he was ready to defend his friend Professor Ashe's honor. Although Noel's Turkish, which he had learned at Oxford, was impeccable, his lessons had not included instruction in the ground rules of friendship, insinuated challenge, and veiled insult. He made the mistake of cracking a little joke about Abdurrahman's hands. "Your hands are famous throughout the city," Noel said. "I was expecting them to be much bigger."

Abdurrahman took this as a challenge to his virility. Eyes flashing, he slammed his enormous fist on the bar. "*Eşoğlueşek!*" he bellowed, "You son of a donkey! *Defol!* Get out!" All conversation in the *meyhane* stopped. Heads turned. Abdurrahman pointed at the door like a malevolent genie.

Noel was rattled by Abdurrahman's extreme reaction. He was not quite able to turn it into an amusing little joke. "Bloody marvelous, your Abdurrahman," he mumbled to himself. They went on to Markiz, where Meredith, Ginger, and Tash had already installed themselves.

Meredith and Ginger were deep into a heated conversation about Claude Levi-Straus, while Tash listened thoughtfully, her head cocked to one side like a bird's. At one point she offered her own opinion on the subject, which Noel disagreed with at length. Stella did not say anything, which she was glad about later, when she discovered that it was an anthropologist they were discussing and not the jeans manufacturer, as she had mistakenly assumed.

At half past seven, they all went back to the Pasaj to see if Leslie and Thomas had turned up. But the men were still nowhere to be seen. Abdurrahman repulsed them with a ferocious stare. On their way out of the Pasaj, a ruffian grabbed at Tash's breasts. Noel threatened to punch him, and he was suddenly surrounded by a crowd of sullen men who had come out in defense of their brother.

Fortunately, a mediator appeared who was able to defuse the situation. After he had placated Noel's opponent, chastised him, and patted him on the back in a brotherly fashion, he escorted Noel and the others out of the Pasaj. "Why you bring women in Pasaj?" he asked. "It is not good place for women. Next time you come alone, you be my guest. But no women, okay?"

"Not bloody likely," Noel said.

The mediator was puzzled for a moment, not sure if Noel had insulted him. Then he decided he had not, because Noel seemed to be a good boy, good-hearted, with an innocent if slightly effeminate appearance, who had risked a sound beating in order to defend the honor of his wife. Such a man would never make light of a man who had stepped out to defend him, thus avoiding bloodshed. So he slapped Noel on the back and said, "My name is Mehmet. I am always waiting for you." Then he disappeared back into the crowd.

"You know, of course, that he did not mean he was actually waiting for you," said Meredith. "It's only a figure of speech, which translates roughly as 'Be my guest.' "

"For God's sake, Meredith," Stella said. "Noel's Turkish is a hundred times better than yours." Meredith shot her an angry look. They proceeded to Rejans in silence.

Rejans, in keeping with the tenor of the evening, was looking seedier than ever. Noel and Tash were clearly disappointed, especially when the old ladies came to them with their famous lemon vodka. "I thought you said this vodka was home-made," said Noel.

"It is," said Stella.

"But this is Turkish Monopoly Vodka," Noel protested. "They've simply gone and stuck some lemon peel into it."

"Well, yes," said Stella. There was a silence.

When eight-thirty rolled by and still Leslie and Thomas had not appeared, they decided to go ahead and order *piroshki*. Tash perked up a little when Meredith told her how marvelous the *piroshki* were. "Oh, I haven't had *piroshki* in years," she said. "It will remind me of my childhood."

"Your childhood?" Meredith asked.

"Tash's mother was Ukrainian," Noel explained. This explanation seemed to make Tash very sad.

The *piroshki* were apparently not up to standard when they finally appeared. When Meredith said, "Aren't they absolutely smashing?" Tash said, "Yes! Yes!" with the nervous haste of someone who is not accustomed to lying. Noel made up for her lack of appetite by wolfing down his portion and then what was left of hers.

"I daresay we should order some more for the men," said Meredith.

"I daresay we should," said Noel. Tash sighed.

"Do you realize that we are sitting at exactly the same table as we did on the original Goosebuying Day?" Stella said.

"I daresay we are," said Meredith.

"When is someone going to tell me the story?" Noel asked.

"Don't worry," Stella said. "Thomas will tell you."

"You might as well tell the story yourself, Stella," Meredith said. "If they've been drinking since noon, Thomas will be too drunk to tell it well when he gets here. If he ever gets here."

"Thomas never becomes incoherent, no matter how much he's had to drink. You know that," Stella said.

"I'm afraid that's less and less true."

"I'm afraid you don't know what you're talking about," said Stella sharply. There was another silence.

"I'm sorry," Stella said.

Ginger smiled that unearthly smile of hers and said, "We're all hungry."

"After another silence, Noel said, "Well! It seems I shall never find out about Hector's goose."

"Why don't you just tell them the story, Stella?" Meredith asked.

"Why don't you?" Stella snapped back.

"Now, now, children!" Noel said.

"If we wait any longer, the story will be anticlimactic," Meredith said to Stella.

"I'm just not a very good storyteller, Meredith. I always leave things out and spoil the punch line."

"For crying out loud, it's not *that* good a story that you have to worry about delivery."

"When Thomas tells it, it's a very good story."

"Don't you think we ought to go ahead and order?" Noel asked, trying to change the subject.

"I daresay that might be a good idea," said Meredith.

"Would you stop saying 'I daresay'?" said Stella. "It's driving me crazy. You're not English. You're an American. Why can't you speak like one?"

"Come, come, now, children," Noel said, this time a bit more desperately. "Let's forget our little differences, shall we? Let's all have another round of vodka." He picked up the vodka bottle. "I'll play mother, shall I?"

"I thought people only said that when they were pouring tea," Meredith said.

Tash sighed.

"Well, perhaps things have changed," said Meredith uncertainly. "When I was going to school in England, this was certainly the case." She turned to give Stella an educated glare. "I did go to school in England for a few years, you know."

"Well, bully for you," said Stella.

"Stella, please don't talk so loud. Those are the Wakefields over there and they can hear every word you say."

"I don't give a damn about the Wakefields," Stella said.

"As well you mightn't," said Noel. "They are a loathsome couple." Willy Wakefield glanced up and gave Noel a withering look.

"Noel, please," Tash said sharply. "That was dreadfully rude."

This time it was Meredith's turn to try and revive the conversation. She did so by trying to draw out Tash. "How interesting that your mother was Ukrainian. Why have you never mentioned this?" Tash gave Noel a pleading look.

"Tash doesn't really like to talk about her mother," Noel said.

"But why?" Meredith exclaimed. "The Ukrainians are such fascinating people. I was just reading an article about them. Is your mother a native Ukrainian or the child of émigrés?"

"The latter," said Tash in a low voice.

"In Paris?" Tash nodded. "Oh, how marvelous!" Meredith exclaimed. "And you were born there?" Tash nodded again. "Goodness, how exciting! But your father was British, I presume?"

"Yes, he is."

"A member of the diplomatic corps?"

"No," said Tash. "He's a farmer."

Meredith turned to Stella and said, "Of course, you know that the English landed gentry call themselves farmers. Where is your estate?" she asked, turning again to Tash.

"Dorset."

"Ah, Dorset! Thomas Hardy country. It is so beautiful there. You've been to Dorset, Ginger, haven't you?"

Ginger nodded.

"Did you spend any of your childhood there?" Meredith asked Tash.

"My father and I went back when I was ten."

"But not your mother?"

Tash caught her breath and gave Noel a desperate look.

"Tash's mother was decapitated in a car accident when Tash was nine," Noel explained.

Meredith's eyes bulged as she choked on a piece of bread.

"They were in Switzerland when it happened," Noel continued. "Somehow she got her head lodged in the fender of the car they had crashed into. The other driver tried to back up a few inches so that they could dislodge her head, but being flustered, he forgot to put the car in reverse. So instead he went forward, and Tash's mum was decapitated."

"Good Lord!" Meredith said. "Oh, oh, you poor dear. And you were there!" Her voice trailed off. Tash blew her nose and gazed sadly at her hands. No one could think of anything to say. When Leslie and Thomas finally appeared at ten minutes to ten, they were still silent.

Leslie came first, looking extremely annoyed. Behind him was Thomas, glassy-eyed, a silly smile on his face. Holding his arm, guiding him among the tables, was Hagop, who was dressed more for a fishing trip than for a restaurant. The ex-ballerinas were not at all pleased to see him. Although they were charming ladies, they were also snobs, and they did not welcome drunken fishermen as customers.

Things continued to go wrong. It was so late that they were out of everything except cold artichokes and tough entrecote. Leslie could not be convinced to stop being nasty. Tash could not be revived from her depression. The greater the tension, the more nervous Noel became. Only Thomas seemed oblivious to the undercurrents. He sat there, smiling, spilling every drink and asking everyone to sing. When no one did, he looked shattered. Finally, he convinced Hagop to sing something. This annoyed the old ladies, who came and told them that Hagop was annoying the other customers.

"I don't suppose you have it in you to tell me the story of Hector's goose," Noel said to Thomas.

Thomas looked bewildered. Then his face lit up and he lifted his glass. "To the goose!" he croaked.

"My goodness, this is turning out to be quite a mystery," Noel said. "I'm going to have to hire a private eye."

Thomas spent the next thirty seconds trying to form a word. "It's H . . . H . . . H . . . Hector's goose," he finally said.

"Oh, I know that," Noel said. "But that's about all I do know."

"Stella, for goodness' sake, tell him the story," said Meredith.

"I guess I'd better," said Stella. "It's really a very amusing story. You see, Thomas and I didn't have any friends when we first came out here. We were very lonely.

But then we were Christmas shopping one day when we ran into Hector, and he brought us here, and we had the most marvelous lunch. Wasn't it marvelous?'' Stella said to Meredith. Meredith nodded. ''It truly was,'' she said.

''And after lunch, Meredith and I went home, but the men stayed downtown, because Hector had lost his goose and he wanted to buy another one. And so they went on a binge, and Hector lost two more geese.''

Noel waited expectantly, not realizing the story had come to an end.

''Oh, I knew I shouldn't have told the story. I ruined it. What else did I leave out?''

''The flag,'' said Meredith.

''That's right, I left out the flag. Oh! And I forgot to mention that Thomas spent all the money for Margaret's Christmas presents on drink.'' She laughed, expecting the others to join in, but they remained silent and looked at her sadly.

At eleven o'clock that evening, while his parents were eating their desserts at Rejans, Eric Lacey almost burned the house down.

It was Susan Duxbury who first heard the suspicious noises, Theo who first smelled the smoke, and Amy who first saw the flames.

Amy had been standing at the kitchen window, thinking about the good time she was missing downtown. Much as she had once dreaded Goosebuying Day, it now seemed like a pleasant mirage.

This was the time of night when Amy regretted how dull their life had become, after all the dishes and waterglasses had been washed and she and Hector had retired to the library with hot lemonade or cocoa or, if Hector was feeling daring, tea, and there were only a few more minutes to go before Hector stood up, stretched, and said, ''Ready for bed, darling?''

This evening, despite the growing tension, there had been no departures from the script. When Hector asked, ''Ready for bed, darling?'' she had answered, ''You go ahead. I'll be up in a few minutes.'' She had then gone into the kitchen for her nightly secret chocolate and her nightly secret cigarette.

He didn't want her to smoke anymore. He said it was unhealthy. So she kept the kitchen window open and blew the smoke outside. Then she brushed her teeth in the kitchen sink. She had a toothbrush and some toothpaste hidden in the drawer where she kept the larger utensils.

That was what she was doing when she first saw the flames—brushing her teeth. Brushing her teeth and wondering if Hector was ever going to ask her where she had been spending her afternoons lately. She had been spending them with Willy Wakefield, drinking secret whiskey. She still didn't like Willy Wakefield, strictly speaking, but she liked the way he appreciated her, how he would sit back in his leather chair and beam at her as if he couldn't quite believe his luck at being in the same room with her. Today, Amy had met his wife for the first time. She was back from law school for the holidays. She didn't seem to mind Amy's visit. As for Willy, he seemed to enjoy the fact that his wife was there to watch Amy come and go.

Did Willy and his wife make love anymore? As she idly watched the flames in the Laceys' window, she tried to imagine it. Then, with a start, she realized what she was looking at. Throwing her toothbrush into the sink, she ran upstairs to wake up Hector.

Hector was sitting up in bed when she threw open the bedroom door. In the half light his eyes looked like two little worry beads.

"You've been smoking," he said.

"No, I haven't!" she lied.

"You're lying. I could smell the smoke up here."

"It isn't a cigarette, for God's sake," Amy cried, "It's the Laceys' house! It's on fire! Get out of bed and help me!"

They found the Duxburys standing hesitantly in the middle of the alleyway. "The house is on fire!" Hector shouted.

"I'll get our extinguishers!" Donald Duxbury shouted. He and his wife went rushing back into the house, while Hector bounded up the steps and pounded on the Laceys' front door. Soon a disheveled Theo threw open the door. He had let himself in through the kitchen.

Following the smoke, they found Eric sound asleep in the middle of the library floor. His correspondence courses were aflame on the desk, as were the curtains behind it. There was an overflowing ashtray underneath the curtain, which was probably, they decided, how the fire had started. At Eric's feet was a bottle of vodka and the famous waterpipe. That, and the faint aroma of hashish, explained why he was asleep.

There was so much smoke they could barely see, but they managed to drag Eric into the hallway by his feet. They slammed the door behind them. They were trying to figure out what to do next when the Duxburys marched up the stairs.

They were both wearing gas masks. When Theo saw them, he let out a yelp of horror. Undeterred, they marched on. Then, crouching like policemen about to launch a drug raid, they kicked open the door and aimed their fire extinguishers like submachine guns.

Smoke poured out of the room, but this did not deter them. Amy wondered if they had once trained in firefighting.

Once he had drenched the curtains, Donald Duxbury turned around and shouted something which no one could understand because of the gas mask. When no one reacted, he shouted the muffled command again. It sounded like German. "Good Lord," said Theo.

Amy noticed Donald's eyes becoming very angry. He pointed at Eric's limp form and then pointed out the window.

"I think he wants us to take Eric outside," Amy said. They picked Eric up and carried him downstairs to the garden.

As soon as they were outside, Eric woke up. But he was still drunk. He showered Amy and Theo with abusive language. "He takes after his father, doesn't he?" Theo remarked. It took three people to get Eric back inside once the Duxburys had cleared the house of smoke.

They tried to settle him into an armchair in the living room, but Eric insisted on sitting on the floor. He was laughing in the most demented fashion, and entertaining them with stories about little men hiding in trees, peering in at him through windows, hiding inside his head and crawling out of his ears. Susan, her brow furrowed with concern, tried to sober him up with a cup of coffee, but he spat the coffee out, spraying Susan's dress. When she tried to force-feed him the coffee, he knocked the cup out of her hands, spilling it on the rug. They decided the best course would be to put the boy to bed.

It seemed risky to leave him alone in the house in a condition they all silently agreed was psychotic, so they decided to wait until his parents returned. Conversation was stilted at first, because the Duxburys and the Cabots had not spoken since the funeral. It was also understood that the conversation was not to focus on Eric, because they were all decent people.

Finally, they found a congenial topic in the Duxbury sons, who were all grown up and back in America, doing interesting things.

"It's wonderful how they've been able to adjust to normal life," Hector said at one point. "How did you bring them up to be so well balanced?"

"Don't ask me," said Donald proudly. "Ask Susan. She's the miracle worker in our family."

"Oh, it wasn't any miracle," Susan said, a little smugly, Amy thought. "I just tried to give them a sound moral framework."

"You know, Amy," Hector said, "I think we forgot to do that. I think we forgot to give them any moral guidelines at all. Which makes it all the more impressive. How did you do it, Susan? When you were absolutely surrounded by bad examples?"

Susan attempted a stoical smile, the kind of smile you might expect from a hunger striker if you asked him where he found his willpower. Donald looked puzzled. "Heck," he said. If Susan hadn't been there, he would have said, "Hell." "We never thought of you as bad examples. We just thought that—" Susan nudged him, and he fell silent.

"I can imagine what you thought," Hector said. "But it doesn't matter. God was on your side."

Amy could not believe her ears. Since when did Hector talk about God with the missionaries? She looked up to see if there was some irony in his eyes, but there wasn't. Then she looked at the Duxburys, both of whom were thoughtfully munching chocolate chip cookies. Suddenly, she had an image of them with their gas masks on. Catching Theo's eye, she saw he had just imagined the same thing. They both giggled.

They were silenced by sober glares from the other side of the room. Theo made his excuses and went down to his apartment. The others remained. The conversation foundered for a while, then regained its balance as Hector discovered even more subjects he now agreed upon with the Duxburys. The conversation was punctuated by smug glances at watches. After midnight, they all became quite grim.

Not long after two in the morning, Noel finally managed to extricate Thomas Ashe and Hagop from a stinking hole-in-the-wall they called "the Gypsy bar."

Since Leslie and Thomas were too drunk to drive and Meredith didn't want to drive at night, Noel ended up having to drive everyone home in his little Hillman. It was snowing by now, which made driving difficult, especially since Hagop took up so very much of the front seat. Every time Hagop turned around to share some Neanderthal joke with Thomas, the Hillman nearly toppled over. They barely made it up the Aşiyan Road.

There, in front of the Ashes' house, there was another foul-up. By now, Thomas had fallen asleep with a childish smile on his face and refused to budge. His wife, the hot-tempered Stella, soon decided that she was better off without him, so she marched up the front steps alone. In the end, Noel had to carry Thomas inside, with Hagop holding Thomas's other arm and blocking attempts on the part of the still-sleeping Thomas to swing at him.

"I cannot *bear* the way they behave toward their servants," Meredith said, as Noel carefully backed down the narrow alley to the Aşiyan Road. Meredith's high-pitched voice sent chills down Noel's spine. "You know, I really do think that one of the golden rules about servants is that you really must command their respect. And I find that we Americans have difficulty in this area. Perhaps it is that we do not respect ourselves sufficiently. Or perhaps we as a nation have too much sympathy for the underdog to assume the terrifying responsibilities of leadership. Even so—and despite their origins—I really do feel that the Ashes take things much too far, don't you?"

"Actually, I don't," said Noel. "Poor Thomas and Stella! It must be awful never to have one's house to oneself. I'm so glad no one can afford servants in England anymore. It makes life so much simpler."

Meredith gave him a long, puzzled look. Then she said, "Aha. You must be a Labourite." Noel cringed and said nothing. He hated discussing British politics with people who knew nothing about British politics.

"Servants aside," Meredith continued, "I really do feel that Thomas' drinking is getting out of hand. He's not looking well. I would not be surprised to hear he had cirrhosis. It beats me how he can get up in the morning and go to work."

"Surely it doesn't affect his work," Noel said. He hated it when Americans turned moralistic.

"Well, you're right, I suppose. I really am jumping the gun. I have no way of knowing for sure. But I do foresee a full-scale disaster with regard to that awful maid and her dreadful husband. Do you know they have the run of the house?" She went on to share a few anecdotes about the Ashes and their servants, together with her own theory of servant-employer relations, and the success with which she herself had applied this theory, which Noel found puzzling, since everyone knew that the Laceys' maid was a prostitute.

There were lights blazing from every window when they reached the Lacey residence. The windows giving out on the balcony looked as if they might be open.

"I didn't realize I left all those lights on," Meredith said. She invited Noel and Tash in for a nightcap, refusing to take no for an answer.

The hallway was full of large, black footprints.

"You're going to have to talk to Eric about wiping his shoes," Leslie said to Meredith.

"I *did* talk to Eric about wiping his shoes," Meredith said.

"I never said you didn't. What I said was that you were going to have to do so again, because he obviously paid no attention to you."

"Oh, Leslie," Meredith said, "you really are the limit.

Any time something goes wrong in this house, you blame it on Eric. No wonder he doesn't improve. And he's been trying so hard lately to please you."

"He has never tried to please me in his entire life."

"Oh, don't be impossible. What about today?"

"Today?" Leslie laughed bitterly. "God, you have a short memory."

By now they had ascended the stairs to the second floor, which smelled smoky. Meredith gasped, rushing into the room with the blackened door. Pushing it open, she revealed a charred desk, charred windowpanes, and blackened walls.

"Eric!" she cried, with a bloodcurdling shriek.

It was than that they all heard a deep voice coming from the living room. "It's all right, Meredith, we got to him in time. He's sound asleep." It was Hector Cabot, sitting in the living room with his wife and those missionaries from across the street.

"Sit down," said Hector, sounding more like a minister than a famous rascal. "There's no need for alarm. Everything's under control."

"That's an understatement!" Noel said cheerfully. No one laughed.

"Sit down," said Hector. "Have some of Susan's cocoa."

"Let me go down and heat it up," Susan said, bustling toward the stairs with the pan in her hands.

"Would you mind awfully if I had something stronger?" Noel asked. "We had a hair-raising drive home, and a shot of brandy would be most welcome."

Hector looked at Noel sternly. "Under the circumstances, I don't think it would be wise," he said. "Now, why don't you sit down."

Noel sat down. So this was the infamous Hector Cabot, the incorrigible womanizer, the good-for-nothing charmer who had once lost an inordinate number of geese. Something had happened to him since that party at the Ashes'. He was no longer the same man.

VIII

Rain

December 21–24, 1969

LESLIE was surprised when Hector woke him up at eleven o'clock Sunday morning and offered to drive him downtown to pick up his car. Leslie was at a disadvantage from the word go, because Hector looked so healthy, while Leslie had the usual Sunday morning hangover. Even before he had brought it up, Leslie knew that Hector had been out running.

That's what they talked about throughout Leslie's rushed, embarrassed breakfast, and all the way to the campus, which was where Hector had left his Citroen. Running, running, and more running. How wonderful it was, how good it made him feel, how much weight he had lost, how his muscles had never had better tone.

What Leslie really wanted to say was, Honestly, Hector, I don't give a damn about your muscle tone. In fact, I'm pissed off at you, damn pissed off at you for the way you let us down last night. But because he was so ashamed about his son, and the fire, and the nasty things he had said to Meredith in front of everybody after they got home, he did not dare say a thing. He let Hector drone on and on about his health, while he marveled privately at how quickly a man could lose his balls.

"You know what I keep thinking?" Hector said, as they drove through the Etiler Gate. "I keep thinking of how many years I wasted. I've spent the last twenty years wrecking my body. And you know how I feel now? I feel as if I've got one more shot. It's now or never."

They took the high road through the new suburbs, with their muddy, unevenly paved sidewalks, their hastily constructed concrete apartment buildings, haphazardly arranged neon signs—for banks, hairdressers, bakeries, dress stores—and lonely, windswept bus stops, empty this Sunday morning except for the occasional woman in her best coat clutching a box of pastries.

Not long after they had entered the city proper, they passed the cemetery where Hector's mother was buried. Scrawled in red on the high wall was a slogan: GODDAMN THE AMERICAN FASCIST MURDERERS. Seeing it, Hector's hands began to tremble, until he could barely hold the steering wheel. He pulled into an empty space at the side of the road. When his shaking was under control, he turned to Leslie and said, "I have a lot to answer for." Leslie did not know quite what he was talking about, his mother or the graffito, or both.

"Come on, now," said Leslie, opting for the simpler interpretation. "You simply cannot blame yourself for her death. It was an accident."

"But you don't understand. She didn't want to be buried here. She had made other arrangements. I just didn't know about them. But you know what the awful thing is? *I never thought to ask*. I just went ahead and buried her here, without thinking." He buried his face in his hands. "What would she think of me?" he said.

"Fortunately, you don't have to worry about that. She's dead."

Hector breathed in sharply, as if this were still a new idea. "But it's typical of the way we've always done things, isn't it? Act now, regret later. And we still haven't learned. No wonder they all hate us. No wonder the children are so mixed up. You know what I can't get out of my mind this morning?"

"What" said Leslie. He really didn't want to know. His headache was killing him. The two aspirins he had taken hadn't worked worth a damn.

"Eric's first drink," Hector said. "I gave it to him. He was ten. Ten! Can you believe it? I thought it was important. You see, my stepfather never let me have a drop and I hated him for it. And so . . ." He punched himself in the temples. "Goddamn it, what a fool I've been!"

Just the sight of someone pounding his temples was enough to make Leslie's own temples throb. "Don't tell me you blame yourself for Eric, too. I know you like to play the martyr, but this is ridiculous. Eric is a problem child. And if you hadn't given him his first drink, it would have been Meredith. Or me."

Hector gave him an incredulous look. "How callous you are."

"Oh, for crying out loud, Hector. Eric was bound to have some problems. How could he be normal growing up around us?"

Hector angrily started up the car again. He darted back into the traffic without looking over his shoulder, causing much honking of horns, which he didn't seem to hear. "What I can't understand," he finally said, forcefully, through clenched teeth, "is how you can just sit there and watch him disintegrate and not even try to do anything about it."

"What can I do, for God's sake?" Leslie said. "I can't get through to him. His mother undercuts everything I do. If this were New York or Boston, I could just cut him loose. But it isn't New York or Boston. I can't turn him out of the house and expect him to support himself. His only hope is getting into some godforsaken two-bit college. That's why I'm so pissed off about the correspondence courses."

"Forget the correspondence courses," Hector snapped. "He needs professional psychiatric help, and right away. Send him back to America. I'll foot the bill."

"Like hell you'll foot the bill," said Leslie.

"Why not? I'm coming into all this money."

"I can pay my own way. I still have some money left, you know. Even after Feza's last Swiss vacation."

"I'm going to take care of that, too, you know," Hector said. "As I said, I'm coming into a lot of money."

"I don't care how much money you're coming into. I'm not going to send my son off to America to be treated by some Freudian idiot who couldn't find Istanbul on the map. Eric's never even been to America. It's a foreign country to him."

"Then the least you could do would be to present a positive role model," Hector said.

"Positive role model, my ass. If he wants positive role models, he can move in with the Donald Ducks. What sort of thing did you have in mind, anyway? Me and him out in the yard, throwing around a football? Going out for a burger? Maybe we could work on a model airplane together. Now, really, Hector. This is not Bergen County, New Jersey."

"You don't have to live in Bergen County to give up drinking," Hector said.

"You can't expect me to give up drinking!" Leslie cried. "My God, what would I do with my hands?"

"Don't be facetious. Of course you don't want to give up drinking. You're an alcoholic."

Hector honked the horn at a car blocking an intersection. "You're going to die soon if you don't watch out. If not from cirrhosis, then from lung cancer. Your skin is gray. You have a chronic cough. But you don't seem to care. You don't want to change. You'll drink yourself right into the grave. And, thanks to your example, your son may end up in his grave before you. But you don't care. Life is one big joke. You're too sophisticated to throw around a football. You're too sophisticated to spend time with him at all. You're so sophisticated, you don't even care that he is teetering on the brink of psychosis."

"Psychosis?" Leslie said in a small voice.

It was at this point that Hector brought up the little men.

Leslie had heard his son talk about the little men. The conversation had terrified him, especially since he, too, had once seen little men staring down at him through an institutional bathroom window. It was in college, at the end of a particularly drunken football weekend, when he got up in the middle of the night to pee. Oh, my God, he had thought, when he had first heard his son—who was drunk, of course—speak of a similar hallucination. It was final proof of what he had been afraid of all along—that Eric was himself reincarnated, himself without the few constraints that had made it possible to make it into adulthood. It made him almost positive that Eric, with his disastrous genetic makeup, would die young—of reckless driving (if he ever learned to drive) or something worse. And before he died, Leslie was sure Eric would publicly humiliate his father by exposing every last flaw in his genetic code. Leslie had been dreading the day when the little men became part of the public record, and now the day had come.

"He said all this in front of the missionaries?" Leslie asked when Hector was finished.

Hector nodded gravely.

Leslie tried to think of something to say in his defense. He couldn't. "I suppose you're right. I'd better give up drinking," he mumbled.

"Of course I'm right," Hector said.

They were driving through the narrow streets behind Istiklâl Caddesi. Just before they reached the parking lot where Leslie's car was, they passed Jozefin Dalman's apartment. Seeing it, Leslie remembered that he had forgotten to visit her. He always visited her during the fortnight before Christmas, brought her a present or two, cheered her up, listened to her tell the same old stories. She took Christmas very seriously, having converted to Catholicism to marry her second husband. She had also, in the course of her life, been baptized into the Congregational Church, the Greek Orthodox Church, and the Armenian Church. During her third marriage, she had converted to Judaism. She had been brought up a Moslem and had preserved the Moslem's grave respect for all prophets.

She was running out of friends these days. The older ones were dying off, and the younger ones were postponing their visits. In a full life it was hard to find time for a woman who was drifting into senility. Her children visited her, but they didn't like her. They made surprise attacks, she said, catching her redhanded with the brandy bottle.

If he went up there now, Leslie thought, she would make him drink some brandy. Just the thought of brandy made him want to weep.

"It's a bad time of year for going on the wagon," he said, hoping Hector might let him off the hook.

"Believe me," Hector said, "any time of year is a bad time for going on the wagon. But you've got to do it. You simply have to. If you don't, you're going to kill him."

"Madame, I doing thinking. Today Monday. When Karismas? Wednesday? Thursday?"

"Christmas Eve is Wednesday," Stella said. "Christmas Thursday."

"Ah, gut. I forgetting. Our Karismas later. January."

"Yes, I know," Stella said. She smiled and bobbed her head. She didn't want to talk to Seranouche and wished she could find a way to get rid of her.

Stella was sitting at the kitchen shuffling through lists. The one at the top was a list of all the people she had planned to send Christmas cards to, except that now it was too late, which was a pity, because she had spent a fortune on UNICEF cards. She made a note for herself (on another list, marked "URGENT") to at least send cards to her family. She wondered if they would mind all receiving identical cards. They all had a picture of the three kings drawn by a child from Uganda. The kings looked very African. Stella wondered if her family would mind that. Then she told herself it didn't matter. She could always turn it into a joke. Underneath the column of "Season's Greetings" in five languages, she would write: "Welcome to the twentieth century! Your loving daughter/sister/niece/aunt, Stella." She wondered if they would mind all getting the same joke.

She thought of her family converging on her mother's house—a little ranch house surrounded by countless other ranch houses, in a suburb indistinguishable from the suburbs surrounding it. The kitchen with its rounded red Formica counters, its picture window overlooking a lawn of half-grown trees, its lace-covered table, its porcelain figurines, its glass cabinet with snapshots of grandchildren stuck along the edges. The Christmas ham and macaroni in the oven. The women taking off their veiled hats and fake-fur coats as they greeted one another. The children, squeaking-clean in their church clothes, running between their parents' legs. The men conferring with one another about the afternoon football game ("For Christ's sake, keep that ham in the oven till it's over. This year I'm not turning off the set at half time for nobody.") One of her brothers taking orders for highballs. The silence as the orders were filled and the women ran out of people to greet, and the children found the channel they were looking for on the upstairs TV (which was the old one; the console in the den was for football). Then her mother would sigh, as she did at every family gathering.

"Too bad Stella's not here," she would say.

The others would agree. "It's too bad. You think she'd get tired of that Turkey place. Wonder if she'll ever come back."

"Don't ask me," Stella's mother would say, adding, "I worry about the kids. She says they have churches there, but . . . I don't know. With that husband of hers, you never know."

"I wonder how she is," her sister Irene would murmur.

"Don't ask me," her mother would say. "She didn't write. No card, no nothing."

"Me neither," Irene would say.

"Same here." This was her other sister, Jean.

"Anyone hear from her?" Stella's mother would ask. The room would fill with sadly shaking heads. "How about you, Bill?" Bill was the one who made the highballs. "Not a word," he would say. They would bow their heads like mourners at a wake. Stella's mother would sigh again. It would be a few minutes before Bill's highballs and forced jollity made it feel like Christmas again.

Stella glanced at Seranouche, who was standing thoughtfully in front of the open refrigerator, her forefinger resting on her chin, her right foot tapping. Returning to the work at hand, Stella wrote, "Date family cards Dec. 2nd." That way she could blame their late arrival on the mails. On her last visit home, she had told her mother that in Turkey they didn't stamp mail for days sometimes. Her mother had believed her. She was ready to believe anything about Turkey. "Guess that's what you get when you hire Muslims," she had said. Stella had guiltily agreed.

Having solved the dilemma of the Christmas cards, Stella was now ready to move on to the greater challenges of the other lists. Lists of chores she could not afford to do until payday. Lists, compiled earlier that fall, in a mood of delirious optimism, of all the Christmas decorations she had planned to make, and all the cakes and pies and cookies. Most depressing was the list at the bottom of the pile. Actually, it was a chart. Names of family members and boxes next to them, labeled, "Major Gift," "Minor Gifts (3 plus)," and "Ideas for Stocking." Half the boxes were empty or incomplete.

For Thomas she had bought, at the Hisar Women's League Bazaar, a pair of those colorful slipper socks they made in some Black Sea village, the ones that itched like hell. Also a book from Yalter's he had since bought for himself. The only thing she knew he'd like was the bourbon. But he already knew about it because she had won it in the Women's Bazaar raffle. In fact, he had been after her to let him unwrap it. It was sitting under the tree, covered in red crepe paper, very obviously a bottle. She was just not good at disguising things. She was sure Susan Duxbury had a nifty way of dressing up presents, but then again, Susan had never given Donald a bottle of anything.

For Margaret she had bought a blouse her boyfriend would probably dismiss as old-maidish, and which she would thereafter wear only to school. She had also bought her a Hittite necklace at Yalter's.

For Beatrice she had bought some lousy toys that would break in a week. They had such crappy toys here. She had been intending to write her a story, too, but so far it was only half done. She had wanted to do color illustrations. Now it didn't look as if she had enough time. On the piece of paper marked "URGENT," she wrote, "B story—possible line drawings? Things to buy tomorrow Bebek: thick paper (white), black ink, construction paper (green), yarn (red). Ask T re whereabouts . . ." What she wanted to ask Thomas was where he had put that thing you used to punch holes in paper. What was it called? This was what happened when you stayed abroad too long. You forgot your own language.

Stella looked up. Seranouche was now leaning against the refrigerator, which was closed. She looked as if she might be trying to think of the word for something, too. Perhaps the English word for raise.

Bambi, the black cat, who caught rats for rewards of beef filet (and who was capable, at least according to his proud owner, Seranouche, of opening the refrigerator and stealing meat from the freezer) was rubbing himself against Seranouche's legs. Seranouche smiled at him indulgently. She now had only half a mouth of teeth. That quack in Bebek she went to had been taking them out one by one since July. She complained often about having to eat mashed food while the rest of her family ate like kings. Hence Stella's premonition that she was going to ask for a raise that would bring forward the day when she might receive her false teeth.

It was a pity, Stella thought, that they were broke.

"Hmmmm . . ." Seranouche kept saying. "Hmmmmmmmmm." With what she mistook for subtlety, she was trying to capture Stella's attention.

"So, Madame. I doing thinking," she began, encouraged by Stella's intentionally blank smile. "You saying Karismas Thursday."

'Yes, I did," said Stella.

"Hmmmmm. Today Monday. Tomorrow Tuesday good shopping day. I doing thinking. I thinking good idea for Madame Monsieur Karismas din-din mebbe lamb leggie."

"Oh, you don't have to worry about Christmas, Seranouche. This year the dinner is at Mr. and Mrs. Lacey's."

"Ahhhh . . . I seeing. . . . I not knowing," said Seranouche. "Madame taking something gut Monsieur Lacey house? I asking Nick big turkey? Ordering wines, ten twenny bottles?"

"There's no need, Seranouche. All they want me to bring is creamed onions."

Seranouche wrinkled her nose. "Kareem and onion?" she asked.

"It's an American dish," Stella explained.

"Ah, I seeing this," Seranouche said, although she very clearly did not see how anyone could eat such a thing. "I seeing this now very gut. Karismas din-din Lacey house." She tilted her head thoughtfully, her forefinger shifting from her chin to the furrows between her eyebrows.

Now I've stumped her, Stella thought. Seranouche had probably invited relatives over for the weekend. She had counted on there being a lot of food around. Whenever she did the shopping, she bought double and kept half. She did the same when she ordered food from Nick's. She thought Stella was too stupid to catch on. But Stella had been wise to it from the very beginning.

"Lemme thinking. . . ." Seranouche murmured. Then she brightened. "Karismas Eve family having big feast, no? Madame, you relaxing. Beauty sleep. I making lamb leggie."

"I already bought a goose for Christmas Eve, Seranouche."

"Goose in freezer?"

"That's right."

"Bad goose. Tough. Not many meats."

"You're right," Stella said. "There's not much meat on a goose. But it's enough for us."

"Then we having many vegetable. Lemme thinking. I making *kabak* . . . *patates* . . . *salata* . . . mebbe *börek,* Madame?"

"Whatever you say, Seranouche."

"So. Wednesday goose plenny vegetable. Thursday Karismas Monsieur Madame Lacey house. Hmmmmm. Friday mebbe lamb leggie?"

She was certainly desperate for that lamb, Stella thought. God only knew how many relatives she had asked over. They were all going to be packed into that little kitchen, glaring at her and the children, willing them to go out for the afternoon so that they could move to the comfort of the larger kitchen . . . and the living room . . . and the library. . . . If Stella relaxed for one moment, Seranouche took advantage of her.

But that didn't mean she was going to give up easily this time. Although she would probably buy the lamb after all, and graciously disappear on Sunday afternoon, pretending not to notice the disappearance of the extra leg of lamb from the refrigerator (which disappearance Seranouche would later blame on the black cat, Bambi), she was not going to commit herself so early in the week. Smiling sweetly, she said, "I'll have to think about it."

As Seranouche left the room, she could barely conceal her scowl. She went into the coal cellar and began banging about with the coal scuttles. It was her son Avram's job to fill them. It seemed he hadn't done so. She screamed for him in Armenian and then let him have it. Stella listened with pleasure. She enjoyed the rare occasions when Seranouche let Avram have it.

That afternoon, in Bebek, Stella had scraped together enough loose change to buy some mistletoe. Now it was sitting in an old newspaper on a chair, waiting to be attended to. Shuffling through the lists, Stella searched for the one entitled, "Things to do Monday." Underneath the note, "Check cleaners re T corduroy jacket," was the note, "Buy mistletoe." She crossed this out with satisfaction, picked up the mistletoe, and went upstairs.

It was four in the afternoon, the only time of day when the house seemed warm enough. Outside, the dull white sky was taking on a bluish tinge. A north wind was bending the trees, and it was still raining.

The lights were on in the living room. The cylindrical stove radiated warmth and a smell that reminded Stella of toasted bread. Thomas was sitting in his chair in the library, reading the *International Herald Tribune*. *Missa Solemnis* was on the record player. Every time there was a scratch, he looked up in annoyance. Stella decided to tack up the mistletoe in the living room first.

"Did you go to the cleaners, by the way?" he called from the library.

"Yes, darling."

"What did they say?"

"They claim they have no record of a corduroy jacket."

"Damnit. Did you check the other place?"

"What other place, darling?"

"Oh, for God's sake. The other cleaners."

"No, I didn't. I'm sorry. It didn't cross my mind."

"Well, check them tomorrow. Please."

"Don't worry, darling. I'll put it on my list."

Margaret was sitting on the living room couch with

Beatrice, reading her "The Little Match Girl." As Stella poked at the coals in the stove and climbed on chairs to tack the mistletoe over the doors, she listened, too.

> She struck her last match. Suddenly she was sitting under the most beautiful Christmas tree she had ever seen. On every branch there was a lighted candle. There were gingerbread men, and candy canes, and brightly colored bulbs, and little porcelain angels smiling down at her. . . .

Beatrice looked solemnly at her older sister, as if she understood everything. It was when she was sitting quietly that she most resembled Hector. Stella wiped a tear from her eye. Margaret continued to read in her normal wooden manner.

> The little match girl stretched out her hands to warm them, but as she did so, the flame went out. And all was darkness, except for the hundreds of Christmas candles, which rose up into the sky and turned into stars. Watching one of them streak across the sky like a comet, she thought, "Someone is dying at this very moment."

They had brought Margaret up the wrong way. They had turned her into an emotional tourist. She had seen so many ruins by her tenth birthday that ruined lives did not move her. She only saw the outside. She was blind to the soul of things. She would never know why it made Stella sad to hear a story about a little match girl whose splendid visions were extinguished. She would never know what was missing in this house. She would never know what was wrong with the Christmas tree.

It was lopsided, for a start. It didn't have enough lights; there was just one string. She had stepped on the other string of lights while she was arranging the first string, and there was no way to fix it. They were low on bulbs this year, too, because Beatrice had sat on the box. To make up for their absence, Stella had ambitiously baked a batch of Christmas cookies with holes in them that she was going to hang on the tree as soon as she remembered to buy the yarn in Bebek. She was also planning to string popcorn. A bowl of it was sitting next to the bourbon bottle under the tree, waiting for Stella to remember what she had done with the needle and thread.

Still, it was better than last year. Last year, Margaret had decorated the tree by herself. On the night they had set aside for this ritual, Stella had been with Hector, backstage in Hamlin Hall, in a huge fake coffin that was a prop in a play they were both acting in. How much fun they had had, trying not to laugh when Amy and Thomas sat themselves down on top of the coffin and tried awkwardly to reassure each other. It was one of Stella and Hector's more cruel moments.

Now Stella was angry at him, angry that he had failed even to phone her since the accident last June. But as angry as she was, she missed him. Life was an empty shell without him, she said to herself. That was why she was overjoyed when she strolled gloomily over to the window to gaze at the rain and saw him scurrying up the garden path.

"Speak of the devil!" she cried, thereby betraying her thoughts. "Look who's come to pay us a visit."

She ran to the front door to let him in. It was only after she had led him through the dark enclosed porch into the living room and had seen the sour look on his face that she thought she might have overdone the mistletoe.

Thomas went through the motions. "Well, Hector! How are you? How great to see you! What a surprise—have a seat. Have a—" Here Thomas showed caution. He did not wish to be seen as pressing a real drink on the man. "Have a lemon and honey toddy. They're delicious. Stella made one for me the other day. How have you been, old boy? We missed you on Saturday. Had a dreadful time. But let's not dwell on that. Have a seat—I insist. Tell me how you've been."

"Awful," Hector said.

Thomas braced himself for the apology. Smiling. Aiming for an expression of warmth and dignity. What was the thing Nixon was always saying? Peace with honor. *I want to make peace with you, Hector. I'm ready to forgive you everything. I'm even willing to forgive you that time you and Stella started giggling in the coffin while Amy and I were trying to find you. Oh, really? So you thought I didn't know? You must think I'm a fool. But I forgot. I forgot why I'm always accepting your apologies. It's because you understand. You understand that we all act like fools. You don't judge me, and all you ask is for me not to judge you. You understand that some things, the things that can't be forgiven outright, are better left unmentioned. You understand that this is important, if I am to command any respect in my own home.*

In my own home, Thomas repeated to himself. *In my own home. Who are you trying to fool, you fool?* He had a wife who cheated on him, a daughter who lied to him, another daughter who wasn't even his, a maid who robbed him and laughed behind his back and thought nothing of requisitioning his favorite corduroy jacket and washing out his favorite stains—the wine stain from Valencia, the inkstains from the leaking pen he had bought at the bookstore around the corner from the American Express in Athens, the bloodstain from the forty-eight-hour bloody nose that had begun in Baalbek. Who respected him in this house? It was only by pretending not to know what went on behind his back that he was able to retain any dignity.

And how to retain any dignity in a place where they no longer wanted him, where he was no longer a man but the butt of slogans? Apologize for living, that's what they all wanted him to do. Apologize for being all the things he had come here not to be. His students, long-faced and angry, looking at him not as a friend or a teacher but as the instrument of repression. He was no longer human to them. He was simply an imperialist whose car deserved to be blown up. Couldn't they understand that it was his city, too, that he loved it as much as they did? Couldn't they understand what it was like to love a place that no longer needed you, a woman who no longer respected you, a child who had never been yours? Couldn't they see how much pain he suffered? He knew his failings. He could see through all the lies he told himself. All he asked was that he be permitted to ignore them. As often as possible, for as long as possible.

Let me pretend to be a man, Thomas thought. Let me

pretend to be the husband of a devoted wife. Let me pretend that I am the master of the house, fair but stern, and never crossed. Let me pretend that this little girl who is climbing on my lap does not sense that there is something lacking between us.

She loves me, Thomas thought. Hector can tell, and to his credit, he'll leave it at that. He knows how important it is to stay quiet about certain things. For all his faults, for all his callousness, he understands.

Or does he? Thomas asked himself. For this afternoon Hector did not look himself.

Stella had brought up hot toddies for everyone. An unnecessary extravagance, Thomas thought. She had also brought up a plate of Christmas cookies—bells, wreaths, Santas, Christmas trees, all decorated with colored sugar. They all had holes in the top, as if she had planned to use them as ornaments.

Thomas looked at her. She was sitting on the windowseat, smiling her fake smile. He wondered if she always smiled that fake smile with Hector, even when they were alone. He wondered if Hector had any idea what Stella was like when she was not trying to be charming. Margaret was sitting next to her, self-possessed as always. You never knew what was going on in her head. Looking at the dark-haired little girl on his lap, Thomas thought how strange it was that he felt closer to her than to his own flesh and blood.

Hector didn't waste any time. "I came here to tell you my plans," he said, "and my reasons for them, before anyone else does. You see, I've been doing a lot of thinking about my life. I've come to the conclusion that what I do here—what we all do here—is wrong. I don't belong here. You don't belong here, either. None of us belong here. And so I've decided to leave."

"You've decided to what?" Thomas asked, flabbergasted.

"Leave. As soon as possible. Most probably in January, after exams."

"You can't be serious," Thomas said.

"Oh, but I am serious," Hector said. He looked at Thomas with blinding earnestness. Thomas looked away, toward Stella, whose fake smile was fading.

"But don't think I'm going to leave you people in the

lurch," Hector continued. "I know the trouble I've caused you over the years, and I plan to make up for it. As you know, I'm coming into a small fortune, so I can pay for my mistakes for a change. I'm referring, of course, to Beatrice. There's no sense beating around the bush. We all know she's mine."

Beatrice laughed, as if Hector had told a joke. Thomas' arms stiffened as he embraced her. His heart began to beat faster. No! he cried silently. No! Don't say it, Hector. At least not in front of the baby, damn you!

"To make a long story short," Hector continued, "I've spoken to that lawyer of mine. He says it won't be difficult to set her up a trust fund."

Outside the rain fell on the muddy playing field; inside the math department, despite the outward appearance of warmth and dryness, it was raining in their hearts. It was two in the afternoon—a gloomy hour. It was Tuesday—a gloomy day. Feza Hanim's legs were aching. She longed to go home. She was happy, at least, that Thursday was a Christian holiday. She was planning to have a friend over. They were going to spend the day removing body hair with lemon putty, and perhaps after that they would make something sweet. *Kadayif,* perhaps, or *yoğurt tatlisi*. Not baklava. Baklava she loved. Baklava she had an indescribable weakness for. But baklava was only baklava when it came from Haci Bekir.

There was silence in the math department. Silence in Professor Edison's office—he had gone home before lunch. Silence in Betül Hanim's office—where she was thinking up treacherous exam questions that would create zeros in the academic records of even her most gifted and hardworking students, thus making Feza's January a misery. The telephone would be ringing for days, interrupting Feza Hanim's peace and quiet with the raised voices of distraught parents and deceived students. "How could my son, my daughter, my niece, my second cousin, be failing? He/she/they have a future to think of. I demand to speak to the professor." "I am so sorry," Feza would be forced to answer. "The professor is attending a conference in Stockholm." Or would it be Munich this year? She did it intentionally, failing hardworking students and then leaving it to Feza Hanim to deal with the families. In Feza Hanim's opinion, this woman had a complex.

From Professor Cabot's office emerged sounds that Feza Hanim could not quite analyze. Desk drawers opening and shutting, file cabinets being moved and unloaded, papers being stacked, papers being crumpled and discarded. Spring cleaning in December. Another mysterious activity for an unfathomable man.

From Emin Bey's office emerged the sounds of a man whose concentration has been broken. Frequent clearings of the throat and scrapings of the chair against the linoleum. Trip after trip to the pencil sharpener. Sighs. Deep sighs. The crumpling of paper. The slamming closed of books.

And, from the desk squeezed into the corner of the foyer behind her own desk, more sighs, these from the man the students called "the Janitor." Halûk Yildizoğlu, the acclaimed revolutionary, the renowned champion of the underdog, the diviner of hidden fascist tendencies, whose avid following had been diminished lately—or so Feza had heard—by the astonishing discovery, at an inopportune moment, of certain deplorable weaknesses in his character. A chink in the revolutionary armor—it had become evident at a moment when the hopes of all his supporters rode upon him, a moment when challenges by enemy forces were in need of being met by an iron will. But instead of iron they had been met by . . . lemon putty. Spinelessness. Womanly behavior. And at a faculty meeting, no less. The consequences would be far-reaching. Feza Hanim needed to say no more.

Ah, for a piece of gum. Feza Hanim added her own sigh to the chorus. If only her comrade, the failed revolutionary, would see fit to lift his sorry frame from his chair and go out for a walk, so that Feza Hanim could enjoy her small pleasure without running the risk of being called a cow. She sighed again, and at that same moment, her wish came true.

Halûk Yildizoğlu rose from his chair, and slowly, sadly, squeezed past Feza Hanim's desk, looking more like an underdog himself than a champion. But what was this? In front of Feza's desk he paused. He reached for his coat, and then paused again, and—what was this? Could it be possible?

—headed for Emin Bey's door, upon which he administered a feeble knock.

"Come in," Emin Bey said. Halûk obediently entered. Who would have known that, less than a week earlier, he had accused Emin Bey—in public, no less, at a faculty meeting, no less—of being a fascist. Could it be possible—could the hope be entertained—that the spineless revolutionary was considering a formal apology?

Feza strained her ears but could hear nothing significant. Still, the fact that the meeting was taking place at all was significant. She considered calling her friend, the college operator, to tell him the news, but before she could do so, before she could even help herself to the longed-for stick of gum, through the door on the opposite side of the foyer came a gloomy-looking Professor Cabot, who said, "I wonder if I could have a word with you, Feza. Why don't you step into my office."

Emin Bey and Halûk faced each other across Emin Bey's desk, both men pretending that nothing was amiss. "Have one of these cheese sticks," Emin Bey said. "They are delicious." "Have a chocolate biscuit. They are sublime." "I am in the mood for some tea. Let me find Rauf *efendi*. You must have some also. I insist."

Halûk accepted each offer in the proper courteous manner. "Thank you." "You are very kind." "Excuse me, I am disturbing you." "Just a small tea. Thank you very much. Only three sugars." He smiled. Emin Bey smiled. Two colleagues having a chat on a rainy afternoon, making pleasant conversation, enjoying a tea break. But underneath the surface, confusion and pain. The memory of shared humiliation. A shared hopelessness about the future. And, in the hearts of both men, doubts about the true intentions of a mutual friend.

The remorseful memories, the hopelessness, the sense of isolation, the doubts—they had been in the air for months. But both men agreed that they had become palpable realities at the previous week's faculty meeting. At least they would have agreed, had convention allowed them to discuss the matter openly.

As they sipped their tea, making inconsequential small

talk, they recalled the darkening sky through the large windows of the library reading room, the bare branches, the dull shine of the mahogany tables, as the faculty filed in for the meeting, taking sides in anticipation of the showdown. The Americans (except for a few earnest ones) in the back, where they could giggle, they thought, without being noticed, and draw cartoons, and catnap. The younger Turkish faculty, gathering to the left or the right (depending, Emin Bey had thought with glee, on which direction you were looking in, forward or backward). The older faculty, balding, slower-moving, dignified, claiming the tables where they always sat, smiling at one another, patting backs, shaking hands, showing their own kind of solidarity.

The fifth item on the agenda was the proposed nationalization of the university. The younger faculty had all signed a petition, which they now planned to present to the faculty as a whole. The man who was to present the petition was Halûk Yildizoğlu.

No one had suspected that he would use this opportunity to continue a personal vendetta. In fact, not even Halûk had known this until the moment arrived.

It had been noticed and remarked upon both by supporters and opponents that Halûk was unusually agitated that afternoon. What was not widely known was the reason. He had just received news that Kirkor, the gifted Armenian student who had been the cause of so much controversy, had tried to take his own life. Apparently some students in the dormitory had ganged up on him and accused him of being unpatriotic. He had tried to hang himself. Halûk took direct responsibility for this desperate act. If it were not for Halûk's opportunism, Kirkor would never have become a cause célèbre. He would be fine now, instead of half dead. But as much as Halûk cursed his own complicity in the tragedy, he cursed Emin Bey a thousand times more, because it was Emin Bey who had suspended Kirkor in the first place—just to cross Halûk. Just to make a point. Just to show his junior colleague who was in charge.

And that was why, when he had finished reading his petition to the assembled faculty, looked up from the paper to survey his audience, and caught sight of Emin Bey, smiling his most ironic smile—smirking, that was the word for it, smirking—he had suddenly filled with an uncontrollable rage, as well as a desire to make everyone in the room see Emin Bey in the correct light.

"And so I come to the end of the petition," Halûk had said. "The time has come for me to add a few words of my own. Before we open the floor to discussion, I would like to give a warning. There are in our midst certain wolves masquerading in sheep's clothing. I shall be more specific. There are among us a number of fascists masquerading as reasonable men, who will do everything in their power to undermine the following discussion. These people will stop at nothing. They will even subject cherished relations to the harassment of prying officials. They have already gone so far as to ruin the lives of their most brilliant students for base political motives. They make a mockery of the principles of our nation's founding father."

"Give names!" someone shouted from Halûk's side of the room.

"There is no need to give names," Halûk said, smiling ironically at Emin Bey. "These people know who they are. They are the ones who will have to live with the memories of their actions."

It was at this point that Emin Bey had done what Halûk was hoping he would do. He stood up and demanded an apology. "I find it an unspeakable affront," he said, "to be accused of betraying the principles of Atatürk by a man whose very political program is based on the nullification of those same principles."

Halûk had laughed, ironically. "We must make one thing clear," he said. "I did not accuse you of anything. I did not name names. You are the one who has exposed yourself in your true colors. It is time to be frank about your fascist agenda." Then, filling once again with uncontrollable fury, he made another accusation, an accusation that gave the discussion a bizarre turn.

"Furthermore," Halûk had added, shouting, his temples throbbing, "as far as you were concerned, it was killing two birds with one stone! It was not only your wish to undermine me that made you suspend the poor boy! It was also the fact that you are a racist! You are prejudiced against Armenians!"

"Hah!" Emin Bey had replied. "The situation is truly ironic. Here we have a young man accusing me of being prejudiced against Armenians, when it was this very man's Mardinli grandparents who were, as residents at the scene of the crime, responsible for the 1915 massacre!"

At this there was a deadly hush. The massacre was not mentioned in polite society. Emin Bey sat down, looking pleased, but even among his supporters it was clear that many people had been offended by his words. Like Halûk, a number of them had originated from the east of Turkey.

The silence was finally broken by Tevfik Erzincan. Standing up, facing in Emin Bey's direction, he said, "What are you insinuating? It was not the Turks who were responsible for the events of 1915. It was the Armenians themselves. They wished to create a nation on Turkish soil."

"That is the official version, I agree," replied Emin Bey. "But I am afraid it is a whitewash. Ask any Armenian. They will tell you what really happened. They will tell you whether or not it was a simple crushing of a political force, or a rampage against defenseless women, old people, and children."

There were uneasy murmurings on Emin Bey's side of the room. Two friends whispered to him that he had said enough, but he brushed them aside. Standing up, he said, "No, I have had enough hypocrisy. It is time we bring this skeleton out of the closet and discuss it like intelligent human beings. I stand accused of a prejudice I do not possess, of a crime against humanity I did not commit. Let the record be corrected. Ask any Armenian what happened in 1915. They will tell you."

Attention turned to the two Armenians in the room, who had turned pale. "It is old history," said one. "Those of us who have decided to remain in this country wish to forget." The other said, "I would like to move that this discussion has been out of order."

Halûk was shaking now, pointing his finger yet again at Emin Bey. "You fascist!" he bellowed, his voice cracking. "You wish to crush me but your ignorance will be your own worst enemy. Let me tell you something about my grandparents, these people you say are guilty of a massacre. In 1915, during the troubles, my grandparents found a little girl hiding in their basement. They took her in and brought her up as their own child. That woman, you fascist, was my beloved aunt! My aunt! My aunt is an Armenian! They took her in, brought her up as a daughter! And you are saying these people are murderers! Shame on you! Shame on you! I demand an apology! I demand . . . I demand. . . ."

Then Halûk did something which his supporters had not forgiven him for, perhaps never would forgive him for. At a time when true seriousness was needed, when the future of many stood in the balance, when it had been essential to meet iron with iron, Halûk had betrayed them. And what was this nonsense about the Armenians? they had said to one another afterward. As Haig Bey himself had said, it was old history. It was an irrelevant issue. It had nothing to do with nationalization. It was nothing to blubber about. Because that was what Halûk had done, in full view of friend and foe, at a time when true seriousness was called for. He had rested his head on the table and burst into tears.

As if a man were not allowed to cry, Emin Bey thought angrily. While he sipped tea and nibbled at cheese sticks and spoke with Halûk pleasantly about the inclement weather (could it be that only a week had passed since that nightmarish faculty meeting?), he remembered how Halûk's supporters had deserted him afterward. One by one, filing past him, saying nothing, on account of a few tears. So that was solidarity! So solidarity was nothing more than the imitation of sheep.

He despaired of these people, these wooden minds with their shocking mishmash of Ottoman obsessions and Marxist posturings. They claimed to be for progress and yet a man was still not allowed to cry because some blockheaded ancestor had died on some confounded battlefield without tears and was therefore said to be a man. Where was the logic in it? Where the consistency? These people were going to bring about the ruination of the country. Not to mention his own so-called allies, who had abandoned him in a similar fashion, on account of his breaking yet another taboo by mentioning the massacre.

And so here they were, Halûk and Emin Bey, tolerating each other because they both understood what it meant to be unfairly ostracized. Tolerating each other because they both felt bad about the Armenian boy—or was Emin Bey misreading between the lines? No, he was not. Halûk had already referred to the boy several times, and insinuated that the suicide attempt was partly due to his own callousness. This could only mean that he wished to apologize for blaming the boy's desperate act on Emin Bey. And Emin Bey was willing to accept such an apology, if only because he wished to show those nincompoops who would no longer eat lunch with him that being a man meant acting from the heart, with courage, and without a moment's thought for appearances.

He was ready to make peace with Halûk. He understood that the boy had been led astray by his so-called friends. He had been naive—and was naive no longer. He had been back from America for only a few months.

He had made his accusations in the heat of the moment, and hadn't Emin Bey done the same in his youth? It was necessary to show sympathy, and so Emin Bey assured Halûk that there was nothing to worry about in the long run with the Armenian boy. As soon as the boy recuperated, they would iron things out, he said. Kirkor would have no trouble getting into a top graduate school. Emin Bey had written him the most glowing recommendation possible.

That said, Emin Bey expected Halûk to take his leave. But instead, Halûk remained. "I have the appetite for another glass of tea," he said. "Perhaps I could go find Rauf *efendi*. I shall bring one for you also, unless I am disturbing you. There is something I would like to discuss with you. It is a very delicate matter. It concerns a mutual friend."

"You are referring to Hector, I presume," said Emin Bey. Halûk nodded unhappily. Once again, their memories returned to the faculty meeting, their joint Waterloo.

What was it Hector had said? Neither of them could remember precisely. Suffice it to say that Hector had acted grossly out of character. Halûk had felt deceived by Hector's speech, increasingly so as the days passed and he had more time to consider the implications. Emin Bey had been puzzled and disturbed, but not surprised. He thought he knew why Hector had been acting so strange.

It stemmed from an unfortunate visit to the mathematics department on the part of his hateful nephew, Policeman Ismet. This has occurred in early December—about a week before the faculty meeting—on an afternoon when Halûk—thank God—had not been in the office. The oily Ismet had visited first Emin Bey, then Hector.

Emin Bey had no way of knowing what went on during the latter interview. He was sure he might have been able to insinuate himself into Hector's office had he had his wits about him, and thereby muted the oily fox's performance, but he had not had his wits about him. He had not had his wits about him because . . . he had been in shock. He had been in shock because . . . of the way Policeman Ismet had greeted his colleague.

He had greeted Hector in English. Fluent English. Not Oxbridge English, by any means. Rather more midwestern. Rather more the sort of English one might learn during training at a certain infamous facility not far from Williamsburg, Virginia. "Well, well, well," Ismet had said. "If it isn't Hector Cabot. Long time no see! Gee, I'm glad I bumped into you. There's something you and I have got to talk about. How about if we step into your office for a moment?"

"I didn't know you spoke English," Hector had said, as he dubiously opened his office door.

"Oh, well, you know," Ismet had answered, with a folksy smile that did not suit his Eastern features, "in my profession, as the saying goes. . . ."

Following Hector into the office, he had closed the door behind him, leaving Emin Bey standing in the foyer with his mouth gaping, recalling, one by one, the months and years of using English to insult and deride his nephew, thinking that the slippery fox was telling the truth when he said he spoke no language other than the guttural bastardization of his native tongue. And to think that all the time he had understood. . . . Emin Bey returned to his office, where he paced back and forth, tormented by his oily nephew's perfectly executed revenge.

In the meantime, he had left Hector at the mercy of who knew what paranoid accusations and clumsily veiled threats. (Or had he abandoned his friend intentionally, failing to appear when needed—just as Hector himself had failed to appear when Emin Bey, unjustly accused of unspeakable political affiliations, had most needed Hector?) But these were nuances. The facts of the matter were that Policeman Ismet had made a visit and that Hector had been acting strange ever since.

He asked himself now if Halûk had somehow discovered the source of Hector's troubles. He stiffened. It was not something he wished to discuss. So when Halûk began to explain what was worrying him, Emin Bey's initial reaction was one of relief.

What was worrying Halûk was this: a recent meeting between his wife and Hector Cabot. A chance meeting—they had found themselves in the same *dolmuş* coming back from downtown. Yasemin had noticed that Hector did not seem himself. Of course, she had been on guard from the start, having heard about his puzzling speech at the faculty meeting. Perhaps if she had not, she might have found other ways to explain away the changes in Hector's behavior—the gruff, almost unfriendly greeting, the non sequiturs and long silences, the monosyllabic responses to polite questions, the way he had stared unabashedly—yes, unabashedly—at her knees.

Poor Yasemin, Halûk thought. Fear was slowly changing her back into a Turkish woman. Now that she was shrinking back into the old mold, Halûk missed the open-minded, independent Yasemin who insisted on running before breakfast, who approached each new day with eagerness, who spoke with raised color in her cheeks about the plight of Turkish womanhood. And to think that he had played a significant part in making her demure again, and mistrustful, and afraid.

What had happened was this, Yasemin told him: the other passengers had alighted at Büyük Bebek. Instead of moving over to provide Yasemin more room, Hector had remained pressed against her, breathing too loud, like a prurient raincoat flasher. Then, when they had themselves alighted at Küçük Bebek and continued to the College Gate on foot, he had also remained uncomfortably close to her. Usually, she said, they discussed psychological theories or other intellectual topics when they walked together. This particular afternoon, however, there had been no conversation at all. Feeling uncomfortable, Yasemin had asked if he had anything enjoyable planned for Christmas.

"Not really," he had said, "not unless you like thinking about cadavers."

"Cadavers!" she had said. "Whose cadavers?"

"Just one," he had said. "My mother's. I have to decide whether or not to dig her up. I'm the one who shot her—it's my responsibility."

"But . . . but . . . but . . . you are pulling my leg, surely," Yasemin had said.

"No, I'm not," Hector had answered. He had continued to speak strangely, until, at one point—halfway across the Bowl, in fact—he had stopped and looked at Yasemin curiously. It was as if, Yasemin told Halûk afterward, as she cried on his shoulder, still hysterical despite the many hours that had passed since the unpleasantness—it was as if he had been considering whether or not to shoot and bury *her*.

In reviewing the conversation in the safety of her bedroom, Yasemin had come to certain conclusions about Hector's mental condition. It was these conclusions Halûk now wished to convey to Emin Bey, as delicately as possible. Hector and Emin Bey were, after all, the best of friends.

"So," Emin Bey said slowly, when Halûk had finished telling him about the puzzling incident, "what are we to make of this? Tell me, does he often make cryptic remarks of this sort when you are with him?"

"I am never with him," said Halûk.

"Never with him?" said Emin Bey. "But you are neighbors."

"This is true," said Halûk, "but only in a physical sense."

"I was not aware of this situation," said Emin Bey. "I thought relations between you were good."

"Unfortunately not," said Halûk. "And to be frank, before I understood the situation fully, I thought I had committed some action that had offended him. But Yasemin . . . I must explain that Yasemin has had frequent chance conversations with him over the past few months . . . purely coincidental, I assure you. It seems they share interests . . . I mean, of course, intellectual concerns—that goes without saying."

"Of course," Emin Bey assured him.

"But ever since their last conversation, which is, of course, the one I have repeated to you in some detail, Yasemin has been afraid to come home from work unescorted, for fear of meeting our mutual friend. Perhaps this is an excessive reaction, but as you know, my wife—your niece, excuse me—has some expertise in the field of mental health. She has, I am afraid, developed certain theories which I feel compelled to repeat to you, as you are responsible for all goings-on in this department."

"And what are these theories?" Emin Bey asked. He had no time for psychological theories, but it was important to appear concerned.

Halûk sighed. "It seems, my teacher, that our friend has been suffering from psychotic episodes."

"*Vah, vah, vah,*" said Emin Bey. He shook his head.

"It seems," Halûk continued haltingly, "that he suffers from paranoia, low self-esteem, and an inability to recall a significant number of his actions. Add to this a history of some violence—I'm sure you have heard the rumors concerning the events of last June—and you have, in the opinion of my wife, many of the unfortunate symptoms associated with classic paranoid schizophrenia."

"*Vah, vah, vah,*" said Emin Bey again.

"I must make it clear that this is, in a sense, the diagnosis of a layman. It is not, precisely speaking, my wife's—your niece's—field. As you may have heard, she has confined herself primarily to clinical studies with rats."

"Of course," said Emin Bey. "That is a far more suitable area for a woman."

"Of course," Halûk agreed, a shade too heartily. "But from her general knowledge of other areas of concern within her discipline, she is under the impression that, given a patient with schizophrenic tendencies, such crises as the one our friend is now undergoing . . ."

"Such crises?" Emin Bey repeated softly.

"She is under the impression that such crises can be precipitated by traumatic events such as the death of a parent."

Emin Bey shook his head. "What a shame," he said.

"I therefore considered it my duty to repeat her analysis to you, seeing as there is a history—among those unfortunates who suffer from this illness—of unpredictable and occasionally violent behavior."

"I appreciate your concern," Emin Bey said. "I shall look into the matter myself at once, and act accordingly."

By the time Emin Bey's door opened, giving her a glimpse of the two former enemies shaking hands, Feza Hanim had managed to make herself presentable again. While Emin Bey and Halûk had been speaking together, Feza had been having a short talk with Hector in his office. After this short talk, she had fled to the ladies' room, where she had cried like a foundling, going through so many tissues that by the time she was ready to clean the rivers of mascara that had flowed down her cheeks, there were no tissues left. She had been forced to use toilet paper.

How cold Hector had been to her. He had treated her like a prisoner asking for parole, when in fact she had asked for nothing. His announcement had been a complete surprise.

He had told her he was leaving—well, so what? What did she care? It was over between them. Years had passed since that time. She had managed without his love. She had a good life. She had friends. She was grateful for the help he and the others had given her. Her requests for assistance had been reasonable. So why now did he no longer trust her? Did he think she was going to take advantage of him simply because his mother had left him a fortune? "I would be happy to continue to support you," he had said. "But I have spoken to my lawyer, and he is adamant about receipts. Any extraordinary needs that you have over and above the monthly allowance you must itemize in a letter, and later justify with receipts."

Justify. Justify. What did he think she was, a liar? Wasn't her word good enough for this lawyer? They were treating her like a thief, or even worse, a bothersome prostitute. Her gratitude, her tact, her years of honest, reasonable behavior, counted for nothing.

She bowed her head to hide her tear-stained face from Emin Bey, who was standing at the door to his office. But as he was an observant man, he saw them.

He saw them, and thought, What has become of our department? One moment my youngest colleague is my enemy, and the next he is my confidant. One moment my secretary is typing contentedly, and the next she is crying.

As for Hector, his confusion was now complete. Who was this man? How to explain his strange behavior? Emin Bey had looked into his office that morning and seen boxes of books, piles of papers, full dustbins—all signs that Hector was planning to take leave of them, and yet Emin Bey had received no formal resignation. Was he thinking of leaving without saying his farewells? And if so, why? Was it because of some unspeakable threat on the part of the oily Ismet? Or was it because he had, as Halûk suggested, lost his mind?

Emin Bey could not believe that Hector had lost his mind. A man did not lose his mind because of the accidental death of an old woman. Not a true man. Not a man like Hector.

On the other hand, neither did a true man run off like a scared rabbit on account of a few oily threats. These were run-of-the-mill crises in which a true man tested his strength.

The inevitable conclusion was that Hector was no longer the man he once had been. The man he once had been would never have stood up in front of the entire faculty and preached like a humorless missionary. The man he once had been would never harass the wife of a colleague by squeezing against her in a *dolmuş* and breathing like a prurient raincoat flasher. The man he once had been would never pack up his office without coming to Emin Bey first with a formal resignation. The man Hector once had been—or had Emin Bey been fooled by this man from the very beginning?

Had he, perhaps, always behaved dishonorably, and deceived Emin Bey as to his true intentions? Had he, perhaps, always made light of his friendships and obligations? Emin Bey scratched his head. He was reluctant to explore these possibilities. So instead he turned to the crisis at hand—his distraught secretary, who was crying unabashedly now, making quite a noise. He went over to her desk and placed his hand on her shoulder in a fatherly manner.

"Feza Hanim, you are making me ashamed," he said. "Have I done something to upset you this afternoon? Was I perhaps too harsh when I dictated those letters?"

Sobbing, she shook her head.

"Well, then, it can't be as serious as all that. Come. Come sit down in my office. I will go find Rauf *efendi* and have him make some tea. Then you will please have some of my cheese sticks. I won't listen to any nonsensical talk about diets. You must have them. I insist. And then, while we are drinking our tea, you shall tell me all your little grievances. I insist that you be frank. And then, I assure you, Uncle Emin will put everything right."

Wednesday, seven P.M., Christmas Eve. Amy was sitting in the Pasha's Library, in an armchair next to the fire, dressed in one of Willy Wakefield's bathrobes, playing footsies with him as she allowed him to refill her whiskey glass. Willy was also wearing a bathrobe, which barely covered his belly. He was glowing pink from their communal bath. His wife, Ruth, forty-five and now only months from a law degree, just back from Chicago for the holidays, was pottering in the distant kitchen, not seeming to mind. Amy, smiling coquettishly at her new lover, thought, Oh my God, what have I gotten myself into?

She knew she should get back to the house to comfort the children. They had sided with her. They didn't want to go back to America either. Hector had shouted at them. "You have no choice in the matter," he had said. "I'm your father. You go where I go. And I'm going back to America." Amy, having had it to the limit with his goddamn moralistic speeches, his silent accusations, his pessimism, his humorless gloom, had finally snapped. Who did he think he was, she had said, making decisions without consulting them, and then losing his temper when they protested? She had no intention of leaving. She had her own job at the Community School to think about. This was her home. If the children felt likewise, they could stay with her.

"Did you actually tell him you wanted a divorce?" Willy asked her now.

"I certainly did," Amy said.

"Well, congratulations! I didn't think you had it in you. To the future, then." They clinked glasses. Avoiding his smile, Amy stood up and strolled out to the enclosed porch.

It was cold on the porch, and black outside, with clusters of sparkling lights marking the shores of the Bosphorus. A yellow-lit ferry was rounding the point, far below them. Amy put her hand to her forehead, fighting dizziness.

She wasn't here, she told herself; she wasn't doing this. Seeking her bearings, she looked away from the endless blackness and the disembodied lights to the cobblestone path below the window. A streetlamp illuminated a small patch of it. It was muddy, as usual—it was muddy three hundred and sixty-five days of the year. The rounded stones glistened in the rain. How easy it was, she thought, to be unfaithful.

A man in a track suit walked into the circle of light. He had his back to the Pasha's Library. He was going downhill. Amy shrank back from the window, thinking it was Hector.

But it wasn't Hector. Hector was at home in his study, his only companion a sad and neglected dog. He was sorting through old papers, packing books, trying to make sense of his life before he ran out of things to do with his hands. There was an old pistol (loaded? unloaded?) in his desk drawer and he was trying not to think about it.

Old photographs sat on his desk. Amy, Chloe, Neil, Thomas, Leslie, Emin Bey, Stella, Ralph, Meredith, his mother—they lay together in neat little rows that reminded him of gravestones in a cemetery. They were from another life. They were all of smiling people. Even Yasemin, two-faced Yasemin, whose picture he had found in an old yearbook, was smiling at him. And his father, in that newspaper clipping—he was smiling, too, urging him to keep faith. But Hector could not keep faith. He stared at the smiling people in the photographs as if they were strangers.

"I can't stand you anymore," Amy had said. And Emin Bey had said, "In my eyes you are no longer a man." "I want a divorce," Amy had said. Emin Bey had said, "I want a formal letter of resignation." What they did not realize was that he had already handed in his resignation. He was already divorced. He had long since cut the thread.

Weeks had passed since that awful meeting that had changed everything, but Policeman Ismet's recitation still rang in his ears. The monotonous, self-assured voice, bringing back to life one wretched evening after another. ". . . And then, on the nineteenth of March 1965, you and your wife had dinner again with the aforementioned gentleman." Ismet was referring to a friend of a friend who had worked with the Egyptian Consulate. A charming man, Hector had long since lost touch with him, and had not even recognized his name when Ismet first mentioned it. "You met at the Divan bar. He arrived half an hour earlier than you, conferring briefly with a gentleman known for his connections with a certain gun-smuggling ring. It was reported that money changed hands. The exchange occurred five or ten minutes before your arrival. You stayed for a drink, then moved upstairs to the dining room. Your wife had beef stroganoff, if I remember correctly. You had a filet mignon, and your host had wiener schnitzel. You had an argument over the bill. You wished to pay, although you had not, in fact, brought enough money with you. Halfway through dinner, your host excused himself to make a phone call. The party he spoke with was later to be found at a neighboring table at the Club Twenty-one, which you all went to after dinner. He and your host for the evening met briefly in the john. At four A.M., they went home together. They had sex upon arrival in Teşvikiye, and then again between eleven A.M. and noon. You and your wife stayed at the Twenty-one until five A.M., in the company of a Mr. White, who was, until last year, a professor of electrical engineering at this esteemed institution, and a Miss . . . Polger, who was destined to marry the aforementioned Mr. White in a Quaker ceremony on the fifth of June 1968. You attended the wedding, during which you fornicated with a Mrs. Thomas Ashe. Good-looking woman—I envy you. You used a rather large closet in the spare bedroom. But I am jumping ahead. To return to the nineteenth of March 1965: you and your wife shared a taxi home with Miss Polger at five A.M. The driver overcharged you. Nevertheless, you tipped him handsomely. You walked Miss Polger to her door, made a pass at her. She was annoyed, although later—to be specific, on the twelfth of October of the same year, and in January 1967—the second, the ninth, the fourteenth, and the twenty-eighth—she reacted in a more favorable manner to your advances. Not to mention your final rendezvous, on June fifteenth, 1968, which was, I must point out, less than two weeks after the wedding."

Stop! Stop! Hector had wanted to say. I repent! Leave me alone to make amends my own way. He did not know why Ismet had chosen to pay him a visit, or what had motivated his recitation. Whatever his political objective, whatever veiled threats lurked behind his words, they had been lost on Hector. Ismet, on the other hand, had had no idea what effect the recitation was having on him. Hector had been clever enough to hide his horror behind a smile, his shaking hands underneath a crossed leg.

"You know more about my life than I do," Hector had said at one point, when (like now, as he sat at his desk with no more papers to sort) the idea of putting a bullet through his temple had become appealing.

Ismet had taken this as a compliment. Bowing his head slightly, he had said, "What can I say? It's all in a day's work. In my job, it pays to have an accurate memory."

"Then do me a favor. Think back for a minute. Can you recall one single good thing that I did during all those years? One small act of kindness? One night when I helped someone instead of disgracing myself?"

Ismet had thought for a moment, and then thrown up his hands in mock exasperation. It was not his own gesture—he had picked it up, perhaps, from his English teacher. "You have me there," he had said.

As Hector surveyed his cluttered desk top, the words still rang in his ears.

He was on his own now. His selfishness had been rewarded. Not even his old photographs could provoke a response in him. When he looked at that picture of himself falling off the boat, it was as if he were looking at a foreigner. And the picture of his mother that he had found in the envelope with the funeral instructions: she was a face in a crowd.

He had no past now: the ambition of a lifetime finally realized. After a lifetime of evasions, he finally understood himself, and his long history of denying his own history. He knew now that it was true what his enemies said about him: it was no accident that he had killed his mother. It was no accident either that he had buried her in the wrong place. He was American, and he had no respect for the dead.

IX

Christmas

CHRISTMAS morning was cold, dry, and clear except for stray flocks of nimbus clouds that raced across the sky, pushed by a fierce wind from Russia.

Hector was up at five without an alarm clock. He spent the next few hours trying on his best suits, most of which were now far too large for him.

Thomas was awakened at six by the sound of the maid's family loading their furniture onto a cousin's truck.

Leslie was up and about by a quarter to seven, having decided that he was to be in charge of the turkey. He was going to do it the Craig Claiborne way.

For once the gas was high enough for the roasting to continue on schedule—even ahead of schedule, because Leslie had allowed for two to three hours of little or no gas. Usually the gas petered out halfway through, and the meal was delayed until the evening. Today, thank God, it was not going to be that way.

He wanted the dinner to be over and done with by sunset. It was to be served at one o'clock sharp. They would all be well into their blasted charades by three, and be played out by five and on their way home. That was if they were lucky and Thomas did not persuade Stella to sing nineteen-hundred Fats Waller songs. There was to be no Jack Horner Pie this year. He was going to ask Meredith to cancel it. It was too time-consuming, and you had to be drunk to laugh at the jokes. He was in no mood for jokes this Christmas. All Leslie wanted was to get it over with.

With the turkey well on its way, Leslie found himself with time on his hands. Meredith and his loathsome children were all sound asleep, and would continue to be for hours. He decided to make the pies.

Damn, damn, damn, he said to himself after he had gone through all the cabinets. They were out of flour and sugar. He consulted with the maid, who hovered like a frightened bird in the doorway. "Do you want me to go to the store?" she asked. She cowered, as if she expected him to whack her. He sent her into the dining room to polish the silver and went himself to the Duxburys' to borrow what he needed.

Susan Duxbury was just taking a squash pie out of the oven when he arrived. Squash pie! His mother had made such wonderful squash pies. For a moment he regretted having escaped from the stranglehold of his parents' vocation. Who were these people he spent his time with? He didn't belong with them. He belonged with people like Donald and Susan, who made squash pies, warbled hymns in bad sopranos, lent sugar and flour to neighbors even if they hated them, and wore themselves out trying to convert Moslems who didn't want to be converted. If only Donald and Susan would peer into his soul. (But they didn't. They dismissed him as being like the others.) How little it would have taken to tempt him back into the fold. One hundred years in Turkey and they hadn't converted one Moslem. But they could have converted him, had they tried. They could have converted him with a little squash pie at the right moment, a few tollhouse cookies, or that wonderful dessert his mother had made from time to time—what was it called?—with carrot and apple peelings.

Ginger was sitting in the kitchen when he returned. She was smoking a cigarette she had rolled herself; it smelled like it might have hashish in it. "Put that thing out," he said testily. To his surprise, she obeyed him.

"Anything I can do to help?" she asked.

"Yes," he said, putting the flour and sugar on the counter. He no longer felt like making pies. "Make the pies. One apple. One mincemeat. The mincemeat's in a disgusting-looking green container in the refrigerator. I'm going upstairs."

"I was sorry to hear about Jozefin," Ginger said.

"So was I," Leslie said. "And I don't want to talk about it."

Leslie took refuge in the living room, so as to be as far away as possible from Meredith's strangled snores. The maid—her name was Sevda—was dusting the furniture. She smiled at him nervously. It wasn't a special day for her. Although she claimed to be the (illegitimate) daughter of a White Russian prince, she had been brought up a Moslem. She had blonde hair, but it was bleached. She was approaching fifty but she still wore pink ribbons in her hair. She was tiny and she limped. She sighed incessantly. She fancied herself a tragic beauty, but for Leslie tragic beauty was something utterly different.

For Leslie, beauty was . . . he looked down at the garden, where Ginger's son Jonas (here for the holidays) was sprawled out on the dead grass. He was wearing tight jeans and a windbreaker. His hair was wet. He kept passing his fingers through it and shaking it whenever there was a strong gust of wind. Twice he glanced over his shoulder, up at the house, and smiled—at Leslie? Leslie could not be sure. He tried to convince himself that he did not honestly—not really, not deep down—want to make love to this beautiful, mindless little teenager.

Jonas was impossible to talk to. His opinions were so mundane, so boring, so very clearly not his own that sometimes Leslie didn't know where to look when he was talking to him. And yet he had been seeking him out all week, afternoon after sober afternoon, evening after sober evening, asking him about his favorite TV shows, singers, and movies. How humiliating for an intellectual in his forties. God, he cried in silence, if you were going to make me fall in love with a teenage boy, couldn't you have sent me a brighter one?

Jozefin would have understood his predicament. She had had a special place in her heart for the Tadzios of this world.

She had been through enough of them herself. He could have taken Jonas down to her apartment for her to see with her own eyes. They could have sighed about him together afterward. "Ah, Tadzio, Tadzio, whither art thou, Tadzio?" she would have said. "Have mercy on your Aschenbachs." They would have commiserated about limp members and wrinkled breasts and all the other defects that had long since put them both out of the running.

Passing the brandy bottle back and forth, they would have reminisced about that distant, awful day—Jozefin called it "the Moment of Truth"—when Jozefin, who had then felt passion for Leslie, had taken matters into her own hands, receiving Leslie in her bedroom, naked, her legs tied to the bedposts with silk handkerchiefs. She had been in her midseventies at the time. "Take me," she had said. "Take me." When he stood there, gaping at her wrinkled flab, trying to figure out whether she had employed an assistant or had actually tied herself up without help, she had said, "For God's sake, man. Take off your clothes." He had obeyed her. Then it was her turn to sit up and take notice.

"Allah, allah, allah." She was looking at his genitals, which the cold and his distaste had caused to shrink. "*Mais non, mais non, mais non!* Excuse me, my friend, but would you please put back on your clothes. You must accept my apologies. You see, I had no idea this barbaric practice existed in other countries. Or did it happen here? *Mon dieu!* What am I implying? Of course it happened here! You have two strapping children!" She had mistaken him for a eunuch.

It had taken him some time to forgive her, although over the years it had become a very special private joke. The eunuch and the vampire, they would call themselves. She had other names for him, too. "Herr Hitler" when he urged her to look after her health. ("What is health in the long run, anyway?" she would say. "A passing fancy.") "Mr. Missionary" when he tried to take her home from a party before she had passed out. And "Mr. Mouse" when he refused to attempt the impossible. For example, the time she was visiting her son in Lausanne and woke Leslie up with a phone call at five in the morning, breathing heavily for half a minute before she identified herself, as the cable crackled.

"I'm thirsty," she had finally announced in a hoarse

whisper. "They are holding me captive. The brandy—they have concealed it behind lock and key."

"I'm very sorry to hear that," Leslie had said. "But what do you expect me to do about it?"

"Something," she had replied.

"For God's sake, Jozefin, be sensible. I can't do a thing for you. You're a thousand miles away."

"What is a thousand miles," she had said, "between friends?"

"I can't bring you a bottle of brandy. Be sensible. You know that."

"But I'm thirsty," she had insisted.

"Drink some water then."

"Ahhhhh . . . *enfin je comprends ce qui se passe,*" she had replied. *"Ce n'est pas mon ami à qui je parle. Non, ce n'est pas lui. C'est Monsieur Souris.* Mr. Mouse. You are not my friend, Mr. Mouse. My friend has failed me."

My friend has failed me. He had heard her say this many times. The time when he failed to make the ice cubes freeze as fast as she wanted them to. The time when she had had a dreadful nightmare, and he had failed to wake up instinctively and rush to her side. The time—in July, which was the last time he had seen her—when they had gone together to a concert of some unspeakably unctuous French pop singer whom she admired greatly, and he had failed to hypnotize the singer into making Jozefin young again with one of his magical smiles.

That had been a bit too ridiculous, he had thought. A bit too unreasonable. By the end of the evening, her demands had lost some of their self-mocking charm. And so he had failed her further, by putting off his next visit. Now it was too late to placate her with flowers, or a cake, or even honesty. She had killed herself over the weekend. A sensible decision, one Leslie could see himself making. She had been diagnosed as having cancer. When he had phoned her apartment on Christmas Eve, he had gotten the son. She had already been buried, he said. "You know how it is, we Moslems. . . ." he had said. "We don't like to delay longer than twenty-four hours. And already when we discovered her . . ." She had not left a note, but if she had, Leslie knew what it would have said: "You have failed me."

Oh, Jonas, Jonas, help me. Take me away. Take me in your arms.

Without even making a conscious decision to do so, Leslie found himself walking down into the garden.

"Aren't you cold?" he asked Jonas, whose hair was still damp.

"A little, but it's worth it," said Jonas. "I love my hair to be wind-dried. It's so much better than blowing it."

"Well, it certainly gives it more bounce," Leslie said.

"You know what I could use, though," Jonas continued. "I could use a brush."

"A brush?" Leslie asked.

"A brush," Jonas said. "But you'll have to promise to be gentle."

"You want me to brush your hair?" Leslie asked.

"So long as you promise not to hurt me," Jonas said. "My tangles are unbelievable."

Leslie was on his way back up the kitchen stairs when Theo popped his head out the door to the garden flat. "Toodaloo!" he said. "And what are you up to this fine morning? Going for Brownie points?"

"I don't know what you're talking about."

"Oh, but I do. He does make demands, doesn't he? Does run one ragged."

"Who?" Leslie asked.

"Our young hopeful over there," he said, nodding at Jonas.

"Fuck off, Theo. You only think of one thing."

"Don't we all," Theo said.

Leslie continued up the stairs, choosing to ignore him.

At first he decided to skip it. He didn't want to brush anyone's hair with Theo watching. But then he decided, what the hell, it would be a chance for a talk, and there was no law against talking, was there? He would take the brush with him and let Jonas brush his own hair. He would suggest a walk. If they took a walk, Leslie could brush his hair on the Bowl. He'd let Jonas decide. He went out the front way and let himself in through the garden gate.

Jonas was gone.

On his way back through the garden gate, he glanced in the direction of Ralph and Theo's kitchen and saw someone Jonas' size and build sitting at the table eating an apple.

Stunned, he walked into the alleyway. After he had closed the gate behind him, he paused to collect himself.

"What's the matter? You look like you just saw a ghost."

It was Hector, somber and drawn in a black suit. He looked as if he were off to a funeral. He was carrying a black umbrella, and in his left arm was a black coat.

"Nothing's the matter," Leslie told him. "I'm just tired. I've been out on a walk."

"On a walk? What were you doing on a walk with a brush in your hand?"

"Oh, do I have a brush in my hand?" said Leslie. "You're right. I do. I must have picked it up on my way out."

"That's strange," said Hector.

"Well, I have to go now. See you later."

"Are you sure you're all right?" Hector asked.

"Of course I'm all right?" Leslie snapped. He walked briskly to the front door. Halfway up the steps, his knees buckled.

"Oh, my goodness!" Hector cried. "Here. Take my arm."

"Let go of me!" Leslie said. "I'm perfectly all right."

"No, you're not," Hector said, and he rang the bell. "I think Leslie should lie down," he said to Meredith when she answered the door. "He almost fainted out here."

Meredith, her eyes still swollen from sleep, gave Leslie a curious look. "What were you doing outside with a brush?" she asked.

"Mowing the lawn," he snarled. He pushed her aside and started up the stairs.

"There's no need to be sarcastic," Meredith called after him.

Leslie turned around to face her. "What else do you expect me to be? It should be fairly obvious what I needed a brush for."

"But you never use a brush. You don't have enough hair for a brush. You always use a comb."

"Well, today I was using a brush, because today is

fucking Christmas.'' He went upstairs to the bathroom, and as he went, he remembered all the stupid things he had said to Jonas outside. ''It certainly gives it more bounce,'' he had said. God! What an idiot I am! God! What I'd give for a drink. He turned the knob of the bathroom door but the door was bolted. Eric was inside. Eric, the source of all his misery. Eric, whose failures and psychoses had forced him onto the wagon. Eric, who slept twenty hours of the day. What good was it being a good example to your son if he spent the whole day in bed? Oh, Jozefin, where are you? Suddenly Leslie understood why she had once called from Lausanne in the middle of the night to tell him she was thirsty.

''Glory be to the Father, to the Son, and to the Holy Ghost. . . .''

Ralph sat glowering at his dining room table, looking up at the narrow window, watching feet.

'As it was in the beginning, is now, and ever shall be, world without end, a-a-amen.''

Hector and Leslie having some sort of scuffle. Hector dressed in a pair of black pointed things Ralph had not seen in years. Leslie in his desert boots, angry as hell. You could tell an awful lot from shoes.

Doors slamming upstairs. Meredith's raised voice, Leslie's snarling one. God, they were all in for a treat this afternoon. With Leslie in that kind of mood, the Horse was going to have one hell of a time playing perfect hostess. Stomp stomp. If they had any idea what they sounded like going up those stairs. God help him if those basketballs fell off the top of the wardrobe again. It would scratch his new record..

And now the Duxburys. Susan's shiny black loafers and—God help us—ankle socks. Don't tell me—I daren't look—did she or didn't she—are her calves shaven or are they not? Thank God I can't tell from here. Now Donald has marched through the gate. Now he's pausing, looking for the keys to the van. Ah, miracles. He's found them. We have been spared a scene.

The Duxbury boarders, filing into the alleyway one by one: meek, respectful, devoid of character except for the blonde one who had the glad eye. In the end they would have trouble with him, Ralph was sure. Donald, muscleman, sliding open the door of the van with ease. Susan, standing back, her feet apart like a soldier ill at ease about being at ease. Probably with her arms akimbo, although Ralph could not see her arms.

Donald opening the front door for her. Susan climbing in. The boarders piling into the back one by one. The boarders and—could it be that his eyes were deceiving him?—the boarders and behind them a pair of black pointed things Ralph hadn't seen in years. Hector's black shoes, first hesitating, and then climbing into the van after all the others. Donald slamming the van door behind him. Donald hopping into the front seat, starting up the engine, overpowering the angelic voices of the King's College Choir, which filled every room of Ralph and Theo's apartment but which no one outside could hear at all.

So what was he to make of this fascinating development, Ralph wondered, as he sipped Theo's poor imitation of eggnog (to think that you could hope to make a decent eggnog with buffalo cream). Could it be that, appearances and attire notwithstanding, Hector was merely getting a lift with the Duxburys as far as Bebek? Or was he actually planning to attend the Christmas service at the Dutch chapel? Dear God, let it be the Anglican place, or even one of the Catholic ones. *Not* the Dutch Chapel, please God, *not* the Dutch Chapel, with those missionary farts sounding off about serving the Lord and those square-jawed women passing around grape juice in lieu of communion wine. No, even the New Hector would have a hard time fitting in there. Even the New Hector, self-righteous fart that he was.

The New Hector had paid him and Theo a visit a few days back. Monday—or was it Tuesday? It had been raining, that much Ralph remembered vividly. Ralph had offered him duty-free whiskey, just for a tease.

Hector had not taken kindly to Ralph's suggestion. "When will you people realize that I'm never going to drink again?" he had barked. "Why is it so important to drag me down with you? Is that all our friendship was, getting drunk together? Why can't any of you accept me sober?"

"Sorry, my darling! Sorry for living," Ralph had said.

Playing the queer. Being nasty and sarcastic, when with a little less self-restraint he would have been crying. When with a little less pride he would have been asking Hector why he had been avoiding his oldest, closest friend for so long. What had he done to deserve such treatment? Ralph wanted to know. Was that all their friendship had been, an excuse to get drunk? It seemed that Hector didn't need his friends any longer, now that he was sober.

But instead of being sincere, Ralph had played the nasty, catty queer. "Of course I don't wish to drag you down with me, Hector," he had said. "Of course our so-called friendship was more than just getting drunk. Furthermore, I must tell you that you are an absolute delight when sober. An absolute darling, and such charming rosy cheeks. Goodness me, I *am* sorry about teasing you, my dear boy. Not for the world would I have you drinking whiskey in my presence. No, no, no. There are better drinks for our Hector. Theo! Snap to it! A Shirley Temple for Hector! On the rocks, of course. And don't forget the maraschino cherry. Or give him two, as an extra treat."

"I'm afraid we're out of maraschino cherries," Theo had said, upon returning from the kitchen with what Ralph could see at once was a very poor imitation of a Shirley Temple.

"Out of maraschino cherries? But how can that be? I brought back two bottles from Alexandropolis. Don't tell me you've eaten *all* the maraschino cherries, fat boy," Ralph had said.

It was then that Hector had started in on his lecture. Goddamn him.

"Why do you think you can order that poor man around like that?" he had asked Ralph. "And you," he continued, turning to Theo, "why do you take it? Haven't you any pride?"

"Of course he hasn't any pride," Ralph had retorted. "How could he possibly? He hasn't been able to support himself in years. If it weren't for me, God knows what black hole he would be subsisting in."

"Is that any reason to rub his nose in the dirt?" Hector had asked.

"Of course it is," Ralph had answered. "It is the price one must pay for charity. Because it is charity, you know.

You can't think I make any sexual demands of this pathetic, overweight boy. He is my manservant. He is here to serve me and put up with me. He is my Jeeves."

"And you go along with this," Hector had said, turning to Theo. Theo had averted his eyes.

"What a waste," Hector had continued. "What a waste of the human spirit. I regret the day—I curse the day—when I brought you two together. Because I did, you know, even though you may have forgotten. I brought you two together. I introduced you. It is all my fault."

"Go fuck yourself, Hector," Ralph had said. But the damage had been done. Theo, goddamn him, had taken Hector's words to heart. He had been uncontrollable ever since.

He had been saying things he had never said to Ralph before. He had been refusing to get things for him. He kept saying, "Hector was right, you *have* been taking advantage of me. You've been rubbing my nose in the dirt. I'm not even fat, you know. I'm only slightly overweight." He had even, on Christmas Eve morning, called Ralph a fart. Ralph, his friend, his benefactor, his savior. It made it hard for Ralph to say, "I'm sorry, don't leave me, I didn't mean it, I was only putting on an act."

Now he was flirting with that stupid stupid stupid boy, Jonas, in the kitchen. It had been going on for days. It was not a pretty sight. A forty-year-old fat boy making bug eyes at an adolescent teetering uncertainly between the last pimple and the first beard. A forty-year-old man—not slightly overweight, but fat and bearlike—giggling, as he offered him apples, asked him asinine questions about his favorite pop stars—God! Ralph despaired of him!—and shuffled his feet about under the table in a game of what Ralph had christened "almost footsies."

This was not the way things were meant to be. Things were meant to be the way they had been when Ralph was a child.

Things were meant to be elegant on Christmas morning. Faithful servants in the kitchen, not outsize pederasts entertaining limp-wristed fuckboys. The table set with all the best silver. The chauffeur in his best, waiting to take them to St. Clements. His parents, stern as they led the children down the front steps, stiff-backed as they led them to the family pews, not because they actually felt stern or stiff but because it was important to keep up appearances. The church decorations, which had filled young Ralph's heart with joy. The choir—no rival to King's College, surely, but sublime. The crèche, which had made Ralph dream of being Joseph, the proud father of a son. That in the days, of course, before he discovered that the likes of him were not destined for Mary, nor Mary destined for the likes of him.

As for the dream for a son, no one could say he had not tried. No one could say that he had not subjected himself to cruel ridicule in his attempts to adopt one. How they had laughed at him, in New York, in London, even here.

Once he had found an agency that didn't seem to care as much as the others. He had allowed himself to hope. Panicking at the idea of a helpless infant, who would need diapering, mothering, constant bottles, endless changes of costume, he had stupidly mentioned—at some cocktail hour—that perhaps it would be better to adopt a four- or five-year-old—someone who, as he had put it, had already reached the age of reason.

"That would be convenient," Amy had said. "You'd have fewer years to wait for the attractive age."

The attractive age. As if that had been his reason for wanting to adopt a son. He had felt like strangling her. He had felt like crying. He had been heartbroken to think that a friend could think such a thing. But instead of letting anyone know how he felt, he had played the queer. Snappy answers. Glib putdowns. My dear girl. My dear boy. My darling little hausfrau, how testy you are this evening. Did you forget, perhaps, to take your menopause pills? He had said it all in the perfect exaggerated drawl. His queer voice, he called it. God, he was sick and tired of being queer.

The record was over now. The sudden silence exposed Ralph to the full indignity of Theo's flirtation. They had entered the confessional phase. Jonas—that stupid stupid positively idiotic boy—did not enunciate his words clearly enough for Ralph to follow him. A blessing in disguise, Ralph was sure of it. But of Theo's half of the conversation, Ralph was spared nothing. "And so what did he do?" Theo asked, in a tone of voice Ralph knew to be false. "He did?

Weren't you scared?'' *Et ita ad nauseam*. Ralph went back into the living room, where he put the needle back to the beginning of his new record. He turned up the sound so that it would block out all ugliness. He went back to the dining room, kicked the kitchen door closed, and sat down once again with his eggnog, staring up at the window, watching for feet with stories to tell, while he sang along in his opera-quality baritone: *''As it was in the beginning, is now, and ever shall be, world without end, a-a-amen.''*

From his study, Thomas could just see the maid's cousin's overloaded truck creaking down the hill. Behind them was a red VW van, whose driver thought the truck should be going faster. He kept honking his horn. Avram, who was sitting in the back of the truck on top of the rugs and chairs and clattering utensils, was waving his arms at the driver in anger. It was the Duxburys' van. They were on their way to church, probably a few minutes behind schedule.

There were some things you thought would go on forever, some people you thought would always be part of your life, if only because they had been part of it for so long. Thomas had never thought he would see the day when Seranouche and Hagop and Avram would be loading their sorry belongings onto a truck, refusing to look at Thomas or anyone else, refusing to say goodbye, refusing even to turn around for one last look after they had taken their seats. The only one who hadn't gone was Bambi the cat. He probably knew that there wasn't much beef filet where Seranouche was headed.

Thomas cleared his throat and took a long swig from his beer. It was nice and cold for a change, because the house was cold; Seranouche had not stoked the stoves this morning, and Stella had not yet risen to this new domestic challenge. He looked down at the Aşiyan Road again. The truck and the van had both disappeared. He already missed Seranouche, as awful as she could sometimes be. He missed her philandering husband and her good-for-nothing son. He missed their undisguised envy, their dull conversations about women and fish, their simple, grandiose ambitions about emigrating to America and marrying Avram off to a millionairess. He was sorry he had had to put an end to all this nonsense. He was sorry he had had to fire them.

He was sorry, too, that he had called Stella a slut in front of the children. Sorry that he had said that he had never loved her. Sorry, most of all, for kicking over the Christmas tree this morning, if only because poor little Beatrice had looked so confused by his sudden violence. He was sorry, but he had been forced to do it, because they had all been laughing at him.

Laughing at him. Imitating him. Manipulating him. Lying to him. Taking him for the fool, misunderstanding his silence. Intimating that he was not man enough to provide a decent upbringing for Beatrice. Well, they wouldn't think that way anymore. He had acted swiftly, and now none of them was in any doubt as to who was boss.

As soon as Hector had taken his leave on Monday night, Thomas had gone downstairs and fired the maid. He had used Margaret as an interpreter, until it became clear that she was softening his words to make them more palatable. The liar. She was just like her mother, always trying to undermine him. Pushing Margaret aside, he had finished the job with his own crude Turkish, which had turned out to be better suited to his aims. He had called them names and accused them of robbing him out of house and home. He had practically torn his corduroy jacket off Hagop's back.

He might as well have let him keep it, because it didn't feel like the same jacket anymore. Even after dry cleaning, it had the shape of another man's body. He might as well have gone downstairs and given it to Hagop as a goodbye present. But he had let the opportunity pass. It was a shame.

Last night he had had a dream. In the dream he was an altar boy again, in his parish church. The bishop was paying a visit to the church that day, and for this reason there was a grand procession. Thomas was at the front, holding incense.

Suddenly, his robes caught on something. The candles on the altar came tumbling down, setting the bishop's robes on fire. In front of Thomas' eyes, the bishop went up in flames, as if he had been soaked in spirits.

For a few moments, the priests and other altar boys watched, aghast. Then, at the sight of the bishop reduced to ashes, they had turned their attention to the culprit. Thomas.

"You . . ." said the priests, (there were three of them), shaking their fists at him. "You . . ." They had backed him down the aisle, threatening him with distaffs. As they menaced him, the congregation joined them, until there was a crowd of more than a hundred people, all shaking their fists at him, pushing him out of the church.

At the door, one of the priests pushed him. He fell backward down the steps. The dream ended with the sound of the doors crashing closed again, as he rolled down the stairs, which went on and on and on, taking him deeper and deeper into the bowels of the earth.

It was a shame about all the promises he had made to the maid that he would no longer be able to keep: the American visas, Hagop's work papers, Avram's education . . . and Seranouche's teeth. Good God, he suddenly thought, how is Seranouche going to pay for her teeth? He had completely forgotten about her teeth.

Rising abruptly from his desk, he stormed into Beatrice's room, where Stella, having given up on the stoves, was dressing her daughter—*her* daughter—for Christmas dinner.

"Why did I have to be the one to fire them?" he said. "You knew what was going on. Why didn't you say anything?" He could barely look at Stella now. The slut. He could barely look at Beatrice either. Her daughter.

"May you go in peace," said Phillip Best to his small congregation. He smiled with genuine happiness as he led the acolytes down the aisle of the Anglican chapel, nodding to the left and to the right almost absentmindedly until he reached the last pew. Here he paused for a second—most people must not have noticed, but Noel did—resting his gaze on a man dressed in black at the far end of the pew. He was the only man in the chapel who was not on his feet. He had his arms resting on the pew in front of him, and his head resting on his arms, so that his face was not visible. He was shaking, as if in despair.

Father Phillip allowed a shadow to fall across his face, but then he collected himself, remembering his duties. He continued out of the chapel. Once outside, he circulated among his parishioners, congratulating some, inquiring after the health of others, laughing heartily, listening with fatherly concern, doing his job.

The parishioners were mostly British, with a handful of Canadians and Americans. They were all lingering outside the chapel longer than they needed to. Like Noel (and perhaps even Tash, although she would never have admitted it), they were reluctant to return to the grimy street, where a normal Istanbul Thursday morning was in progress.

It was half past eleven. Noel and Tash were due at the Laceys' at one o'clock for Christmas dinner. They both dreaded it equally, which was why, when Nikolai Kadinsky (a charming fellow, whom they had met here at the consulate on the Queen's birthday) invited them back to his flat for a quick drink, they accepted, even though they knew very well that this would make them late.

"You're welcome to stay to dinner," Nikolai went on. "I'm afraid I got carried away yesterday and made rather too much food. But you don't have to let me know just yet. Let's round up our lot and be off. Have you a car? Well, we'll put half in mine, then, and half in yours. Parking's a bit dicey in my area, but we'll manage somehow."

It was cold outside. They could see their breath, and Noel found that he had misplaced his scarf. He went back into the chapel to look for it, and found it lying under one of the pews. It had a woman's footprint on it, which Noel stopped to dust off. While he was standing there, he saw Father Phillip coming back into the chapel.

Father Phillip did not see Noel. He was looking at the man dressed in black, who was still bent over and trembling at the far end of the last pew. There was pain on Father Phillip's face as he slowly approached this man. He paused for a moment behind him. Then he reached out and put his hand on the man's shoulder.

The man startled and looked over his shoulder. Noel could still not see his face.

"Father," said the man. His voice was hoarse—and familiar, although Noel could not quite place it.

"Father," the man said again. He stood up and took Father Phillip by the hand. They looked at each other for a few minutes, and then Father Phillip said something very strange.

His voice cracking, he said, "My son."

"I was hoping you'd come back one day," Father Phillip continued after a brief silence. He had regained some of his composure. "But I must say I had begun to lose hope. Well, never mind. Better late than never. Come along with me now, why don't you." Putting his arm around the man's stooped shoulders, he led him out of the chapel. Noel followed them out at a distance, embarrassed to have witnessed their reunion.

Nikolai lived in a grand old building in a rabbit warren of a neighborhood known as Cihangir. His flat had large windows overlooking the sea, as well as a small wrought-iron balcony, the doors to which were closed today on account of the cold weather. The furniture was comfortably shabby—old green settees over which had been strewn cushions from Liberty's; antique lamps and tables, some priceless, some merely serviceable. On the sitting room floor was a large Bergama carpet. On the wall, across from the antique mirror, was a *kilim* Noel was sure was from Manisa, although he had never seen anything quite like it. The other walls were taken up by bookcases. Some were reserved for paperbacks, others for leatherbound editions of scholarly works. Sitting on an old lectern next to the balcony was the compact OED, open, with the magnifying glass lying on the page.

In the dining room was a long table set with china and silver on a linen tablecloth. The china was not a complete set. It consisted, rather, of three or four patterns, as did the silver. On the sideboard was a magnificent candelabra. Above it was a collection of framed eighteenth century prints—one of a harem, another of a flotilla, a third of a bazaar scene, and a fourth of Ithaca.

Nikolai served his guests *glog*. He had gotten the recipe from a Swedish friend he'd known in Budapest. Noel drank too many glasses of it. Before he knew it, it was half past two and they were disgracefully late for the Laceys'. Noel did not need much convincing to decide he was in no shape to drive. Bracing himself with yet another glass of lovely *glog*, he made the necessary telephone call to Meredith and told all the appropriate lies.

It was with great relief that he returned to the kitchen, where he was pretending to help Nikolai carve the geese.

It was an old, austere kitchen with yellowing walls and a stone-tiled floor. On the shelves were arranged Nikolai's modest supplies—a porcelain canister (turn-of-the-century German?) labeled "Sacher" and another, larger porcelain canister labeled "Riz" with a similar, though not identical, floral pattern. Smaller plastic containers for spices. Carefully stacked matchboxes. An unopened box of Turkish tea, and beside it four containers of Twinings tea.

The geese were sitting on the table. On the counter was a *bulgur* salad, a plate of homemade French pastries, various curried vegetables, a bowl of Cumberland sauce. The carrots and potatoes and brussels sprouts were heating up in the oven. Nikolai had just finished stir-frying the broccoli in his wok, which he had set at the back of the stove while he heated up a second sauce for the geese.

"It's a medieval recipe," he explained. "Made with strawberries. The strawberries are courtesy of Celia, I must add. She freezes them every summer; formidable woman. It's meant to be eaten with chicken, or rather, capon. But I thought I'd be daring and try it on the geese. I am so glad you've decided to stay," he added.

"Phillip called a while ago," he went on. "He should be arriving shortly."

"Did you see that man he was speaking to at the chapel?" Noel asked.

"No . . . no . . . I'm afraid I didn't," Nikolai said.

"The one dressed in black, at the very back. You may have seen him engrossed in abject prayer as we were filing out."

"Ah, yes," said Nikolai. "*That* one. Oh, yes, I certainly did see *him*." He paused, as if he were going to tell Noel more about the man, but then he caught himself. Despite his idle curiosity, Noel was relieved. How wonderful to be among people, he thought, who knew how to be discreet.

How wonderful to be among people who knew how to arrange their lives and their sitting rooms in an orderly fashion, who knew when it was appropriate to speak of private matters and when it was not. Noel sauntered into the sitting room as if on a cloud. Surveying Nikolai's other guests, he felt something close to ecstasy, because even though most of them were strangers, he knew them all well.

There, leaning against the balcony door, was Fiona whatsit, gaunt, sharp-nosed, hung over, looking rather fleabitten in a worn velvet trouser suit. She was here to do research for a book on Iznik tiles. Fingering the interesting Manisa *kilim* was Simon so-and-so, dear, dear friend of Nikolai's, up-and-coming young director in his uncle's Cork Street art gallery, in town for the holidays. He was talking about "the astounding fluctuations in price for Botticellis during the nineteenth century" with Alistair whatever-his-name-was, jaded television journalist, who was off to Beirut the next day to do yet another documentary on the latest British double agent.

Sitting at the other end of the room were the Grubbs. Gordon was thin and balding with a florid complexion and a bitter mouth. Celia was rather larger than he, with a head of tight, silver curls and a substantial bosom that was nearly matched in size by her backside. He was the commercial attaché at the consulate, only a few years from retirement. Celia was leaning forward in her chair, lecturing Tash on the subject of thrillers. "I've always enjoyed thrillers," Celia was saying, almost belligerently. "Ever since I was a girl. Three a week is my normal ration. I have an account with Hatchard's, you see."

Tash smiled wanly at Noel. "So you rang them, did you?" she asked. Noel nodded.

"I hope they weren't too dreadfully offended," she said.

"Oh, no, not at all," Noel said. "I told them you had a touch of Turkish tummy, which fabrication sent Meredith into paroxysms of sympathy. She even wanted to bring us over a 'CARE package,' as she called it."

"Goodness!" Tash said. "I hope you talked her out of it."

"Well, I had to, didn't I? I had to tell her we weren't at home."

"Oh, dear! And what did she say about that?"

"She said nothing. I merely told her we had stopped here after church for a quick drink, when you were suddenly taken ill. I said you were having a lie-down, after which we would be going home."

"Oh, dear," Tash said regretfully. "I do wish you had come up with something *slightly* more plausible. They must be frightfully offended. We did promise them we'd be there."

"Who are these people who were expecting you?" asked Celia Grubb.

"Neighbors of ours in Hisar," said Noel. "Man named Lacey."

"Not Leslie Lacey?" Roland asked. "Thin, balding chap? Bad cough? Red nose when he drinks?"

"That's the one," said Noel.

"Goodness, then," said Roland. "You're well out of it."

"Do you know him?" Noel asked.

"Do I know him? Oh, yes, I'm afraid I do. Nasty sort of fellow. Used to play darts with us at the club on occasion. Tried to fiddle the scoreboard. Friendly with a blackguard named Hector Cabot. Two of them three sheets to the wind in no time. Second fellow—Hector—threw a dart at Julia Parsons, missed her by this much. Jason—you must know Jason, ex-India Police, burly sort of chap—Jason had to throw them out. Disgraceful pair. Especially the second fellow. Hector. Glad to hear you put them off. In my opinion, you're well out of it."

"Actually," said Noel, "you'll find that Hector Cabot has changed dramatically since you last saw him. He's gone on the wagon—for good, apparently. And now he's gone to the other extreme."

"The other extreme?" Celia exclaimed. "What could possibly be the opposite of throwing darts at typists?"

"No longer throwing darts at typists himself, and suspecting everyone else of it. What I mean to say is that he's turned into a frightful prig."

"Hector Cabot? A prig?" Celia exclaimed. "I must say, Americans never cease to surprise me." Then she turned away from Noel to greet Father Phillip, who was standing in the foyer handing Nikolai his coat and apologizing, in his loud, professional voice, for the unavoidable delay.

Noel glanced at his watch. It was three o'clock.

* * *

Meredith glanced at the clock on the far wall—a cuckoo clock from Lucerne, a souvenir from a time when she and Leslie were happily married. It was half past three.

There was silence in the dining room, except for the occasional clearing of throats and the quiet scraping of forks against dishes as the guests ate their Christmas dinner. Meredith closed her eyes and gave herself a silent lecture. Pull yourself together, old girl. Stop feeling so sorry for yourself. You must think instead about the others. They are depending on you, their hostess.

Of the nineteen people Meredith had set places for, only eight were now seated at the tables. The children had left when the fighting became too much for them. They were up in the bedrooms now—except for Jonas, whose late arrival had caused so much of the trouble. He was eating with gusto now, alone at the children's table, coolly examining the paper snowmen and angels Meredith had made as place markers, which she had spent so much time decorating and which no one had commented on.

On the sideboard, to Meredith's right, between the turkey carcass and the creamed onions, underneath the stain on the wall where Leslie had thrown the cranberry sauce (black market: it had cost Meredith an arm and a leg), lying on their sides, splattered with gravy, were the place markers Meredith had made for Noel and Tash. Noel's was a choirboy, Tash's a choirgirl. On Noel's choirboy she had written the first two verses of the Christmas carol of the same name, thinking he would appreciate that touch, although now she thought otherwise. On Tash's choirgirl she had written (out of deference for Tash's academic subject) the first verse of "O Tannenbaum" in German (in Gothic letters, which she had learned to write as a child at a summer camp).

How cold Noel had sounded on the telephone. How short he had been with her when she had suggested, out of the kindness of her heart, that she send over a CARE package. He had acted as if CARE packages were in bad taste. But surely it could not be in bad taste to offer kindness. "You are very kind," Noel had said stiffly. "But it won't be necessary. You see, we are not at home. We are at Nikolai Kadinsky's. We ran into him at church and came home with him for a quick drink. We were just on our way when Tash was taken ill. She's having a lie-down now." In the background Meredith could hear the tinkling of glasses and hearty laughter, and Tash's voice. "As soon as she's up to it, we'll be going home."

Meredith had not believed him for a moment. They had found a better place for their Christmas dinner. Surveying her own sorry table, she could not say she blamed them.

Were these the people she had devoted her life to? Were these the people she had been cooking for, planning for, wrapping presents for, all week, all month along? Was that hateful, thin-lipped man sitting at the other end of the table really her husband? And were these ingrates sitting to either side of him really her closest friends?

How cruel Leslie had been to everyone. And just because he was too pigheaded to let things slide for a day and pour himself a drink. He had been shouting at Meredith since the moment she woke up. Insulting her, calling her lazy, accusing her of drinking the cooking sherry on the sly. Imitating her, wincing when she laughed, telling her not to spell things out, that people weren't quite as stupid as she thought they were. Insulting everyone else, too. Insulting Stella. ("Oh, how thoughtful," he had said, "you remembered to bring those awful onions in white sauce.") Insulting Thomas. ("Oh, so I take it you decided not to bring along the maid and her delightful husband.") Taunting Ralph when, at half past two, Theo and Jonas had still not appeared. ("They're probably downstairs fucking their balls off," he had said. This had also antagonized Ginger.) Taunting Blake. Belittling Amy. ("Willy Wakefield!" he had snarled at her, before she even had a chance to take off her coat, before she even had a chance to ask him not to talk like that in front of her children. "Willy Wakefield!" he had said, over and over and over. "Of all people, why did you have to choose him? I know Hector's been a pain in the ass lately, but really, it's no reason to scrape the bottom of the barrel.") Amy had been rendered speechless by his attack. She had spent the hour before dinner (or rather, the two hours before dinner, as they waited for Theo and Jonas, for Noel and Tash, and for Hector, Goddamn him, who had not even been considerate enough to make a call)—she had passed these empty hours gazing out the window, clutching her drink, sniffling, wiping stray tears from her eyes as she puffed cigarette after cigarette.

This year Meredith had been in charge of Jack Horner's Pie. Leslie had opted out of it. She had gone out of her way to make both the gifts and the accompanying limericks tasteful, as she did not quite approve of the nasty ones Leslie had given in the past. This had been partly out of a (misguided!) desire to impress Noel and Tash, and partly out of a genuine desire to show mercy. She had the goods on them all. Now she was sorry she had held herself back.

She thought of all the things she could have given Leslie. A toupé. An aphrodisiac. A collection of dirty pictures involving decrepit men and young boys. A subscription to *Screw* magazine. How she would have enjoyed writing the limerick to go along with it. How she would have enjoyed reading it to the assembled company:

There once was a would-be whoremonger
Who could not make his dick any longer
So he turned to the joys
Of pursuing young boys . . .

How she would have enjoyed watching him squirm and blush. How she would have enjoyed watching his friends laugh. Because they hated him. They hated him as much as he hated them. They all hated each other. Oh, how much hatred they had shown for each other this afternoon. The things they had said to one another. Meredith could not remember how it had begun.

Memories of venomous insults swirled in her head. "Fuckboy. Fat boy. Liar." That was what Ralph had said to Theo when he appeared late, hand in hand with Jonas. "You're filthy. You're obsessed. You only think of one thing." That was what Amy had said to Ralph when Ralph wouldn't let up. "Harridan. Hausfrau. Menopausal mother hen." That was what Ralph had said back to Amy. "You still can't convince yourself I have absolutely no interest in your hairy son," he had continued, "and do you know why? I'll tell you why. It's because the one who would really like to fuck him is you."

"You filthy, filthy man," Amy had cried.

"You goddamn hypocritical harridan," Ralph had retorted.

Meredith, still trying to play the placatory hostess at that point, had said, "Do you think we could have an entire meal in which beardless youths are not discussed? If I have to hear one more comment about the relative hairiness of another youth, I for one am going to scream."

But no one had listened to her plea for peace. The insults had continued flying, as had the demands for apologies. One by one, the others had been drawn into the battle. How had it happened? Meredith could not remember the details. She could only remember Ginger standing up and saying, "I resent the way you all assume my son is a homosexual." She could only remember Blake breaking down—poor Blake, who had come all the way from his muddy little village to join them on this special day, and for this!—Blake breaking down and saying how bad he felt about changing his mind about the *muhtar*'s daughter. And Leslie making fun of him. And Ralph making kissing noises at him, his queer act completely out of control. And Stella railing Blake for his hypocrisy. That was all Meredith could remember. That and her growing desperation as the fighting grew worse. "Could we please carry on this discussion some other time?" she kept begging. "This is Christmas." But no one had listened.

What else did Meredith remember? She remembered Ginger taking Blake aside, leading him to the front stairs for a heart to heart. She remembered every word of this heart to heart. She had been in the kitchen at the time.

The pain, the pain of discovering what your friends really thought of you. The cruel misunderstandings, even after years and years. How long had she known Ginger now? More than half her life. And still she could write Meredith off like that, so quickly and so thoughtlessly, to a perfect stranger.

Who was Blake to Ginger? A Peace Corps worker facing a dilemma. A confused young man. A man. Perhaps that was the full explanation. She would still, after all she had been through, do anything to get a man.

This was how Ginger, earth mother par excellence, had comforted her young charge.

"You must learn to permit these people their little games," she had said. "It is all they have left. They don't have full lives to look forward to like you and I. They have cut themselves off from their roots, and when you do that, you become a caricature of yourself. Look at Meredith. I've known her for more than half my life. And let me tell you, she hasn't learned one thing since the day she set foot on this hill. And it's a pity, because she had potential. Now she reminds me of an ingrown toenail, turning in instead of out."

"What an interesting metaphor," Blake had said, cheered up now.

Ingrown toenail! Meredith thought indignantly. But as hard as she tried to be angry at Ginger, instead she felt as if someone had stabbed her in the chest. Ginger, to whom she had shown so much kindness. Was this the thanks she deserved? Ginger, whom she had once worshipped like a goddess, whose embraces she had longed for but never received. Ginger, whose decline into sordid American adulthood she had watched with silent sorrow, telling herself all the while that she would be there to lend support when Ginger—who was too brilliant for all that—opted out of it. And she had been there. All she asked for in return was gratitude.

Instead she had become the object of contempt.

Contempt. What contempt Leslie must feel for her to treat her Jack Horner's Pie the way he had. Her Jack Horner's Pie, which she had spent all month preparing. One by one he had taken her carefully wrapped presents out of the basket, and ripped the tasteful limericks out of them, and read them aloud, grimacing, stopping from time to time to ridicule their author. "Oh, Meredith. Come, come, now. You could have been a shade more risqué. A shade less nursery school. Come, come, now. A cookbook for Stella? Why not a diaphragm? God knows she needs one. . . . And for Amy, a cigarette lighter? Why not a dildo, or a hairpiece for her paramour? . . . And a record cleaner for Ralph. How sweet. How very elementary school. But you ought to have bought him a whip, and perhaps a leash for Theo. And as for our precious little failed priest here, how lightly you have let him off. A *Poetry Primer*. Was that the best you could come up with for pious old Thomas? What has become of your comic sense, my dear? Why not *How to*

Overtip, or *How to Make Friends with Your Maid?* Or *Grin and Bear It: A Cuckold's How-To*."

More insults now. Thomas inviting Leslie to step outside for a fight. Leslie declining. Thomas calling Leslie a coward. Leslie once again calling Thomas a failed priest. Stella stepping in to defend Thomas. Calling Leslie a closet queen, a bad father. Calling Meredith a nymphomaniac, a bad mother. Meredith seeing red now. "How dare you call me a nymphomaniac with your track record, you goddamn hypocritical two-faced Catholic?"

Thomas stepping in to defend his wife. "Don't you call my wife a hypocrite, you slut."

"Don't you dare call me a slut," Meredith had cried. "Leslie! Aren't you going to come to my defense? He called me a slut."

"Don't call my wife a nymphomaniac," Leslie had said. Wearily.

"Why shouldn't I?" Stella had said. "She *is* a nymphomaniac. No wonder her children are such disasters. All she does all day is make eyes at Ginger."

"You take that back!" Meredith had screamed. Alone again. Undefended.

"No, I won't take that back. You think that just because I haven't read Levi-Straus I don't notice anything? Well, I've got news for you. Not only have I noticed everything, but so has everyone else. Everyone knows you have a crush on Ginger."

"I'm not in love with Ginger, you slut!"

"Don't call my wife a slut."

"Then tell her not to call me a lesbian."

"But you are a lesbian," Stella had said.

And Ginger had added, "So what if she is? It would do us all some good to fuck a few women."

And Meredith had cried, "You fucking bitch! Why can't you stay out of this? I hate you! I never want to see you again!" And she had thrown her glass across the table, not at Stella but at Ginger. Seeing red, she had aimed badly, and ended up hitting Blake instead. She had cut his forehead. The glass was still all over the floor. He probably thought she was crazy. He probably dismissed her as menopausal. He had come all the way from that village for this.

He was probably thinking, So this is their idea of a civilized Christmas dinner. At one end of the table Scrooge, at the other end a hysterical middle-aged woman who throws glasses at her guests. And what charming friends they have—a pair of ageing homosexuals who are about to cut each other's throats. And a slut and a failed priest, who are silent now, put to shame by little Beatrice, who has been the only one to speak during dessert. "Mommy? What is a slut, Mom? Daddy? Daddy? Why did you kick over the Christmas tree? Why? Did it do something bad? Why, Daddy, why?"

So this is Christmas dinner chez Meredith Lacey, perfect hostess. Shame on you, old girl, shame. Pull yourself together. Say something bright and cheery. Pretend it never happened. Pretend you are all friends. Smile now, as Leslie rises to his feet and says, "I don't know about the rest of you, but I'm going to have a drink." Smile instead of saying, "It's too late now, Scrooge. A drink won't help us now." Smile, and offer seconds, and think of some way to salvage the rest of the afternoon.

"Does anyone want seconds?" Meredith asked, smiling. Smiling bravely, perfect hostess, hostess par excellence. "Why don't we just cut everyone another piece? There's more than enough to go around, as I suppose you all can see."

Silence, as Leslie came back into the room with the wine.

"Well! Who's for seconds, then?"

Silence, as he poured himself a glass and passed the bottle down the table.

"No one? Are you sure? Perhaps the children would like some. Jonas, would you. . . . Oh, never mind. It doesn't matter. It's just so sad!" she blurted out, surveying the ruined meal around her—the half-carved turkey carcass, the half-eaten casseroles, the congealed gravy, the pies with only one piece taken out of them, the tasteful limericks and careful gift wrapping strewn all over the floor, her thin-lipped husband, her ungrateful friends all staring into their wineglasses. "There's so much extra food! Well, I suppose we can count on Hector to eat some of it. He never called, you know. He must be on his way. He must have been held up somewhere, that's what I think. He should be arriving soon. I wonder," she said, breathing in sharply to keep her voice from cracking, "I wonder what became of him?"

It was ten minutes to four when Sevda the maid glanced out the window and saw a man dressed in black climbing the hill. Despite her failing eyesight, she immediately recognized this man as Hector Cabot. She was overjoyed, because no matter what people said, in her eyes Hector Cabot was a good man. He would bring to an end this nonsensical fighting at the dining table. He would force them all to apologize and become friends. Then it would be safe for Sevda to go downstairs and do the dishes. She was anxious to get the dishes done because she was expecting a gentleman visitor at five. A truck driver with a proven temper, he would be angry if she was not there to greet him.

She was stretched out on the radiator in Winifred's bedroom, which was, because of its feminine furniture, her favorite room in the house. Sitting on the floor at her feet were her three friends, Winifred, Chloe, and Margaret. They were all upset, poor things, because of the terrible fighting in the dining room. Despite the fact that they were fast approaching middle age, they still possessed an innocence which broke Sevda's heart when she looked at them. They were still surprised when life was unkind to them. Thinking of the crushing blows that awaited them when they left home to enter the real world of men, she wished she could be with them always, cushioning the impact of life's inevitable bullets, bandaging the wounds, offering rare words of solace and unquestioning companionship.

Oh, if they would only listen to her warnings about the evil men who lurked in every shadow and preyed on innocent virgins. Oh, if they only learned from her example and put their faith in good men. Innocent young girls were too weak to fight evil single-handed. They needed good men as their champions. If only she could make them see this. In the old days, when they were still children, they had believed her. Now they told her that there were no evil men in the world, or good men either. Everyone was a combination, they said.

When Sevda turned to Chloe (red eyes, swollen face) and said, "I have good news. Your father is arriving. He will end this nonsensical fighting,'' she merely shrugged her shoulders. She was angry at him, she had confessed earlier to Sevda. He was divorcing her mother, Chloe had said, and taking the children back to America with him. ''I don't want to go back to America,'' Chloe had said. ''It's not my home. This is my home and I want to stay here.'' What she didn't realize was that it was sometimes necessary for good men to take drastic measures. You had to trust in their greater wisdom. If only Sevda could make young Chloe understand this.

When Sevda was sixteen, she was corrupted by a bad man, and later rescued by a good man who had taken pity on her. The good man, wishing to restore her to virtue, had taken away her fine clothes and jewelry and put her to work in his factory, saying it was important for her to learn the value of honest money. But Sevda, careless Sevda, had not understood the wisdom of his drastic measures. In pursuit of more fine clothes and more fine jewelry, she had returned to the bad man and become a bad woman.

She had often longed to tell her young friends this story so that they could learn from her example, but she did not have the heart to disappoint them by revealing the badness that lurked inside her ravaged soul. No, it was important for them to continue to believe in her, to trust her as a caring, worldly confidante. And so she prepared to tell them the more inspirational story of her life as it should have been. She sighed deeply and flicked back her hair, which was ten thousand gold threads today in the fading afternoon sun. (In anticipation of her gentleman caller, she had had it tinted to a richer shade the previous afternoon.) She looked at her worn hands and her frail, tired legs, which had been made for silk-covered divans and not for housework. She smoothed out her faded dress and felt the large pink ribbon in her hair. She looked at the gold ring on her finger, which she wore to convince her neighbors that she was a respectable woman who had been tragically widowed.

Downstairs, the doorbell rang. She could hear Madame Lacey exclaim something in her high-pitched voice. Then rapid footsteps, followed by the door opening on its unoiled hinges, and more of Madame Lacey's exclamations, followed by the low, reassuring tones of Monsieur Cabot's voice.

Monsieur Cabot followed Madame Lacey back into the dining room. Sevda sighed with relief. Now her evening would go according to schedule. She would tell her story and then go downstairs to do the dishes. She would be home before her gentleman caller arrived, and therefore not be subjected to a beating.

"Let me tell you," she said, turning to her three young disciples. "Let me tell you how easy it is for a young and innocent girl to be corrupted.

"Let me begin on a perfect spring day, when a young girl with blue eyes and ten thousand gold threads for hair takes leave of her mother and goes out for a stroll along the sparkling waterfront. . . ."

Sevda stopped to sigh, as she always did when she spoke of blonde, blue-eyed girls. It was just like the old days, Margaret thought. She looked around her at Winifred's stuffed animals, her stacks of *Seventeen* magazine, the photographs of movie stars on her wall, and her neatly arranged makeup on the vanity table. Little had changed in the three years since Margaret had last visited the room.

In the old days, they had spent all their afternoons up here, scribbling notes which they slipped under Eric's bedroom door, waiting for him and his friends to respond with water balloons, making truces so that they could combine forces for a game of Ghost or My Poor Toe. In the old days, they had thought they would play these games forever. Then Eric had gone away to school, and Winifred had embarked on a successful diet, turning almost overnight from a rambunctious child into a thin teenager with no time for horseplay.

It had taken a year or two for Chloe and Margaret to follow in her footsteps. Now they were all thin teenagers, and suddenly all friends again, as they listened to Sevda spin them a fairy tale they had heard her tell many times before and long since outgrown.

". . . And so she is strolling along the sparkling waterfront, which is, oh! so nice, and she is admiring the fine boats and the elegant strollers and the deep blue cloudless sky and the sea, which is smooth like a scarf. She looks this way, she looks that way, she says, 'Ah! Oh! How lovely! How nice!' She is innocent. She is happy. She trusts everyone, thinking they are all as good as she.

"And then, along comes a wicked man.

"He is dressed in a tuxedo of the finest cloth. He has black hair—oiled black hair—and thick eyebrows that meet over his nose, and dark skin like an Arab. He has flashing white teeth and a thick black mustache which he fingers as he smiles. At the sight of the blonde, blue-eyed angel . . ."

Sigh.

"At the sight of the young girl he stops short, dazzled by her pure beauty. Then he fingers his mustache and says to himself: Heh, heh, heh. He has a plan.

" 'And a very good day to you, my beauty,' he says. She smiles, because she is innocent and smiles at everyone. When he invites her to accompany him to a pastry shop, she accepts, not suspecting his intentions.

"At the pastry shop he buys some baklava. He has them put it into a box. 'I have an idea,' he says. 'It would be a shame to enjoy such luscious baklava amid such commotion. I would like to invite you to my home. My mother is waiting for me. I am sure she would like to meet you.'

" 'Your mother?' says the innocent girl. 'But of course. It would be unthinkable to keep your esteemed mother waiting.' They go back to his apartment, a grand apartment with the finest appointments. The girl is impressed. But the mother, where is the mother? 'My mother, I am sad to say, was feeling unwell and retired to her bed.'

" 'But you must stay. I insist,' says the crafty gentleman. 'I would like to show you my etchings. Did I tell you I was an artist? Yes, I was trained in Paris. Why don't you look at them, while I have my servants prepare the coffee.'

"And so the young girl wanders from etching to etching, saying, 'Ah! How beautiful!' and 'Oh! How nice!' In the meantime, the servant arrives with the coffee on a silver tray. While the girl's back is turned, the wicked man takes a vial of sleeping potion from a hidden pocket in his coat and empties it into the young girl's cup.

" 'Oh! What delicious coffee,' says the girl.

" 'Yes, isn't it?' says the crafty man. Heh, heh, heh.

"The next thing the girl knows, she is waking up in an unfamiliar bed. She knows right away that several days have passed. She immediately thinks of her mother. How worried she must be! She pulls off the covers and sees that she is naked.

"The crafty gentleman appears at the door. 'How are you, my little paramour?' he says. Heh, heh, heh. Heh, heh, heh. It is then that the girl realizes that she has become a woman.

"She cries. She pleads with her corrupter. 'Let me go,' she cries. 'Let me return to my mother.' But he refuses. He keeps her under lock and key. For a year he keeps her there. In the beginning, he brings her expensive gifts. But then, as he tires of her, the gifts come to an end. Sometimes he does not visit her for weeks at a time. Finally, he throws her out. Too ashamed now to return to her mother, she takes up residence in a house of ill repute.

"Here, because of her beauty, she enjoys great success. But still her heart bleeds. No one cares. She is a prostitute. No one cares . . . except for one person.

"This person is a fair-haired gentleman with a stern expression and kindly eyes. Every evening at seven, he strolls past the house of ill repute and looks up at her window.

"One day, he comes inside and has a long private meeting with the madame. At its conclusion, the madame comes upstairs and says, 'Gather your things, you lucky one. You have been sold.'

"At first the girl—the woman—assumes she is to be the kindly man's mistress. But no, the man does not wish for anything in return for his kindness. He takes her to a beautiful villa overlooking the sea. Next to the villa itself is a tiny little *konak* the size of a doll's house. This is where he installs her. He tells her that he is a teacher. He is going to educate her so that she can make an honest living. It will take a long time, he warns her. 'But I promise you every luxury in the meantime. When you are capable of earning an honest living,' he says, 'I shall set you free. Until then, I shall be keeping you under lock and key.'

"And so, the months pass. The girl—the woman—works hard at her lessons with the kindly gentleman, but she is lonely sometimes, especially on days when more important engagements prevent her master from coming to teach her.

In the summer, things become even more difficult. She develops a longing.

"This villa she is living in happens to be in Kanlica, and the longing she develops is for Kanlica yogurt. 'Ah,' she says, 'for one dish of Kanlica yogurt!' And so she forgets the warnings of her kindly master. One sunny afternoon, she climbs out the window and sets out for the café next to the ferry station. Here she orders a luscious Kanlica yogurt. As she sits looking at the sparkling sea, she dreams of her future as a schoolteacher. She dreams of her adoring pupils, and she dreams of the man she comes home to every evening. Who is it, you ask? It is, of course, the kindly gentleman who is her master. By now, of course, she is hopelessly in love with him.

"She returns to the *konak* and her studies. The next time she sees her master, she feels badly for having gone against his will. She vows never to do so again. But as is always the case in life, one longing leads to another. Her outings to the Kanlica café continue, first once a week, then almost every day. And the inevitable day arrives when the unparalleled yogurt of Kanlica, the sparkling marine vistas, the dreams of her future as a schoolteacher, are not enough to satisfy her hungry soul.

"One afternoon in late summer, as she is sitting alone at a table overlooking the water, she develops a sudden longing for baklava. Not any baklava, but the baklava from a certain sweetshop in her old neighborhood, the neighborhood of her undoing and disgrace. Ah, for some of that baklava! she says to herself. Ah, for one small piece. And so she buys a ticket for the next ferry going into the city.

"She returns to her neighborhood. She returns to the sweetshop, where she enjoys a plate of baklava. And then she sets off on her return journey.

"She is about to descend to the ferry station when suddenly a curiosity overcomes her. She decides to take a longer route, past the house of ill repute where she once was a prisoner. She wishes to see it one more time, from without. And so she walks down the familiar street in all her finery. Before she has even reached the house of ill repute, people have begun to recognize her.

"Street urchins, beggars, pimps, and, looking down from

their windows, whores, all whispering to one another, saying, 'Did you see her? She has come back in all her finery to let us know how well she has done for herself. Look at the shoes she is wearing, look at the dress, look at the rings on her fingers, look at her parasol. Look at the way she lifts her nose in the air, as if we smelled bad. Shame, shame on her for looking down on her own kind. She is no better than us. Once a prostitute, always a prostitute. Shame on her, shame on her. Whore, putting on airs. Whore, masquerading as a lady.' As she passes by the house of ill repute where she once was a prisoner, the first stone falls at her feet.

"Who is to know who threw the first stone? A street urchin, a pimp, a jealous former friend . . . it could be anyone. It is followed by a second stone, and a third, and a fourth, which hits her in the chest, drawing blood. The malicious whispers give way to mocking laughter, jeers which grow ever louder, and deafening insults. A crowd of men forms behind her. Ten men, twenty men. Soon there are too many to count. She runs, she hides her face with her arms, she screams, but they continue to pursue her, hurling stone after stone, while whores leaning out of their windows cheer them on. Just as she reaches the corner, a large rock hits her on the head and she falls to the ground.

"She has given up hope for herself, when who should suddenly appear out of nowhere but her kindly master! He tries to save her, but it is too late. The riot has grown to unmanageable proportions. 'Stop!' he cries. But now they are both being pelted with rocks. He takes her in his arms and tries to stop her bleeding with his handkerchief. But it is too late. She is dying.

"Her soul leaves her body to float up to heaven. She looks down on the heads of her attackers, who are sneering at her and shaking their fists. Higher and higher she goes. As she ascends, she desperately searches the crowd for her benefactor. Her kindly master, who risked his life to save her. Her kindly master, whom she loves. But she can find him nowhere.

"At last she reaches the gates of heaven. She looks down once again on the heads of her attackers. Although they are far, far away by now, she can see them clearly, as if they were only an arm's length away. To her surprise, they are no longer sneering but angry and envious. Then she turns around and sees why. Waiting for her at the gates of heaven is her kindly benefactor.

"They embrace. They are so happy that they smile down on the heads of their attackers and forgive them. This makes the attackers even angrier. They cannot bear to see their victims delivered from their misery.

"The lovers turn to face each other. They embrace, ignoring the howls of envy from below. And then, arm in arm, they glide through the open gates of heaven.

"And that, my dear girls, is the end of my story." Sevda sighed, glanced out the window, and lit a cigarette.

After Sevda had finished her story, Margaret went downstairs to see if conditions were favorable for Sevda to do the dishes. It sounded as if they might be: there were no raised voices coming from the dining room. "They have made peace," Sevda predicted. "They have buried their hatchets." But Margaret, who had been tracking omens of impending disaster for longer than anyone, thought otherwise.

Perhaps they are all dead, she thought, as she walked down the stairs. Or perhaps they have all sneaked out through the back door and abandoned us, left us with nothing to do but pick up the pieces. Being only seventeen, she still thought that when things ended, they ended in catastrophe. What she heard when she reached the kitchen, therefore, was not what she expected.

Hector was talking. He had a new voice: loud, clear, and resonant. Propping her elbows on the kitchen table, she listened to him.

". . . And after my father and I had sat together for an hour, we went to the cemetery. There I lit a candle next to my mother's grave. Together we said a prayer for her soul. And you know—this sounds embarrassing, I know, but I have to say it—I suddenly realized that it was my soul that was buried in that earth, and that my prayers were bringing it back to life.

"I know it's the wrong time of year to be talking about resurrection. I suppose I'll always be unorthodox. A lapsed Christian in a Moslem country—what do you expect?

"You know I've never believed in God. Not really. Not

since I was a child. So you can imagine my surprise when I felt this . . . soul returning to me. And I mean my soul. My soul. I'm sorry, but there's no other word.

"And now suddenly I believe in God again, just as I did when I was a child. Suddenly it is all real—Jesus, his teachings, his sacrifice . . . all of this is living inside me. I wish I could explain it better.

"And so that is where I was today. I am sorry if my absence ruined the dinner, but now we can try to forgive each other and begin again.

"I have a request to make. It is a bizarre request, I know, but I think it is only right under the circumstances. I would like to give thanks before I eat. I hope you don't mind.

"Let us join hands.

"Dear Lord."

Silence.

He cleared his throat and tried again. "Dear Lord.

"No. I don't think I can do this. I'm too self-conscious. I'm afraid I might laugh. I guess you can't sit down and say a good grace after the kind of life I've been living. I'm sorry. I've kept you all waiting. You must want your desserts. Well, I'd still like to say something, nonetheless. Perhaps I should just say a simple prayer."

He cleared his throat. Margaret peeked around the corner just in time to see him bow his head.

I am the resurrection and the life, saith the Lord;
he that believeth in Me, though he were dead, yet shall he live;
and whosoever liveth and believeth in Me shall never die.

I know that my Redeemer liveth,
and that He shall stand at the latter day upon the earth;
and though his body be destroyed, yet shall I see God;
whom I shall see for myself and mine eyes shall behold,
and not as a stranger.

For none of us liveth to himself,
and no man dieth to himself.
For if we live, we live unto the Lord;
and if we die, we die unto the Lord.

Whether we live, therefore, or die, we are the Lord's.

Blessed are the dead who die in the Lord. . . ."

He was sitting at the head of the table. Margaret could only see his back. The others were watching him. Her parents and Leslie on one side, Ralph and Theo on the other, and at the far end of the table, Meredith, whose face was, like all their faces, tearstained. Their mouths were hanging open. They were all holding hands.

They looked betrayed, as if he had already moved beyond their reach, as if he had forsaken them for the gates of heaven. Too civilized to throw stones, they were nevertheless devastated to see him delivered from his misery.

X

Hector's Odyssey: The End

July 6, 1982

THESE were the same people who reassembled thirteen years later, except for Leslie (dead of lung cancer) and Theo (long gone, last heard of in San Diego).

There were other differences. Beatrice was no longer a baby but a subdued adolescent, Margaret no longer a subdued adolescent but an adult. Margaret's husband, Peter, was another new face.

It was not a winter afternoon this time but a pleasant summer evening. And they were not gathered around a ruined feast in the Laceys' dining room but sitting on the Ashes' wisteria-covered terrace, sipping their *rakis* and Hill cocktails in the failing light.

Hector was the only one who had aged—thirteen years of sensible behavior, Margaret thought. The others—Stella, Meredith, Ralph, even Thomas—were deeply tanned and radiated the youthful optimism of midsummer. There was no hatred, no envy, no bitterness in their expressions as they looked at their old friend. Rather, they were delighted at his surprise visit—a welcome break in their dull, though pleasant, summer routine. They held nothing against him now.

Time had proved that, for the time being at least, Hector was not bound for heaven nor they for hell.

Though of all the people present, Margaret was the only one to remember how they had once feared this was the case. For the others, the trials of the intervening years had erased their memories of that Christmas dinner the way a wave erases writing on wet sand.

"So you're happy with your new life," Meredith said.

"It's hardly new," said Hector.

"How right you are," Meredith agreed. "I'm losing my sense of time in my dotage. Years have a way of blending into one another here, with the exception of that ghastly winter when we didn't have any heat. That was quite dreadful, wasn't it, Stella?"

Stella nodded but said nothing. Nor did anyone else wish to dwell on the horrors of the heatless winter. There was a silence, broken finally by Ralph. "And how is your father?" he asked Hector.

"He's fine," Hector said. His father, retired now, was living with him in Woodstock, Connecticut. "He's taken up gardening," Hector added.

"How nice for him," Ralph replied. He lit a cigarette, inhaled, and then smiled at Hector as he exhaled.

"More tea?" Amy suggested.

"Thank you, that would be lovely," Hector said.

"It's Twinings," Stella said. "I hope it's not too stale."

"No, it's not stale at all," said Hector.

"Oh, good," said Stella. When it became clear that Hector could find nothing to say, she added, "I wrap the tin in plastic."

"What a good idea," said Hector.

Stella knocked back the rest of her drink.

"I didn't want to write," Hector explained, "in case our plans changed."

"How long has it been, all in all?" Meredith asked.

"We've already been through that," Ralph reminded her.

"Yes, but I forgot," Meredith said.

"What *is* becoming of your memory?" Ralph said.

"Goodness gracious, yes," Meredith said. "Let me see if I can redeem myself. Let me do my calculations." She closed her eyes. Her mouth moved as she did her calculations. "Thirteen years," she said finally. "Or rather, it will be come January."

Stella coughed. Ralph, turning to Hector, gave him that strange, glassy smile again. He winked—voluntarily? Involuntarily? Hector did not know what to say.

This time Thomas rescued him. "Will this be your first trip to Jerusalem?" he asked.

Hector was taking a group from his church in Connecticut on a tour of the Holy Land. They had been in Istanbul for three days. Tomorrow they were to fly to Jerusalem. This evening he had left them to their own devices so as to be able to make his pilgrimage alone.

Ever since he had planned the trip, he had been dreading this reunion. He had foreseen the stiffness, but not that they would be happy to see him.

It was as if they had never hated him, ostracized him, failing even to come say goodbye to him on that bitter January morning in 1970 when he had loaded his suitcase into the trunk of Hamdi *efendi*'s taxi and left his life behind. His father had been the only one to come to the airport to see him off.

The last time Hector had seen Amy, she had spat at him. But now, when the time came for him to take his leave, she seemed almost offended. "Surely you can't be leaving us so soon. There's so much we haven't talked about." It was as if they had never been married, let alone divorced.

"I'm afraid I have to go," he said, rather stiffly, because it was a line he had rehearsed. "I'm meeting Emin Bey at seven at Osman's."

"Are you really off tomorrow?" Amy asked.

He told them he was afraid this was so.

What a shame, they all said. Couldn't he put it off? "What about on your way back from Jerusalem?" Meredith suggested. "Couldn't you put your church people on a plane to New York and come back by yourself?"

"No," he said. "My father needs me." Furthermore, there was a mission he was supposed to go on, to the Philippines.

"Then you must come back quickly," Meredith said. "Things are so much better now. The military—oh, dear, you and your human-rights friends must think dreadfully ill of the military—but the truth is, they have done some good for the common man. Do you remember how impossible it used to be to walk along the waterfront in the summer? All those street boys using the pavement like a beach, making such nuisances of themselves. One can tire so easily of drawn and hungry faces underfoot—I suppose men don't have this problem, although you did say *you* did, Thomas. You remember, that day you wore those light blue corduroy trousers to Bebek to get the paper, and they all thought you were a queen. As for myself, I never *could* see what could possibly be so thrilling about a glimpse at my boring old underpants. Well, that's all over with now! The military's banned swimming along there. Their beautification program has been most successful. Did you notice how they've fixed up the benches along the shore as well? And I suppose you took your group to the bazaar. You noticed, then, how they've cleaned things up *there?* Although I must say I miss the riffraff."

Before Hector left the garden, he paused to look at the view, because he did not plan to ever come back again. It was just the same, or almost. The hills were that misty blue-green of midsummer, the crenelated walls and towers of the castle as formidable as he remembered them, the Bosphorus just as blue. The garden was in bloom except for one former flowerbed, where, Amy had explained to him, the gardener had been permitted to grow vegetables for his family.

At the end of the garden there had once been a low green gate leading to the Bowl. Now in its place was a high wall built by the new rector of the university, a man with a fondness for defined boundaries and cement. Now it was impossible to get onto the campus unless you went around to one of the gates. They didn't let you in without a university identity card. But this was not of immediate concern to Hector. He was going in the opposite direction.

Margaret and her husband accompanied him down the hill. When they reached Osman's, the husband (Peter?) asked if they could join him for a beer. Hector said of course, although he would have preferred them not to. It would make things more complicated when Emin Bey arrived, and he needed things to go well with Emin Bey.

He needed Emin Bey to see that he was a changed man.

"I want you to know," he had written to Emin Bey, in a letter he now realized had been too earnest, too humorless, too American Protestant:

> I want you to know that the man who cuckolded dear friends, the man who neglected his wife and his children and failed his colleagues in their hour of need—the man who failed to give a thought to anyone but himself—this man is no longer. I deserved those harsh words of thirteen years ago, Emin Bey. And I want you to know that I took them to heart. I've changed. Now I pride myself on thinking of other people more than I think of myself. I take good care of my father. I've provided for my children. I give much of my time to volunteer work. I think I've learned, also, how to give to people, and when not to, and how to offer help without injuring a man's dignity. And as for my private life, I assure you I have not repeated my past mistakes. I still don't drink. I regard this as essential. There is a woman I see from time to time, a wonderful, understanding woman, but she has her own life and I respect this. We see each other twice a month, on Tuesdays.
>
> You see, Emin Bey, I came to the conclusion long ago that I committed my most heinous crimes while under the influence. When I am drunk I am completely uncivilized. This is why I continue to abstain. It is absolutely essential, as I said.
>
> As for those other things you said to me thirteen years ago, I have given much thought to them, too. And I think in a way you were right. Perhaps we never did belong there. Because we did abuse our privileges. Perhaps it is true that Western education has brought much unhappiness to Turkey, but surely this was an accusation you made in the heat of the moment. Surely you, a mathematician, will agree that education is necessary.
>
> There is another thing I think about often, and that is that I do not regret my years in Turkey. All moral issues aside, I do not regret it. If I had never come to Turkey, we would never have been friends.

* * *

He should never have sent the letter, he now saw. When he had called up the day before to arrange a meeting, Emin Bey had been distant, almost rude. Perhaps he didn't even intend to turn up this evening. As Hector awaited his long-lost friend's arrival, he found himself becoming more and more nervous, and less and less able to answer Margaret's husband's questions with conviction.

He was an intense young man, this Peter, very much the earnest American, although he had picked up some Hill mannerisms, and would pick up more, Hector was sure, as time wore on. He wanted to know about Hector's work, and so Hector told him about the various agencies he was involved with, trying not to bore him with details. He had done some important work, actually, especially over the last four or five years. But he was careful to be modest about it, and he stressed the importance of other people's contributions, even when they weren't so important. He was careful about everything these days, so worried about stepping on other people's toes, that he resorted to constant, petty dishonesty in order not to. Sometimes he hated himself for it.

Peter was interested in politics. He asked good questions, although this would not last, not if he stayed on the Hill. Sooner or later he would reach the point of no return and become an expatriate. Hector could see the signs already: the way he held his cigarette, the way he laughed, the way he sprinkled his sentences with Turkish expressions that were somehow more apt, the way he mistook a waiter's smile for a sign that he was welcome here. Hector could foresee the day when Peter discovered, as they all had had to discover, that he was a foreigner.

Hector was tempted to say something, but then he reminded himself: what this young man did with his life was none of his business. Peter could look at Hector's example if he wished. If he wished, he could learn from it. But as for Hector's private thoughts, he would have none of them. To each his own damnation.

The evening was perfect—exactly as he remembered evenings at Osman's. The little ferry station across the road was empty except for the ticket seller, who stood at the edge of the wharf gazing contentedly at the water. The first fishing boats were going out. Across the Bosphorus, the windows on the Asian shore were golden with the light of the setting sun. It was hard to believe all the horror stories about torture and political prisons amid such peace. He could almost convince himself that time had stood still along this small stretch of the Bosphorus, preserving all that was best about the old days. Then something happened to show him that time had not stood still here, not even for a second.

A cream-colored Mercedes-Benz pulled up onto the sidewalk and parked right in front of their table.

The driver was a chauffeur. He came around to open the door for the passengers—a man in his midforties with lean, ratlike good looks, and a schoolgirl who could not have been more than sixteen. She was wearing loafers and bobby socks and had her hair in a braid. She was excited, as if she had never been to a restaurant without her parents before. The man was pleased to see that she was turning heads. He put his arm around her as he dispatched the chauffeur and led her into the restaurant. He chose a corner table. As the waiters scurried around them, he squeezed her hand and gave her an amorous look. It was very important, apparently, that no one mistake this schoolgirl for his daughter.

Hector could not take his eyes off the couple. The man looked familiar to him, although he could not place him. It was clear that he was a man of importance. An official of some sort? Hector watched the waiter bring them a bottle of *raki*. The man poured out two glasses. He added water to the girl's glass but none to his. They lifted their glasses and said a toast.

Then the man turned abruptly and stared Hector straight in the eyes, like a cat about to pounce. He bared his teeth, as if to smile. He lifted his glass. Then, just as abruptly, he returned his attentions to the schoolgirl.

Hector broke out in a sweat. He knew this man, he knew this man, but who was he? As if in search for an answer, Hector reached into his pocket. Then he panicked, because his wallet wasn't there.

His heart pounding, he felt his other back pocket. The wallet was there, thank God, and his passport was still safe in his shirt pocket. In the front pocket of his trousers were his housekeys, for some reason, and loose change—some Italian, some English, some Turkish. Everything was in its place, he assured himself, as he returned his attention to Margaret and Peter. But he could not rid himself of the fear that he had lost something.

At half past seven, Emin Bey surveyed himself in his bedroom mirror. It was a large mirror that took in the entire room, from the garish pillows on the bed he shared with his wife to the collection of foreign cosmetics on the vanity table, whose names he could read backwards.

To the right of the vanity table was a shelf of knick-knacks; behind it was a wardrobe of clothes Roksan would never wear again. On the other side of the room was a bookcase filled with weighty volumes neither he nor she would ever read. Next to the bookcase were his shiny brown leather bedslippers. Everything, Emin Bey thought gloomily, was in its place.

Everything, he thought, except for that blot in the middle of the mirror, that sorry figure staring back at him, mocking his dignity—the reflection of Emin Bey, the Sick Old Man of Europe himself.

His shoulders were hunched now. His complexion was yellow. He wondered how long it would take for Hector to realize he was dying.

"Don't forget to take your pills," said his wife, standing in the hallway, anxiously examining his eyes, straightening his collar, temporarily blocking his way. "And try not to eat anything salty. Make sure that madman does not make you drink any alcohol. Remember what the doctor said. For God's sake, for Allah's sake, remember his warnings. Are you sure you wish to go? There is no need for you to go unless you want to. You owe this madman nothing."

But he did want to go, if only to prove to himself that the reflection in the mirror was a lie. Those hunched shoulders, those bloodshot eyes, that yellowing complexion, these were all elements of a disguise. Inside he was still Emin Bey, still the fearsome lion, master of every situation, yachtsman, scholar, honorable friend, dutiful husband, feared enemy.

Be frank with yourself, sick old man, Emin Bey told himself. Perhaps not so honorable, not so dutiful, not so feared. Which was not to say he had not enjoyed a few successes.

Feza, for example. Now this was a success story. He had married her off to the son of an old schoolfriend—a shy, unworldly boy named Feridun whose young wife had died in the DC-10 crash outside Paris. He had been left with two infants. Feza had fallen in love with them at first sight. They now lived in New York, where Feridun ran an import-export concern.

Yes, with Feza he had worked a miracle. But what had he been able to do for Halûk and Yasemin, when, during the 1971–72 martial law, they had been imprisoned? Some money, some clothes, some food, some books, some inconsequential visits during which they had all pretended that they would not be marked for life by the experience. His niece, Yasemin, in prison. His colleague, Halûk, in prison. Yasemin had given birth in that hellhole not fit for a dog, and the child had died there two weeks later. They had counted on him to do something. He had tried, but he had achieved nothing. How he had groveled at the feet of Policeman Ismet, trying to extract favors from his oily hands, trying to squeeze compassion out of his coal-black heart. The Eastern fox, then at the summit of his power, had made half promises but had done nothing. He now had a dead child on his conscience.

A dead child and broken parents. They were in California now. They had lasted in Istanbul through the worst years of the Anarchy, enduring many dangers and indignities, but finally, in 1979, they had awoken one morning to find bullet holes in their bedroom window. They were Rightist bullets. Emin Bey had not had it in him to urge them to stay.

Oh, the things he had dreamed of saying to Ismet. *Is this what you wish for your country, to chase away the flower of our youth, and if they remain, to torture them, imprison them, rob them of every nuance of human dignity? Is this your idea of bringing a nation into the twentieth century?* But he said none of this, because once again there was martial law. The new reign of terror had enhanced Policeman's Ismet's significance. Emin Bey had his wife to think of. He had his other relations. He had to keep his burning anger to himself.

It was from Ismet that Emin Bey had first learned of Hector's return. He had called two days earlier, his intentions unclear but ominous. "I thought you would be interested to learn of the arrival of a mutual friend," he had said.

Emin Bey had been unable to refrain from insinuated insult. "I did not realize I had the honor of being friendly with someone upon whom you looked with equal affection," he had said. "I thought our tastes were incompatible."

"Yes, you are right," Ismet had said, in his even, oily manner. "Perhaps the term 'mutual friend' is an exaggeration. In fact, the term 'friend' may also be excessive. In my understanding, relations between you and this man have been strained. I am referring, of course, to Hector Cabot."

"Ah, Hector, my dear friend and former colleague," Emin Bey found himself saying. "I have been waiting for him."

"You have corresponded?" Ismet asked. Emin Bey noted with pleasure the surprise in the man's voice.

"Yes, we have corresponded," Emin Bey lied. Because although he had received a puzzling letter from the man, he had never answered it. "But I am sure this is no surprise to you, with your observant connections."

"Alas," Ismet agreed. He was easier to flatter now. "Alas, for a man in my position, there are few surprises."

And this from the lips of a man whose only trip abroad had been to the infamous facilities not far from Williamsburg, Virginia.

It was necessary to keep up appearances, to show that oily fox that no matter how far-reaching his power, he could not prevent a dying uncle from seeing whom he wished. What were threats and insinuations to a man who had less than a year left on this earth? It was with Ismet in mind that Emin Bey set out to meet Hector.

The sun had just fallen when Emin Bey arrived at the Bebek taxi stand. As it was the month of Ramazan, the muezzin was making a dreadful racket. What hope was there for his country, Emin Bey wondered, with this man and so many thousands like him infesting the land like flies, buzzing, whining from every minaret, coaxing the faithful to forget all they had learned and return to the ignorance of the middle ages? It was too much for a scientist like himself to contemplate.

The taxi drivers all looked hungry. They had been fasting since dawn. Emin Bey thought fasting was unadulterated stupidity, although he did not hold it against taxi drivers, whose ignorance was the fault of others. He himself never fasted. In fact, in recent years he had made a point of indulging in fat, pink, smoked pork chops and full-bodied red wine during Ramazan—just to annoy his wife, who tried to fast if she was in good health. A strange quirk, Emin Bey thought, in a woman so sophisticated that she spoke her own language with a French accent.

"It is good for you," she always said. "You sacrifice one small thing and you gain something much greater. A day without food is a small price to pay for spiritual satisfaction."

"I want satisfaction of the appetite, not of the spirit!" Emin Bey would retort. But to his wife. Never to the likes of Hamdi *efendi,* whose ignorance he forgave, whose dignity he respected. The poor man was leaning against the side of his taxi, looking wan and tired after a day without food and water. Wasn't he too old to be subjecting himself to such hardships? Emin Bey knew better than to ask him this question.

Hamdi *efendi* was on his way home. He said he would be happy to drop Emin Bey off in front of Osman's.

And so it was at a few minutes past eight that Emin Bey joined his former friend and colleague, who was sitting at an outside table at Osman's in the company of Thomas Ashe's daughter, Margaret, and her husband, Peter Brooks.

Hector jumped to his feet at the sight of Emin Bey. He ran out to embrace him. "How wonderful to see you again," he said. "How wonderful to see you," Emin Bey replied, with a shade less spontaneity. But all in all, it was an excellent performance. A detached observer would never have guessed at the treachery Emin Bey had suffered at the hands of Hector, nor the wrath Emin Bey had showered on this man when the treachery was discovered.

Now, as they exchanged pro forma compliments and asked each other about the health of people they did not care a whit for, they pretended that nothing untoward had ever occurred between them.

Hector looked older, but not too much older. He was fit and tanned, with the same engaging smile, the same deceptively clear blue eyes that had once fooled Emin Bey so completely. So this was the new Hector. He did not look as different as he had hinted in his peculiar letter, this reformed character who now devoted his life to prying into the internal affairs of Third-World nations, this joyless missionary man who had the gall to think he could change peoples' hearts, this milquetoast who allowed his woman friend to have a life of her own, meeting with her on alternate Tuesdays. What kind of nonsense was this? It was merely a disguise. Underneath it was the same treacherous man.

A man might seek to advance himself by altering appearances like a chameleon, but the heart he concealed inside him never changed. It was either good or bad, strong or weak, faithful or treacherous. The heart was a mystery, but it never lied. Appearances lied. Emin Bey's gracious manners lied. Hector's engaging smile lied, as did his bright blue eyes. What liar had written that the eyes were the windows of the soul? These eyes were curtains. They hid the truth, just as the beautiful night closing in on them hid the truth, the dreadful secrets about his doomed country.

Hector asked him what he wished to drink. Emin Bey said he would have to make do with soda water. Doctor's orders, he explained. Hector ordered more *mezes*. They were almost all salty, and so Emin Bey had to content himself with picking at them like a flighty woman.

The conversation dragged. Emin Bey asked after Hector's children and then was forced to listen to the man's embarrassing apologies. They were not doing well, it seemed. Then Hector asked after a number of his former colleagues. Almost all of them were living abroad now. Emin Bey made light of this. "After all, we are a backward country," he said with a nonchalant smile. Hector nodded sadly. Despite his outward calm, Emin Bey felt a pang of shame that Hector should agree with him so readily. He asked himself what he hoped to gain by continuing this charade.

Why was he always having to pretend, pretend, pretend, and never reveal his true feelings? No wonder there were rings under his eyes, no wonder his skin was growing yellow and his shoulders hunched. A lifetime of concealing a thousand passions and hatreds had exhausted his poor constitution. All his life he had been attempting to be reasonable, honorable, dutiful, while inside his heart smoldered like the eternal flame. What was the point of such deception? What was the purpose of reasonable behavior, if it bred such misery?

It was at this low point in the conversation that Emin Bey glanced over his shoulder at the corner table. He was not surprised at the sight that met his eyes. Enraged, yes, but not surprised. The man was capable of anything.

Emin Bey recognized the schoolgirl Ismet was sitting with. She was the daughter of an acquaintance of his wife's. She went to the German Lycée. She lived in Bebek. He had seen her coming home from school with her classmates. She could not be more than fifteen, and here she was allowing this oily Eastern fox, this torturer, this murderer, to fondle her hand and ply her with *raki*.

It did not take long for Ismet to sense his uncle's eyes upon him. Looking up, he bowed his head in mock respect and lifted his *raki* glass. He bared his teeth as if to smile, as if to say, I shit in your mouth, I shit in all your mouths. You can do nothing without my knowledge. Once you used to laugh at me, but now you cower. You are like ants about to be crushed. And you will be crushed in the end, all of you. The future belongs to me.

"Who is that man?" Hector asked. "I know him from somewhere."

"He is not worth talking about," Emin Bey said. It was all he could do to keep his voice from shaking.

"But you know him?" Hector asked.

"Yes, I know him," said Emin Bey.

"He looks important. The waiters seem terrified of him."

"He is a nobody, a parvenu. He is not worthy of our attention. He is . . . he is married to my wife's niece. It is not a happy marriage. She has long been aware of his infidelities."

"He's not Ismet, is he?" Hector asked. Emin Bey said nothing. "Yes, of course. Of course he's Ismet. What was his last name? I don't think I ever knew it. Well. He looks like he's done quite well for himself. I'm not surprised."

"He may look important," Emin Bey repeated, "but in reality, he is nothing."

"What is he up to these days?" Hector asked.

"I do not wish to discuss it," said Emin Bey.

"Why not?"

"It has no relevance to the purpose of our meeting. He is a nonentity, I repeat. In short, he is a scum. This girl, I know her also. He is trying to provoke a reaction from us. Let us not give him this satisfaction. Please. We must continue as if everything were normal."

"As you wish," Hector said. For a moment, Emin Bey thought he understood. But then he did something to reveal the depth of his callousness.

In an attempt to change the subject, Emin Bey asked Hector how Istanbul appeared to him after his lengthy absence. To Emin Bey's dismay, Hector broke into a broad smile. He said it looked wonderful. "And I've been extraordinarily lucky with the weather," he said.

It's wonderful, is it, my fair-weather friend? You go away, you forsake us, and thirteen years later, you come back and say that everything is the same. The humiliation of this last decade means nothing to you. The martial law, the anarchy, the bombs, the riots, the shortages, the terror, the witch hunts, they are of no consequence. You think only about the beautiful scenery. You stay away while the tragic fate of our nation is apparent on every streetcorner. You come back only when it is once again concealed behind bars.

To think of so many of his compatriots seeing conspiracies inside conspiracies, linking so-and-so with the CIA and so-and-so with U.S. Naval Intelligence, dreaming up ulterior motives where none existed. Americans were in Turkey for a reason, they were sure of it. What would they have thought if they had learned the real reason—would they have laughed or cried? These Americans Emin Bey was sitting with were here because they could afford the restaurants.

Vallahi billâhi, he had had enough of them. Beside himself with frustration, he pushed his chair back from the table.

"I have had enough of this nonsense, very frankly," he said.

"What nonsense?" Hector asked. He looked surprised.

"The entire charade," Emin Bey said impatiently. "You. Her. Him. Myself. It is utterly pointless." He paused to look at his captive audience, agreeably surprised by his sudden power.

Not since his retirement had a group of people hung onto his words like this. He had forgotten how enjoyable it was to be the master of the situation. These days the master of the situation was his doctor. It was his doctor's words people hung onto. "No more salty food," he would declare. Oh, yes, my *padişah,* oh, certainly, my *beyefendi.* "No more oily foods either, for that matter." *Hay hay efendim,* of course, sir, anything you say, sir, your wish is my command. "No more *raki* or wine." And beer, my most honored sir? "No beer either. No alcohol whatsoever. It is essential to observe a strict regimen."

Oh, yes, sir, anything you say, sir. But sir, you are—are you not?—on holiday at this moment. You are on your lovely yacht, which once was my yacht, and you cannot see what a lovely, oily *dolma* sits in front of me. A lovely, oily, salty *dolma* which I am lifting to my lips at this very moment. Ah, my doctor, my *padişah,* my most respected sir. I must tell you something. It is delicious.

So what if it kills me? What is health but a transitory thing? My health has, I fear, long since transited. Ah, how good that was. And now for a fried mussel. My soul longs for a fried mussel. One fried mussel, and then I shall leave this gathering of false friends and go home.

It was while Emin Bey was eating the fried mussel that Hector interrupted his pleasurable thoughts. "Why do you feel this meal we are having is a charade?" he asked, in a thin voice that was not entirely his own. "And why is it pointless?"

"It is a charade because we are not doing or saying as we wish," Emin Bey said, reaching for a succulent-looking *börek*. "And it is pointless because we stand to gain nothing from the deception. But, oh, my word, how delicious this *börek* is," he said, with exaggerated lightheartedness. "You really must have one. I must say, this establishment has improved over the years. Wouldn't you agree?'' Emin Bey looked up, and that was when he saw something that surprised him.

His false friend's deceptively clear blue eyes were bloodshot, and on his cheeks there were two unmistakable tears.

It reminded Emin Bey of another occasion, when he had been similarly surprised. Not at Osman's but at Nazmi's, which had been torn down to make way for an apartment building. When had it been? Just before Hector's mother's death, Emin Bey seemed to remember. They had been, if Emin Bey remembered correctly, discussing Hector's father. And Hector had suddenly started to cry.

What was this womanly behavior, Emin Bey asked himself now, as he had also done on that earlier, happier occasion. He fought back his own tears as he told himself that this was one more proof of Hector's weak character. Men did not cry. Not outwardly, in any case.

''Please, dear boy, please! Do remember we are in public! Try and contain yourself!'' he cried, mimicking the alarm he had once genuinely felt. What he would give now for the ignorant bliss of those earlier days.

But his own womanly tears. What was the explanation for them? He did not understand this sudden weakening. Could it be that he had judged this man too harshly? he asked himself.

No, Emin, my child, don't allow yourself to weaken also. You have already given this man too many chances. Why did Americans always ask for more chances than they deserved? Why had Hector asked him here? What did he hope to achieve? Who was this man sitting across from him? After all these years, he had a right to know.

After all these years . . . he could feel the wretched Ismet's eyes resting on his back. He could sense his mocking smile. He could read the report that the oily Eastern fox was already writing in his head as he fondled the hand of an unsuspecting schoolgirl:

> On the evening of July 6th, 1982, there occurred at Karaca Restaurant in Rumeli Hisar (which establishment is known to its habitués as ''Osman's'') a reunion between the aforementioned subject and his old col-

league, Hector Cabot. It was an uneventful meeting, during which both men drank water and picked at their food like flighty women. There was a brief period during which the aforementioned exhibited rebellious behavior. Several prohibited substances were consumed. Afterward, certain words were exchanged and both men were observed to shed womanly tears. It is the opinion of the surveillance officer that . . .

Enough, Emin, my son! He silenced his thoughts. He hailed the waiter, suddenly aware of what he had to do.

At first Hector did not know what to make of it. Emin Bey had lost his touch. His efforts to manipulate Hector were so transparent it was embarrassing.

"My friend," he was saying (his use of the word was purely rhetorical), "this is nonsensical. How long has it been? Thirteen, fourteen years? What harm will it do? You are leaving tomorrow. We shall probably never see each other again. I am inviting you to join me. It will make me happy if you do. It is a small thing to do for an old friend. It is a tiny sacrifice, a small price to pay for . . ."

"For what?" Hector asked, although he knew the answer.

"For . . . how shall I put it? An enjoyable evening. A successful . . . reunion." He smiled and sat back, awaiting Hector's decision. He did not look over at Ismet, but it was clear that the performance was for his benefit. Hector was annoyed that Emin Bey had seen fit to drag him into a Byzantine feud that was none of his business.

"I'm sorry," Hector said, "but I can't. If I did, I would be going back on a promise I made myself years ago."

"What is more important," Emin Bey said impatiently, "a selfish promise or a friend?"

"It's not a selfish promise," Hector protested. "It's an obligation to myself and to everyone who depends on me. And it's . . . and it's the principle of the thing."

"Then let me ask you this question," Emin Bey said. "What is more important, a friend or the principle of a thing?"

Hector said nothing. Emin Bey's flashing eyes left him in

no doubt as to how Emin Bey would answer his own question.

"So you are telling me," Emin Bey said in a menacing voice, "that if you have a dying friend, if this dying friend made a last request, you would think first of the principle of the thing. We are speaking, of course, in abstract terms. . . ." Emin Bey's voice trailed off. He stared hard at Hector, and then, seeing that Hector was not going to change his mind, he said, with the grimness of an undertaker, "So. This is very interesting." He pushed back his chair, as if he intended to leave.

"I'm sorry, Emin Bey," Hector said, trying not to sound annoyed. "I'd do just about anything for you, but not that."

"Of course," he said. He was wearing his stiffest, most infuriating smile.

"And as far as your nephew is concerned . . ."

"Yes?" said Emin Bey. He picked up a toothpick. Covering his mouth with his left hand in the proper gentlemanly fashion, he began to fiddle with his teeth.

"Well, you know what I want to say. There's no need to impress him."

"Ah," said Emin Bey.

"No matter what we do, he's still not going to be impressed."

"Hmmmm." Emin Bey gave him a supercilious look, then went back to his teeth.

"And anyway, you shouldn't be wasting your time on that little policeman. You're too much of a man to be making a fool of yourself this way."

"I am obliged that you have seen fit to grace me with your opinions, but, excuse me, I think I am the best judge of that."

"No, you're not," Hector cried, unable to conceal his annoyance any longer. "You're so immersed in this ridiculous vendetta that you can't see what you're doing anymore. For God's sake, what is wrong with this place? You people do nothing but put on ridiculous shows for each other. No wonder this country is in the shape it's in! No wonder there are . . ." His voice trailed off, as he realized he had gone too far.

Emin Bey looked away, pretending to be distracted by the

lights of a passing tanker. From his corner table, Ismet gave Hector a conspiratorial sneer. He lifted his glass. There was something about the unnaturally American way Ismet nodded in the direction of his uncle that reminded Hector of that awful day thirteen years ago when Ismet had showed off his memory to him. He shuddered, and asked himself once again why Ismet had bothered. Hector had been on his way out by then, Ismet or no Ismet. There had been no need for Ismet to deal the final blows to his pride.

Turning away from Ismet, pretending not to have noticed his unpleasant smile, Hector looked at Emin Bey, with his painfully correct posture, his labored breathing, his studied air of nonchalance and the glassy eyes, the trembling lips that threatened to betray it. How hard he was trying to appear invincible. How frail he really looked. Suddenly the high and mighty principles that had meant so much to Hector only moments earlier meant nothing to him. All he knew was that he could not leave his friend to the mercy of the Ismets of this world, those merciless vultures whose special talent was to finish off what were already dying breeds.

"I'm sorry," Hector said. "I don't know what came over me." Emin Bey said nothing, but Hector knew what he had to do. He picked up the *raki* bottle Emin Bey had ordered and poured out four glasses. "Here. Let's have a drink and forget about politics. I don't know why I've been such a crank. One small drink never did anyone any harm.

"To your health," Hector said, as they all clinked glasses. Then he realized that this was hardly the thing to say to a dying man—or to anyone with a glass of *raki* in his hand. It was, in Hector's opinion, pure poison. It had traces of wormwood in it; it could drive you insane. But for once Emin Bey did not catch on to the unintended irony of the toast.

He smiled graciously as Margaret and Peter echoed Hector's toast—"To your health," they said, in mournful unison, reminding Hector of the chorus in a Greek tragedy. Emin Bey breathed in deeply, like a man facing a firing squad. He glanced over his shoulder, giving his policeman nephew a victorious smile. Then he turned back to his dinner companions and said, "And to your health also."

* * *

The dinner party on the Ashes' terrace broke up at half past eleven. It had been a spur-of-the-moment thing. After Hector left, no one had seemed to want to go home, and so Stella had made a large omelette and a salad. Then they had finished off the lemon sponge cake Beatrice and her friends had made the previous afternoon. They had all enjoyed it.

Ralph had grown quite silly by the end of the evening. He had started off with grand hypotheses. "I wonder how Hector *feels* about this place after so many years," he had said not long after Hector left. "I wonder if he has any *regrets*. You know what *I* think, don't you? I don't mean to intimate, of course, that his life now is at all empty. For how could I say that? How indeed? Our Hector is an important man now, flying here, there, and everywhere, writing reports, meeting the press. But I have the feeling that this visit was more important for him than he would have us believe. You know what *I* think, don't you?" he said, pausing as he lit his cigarette to stare with satisfaction into the flame of his Bic lighter. "I think that, in a way, he wishes it had never happened."

"Wishes *what* had never happened?" Meredith asked.

"The entire affair," Ralph said, with a sweeping gesture. "This . . . this . . . new life of his. A part of him wishes he was still living here, with us. You see, I think he's lost something. I do not mean to imply that he derives no satisfaction from his good works. No, that would be presumptuous of me. It's more that I find him more *constipated* than he used to be. More *inhibited,* if you follow my reasoning. The heart's gone out of the man, you see. I really don't think he's capable of actually feeling anything anymore. He's forgotten how to enjoy himself. It's a knack, you know. You can lose it, just the way a child loses its imagination."

"He seemed perfectly happy to me," Meredith had said.

"Yes, of course he would, to you," Ralph had answered. "But that does not surprise me. You are always gauging the spiritual depths from the elusive sparkle of the surface."

He had felt he'd scored points with that remark. He had been very pleased with himself. But as the evening progressed, his imperious manner had crumbled. He had succumbed to puns and jokes they had all heard a thousand times. He had lost his coordination. He had knocked over his glass when it was full of wine. While Stella poured salt on the stain, he had said, over and over, "Good Lord, who would have ever thought it? My cup runneth over. Oh, dear, my cup hath been runnething over again. Dear, dear Stella, I am so sorry. I have ruined your lovely tablecloth. Thank God Hector did not stay to witness this sorry scene. Do you think he noticed my tic?"

Meredith had taken it upon herself to escort him home. She had to put him to bed with his socks on, because he had threatened to kick her when she had tried to take them off.

It was a good thing he had agreed to move in with her come September, she thought, as she climbed the stairs to her own bedroom, pausing for a moment on the landing to gaze out the window at the stars. She thought he might have one of those nervous disorders, although she could not for the life of her get him to the doctor. It was getting to the point where it was dangerous—especially on nights when he had been drinking—to leave him alone. Although one could hardly blame him for overindulging tonight, Meredith thought.

What a surprise, Hector suddenly appearing after all these years. He had looked wonderful. He had been so very polite about her embarrassing memory. God, what a fool she had made of herself. He probably thought she was senile, although he was too polite to say so. She had caught him looking at her.

So had Stella. She had caught Hector looking at her during one of the awful silences, right after she had made that stupid remark about wrapping the Twinings tea tin in plastic. What had he been thinking at that moment?

He had looked very well. He had, after all, done well for himself, while the rest of them had lingered on here achieving nothing in particular. Well, she was happy for him. She was relieved to be happy for him. She couldn't remember why she had once been so angry at him. She supposed it was simply because he had ignored her. Injured pride, that's what it had been. Hell hath no fury, and so on. But even fury died down after a time. She was sorry he had not stayed for the omelette. Her omelette technique was one thing that had definitely improved.

Stella had also caught Hector looking at Beatrice. He could not possibly think that Beatrice was his anymore. She looked too much like Thomas. He had not seemed happy about that. He had not seemed happy, either, at the prospect of Margaret and Peter accompanying him down the hill. She could not imagine why. It wasn't as if they were unpleasant company. Stella was proud of her son-in-law. Perhaps Hector thought that they should be back in America, doing great works. But as far as Stella was concerned, she was happy to have them so nearby. It was a comfort knowing where her daughter was and what she was probably doing at any given time. As Stella carried the last plates into the kitchen, she pictured Margaret and Peter sitting on the balcony of their Bebek apartment, enjoying a nightcap before retiring to bed.

But she was wrong. They were sitting in Emin Bey's apartment, watching helplessly as Hector tried to comfort Emin Bey's wife.

Roksan was sitting on a blue velvet sofa. In front of her was a glass coffee table covered with porcelain shepherdesses and ceramic ashtrays, some of which had been pushed aside to make room for a cold, untouched cup of tea. She was having trouble breathing. She kept putting her hand to her throat as if she were about to choke. Her nails were long, perfectly manicured, and blood red; the first time Margaret saw them sliding across her powdered neck she thought Roksan was clawing herself.

Hector was sitting next to her. Each time she burst into tears, Hector put his arm around her. His movements were measured, almost tentative, like a man picking his way among landmines. It was as if he feared that one heartfelt, uncalculated gesture would shatter all that was fragile in the room.

His eyes were bloodshot. Tears swam inside them unable to escape. The doctor had come and gone by now. Emin Bey was officially dead. He had succumbed to a heart attack at approximately half past ten that evening, after sharing three bottles of *raki* with his dinner companions and drinking a fourth bottle by himself.

No one had been able to stop him. After Ismet and his

schoolgirl girlfriend joined their group, the dinner table had turned into a battlefield. Emin Bey had been determined to drink his nephew under that table at any cost.

The hostilities had begun with the typical backhanded compliments. "I was not aware that you were in the habit of picking roses before they bloomed," Emin Bey had said after being introduced to the schoolgirl. Ismet had countered with an exaggerated concern for Emin Bey's health. "You are overtaxing yourself, my uncle," he said. "My esteemed aunt must be worried about you. Please. Let me have my chauffeur take you home."

Emin Bey's response had been to order another bottle of *raki*. "Nonsense. Women worry too much. Let us enjoy the evening while it lasts." For a while, they had all pretended to do so. Hector, Margaret, Peter, and the schoolgirl had watched, aghast, as Emin Bey and Ismet downed one glass of *raki* after another, as casually as if they were drinking water.

The compliments had continued. "Honestly, my uncle, with all this talk of your heart condition, I have been underestimating your capacities. You are truly a lion."

"You are trying to flatter me," Emin Bey had responded. "But what is a lion compared to a man with a thousand pairs of eyes?"

"My uncle," Ismet had protested. Emin Bey had silenced him with a gently raised hand. "Please, Ismet! This is no time for modesty. We all know that a thousand pairs of eyes are scarcely sufficient for the successful completion of your sacred mission. Why not two thousand pairs of eyes, or three, or four? The strivings of patriots should not be subjected to the petty constraints of economics."

"This is not a suitable conversation in the present company," Ismet had said, his face going rigid.

"My child," Emin Bey had replied, "such modesty is a commendable virtue, but allow me to say that it is entirely unnecessary in the circumstances. Why should your charming young companion not be aware of your distinguished history of heroic acts? Why should she not know how many murderous anarchists you have uprooted, how many Lenins and Stalins you have massacred in their cradles? Truly, it is a shame that such accomplishments must forever be shrouded in mystery. If the world were a just place, Ismet, my son, you would be awarded a thousand medals at a public ceremony. You would be a national hero. You would be on television."

"But why?" the schoolgirl had asked. At that, Ismet had planted his fist firmly on the table. "Enough," he said, in a menacing voice. "We shall continue this conversation when we are not in the company of women and foreigners."

"My dear Ismet," Emin Bey had persisted. "Such xenophobia. Again, a commendable virtue, and one that will continue to be necessary as we battle to restore our national purity. But again, completely unnecessary in the circumstances. Although it may seem inevitable to someone with your Kurdish sensitivities, it is not actually true that whenever Turks and foreigners meet, they do so to plot the overthrow of governments."

"I am not a Kurd," Ismet had shouted. "How dare you insinuate that I am not a true Turk? You, with your Bulgarian mother and your Greek concubine of a grandmother!"

Emin Bey had countered with an insolent smile. "My dear nephew, it does not matter what my mother and grandmother were, just as it does not matter that your parents and grandparents slept in the same room with their cows and sheep. We are a democracy now and everyone is equal. Or are we a democracy? Perhaps you, with your special connections, could tell us."

"Do you know what I tell you?" Ismet had said. "I tell you this." He spat at Emin Bey. The spittle landed on his shirt.

Ismet's schoolgirl friend put her hand to her mouth and let out a short, high scream. "Be quiet," Ismet barked at her.

After he had wiped his shirt clean with his handkerchief, Emin Bey had turned to the others with a benevolent smile. "Please allow me to apologize for my nephew's uncivilized behavior. The Kurds, alas, suffer from a low level of enlightenment. Did you know that in the Kurdish language there are forty-seven different words for horse manure?"

"I shit in your mouth!" Ismet had screamed. "I shit in all your mouths. Your future is nothing in this country! I shall butcher you—I shall butcher you all before it is over!"

"My dear Ismet," said Emin Bey, "I am afraid you are about to run the risk of betraying your entire agenda. You are in danger of forgetting that enemy ears are at large. You are overtaxing yourself, my boy. You have had too much *raki*. Allow me to arrange for your chauffeur to take you home."

"I am not the drunk one," Ismet had snarled. "We shall see who is the drunkard among us." Hailing the waiter, he had ordered another bottle of *raki*. When it arrived, he poured himself a large glass and knocked it back in one gulp. Then Emin Bey did the same thing. But after that, he drank with greater caution. He was as tense and alert as a cat about to pounce as he watched his nephew knock back one drink after another. From time to time he threw him a compliment. "Honestly, my dear Ismet, I have been underestimating your capacities. You are truly a lion."

First Ismet lost control of his tongue. He was no longer able to finish his insults. Then came the time when he could no longer light his cigarettes. Finally, his head began to wobble from side to side. He knocked over his waterglass. As he tried to mop up the water, he knocked over his drink. Exhausted from the effort of mopping this one up, he rested his head on the table. Soon he was sound asleep.

The schoolgirl tried to arouse him, but Emin Bey motioned for her to stop. He paused for a few moments, watching Ismet closely, and then he gently pulled the table toward him, causing the sleeping Ismet, who was sitting opposite him, to slowly slide off it. He slid like a rag doll to a heap on the ground.

Emin Bey looked lovingly at the snoring heap underneath the table. Then he turned to Hector, Peter, and Margaret. "My friends," he said, "you do not know how long I have been waiting for this moment." Sighing deeply, he crossed his legs and propped them on the sleeping Ismet's head.

The schoolgirl had gone hysterical at this point. Emin Bey had arranged for Ismet's chauffeur to take her home.

Emin Bey's heart attack had come an hour and a bottle of *raki* later. No one had been able to control him, not even Hector, who had tried hard. At the time of his collapse he had been singing an old tango melody, whose words he had changed to fit the occasion.

"Oh, your dimples," he had sung, waving his glass at the snoring Ismet, "I could die for your dimples, I could shit in your mouth for your fascist dimples. . . ."

A doctor at a neighboring table had tried CPR on him, but to no avail. They had taken him home in Ismet's Mercedes-Benz, with Ismet, still sound asleep, in the front seat.

Nilüfer, who came to relieve Hector, Peter, and Margaret not long after midnight, was a slight woman with black hair that was cut in such a way that she was constantly having to push it out of her eyes. It was rumored that she was soon to become a widow. Her husband, Tevfik, who had once taught at Woodrow College, was in prison awaiting trial, and it was said that he and his codefendants were to receive the death penalty. They were charged—unjustly, people said—with plotting to overthrow the government.

Which was how Nilüfer and her two children came to be staying with Nilüfer's parents, who lived next door.

When she arrived, she apologized for not coming sooner. She and her parents had been at a reception in honor of Nureyev, she explained. He was in town for the week, the star attraction of the summer festival. Despite the fact that she had not changed out of her evening clothes, she had the abrupt, efficient air of an overworked registered nurse. What little mercy she had she reserved for Roksan. After she had put her to bed, she came out to the living room, where Hector, Margaret, and Peter were waiting, at a loss. Lighting a cigarette, she looked the three of them over from head to toe, as if she found fault with their clothes. "You may go now," she said. She sauntered back into the hallway and opened the front door.

On his way out, Hector paused to tell her how sorry he was. "It is a terrible tragedy," he said. "Emin Bey was a dear friend."

"Friend," she said with a bitter laugh. "Is that what you do to your friends in America? Let them kill themselves before your eyes?"

"There was no stopping him," Hector said. "It was a matter of pride."

She took a drag from her cigarette and looked at him, her eyes full of contempt. She flicked her hair out of her eyes and exhaled. "Go," she said. "Just go. We don't need you anymore."

She stood at the door watching them go down the stairs. Just before they left the apartment building, the hall lights went off. They heard her laugh. They continued to Bebek in silence.

Margaret and Peter were not ready to go home after they had seen Hector off in his taxi, so they went for a walk. Bebek was almost deserted by now. The restaurants were closed, the stores dark behind their iron mesh grills. Only the neon-lit nightclubs at the far end of the town showed signs of life. Margaret and Peter did not walk that far. Instead they ambled out to the ferry station to look at the bay. All but one of the boats that were moored there were dark and empty.

The boat that was lit up was a sleek, thirty-five-foot yacht. There were a dozen people on board having a party. Tom Jones was singing "Delilah" on a cassette recorder. One couple was trying to dance to it while the others laughed quietly.

A gigantic, dimly lit Russian naval vessel slid into view, traveling in the direction of the Black Sea. The large, radar-equipped motor launch that locals called the CIA boat was moored less than twenty feet away from where Margaret and Peter were standing. It sprang to life and zoomed out of the bay in pursuit of its prey.

It would pursue the Russian ship for a few hundred yards, taking pictures and doing radar scans. Then it would return to Bebek. Two dark-suited officials wearing sunglasses would step off the boat clutching briefcases and manila envelopes. Glancing furtively to either side, they would sneak through the bushes to their cars, and then drive off satisfied that no one knew what they were up to. Margaret had seen them go through this routine hundreds of times, even in broad daylight. It was embarrassing to share a nationality with them, especially at a time when her welcome in the country she called her home was so precarious.

The CIA boat left behind it waves that made the party yacht rock. Then came the larger waves from the Russian naval vessel. The dancing couple nearly fell overboard, but they rescued themselves at the last moment. There was more laughter, and the pop of a champagne cork. Peter squeezed Margaret's hand. She knew without asking him what he was thinking.

He was thinking about Hector, and so was her father.

Having given up on counting sheep, Thomas had turned on the light and was pretending to read a thriller. Where was Hector now? he wondered, trying to chase from his mind those nagging philosophical questions that plagued him whenever something happened to upset his daily routine.

He placed Hector, incorrectly, in his room at the Pera Palas, sleeping the righteous sleep of the sober.

Tomorrow Hector would rise early, Thomas predicted. He would join his church group for breakfast in the dining room. "How did your visit go?" they would ask. "Oh, very well, thank you," he would say. He would not go into the details. He would not mention wrinkles or shaking hands or bad legs. It would not be in good taste.

And then he would leave them again, moving on to better and more important matters. Thomas pictured him a crusader, galloping off on a horse. Hector the dashing crusader, and Thomas the crippled friend who had hoped to accompany him, who was unable to accompany him, who was hiding his disappointment well, whose false cheer Hector accepted without question, whose gallant farewells were drowned out by the pounding of horses' hooves. There were many things in the world that were more important than the feelings of a crippled friend.

Enough self-pity. He had no business thinking of himself as a cripple. Because he wasn't crippled. All he had was a limp. It was not any old limp, either. He was proud of his limp. He realized he had forgotten to tell Hector what a very special limp it was.

He had been caught downtown in crossfire, in 1978. He had been written up in the papers. "Loyal university professor, much loved by his students . . ." It had made him feel less of a foreigner.

He had given Hector the wrong impression. He had not risen from his chair once. Hector had probably gone off thinking his old friend was a cripple. It was a pity he had not stayed for dinner.

It had gone well, the visit, short though it had been. It was good to see they could all be friends again. Though why they had not corresponded all these years, Thomas could not really say. Thinking back, he truly could not remember why they had all been so angry at Hector. The reason for their anger had, like everything else, slipped away.

Hector had acted strange that last year, certainly. At the end he had meddled in everyone's private affairs. But he and Hector hadn't had an out-and-out fight, had they? Thomas remembered thinking he'd like to punch him (why?) but he had never actually done so. It was strange how one's memory edited itself. There was so little left to go on.

In any event, it had been good to see him. And yet, there had been something missing. It hadn't been like the old days, because Hector was so different now. So careful, so reserved. What had become of the man in the fishing boots and the Astrakhan hat who had swooped down on them like an angel in search of lost souls on that wonderful rainy afternoon so many years ago, who had insisted on paying for everything, who had swept them off to Rejans and then off on a wild binge, losing geese right, left, and center, and changing Thomas' life forever? This man was gone, and with him his dreams. The new, sensible Hector was no replacement. It broke Thomas' heart even to think of it.

He sighed. He pulled himself together. "It was good to see Hector again, wasn't it?" he said to Stella. Stella, who was pretending to sleep, nodded drowsily. "It was just like the old days, wasn't it?" Thomas said. He was still in the habit of lying to his wife. It had come in handy during the bombings and killings and fuel shortages, this false cheer of his. Both he and Stella had come to depend on it.

The ceiling creaked above their heads. It was Amy, who lived now in the apartment upstairs. She was still up, still pacing the floors.

She couldn't sleep. She didn't know what to make of the whole thing. In a way, it had been a pleasant surprise, his sudden reappearance. But in the end he had succeeded in annoying her.

It was while she had been showing him around the

garden. Up until then, he had been suitably respectful. He had complimented her on her new rugs, he had thanked her for writing Chloe that letter urging her to go back to med school, he had listened sympathetically to her stories about the Community School and told her they were lucky to have her. He had stayed away from the subject of their son, Neil, and thus avoided an argument. Time had passed more quickly than she had expected.

But then she had shown him the wall where the gate leading to the Bowl had once been, that ugly cement thing that sent her blood pressure up just to look at it. And he had said, "So this is the famous wall. Well, it's not as bad as you made it out to be in your letters."

"Not as bad as I made it out to be?" she had exclaimed.

"I was expecting something taller and uglier."

"It's not the height of the wall that bothers me," she had tried to explain. "It's the principle of the thing."

He had shrugged his shoulders. "It will look all right in a few years, when the ivy covers it."

She could not understand how he could be so callous. Didn't he realize how insulting it was for her to be walled out of a university that had been the center of her life for a quarter of a century? How humiliating it was when they stopped her at the gate and asked her for her identity card? They didn't even let her use the library anymore. They would have liked to pretend that she—and everyone else who taught at the Community School—did not exist. It was a bad sign when people built walls where gates had been sufficient.

Hector had never cared about her feelings—that was the problem. Even when they were married—especially when they were married—he had never stopped to put himself in her shoes. If she ever saw him again, she would make sure to tell him that.

It was midnight. It was time to go to bed. Amy went from room to room, doing the things that she did every night before retiring. She put on her nightgown. She removed her scant makeup, pausing a little longer than usual to see if she looked older. She gathered up stray coffee cups and put them into the sink. She adjusted the photographs of her children on the mantelpiece and said goodnight to them:

Chloe, who looked so breezey in the picture but who had been through such difficult times—she had ditched that awful man, thank God, and was off to Guadalajara in the fall to finish up her medical studies—and Neil, who looked so sad in his picture but who had sounded so cheerful in his last letter. He was married and living in San Francisco. He had left that security firm, thank God, and was washing dishes for a living while he worked on his novel.

Kissing them both, she continued on her rounds. She checked to see if the stove was off, the doors locked, and the windows closed. She checked on poor old Lazarus, who was asleep in his usual place, next to the door. That was another thing that had bothered her. He had not been surprised that Lazarus was still alive. In fact, he had even shown alarm at how mangy he was. When he should have realized that it was a miracle, an absolute miracle, that the decrepit thing was still alive.

As long ago as 1969, when they were still married, Hector had predicted that Lazarus was not much longer for this world. And yet here he was, still hanging on, as always.

Priding herself on the care she had given her Lazarus, she got into bed. She turned off the light, but then she turned it on again. Something was wrong. There was something she had forgotten.

The doors? The windows? The stove? She checked them all again but could find nothing amiss. She checked Lazarus again. He was snoring peacefully, his back against the door. It was on her way back to bed that she heard the noise outside.

In the old days, Lazarus would have been up and barking. He was not much of a guard dog these days. He could barely see. He was hard of hearing. He had lost his sense of smell. And yet he still had his pride. That was why Amy couldn't even think of getting a second dog for protection.

Without turning on any lights, she tiptoed across the living room to the balcony. She reached it just in time to see a man struggling over her hated wall. It was Hector.

He was having a hard time getting over it. Now, that was poetic justice, she thought. "Goddamn this thing," she heard him say.

He had a bottle of something in his left hand. So, Amy said to herself. This was very interesting. So much for his high-minded resolutions. One night back in Istanbul and he falls off the wagon.

No wonder he couldn't get over the wall. You couldn't get over a wall with a bottle in your hand. At first she just stood there, watching him slip and fall and try again. She just stood there, her arms akimbo, just as she had done on the night his mother had died, which was the night when she had lost him.

That awful night, when she had lost him.

What are you so sorry about? she asked herself. You were bound to lose him sooner or later. You were never happy with him. You're far happier living alone. You don't need him. You're independent now. You can't bring back the old days no matter what you do. This man who is having such a hard time getting over the wall means nothing to you. Close the door and go back to bed.

She closed the door. She went back to her bedroom. Then, on an impulse, she threw on her robe and rushed outside. "Hector!" she whispered when she reached the wall. "It's Amy. Give me your hand and I'll help you over!"

Ten seconds passed. Twenty. Thirty. Amy had just about given up hope when there was a rustling in the bushes. A hand appeared. Then another hand. Then Hector lifted his head above the wall and looked at her. There was so much pain in his face that Amy gasped, thinking for a moment that he had been wounded.

She looked so tired and tense, even in the muted light of her bedroom, which had the desolate neatness Hector associated with old maids. There had not been a man in here for years. At first she flinched, as if the feel of a man's hand were a shock, but then she relaxed as he smoothed the worries out of her face. The more smoothed-out her face, the younger she looked to him, until she looked no different from the way she had looked on the day he had met her. As he caressed her back and kissed her breasts, he wondered if it had felt this way the first time they had made love, before the barriers went up between them. He could not, of course, remember.

Afterward, they talked. Eventually Amy fell asleep with her head on his shoulder. Once he was sure she would not wake up, Hector gently extricated himself and tiptoed into the kitchen, where, after a brief search, he found a bottle of brandy and poured himself a double, taking pains that his loose wrist did not turn it into a triple.

He was walking the tightrope. He knew he would have to stop soon—either that or end up in the gutter. In the meantime, he had to keep on drinking, just enough to keep believing in his plan.

He was going to take them all back with him. They would live happily ever after in his house in Connecticut. They would start a school, if that's what was needed to keep people feeling useful. Money was no problem: they could do any number of things. He would let them decide about the details. The important thing was to talk them into going back.

He would tell them that they were no longer welcome here. They had no future here, he would say. It didn't matter if he turned out to be wrong. People usually were wrong when they predicted the future. So long as he could convince them he was right, that was all that mattered.

Amy did not take his plan very seriously. She did not know yet that he planned to propose marriage to her again. She thought that because he was drinking, he would black out and have no memory of his plan in the morning. But she was wrong. Although he was drinking, he wasn't drunk. In the morning he would remember everything.

"They'll never agree to it," Amy had said. "They're determined to stay here, and they have a right to do so. This is our home."

"I'll make you a better one," he had insisted.

"You think you can bring back the old days, but you can't," she had continued. "The party's over."

"No, it's not," he had said.

"And even if they did go along with it, it would be a nightmare. Think of the fights we would have!"

But Hector refused to think of the fights. He had plenty of time to think about them later. What he wanted to think about tonight was his vision of their future together, under one roof. Amy dishing out the eggs and bacon at the breakfast table. Thomas reading the paper as he ate. Stella getting up to open the windows, to let in the morning breeze. Meredith coming in from the garden, where she had been gathering blackberries. She would be wearing a wide-brimmed straw hat that Ralph would be sarcastic about. She would smile brightly, as determined as ever not to let him get the better of her. "Such a beautiful morning!" she would exclaim. She would give the blackberries to Hector, and he would take them into the kitchen to wash them. And looking out the window he would see his father pulling weeds in the garden, and the children, who were married with their own children by now, sunning themselves on the lawn.

The vision faded. In the hope of bringing it back, Hector poured himself another double brandy. He turned his back on the living room because it was too painful to look at. It was filled with all their old furniture, but everything was in the wrong place. Instead he looked down at the Bosphorus. It was almost dawn.

A caique appeared from behind the dark walls of the castle. Seeing it, Hector remembered the days when he and Emin Bey would go out on their fishing trips. They would leave at such an hour. They would use the motor until they reached the Marmara Sea.

By then the sun would be high in the sky. Emin Bey would put up the sails and they would race across the sparkling blue water. Behind them, the silhouette of the city would turn gray and finally disappear.

It was only when they were in open sea that Emin Bey would relax. Opening his arms to the sky, breathing in the sea air, he would sigh happily and say, "My friend, I am telling you. There is nothing more difficult than being a modern Turk.

"The contradictions!" Emin Bey would exclaim. He would take out some fruit and cut it up and force Hector to eat most of it. He would stretch out on the bench to take full benefit of the sun, while Hector took over the rudder. They would exchange ideas. In those days, before Emin Bey discovered that Hector's motives for being in Turkey were selfish rather than noble, Emin Bey had thought the world of his opinions. Even in those early days, before he had done any irrevocable damage, Hector had felt like an imposter: a child who has been mistaken for an adult.

I didn't mean to kill you, Emin Bey. If I had known this was going to happen, I would have stayed away.

Fighting tears, Hector poured himself another brandy. He forced his mind to the scene before his eyes. Looking at the dark, crenelated walls of the castle, he remembered the time he and Amy and all the others had had a picnic up there on the ramparts. Those were the days when their idea of fun was having picnics in forbidden places. They had also had picnics on the roof of Aghia Irini and the dome of Aghia Sophia. They had tried, unsuccessfully, to picnic in a minaret. The most important part of these picnics had been the wine, and Hector had always drunk most of it. The Saturday of their castle picnic had been no exception.

Hector had felt on top of the world that day. Looking down at the meek museum guards who had failed to apprehend them, Hector had thought how ironic it was that he was drinking wine on the same ramparts that had once been patrolled by the army of Mehmet the Conqueror. All through his childhood, his mother had terrified him with stories of this bloodthirsty sultan, who had used this very castle as a base from which to lay siege to the city. The siege had lasted a year, she had told him, causing starvation and despair. It had ended on a Tuesday, which was why all Tuesdays brought bad luck. Mehmet the Conqueror and his men had stormed through the city gates, stealing the city from the Greeks, its rightful owners. "But one day we shall take it back," she would always say, showing her son a clenched fist. Standing on the ramparts, invigorated by the sharp north wind, switching from wine to a flask of brandy, Hector had recalled his mother's vow.

He had turned to his friends and said, "Let's take the city back. Let's lay a siege."

It had started as a joke, but before long he had started believing it. He had begun to shout and make speeches. Thomas and Leslie had had a hell of a time getting him down the narrow steps and out of the castle. They had told him later that he had come very close to being arrested. He had continued to make a scene all the way home.

Once he was home, he had broken down. "Why are you thwarting me?" he has asked Thomas and Leslie. "I have to take the city back. My mother is counting on me. It's why I'm here. It's my sacred mission." They had teased him about it for months afterward. Hector remembered how mortified he had been—and how worried that his Turkish friends would hear about his drunken tirade and think he had been serious. But he also remembered his exhilaration on the ramparts when, for a few minutes, he had been able to believe in filial duty and divine missions and moral righteousness, and a lot of other things you had to be drunk to believe in those days.

So that was what it was like all those years, Hector said to himself. All those lost afternoons, all those drunken nights, he had been dreaming up glorious missions for himself and his followers. All those years he had been going to bed a hero with a long agenda, and waking up a shattered man whose only quest was for the aspirin bottle.

All those lost dreams! As he watched the world around him turn gray with the approaching dawn, he wondered what had become of them. He wondered how different his life might have been had he been able to remember them in the morning. He mourned their passing.